PROSPECT STREET

EMILIE RICHARDS

PROSPECT STREET

ISBN 1-55166-921-8

PROSPECT STREET

Visit us at www.mirabooks.com

Printed in U.S.A.

First Printing: July 2002
10 9 8 7 6 5 4 3 2 1

AUTHOR'S NOTE

My fascination with Georgetown began when I was a college student at Florida State University. My mother, who lived in Washington, took an apartment on W Place at the edge of Georgetown and I joined her there for the summer of my freshman year. The heady mixture of college students, society grandes dames and street people made a strong impression on a relatively unsophisticated young woman, much as it does on the characters of this book. Georgetown was forever rooted in my imagination and heart.

When I moved back to the Washington area several years ago I rediscovered Georgetown and fell in love all over again. My thanks to all the "guides" who showed me the city, particularly Vera Tilson for the wonderful tour, Margaret Ogden for a visit to an authentic Georgetown showplace and Jerry Neilsen, who invited total strangers into his Prospect Street row house to sample the view. Thanks to Michael and Shelly McGee, who rambled through back streets and alleyways and never complained.

Those of you who have had cause to do research here will realize that I've taken liberties with the hours of the Peabody Room at the Georgetown Regional Library, as well as invented new personnel because I didn't want to put words into the mouth of Jerry McCoy, the gracious and hardworking librarian. The Peabody Room is a wonderful repository of local information, just as Faith discovers in the story.

This book takes place just before the acts of terrorism against the World Trade Center and the Pentagon. I am grateful to be living in the Washington, D.C., area with so many thoughtful, interesting and courageous people.

 Prologue

December 1999

Driving past Granger's Food and Gas, the country store just two miles from the Bronsons' weekend cottage, was like crossing the finish line in a marathon. For Faith Bronson, Granger's was a promise that the cultural journey from sophisticated Northern Virginia into rural West Virginia was about to end. By then Alex, the Bronsons' son, had pestered his older sister Remy to her breaking point, and even Faith—who secretly cherished Alex's boundless energy—was ready to pack him in the trunk with the suitcases and groceries.

David, Faith's husband, always claimed that Granger's, with its antique gas pumps, its tow trucks and tire mountains, was the point in their trip where his breathing and heart rate finally slowed. As the family passed the store he invariably tugged at his collar and slumped in the driver's seat, as if some unseen judge had looked away and David was out from under surveillance.

This morning, just ten days before Christmas, Faith was alone in the family's Volvo when she sighted Granger's—decorated in what seemed like miles of tinsel rope and fringe. By the time she pulled in for gas, the hour and a half of silence, which had seemed so promising when she'd climbed behind the steering wheel, felt hollow and unwelcoming.

"Morning, Miz Bronson. And Merry Christmas." As she stepped out of the car, Tubby, Granger's proprietor, lifted a gnarled hand in greeting. Tubby was rail-thin, with overalls draped in folds off sloping shoulders. The fact that the straps defied gravity had always mystified her.

"Merry Christmas, Tubby." She unlatched the gas cap and went to the pump, but Tubby took the nozzle from her hand.

"Gives me an excuse to stay outside. Last pretty day before winter really hits, I reckon."

Faith reckoned the same thing. The weather was unseasonably warm and thoroughly welcome. At dawn an infusion of sunlight had bathed her face and shoulders, and she had thrown off the covers and padded to the window to look out on the most perfect sunrise she remembered. David, away on his final business trip of the year, wasn't there to share it, and even Alex, who usually reveled in Mother Nature's excesses, complained when she shook him awake to see it. Now that Alex was eleven, she supposed she had years of complaining ahead of her.

Even when she saw both children off to school, Faith was still immersed in the morning's magic. Before the day could become like every other, she impulsively called her mother and asked Lydia to stop by the children's school that afternoon and take them to her house for the night.

Lydia Huston, obsessive senator's wife, checked her calendar, eternally packed with charity luncheons, visits to the salon and political photo opportunities. Although Christmas was her busiest holiday—as she pointedly reminded her daughter—she would come so Faith could go away for the night. But Lydia recommended that Faith not make a habit of this kind of reckless spontaneity.

Despite a fear that she was being foolish, Faith had canceled a final planning meeting for the teacher appreciation Christmas party, packed the car and taken off for the country.

"You see that sunrise this morning?" Tubby asked. "Woke me up, right out of my bed. My daddy always said a sunrise like that brings big changes. God's way of making an announcement."

Faith was delighted to find a fellow enthusiast. "He must have something big planned today."

"Just for the folks who seen it. Not for just anyone. Nuthin' like the end of the world, not that sort of thing."

Faith glanced at the pump and fished a twenty-dollar bill from her wallet. "I'm glad to hear it. I thought I might have to drop down on my knees here and now."

"Me, I got another grandbaby coming. I figure this'll be the day." He shook the nozzle and put it back in the cradle, then he screwed her gas cap back in place. "How about you?"

"Are the changes always good ones?"

Tubby screwed up his face like a sponge being wrung dry. "Nope," he said at last. "Day my daddy died started with a sunrise so bright it like near to have blinded me."

She was caught now. Tubby was waiting, and suddenly months of worry clamped her chest like a vise. Faith could feel the old man staring expectantly at her. "Well, I guess I'll just be surprised."

"Don't say I didn't warn you, something big turns up." Tubby took her money and made change. "You need anything from inside? Or'd Mr. Bronson get everything you need?"

The question confused her. "David? No, he's away on a business trip."

"And here I thought you and the mister were havin' some time away from the kiddies."

"I'm hoping he comes here from the airport this evening." She hadn't been able to reach David at his hotel in Seattle, but she'd left a message on his cell phone and another with his secretary. From Dulles Airport he could be at the cottage in an hour.

"Thought I saw him drive by last night." Tubby rubbed at a smudge on her windshield, wet his index finger and tried again. "My mistake."

"He's in Washington state, speaking at a conference."

"School prayer?"

David and Tubby engaged in endless friendly conversations about the state of the world. Harvard-educated David, director of Promise the Children, a conservative organization that lobbied for family values and social change, liked to share his philosophy with anybody who would listen. High school dropout Tubby could hold his own.

"Actually, this time I think he's talking about the need to police the media," she said.

Tubby stepped away from the windshield, satisfied. "God bless him."

God had blessed all the Bronsons. Faith knew it and was grateful. Beautiful, intelligent children, good health, prosperity; and a marriage built on common values. If lately it seemed she and David were no longer connecting, wasn't it a small thing and easily remedied with a little work?

Beginning tonight?

"Well, I'm off," Faith said. "Thanks for your help." Once she started the engine she gave a quick wave, and Tubby waved back.

Out on the road again, their conversation nagged at her. She had spent the drive trying not to think about the problems in her marriage, but clearly they were coiled under the surface. Just a casual comment or two and they had sprung to life again.

Faith loved David. In fact, he was the only man she had ever loved. At twenty-two she had fallen head over heels for him, and she still pinched herself when she realized that elegant, charismatic David Bronson had chosen her as his wife.

David loved her. That wasn't in doubt. David had never looked at another woman during their fifteen years of marriage. He worked too hard, and he was often away from home, but he was a devoted husband and father. She was the envy of most of her friends. David lived the values he preached.

The recent problems in their marriage were subtle. Their relationship had always been more about love than passion. They had clicked at their first meeting, talking until dawn and every night after until all the things they'd never told anyone else had been said. She had been thrilled by his touch, but even more thrilled by his rapt attention. For the first time in her life someone had found her fascinating, and she had melted gratefully into marriage, a warm puddle of unending devotion.

If their sex life had quickly grown routine, Faith had been philosophical. She and David were soul mates. She would gratefully trade the emotional excesses other women claimed to experience for the stability and tenderness she and David had built. She found satisfaction in their lovemaking, and more satisfaction in their life together.

Until recently.

Faith slowed the car to take the long curve on Seward Road that led to the gravel drive to their cottage. Ten years ago David had bought the cottage, with its fifteen wooded acres, as an anniversary gift. He had promised they would steal occasional weekends without the children, but they never had. Instead, she had contented herself with making the cottage a second home for all of them. Someday in the future, when the children were grown, she and David could come here whenever they wanted to rekindle the spark of romance.

But this morning, as the sun lifted from the horizon, she'd wondered if her patience was partially at fault for the way the spark had gone out. In the last months their sex life had gone from routine to nonexistent. David had been away more than usual, but even when he was home, he claimed exhaustion when she cuddled close. He held her off with promises, but she was fast becoming aware that, for once in his life, David was not living up to his word.

The fault had to be hers. Not enough patience, or too much? Not enough compassion for the pressure he was under, or too much compassion and too few demands? David was a man who responded to the needs of others, and maybe he had to be reminded that his own needs shouldn't be pushed aside.

With a resulting burst of enthusiasm, she had planned this night away. Faith had packed her car with candles and gourmet food, fresh flowers and massage oil, then topped it all off with a gift she'd bought for herself and never worn, a sheer lace teddy with ribbon bows that were just waiting for the right masculine fingers to untie them.

She made the turn into their driveway and slowed to a crawl. In the distance the highest peaks still sparkled with a post-Thanksgiving snow, but the winter-brown clearing where the cottage stood was carpeted with pine needles and dried leaves.

The same winter-brown clearing where David's silver Honda Accord peeked out from behind a tree.

Faith pulled up to the cottage and turned off the ignition. She had missed David at his hotel that morning, but she assumed she had missed him by minutes, not some portion of a day. When Tubby claimed to have seen him last night, she had thought nothing of it. But David *was* here, and clearly had been for a while.

She sat in the car, her cheeks warming in embarrassment. She had counted on time to set the scene. She'd planned to have candles flickering and soft music on the stereo. Now she felt foolish. What could she do? Walk into the cottage with seduction in multiple shopping bags and hope he didn't laugh?

Her embarrassment segued into something darker. Obviously David had finished his meeting sooner than planned and taken an earlier flight back. Instead of coming home to help her make Christmas for the children, he had used this bonus time—as he sometimes did—to come to the cottage, where he could work undisturbed.

David hadn't thought that she might welcome his help, or that she might welcome another adult in the house for a change. As he did all too often lately, David had thought first of his job.

For the moment she decided to leave the bags in the car. It was time she and David had a talk. She believed their marriage was more her domain than his. If problems had to be explored, she would have to be their emotional Lewis and Clark. If all went well, he could help her carry the bags into the house and unpack them.

She decided not to announce her arrival, because his first reaction would tell her everything. She opened and closed the car door quietly, although the cottage was built of stone and nearly soundproof. She could picture him holed away in the knotty pine study. It was the first room he'd furnished. She wondered if this was the first time he had come here to work without telling her.

What else didn't she know about her husband?

The door was locked, and she fished for her keys. It creaked when she pushed it open, but David didn't come into the living room. The family hadn't come often since school began. The house was silent and musty, as if he'd been too busy to open the winter-smudged windows and air out the rooms. Now she noted dust on the fireplace mantel and one labyrinthian spider's web hanging from an exposed beam in the corner. The cottage was warm enough, but no fire burned on the hearth. She padded across the oak floor to the hallway at the right and started toward David's study.

A moan stopped her. She froze. She wasn't sure where the sound had come from, but surely not from the study, which was just ahead to her right. The sound had come from one of the rooms at the hallway's end.

Faith couldn't seem to make her feet move. She listened intently, not daring to breathe. Just as she was about to call out for reassurance, she heard the sound of something scraping across the floor, then a low laugh.

Gratefully she closed her eyes and pictured her husband in their bedroom. David was moving furniture or trying to open a window. One window was out of reach without using a step stool they kept under the bed. She couldn't count the number of times he'd banged his toes on it when he kicked his shoes out of the way at bedtime. He had probably decided to take a nap, taken off his shoes...

She finished the scenario in her head as she started back down the hallway. This time she made enough noise to wake bears sleeping in the forest. She was close enough now to gauge his reaction when he saw her.

"David? Are you in there?"

Hand on the knob, she paused. She wasn't sure why. She had a sudden vision of that morning's spectacular sunrise. God's announcement.

And a premonition that she wasn't going to like the news.

She opened the door anyway. Sunshine flooded the room and the two men basking in it. One was her husband, naked from the waist down, standing in front of a pedestal mirror that had been dragged to that spot. The other was a man she had seen before, but never like this, never naked, with his body embracing his lover's. Abraham Stein, the liberal journalist who had so often bedeviled Promise the Children, cradled David in his muscular arms, like a child with his favorite holiday gift.

David's patrician face drained of all color. As a stunned Faith watched, he crossed his arms, covering his erection with his hands.

In the last lucid moment she would have for the rest of the day, Faith realized that David was not protecting himself from Abraham Stein's embrace. He was protecting his sexuality from the unwelcome stare of the woman he had been married to for fifteen years.

 1

How often in one lifetime does a woman sign away her dreams? How many times will she date and initial the ending of the world as she knows it?

"And, Mrs. Bronson, if you'll just put your signature right here..." Carol Ann, the representative from the settlement company that was finalizing the sale of the Bronsons' house, shoved one more piece of paper at Faith. "Don't forget the date," she said for what seemed like the fiftieth time that afternoon. "August 7th."

"Thank you. I'm not in much danger of forgetting." Faith didn't look up. She concentrated on signing away her past in neat, private school script.

"We're nearly done." Carol Ann—who didn't seem to have a last name—patted the table near Faith's hand, as if that would make Faith's task easier.

Faith supposed Carol Ann meant well, but she'd taken an instant dislike to her. She wore mauve eyeshadow that stopped just short of thinly plucked brows and a smile that could turn steam to snowflakes. Carol Ann just wanted one more settlement. One more house signed, sealed and delivered. One more life set adrift.

"Now, Mr. Bronson. One last signature for you. Then I think we're finished."

Faith slid the paper across the table to David. He was sitting still, as if by not moving a muscle he could keep Faith from remembering he was there. In the few encounters they'd had since she'd found him in his lover's arms, David had assumed the same lifeless posture. She didn't know if he was afraid he might fly apart, or if he simply no longer knew what to do with his body. It was a whole new body, after all, a whole new life, a whole new world he lived in.

Her husband, a gay man.

David signed the paper in script that strongly resembled Faith's own. Once they had laughed at how similar their handwriting was and how easily they could forge each other's signatures. Now the similarity seemed deceitful. Foolishly, she had taken it as just another sign that she and David breathed in the same rhythm. She had wanted to believe that. After all, how could a man who was so like her in temperament, who valued everything she valued, ever hurt her?

"Well, that went smoothly." Carol Ann sharply tapped the papers on the table, like a judge pounding her gavel. "I hope you'll find everything in order," she said to the young couple at the other end of the table, who had just bought the Bronsons' house. "If you have any questions, don't hesitate to call."

Carol Ann's smile warmed marginally when she turned it on David, although she wasn't flirting with him, a useless endeavor under the circumstances. Faith was sure she knew the story behind this sale. As far as Faith could tell, the whole world knew. David's forceful ejection from the closet had been reported by every scandal sheet in the free world.

Faith hadn't been the only interloper at the cottage that infamous day in December. After hearing one too many snippets of gossip about the two men, a particularly heinous colleague of Abraham Stein's had followed them from the conference in Seattle and parked in the woods nearby. If the reporter had harbored any doubts about what was happening in the cottage before Faith's arrival, her tearful flight to her car and David's tardy shouts from the doorway had confirmed his suspicions.

One more Washington role model tarnished beyond redemption.

Carol Ann stood. "Mr. and Mrs. Bronson, if you have any questions..."

"Thank you." Faith gathered her purse and a navy blazer her mother had given her on the worst Christmas morning of her life. Faith had carefully packed away everything David ever bought for her, as if wearing clothing he had chosen would be like leaping back into his arms.

The young mother who was the new owner of Faith's house sidled in her direction. "You're sure you'll be out by the end of the month?"

The new owner was a little whiny, a little imperious. Faith could not imagine her standing at Faith's own AGA cooker every morning, heating water and boiling eggs for her husband and three small children. She was not kind enough for the house, not properly grateful for the weed-free lawn or the elegant stencils on the master bedroom walls.

"You don't have anything to worry about." Faith slipped the blazer over her shoulders. She took a breath and lied politely—the way every senator's child is taught in the cradle. "I hope you'll love living there."

"I guess we'll manage. The market is so tight, it was the best we could do under the circumstances. "

Faith was glad she'd taken a deep breath. Because suddenly she couldn't breathe at all. Her lungs had turned to stone, which was just as well, since if they began to work again, she didn't know what might spew forth.

She caught David's eye, something she'd tried not to do throughout the whole ordeal. He looked shaken. For a moment they were bonded by their sorrow. David loved the house as much as she did. They had built it with the help of one of Washington's most talented architects. David had landscaped the extensive yard, installed a sprinkler system, even dug a fishpond last fall. They had planned to buy koi and water lilies this summer. Instead, the new owners had asked them to fill the hole as a condition of sale.

"Do you need a ride?" David asked before Faith could avert her eyes.

She found her breath and voice. "My mother's coming."

"I could take you—"

"No." She slung her purse over her shoulder and turned to say goodbye to Carol Ann and the Realtor who had represented the

Bronsons' interests. Then, before David could say another word, she left for the parking lot.

Her refusal to be alone with him wasn't new. Since that morning in December they had spoken only when their attorneys or her father were present. Joe Huston, Virginia's senior senator, had been with her on the day David explained that the board of Promise the Children had fired him and invoked the morals clause of his lucrative contract. The bonuses he had carefully invested through the years had to be returned, and the downturn in the stock market had taken care of the remainder of the family's assets. The house in McLean and the vacation cottage in West Virginia, both mortgaged, were almost all they had left.

At least Faith hadn't been sorry to sell the cottage.

The closing had finished early, and Lydia hadn't yet arrived to provide a clear escape. The lease had come due on Faith's Volvo the previous week, and she hadn't had the cash to purchase it outright. Now, on top of everything else, she had to find a reliable used car she could afford.

Despite her efforts, David caught up with her. Reluctantly she faced the man who was still, until their divorce became final, her husband. She knew it was important to make this look like a casual conversation. She knew too well that outsiders were always watching.

Her voice was low. "Please don't say anything. I don't want to hear how sorry you are, or how bad you feel. It doesn't matter."

"I'm sorry you're upset."

She was dry-eyed, because her tears had all been cried. For eight months, whenever her children were out of sight, she had indulged her sorrow, and now she wanted to move on. "You should leave. The children don't want to see you, and they'll be in the car with my mother."

"That will have to change."

As usual, David was wearing a suit. He had a Brooks Brothers wardrobe that might last him for several years of fruitless job searches unless he continued to lose weight. He had always been thin. He was thinner now, almost gaunt. His blond hair was threaded more heavily with gray.

"I don't know how to change anything," she said. "I'm not poisoning them against you. I try not to mention you at all. But both Remy and Alex understand what happened and why. Neither of them is ready to face the new you."

"Not a new me."

"That's right. Nothing new. Just something you forgot to mention."

"Something I forgot to face, Faith."

She didn't know what possessed her. She had just signed away her home, and the loss was immeasurable. By the same token, she felt newly unburdened. "You mean when you and I were making love and you were disgusted by my body, you refused to acknowledge it?"

"For Pete's sake, this isn't the time to imagine things that never happened. How can you believe that's true?"

"I believed a lot of things were true that weren't, didn't I?"

"I tried to believe them, too." He moved a step closer. "I want you to understand that. I locked away who I was. Not just from you and the rest of the world, but from myself. Maybe I was in the closet, but I liked the view well enough to stay there the rest of my life."

"Until Abraham Stein came along. A liberal journalist, David? Certainly not a born-again Christian. How many about-faces can one man make?"

"*Not* until Ham came along. He didn't cause this. I was living a lie, and it was wrong for you. For both of us."

"Really? That's funny, because I sort of liked it. I was married to the man I adored. I had two beautiful children, a home, respect. Now I have the truth and nothing else—except the children, who are falling apart. And at the end of the month we won't even have a place of our own. We'll be moving in with my parents."

"You were married to a man who couldn't love you the way you deserve." He put his hand on her shoulder, and when she tried to squirm away, he tightened it. "Listen to *me* for once. You deserve better. You deserve a man who can't keep his hands off you, somebody who can't wait to get home to you and doesn't want to leave you every morning. Not a best friend. A lover."

She stood very still, but contempt colored her voice. "You did this for me? Out of charity?"

"That's not what I'm saying."

"I would appreciate it if you *never* touched me again."

He dropped his hand. "What I have isn't catching."

"No? Some things associated with it certainly are."

"My attorney assured you, Faith. I didn't make love to you after Ham and I became lovers. And I was always faithful to you before then. You were never at risk for HIV."

"I've been tested anyway. Why should I take your word?"

He looked distressed. "Because if you can believe I was faithful, you'll understand what a struggle I put up. I wasn't the man I wanted to be, but I tried to be that man for you. For all the years of our marriage, I tried."

She was rarely sarcastic, but she couldn't stop herself now. "Oh, thanks so much. Just for me?"

"Faith—"

"Or was all that self-denial really for your father, or maybe mine? Until the day he died, your father thought he'd raised the perfect son. And my father? My father was grooming you to take his place in the Senate one day."

"That was Joe's idea."

She continued as if he hadn't spoken. "Or maybe you struggled for that world you created for yourself. The paragon David Bronson, family values czar. The man everyone looked up to for guidance."

"I wanted to be that man, Faith. For all of you."

She wasn't angry enough that she couldn't feel a flutter of compassion, despite wishing it weren't so. Perhaps her tears weren't all dry, because she wanted suddenly to cry.

"Why didn't you just tell me? At the beginning? Before... Before everything."

"I couldn't tell you what I couldn't tell myself."

"You're saying that before we were married you weren't attracted to men?"

"Homosexuality was a sin. I couldn't believe I was..."

"Gay," she snapped, to keep the tears from her voice. "The word is gay. One of the better words, as a matter of fact. Not the one Alex heard at school when the story got out. Not the one Remy uses every time she sobs her heart out."

He flinched. "I never meant to hurt them."

Even before the newspaper exposé, the infrastructure of their lives had collapsed and could never be reconstructed. But now she asked the question that had haunted her.

"Then why didn't you just *stay* in the closet, David?" Despite her efforts, she could feel tears filling her eyes. "Would you have, if I hadn't discovered you with Ham? If I hadn't come to the cottage that day, if the reporter hadn't come, would you ever have told me? Or would we still have everything we lost?"

"Would you want any of it? Knowing what you know now?"

She couldn't answer, because she didn't know.

"I was going to tell you. As soon as I found a way." He tried to smile, but it was ghostly and fleeting. "I was still working on an opening sentence. It would have been the toughest speech of my life."

"One picture was worth a million words."

He reached into his suit pocket and pulled out a handkerchief. He always had a crisply ironed handkerchief. Once upon a time she had seen to it. David offered it to her, but she shook her head.

He stuffed it back in his pocket so that it hung askew, like a distress flag on a sinking ship. "I'm going now, but you know where to reach me. I'll be there if you need me."

"Can you help me put my life back together?"

"I can offer friendship."

There was nothing she could say that could be said in public. She turned toward the road and away from him. "Worry about your children, David. That should keep you busy enough."

2

A woman who suffers nightmares prefers not to sleep, but years of sleeplessness take their toll. For nearly four decades Lydia Huston had been afraid to close her eyes.

The all-pervasive fatigue had started before menopause, and her joy in life had fled long before even that. Lydia ate only when she had to and found the simplest tasks daunting. In the last months she had watched her blond bob thin, and her carefully cared-for skin pucker and fold.

Of course, in the nightmare she was always young. Not a golden-haired debutante leaning proudly on her ambassador father's arm, not an eager bride leaning on the arm of her congressman husband, but a young mother, frightened and alone, for whom no arm could ever be support enough.

In her dream the house surrounding her was dark. Despite tiny rooms and a narrow hallway, she could not find her way through it. She felt along walls, stumbled over carpets, fell to her knees and lost what little sense of direction she had.

Music sounded, echoing off walls and stretching toward the attic. Arpeggios rippled; chords crashed like waves on a storm-tossed sea. She stood an inch at a time, not certain what was above or below her, and began to move again.

She stumbled over the bottom step of the staircase and grabbed the banister to break her fall. One foot on the step, pulling herself upright. The other foot beside it, swaying, reaching into darkness, swaying again.

The music crescendoed until she wanted to cover her ears. She tried to focus on the darkness, to single out a whimper, a murmur, but now scales soared, then descended, octave after octave.

She accomplished the third step with difficulty. On the fourth the banister ended suddenly and she nearly fell. The banister should have been there—it had always been there before. But not today.

Today. Not *tonight.* It was daytime, even if there was no light. She was getting closer, but not quickly enough. The unseen musician began a spirited polonaise, Liszt or Chopin. She had hoped for a waltz, a nocturne, anything that might allow sound from upstairs to filter through. She listened between phrases, during lengthy fermatas, hoping that in the pause between one musical thought and another, she would hear the sound she most longed for.

But there were few pauses and no sounds from upstairs.

She took one more step, and something, some*one,* brushed past, nearly throwing her backward into the void. She threw herself forward, teetering wildly, and just as she found her balance, the music ended.

On the floor just below her she heard laughter. One terrible, demonic laugh, then the wail of a newborn. A thin, piercing wail, followed by the most profound silence imaginable.

She tried to follow. She tried to scream for help. And when she did, as she always did, she awoke.

"Hey, the light's been green forever, Grandmother."

Nightmares could follow a woman into her waking hours, too, and Lydia had allowed it to happen again. She stepped on the accelerator and shot into the intersection just as the light changed to amber. "I can drive perfectly well without your help, Alex."

"Well, you weren't paying attention. And Remy won't say anything. She wants *me* to get in trouble."

Lydia had been transformed by the nightmare and the event that sparked it. Both tolerance and patience had disappeared with her energy, but most of the time she had learned not to show it. She could visit inner city schools, throw impromptu dinner parties for fifty, pretend her husband was God's gift to the United States Senate. But she could not find pleasure or comfort in the people she was supposed to love. Taking care of her grandchildren, a job most grandmothers savored, was like being thrown into a lion's den.

As she steered her Mercedes into the narrow lane where Faith waited, she snapped at her grandson again. "I won't tolerate another word from you, Alex. I've heard enough. Your sister just wants to be left alone." And so do I, she added silently.

"You always take her side."

"Her side rarely involves pushing and shoving."

"I didn't touch her." Alex paused. "Not for a while."

Alex was nothing if not honest. She had to give the child that. She glanced over her shoulder at the mop of auburn curls, broad face and temporarily sullen expression that was her grandson. "Do you want to walk home? Because if you do, you're well on your way."

He didn't answer. For the short term, at least, she'd won.

Lydia pulled to a halt beside her daughter and unlocked the door. Faith's dark blond hair shone in the summer sun, a sleek bell that almost touched her shoulders. She looked pale, but, as required from childhood, her spine was as straight as a flagpole, and when she got inside, she mustered a smile for her children.

She had been taught well, this daughter of Lydia's.

"Hi, you two. Did you have a good day?" Faith turned around to address them.

"Like that's possible," Remy said.

Lydia's fourteen-year-old granddaughter strongly resembled Faith and, for that matter, Lydia herself. Petite and golden-haired, Remy had clear skin and naturally straight teeth, putting her a step ahead of some of her friends. Lydia hoped Remy used this God-given lead wisely.

"How about you, Alex?" Faith asked.

"I can't talk!"

Faith shot a quick glance at her mother. "And the reason would be?"

"Because he can't say anything we want to hear."

"How long has he been cooped up in the car?"

Lydia sent her daughter a warning glance. "Doing errands in a Mercedes is not exactly being cooped up."

"Alex, hang in there," Faith told her son. "We'll be home before long."

"You spoil him," Lydia said.

"Who wouldn't? He's irresistible." Faith winked at her son.

Lydia took her foot off the brake, and the car rolled forward. She turned into traffic. "As a matter of fact, we aren't going home. Unless you absolutely have to."

Faith settled back against the leather seat. "Where are we going?"

Lydia ground out her answer, gnawing at the "r's." "Prospect Street."

Faith was appropriately surprised. "Now? What for?"

"The house is empty."

"Empty? Don't you have Georgetown students renting it? The school year's about to start."

"They took off. Last week, it seems. The property manager went to see about repairing an attic window—something she was supposed to do months ago—and found the place empty."

Lydia switched lanes and sped up to avoid an accident. "I spent the entire morning on the telephone tracking down the students. It seems one of them got an internship somewhere out of D.C. Another one moved in with a girlfriend. The third boy couldn't find roommates to share the place, so he's commuting from Maryland."

"And no one thought to mention this to you?"

"After the first year, our agent never renewed the rental contract. Seems she thought this would never happen, since housing near the university is so difficult to find. So she didn't worry about the lease."

"What about a security deposit?"

"There was no reason to think the students would get the money back, so they didn't bother to try."

Faith glanced at Alex—who was beginning to pick at Remy again. Lydia wished her daughter would discipline the boy. He was rowdy and rude, not at all the sort of child she had expected quiet, orderly people like Faith and David to raise. The fact that he and his sister would soon be living with her didn't boost her grandmotherly impulses.

Faith turned around in her seat. "I gather the house has been trashed?"

"A colorful way to put it. Yes, apparently it has." Despite everything that had happened in the house on Prospect, Lydia's heart was heavy at the thought. "I discovered what I could from the agent before I fired her. But I thought I'd better see for myself."

"I don't see why *we* have to go." Remy leaned forward. Lydia could just see her head in the rearview mirror. "I'm supposed to go to the movies with Megan."

"Because I don't have the time to take you home first," Lydia said. "For heaven's sake, Remy. It certainly seems with everything else I've done for you, you could do something for me."

Remy's head disappeared from view.

Faith spoke in low tones. "Mother, this is a tough time for all of us. Let's give Remy and Alex the benefit of the doubt, okay?"

"I've done little else all day, or most of the summer, for that matter." Lydia heard her own sharp tone and wondered for a moment who was speaking. When had she made room inside herself for that voice? When had the gentle, soft-spoken young woman changed into the shrewish, unfeeling matron?

The answer was simple. The transformation had begun on Prospect Street.

"We're all grateful for your help." Faith sounded anything but. She sounded wounded and vulnerable, exactly as anyone else would under the circumstances. The life she had built for herself was over, and the future couldn't be more uncertain.

Lydia reached deep inside to find some remnant of the gentler woman. "Going to Georgetown is never easy for me. I wanted..." She didn't know what else to say.

"I'm sorry. We'll be happy to come and give you some support." Faith touched her mother's arm. "Or at least I will. The kids can be our prisoners."

Lydia remembered when Faith was the tiniest little girl, how she would rest her fingers on Lydia's arm. How she would look at her with eyes as big as tomorrow, as if Lydia had all life's answers right under her skin. She remembered brushing off that tiny hand, afraid, oh so afraid, that the answers she had found in her own short life would destroy her daughter.

She pulled into the turn lane so she could take Chain Bridge into D.C. "It won't take long. It's not as if I can do anything today. I just need to take stock. I wish the timing were better. School starts in a few weeks, and there won't be time for serious repairs. I doubt I'll find renters before second semester."

"I wish you'd just sell the house," Faith said. "I've never understood why you keep it."

"That house has been in my mother's family since it was built, and it will be yours one day. Hopefully someday it will be Remy's."

Faith leaned closer. "It's not worth the pain it causes."

Lydia slowed to a crawl, inching along the bridge in a line that seemed to extend to the capital's center. She came to a traffic-induced halt. "You really don't understand, do you?"

"I'm sorry, but no."

Lydia turned to look at her. "Prospect Street was the last place I saw your baby sister. How could I sell the house to strangers, Faith? How could I ever?"

 3

The house on Prospect Street was cherry-colored brick of modified Federal style, a description that hardly did it justice. A survivor of wars and warring political parties, the century-old row house nestled snugly against its neighbors, like an elderly socialite drawing comfort from surviving members of her women's club.

The house held a forbidden allure for Faith. She had rarely come here, but each visit had made a strong impression. To a child, the ceilings had seemed as high as the clouds. As a teenager, she had been embarrassed by this monument to the tragedy that set her family apart and made her forever "different." As a young mother, she had tried not to bring her children within miles of Georgetown, unwilling to be reminded that in the end she had little control over what happened to their precious lives.

"I haven't been to Prospect Street in a long time," Faith told her mother as Lydia parked on the street a block and a half from the house. She was lucky to find any parking place at all.

"You have no reason to come."

"Alex and Remy haven't even been inside, have you?" She faced her son and daughter, trying to keep her voice buoyant. Remy rolled her eyes. The strain Faith had read on Alex's face began to ease at the thought of abandoning the car.

"Can I get out now?" he demanded.

Faith was surprised her son had asked, chalking it up as one of the day's few good signs. "Just stay with us. Don't take off on your own." She winced as his door scraped the curb.

"I'm not going inside," Remy said. "I have to call Megan. Can I have the cell phone?"

"May I," Lydia corrected her. "And you will come inside, Remy. I don't want you sitting out here by yourself. We're in a city, and nice girls don't sit in cars waiting for goodness knows who to come along."

Privately Faith thought her daughter would be fine. Georgetown was hardly D.C.'s crime-plagued inner city, and Prospect Street was well-traveled enough to make serious crime in broad daylight unlikely.

She tried for a compromise. "I'll let you have the cell phone once we're inside. Or you can sit on the front steps, if that's all right with your grandmother."

"She can come inside with the rest of us." Lydia opened her door and started toward the house.

"Why does she get to make all the rules?" Remy asked her mother.

"Remy, be polite, please."

"Oh, what's the point of talking to you!"

Sometimes Faith wondered that, too. "This is your grandmother's house and your grandmother's car. And you will be polite."

By the time she joined her son and mother on the sidewalk, Alex was swinging on a tree limb that didn't look strong enough to hold him. When Lydia made him stop, he launched himself across the uneven brick sidewalk, jolting to a stop at a low iron fence. "Look at the flowers growing between these bricks." He dropped to his knees to yank out dandelions.

"Leave him alone, Mother," Faith said, before Lydia could stop him. "He's doing the owner a favor."

"He can't stand still for ten seconds."

"He's a boy. He's supposed to run and jump. Girls, too, only we get it squeezed out of us pretty fast."

"I suppose that's a complaint about the way you were raised."

"Social commentary." Faith watched the daughter *she* was raising emerge slowly from the car. Remy was everything her brother was not. Sedate, eager to please, polite. Or at least she had been until her world fell apart.

"Megan's probably gone already, anyway," Remy said. "She *probably* asked Jennifer Logan to go with her to the movies, since I'm not there."

Megan lived on their block, and she and Remy had been best friends since they were pre-schoolers. In many ways the move was going to be hardest on Remy, because her entire life revolved around her social group.

Faith tried to help. "Maybe she can spend the night tonight. If you reach her, ask her. We can order pizza."

"Nobody wants to come to our house anymore."

"Ask her anyway." Faith was surprised at how stern she sounded. "We won't be living there much longer. You won't have many more chances."

"What's the point? She's not going to come all the way to Great Falls to see me after school. We won't be friends anymore once I move."

Faith didn't have the strength for an extended battle. "Come on, Alex."

He got to his feet, his hands dirty and filled with dandelions. As they walked toward the house he popped off the fluffy heads with a flick of his index finger, aiming them in the lagging Remy's direction.

"Stop it, Alex!" Remy said. "Mom, do you see what he's doing?"

Faith shook her head at Alex, who grinned back at her, dropping what was left of the dandelions and dusting off his hands in victory. Remy moved in close enough to shove him, but not hard enough to make him fall.

Lydia's lips were a straight, thin line, but, remarkably, she kept silent.

They passed more row houses like the one Lydia owned. Prospect began at bustling Wisconsin Avenue, with its chic shops and expensive restaurants, and extended toward Georgetown University, growing more residential with every block. Some of the properties were historic, elaborate edifices sheltered by enormous trees and blocked from view by brick walls. Others were modest by Georgetown standards, rentals for students or young professionals. Many of the houses sat almost directly on the sidewalk, looming like the bygone tales of former inhabitants, just out of reach.

A Georgetown address was prestige in itself, but absentee landlords held some of the property, much as Lydia did, depending on the area's reputation instead of meticulous upkeep and updates. One house they passed had trim that badly needed painting. Another's postage-stamp front yard was in need of a chain saw to clear deadwood and shrubs that no longer thrived.

"I ought to sue the rental agency." Lydia put her hands on her hips and gazed at the house they'd come to evaluate.

Faith stopped, too, the children well behind her. She had never lived here. But she felt ashamed.

A woman's voice floated toward them from the house next door. "It's about time you came to see the place, Lyddy. Before the city condemns it."

Beside Faith, Lydia went rigid. Faith followed the voice with her eyes, but it took a moment to see the woman in question. She stood at one of the tall windows on the second floor, just inside an iron railing extending over the narrow yard. She appeared to be as old as a Supreme Court Justice and as brazen as a certain White House intern. Even though it was well into afternoon, she wore a brilliant blue wrapper over a nightgown—at least Faith hoped she was wearing a gown—and her head was wrapped in a matching turban.

"Ignore her," Lydia said, for Faith's ears only. "She's the wrong kind of woman to introduce to your children."

In a louder voice Lydia went on, as if the woman hadn't spoken. "I am going to sue the rental agency. This is disgraceful. They were responsible, and no one told me."

When the woman disappeared inside, Faith reluctantly pulled her attention back to the house. "When was the last time you stopped by?"

"I don't stop by. Why should I? I hire people to take care of the property. Do you think I want to hobnob with the tenants?"

Faith was accustomed to Lydia's sarcasm. She wanted to believe that hiding somewhere inside her mother's frozen heart was a compassionate nature, that under her rigid self-discipline and even

more demanding expectations a warmer, more tolerant woman
hid. She thought she saw signs of one occasionally.

But the Hustons hadn't named their daughter Faith for nothing.

"Will you look at the door? At the yard?" Lydia shook her head.

Faith had no other place to look. The house was three stories high
and one room narrow. Like many of its neighbors, architectural details were minimal. A wooden door surround with a semicircular
fanlight over it. A cornice with toothlike dentils underscoring the
slate roof. Shuttered windows with double-hung sashes. An iron
stair rail enclosing four wide steps to the door.

The only adornment was an antique iron plaque, or "fire mark,"
placed well above the fanlight to show that the family's credit with
the local fire department was good. The house wasn't old enough
to have needed one, but one of Lydia's ancestors had probably res-
cued it from another street and added it for effect.

Silently Faith catalogued the problems. The brick needed cleaning. The peeling gray trim needed paint or, in a few cases, re-
placement. A pane of glass was missing in the attic, and another
on the second floor had been patched with duct tape. The stair rail
needed sanding and rust inhibitor—if enough of it was left to paint.
The shrubs hugging the house were dying.

"From the outside, anyway, there's nothing wrong with it that
some hard work won't fix. For starters, we ought to ask those people on the next block to go in a chain saw rental," Faith said.

"I fail to see the humor."

"I'm learning to find it in the least likely places."

"Woo-woo..." Alex said, and not like a train. "It's haunted!"

Faith whirled to silence him, but Lydia reached him first, grasp-
ing his shoulder. "You will never say that in my presence again.
Do you understand? Your mother may think your behavior is cute,
but she's the only one who does."

Alex stood perfectly still, but his expression said everything.
Faith couldn't let it pass. "Mother, he didn't mean—"

"I don't care what he meant!" Lydia dropped her hand with obvious reluctance.

Faith drew herself up to her full five-four. "Mother, you and
Remy go ahead." She fished in her purse and found the cell phone,

holding it out to her daughter. "Alex and I will join you in a few minutes. Somebody needs to explain to him why you're so angry."

For a moment Lydia froze in place; then, without a word or glance, she hurried up the steps.

"Oh, come on, can't I sit out here?" Remy said.

"Not a chance. Go on." Faith nodded toward the house. "And stay out of your grandmother's way until I get in there."

"I don't care why she's mad," Alex said, when the others were gone. "She's always mad. She hates me."

"She has very little patience today." Faith settled herself on the third step and patted the space beside her, wondering how much more honest she should be.

He joined her, leaning against her for comfort, his auburn hair brushing her shoulder. She put her arm around him. "I'm sorry, sweetheart. Your grandmother doesn't have much experience with children, and none with boys."

"How come making ghost noises upset her?"

Faith tried for the basics. "You must remember the story about my sister? I'm sure you've heard it a million times."

"She was kidnapped." He shrugged, rubbing his shoulder companionably against hers. "That's all I know."

"Your grandmother and grandfather lived in this house a long time ago."

"Well, it looks like nobody's lived here since. Except maybe ghosts. That's all I meant."

Faith patted his denim-clad knee. "Nobody who cares about the place. But my mother's family had always owned this house, and after they married, she and my father moved in. Not too long afterward, they brought their first daughter home from the hospital."

"Hope." Alex brushed his foot back and forth on the bottom step. "I know that part."

"That's right. My mother put baby Hope in a crib in the nursery and left her to sleep. Later, when she went in to check on her, she was gone."

"And nobody ever found her." Alex's foot moved faster.

"They never did. Even though it was national news for months and months, and hundreds of police officers worked on the case. Nobody ever discovered what happened to her."

Alex was trying to make sense of it. "That was a long time ago. And *I* didn't kidnap anybody. Why's she angry at me?"

"She's not. She just... She always feels sad when she comes here, because the house reminds her of Hope. Maybe it wouldn't be so bad if we knew what happened to her, but we don't. Nobody does. So your grandmother never really put it behind her. Can you understand that?"

"I understand a lot more than you think."

Faith heard the voice of the man Alex was going to become. She heard those echoes more often now. "I'm glad."

"So when I said the house was haunted, she thought I was talking about Hope?"

"Exactly." Faith paused. "There's been a rumor for years that sometimes, late at night, you can hear a baby crying up on the third floor."

"Spoo—ky!"

"Yes. Well. It's just one of those gruesome stories people like to tell. The tour groups who come by have kept it going."

Alex got to his feet, anxious to move on. "I'd like to live here. I think it would be neat to see if the story's true."

"Don't mention that to your grandmother, okay? She would most definitely not think it was neat."

"I didn't mean to make her sad."

"Maybe when she's feeling better you could tell her that."

"She doesn't hear anything I say."

Faith was afraid he was right. "Maybe she just doesn't hear *as much* as you'd like."

"You're sad, too. All the time now."

She made a point of not lying to her children. "I'm sorry. I *am* sad."

"Me, too."

She reached for his hand. "I know. You wish things were the way they used to be."

"How could Dad do this to us? It's killing Remy. I can take it. I'm a guy. But she hates him, and maybe I do, too."

She couldn't explain what she really didn't understand. "Being...gay, well, it's tough. And when your daddy was growing up, it was even tougher."

"Yeah. Grandpa Bronson would have knocked him silly for the Lord."

David's father, a renowned evangelist, would have done exactly that. Arnold Bronson was dead now, which was just as well, because David's announcement would surely have killed him.

"How do you know what your grandfather would have done?" Faith got to her feet, squeezing Alex's hand before she dropped it.

"I can draw conclusions, you know. I'm not stupid, even if everybody thinks so."

"I don't think you're stupid. You know I don't. You're very smart. You just like to think outside the box. You're going to do big important things with your life."

"I want to see the house. I'll stay away from Grandmother."

"Good thinking."

"If I was really smart, I'd think of a way to make Dad come back."

Her throat tightened. "You didn't do anything to drive him away, and you can't do anything to bring him home."

"I don't want to see him." He folded his arms. "He probably doesn't want to see us, anyway. He probably doesn't care."

"He wants to see you. When you're ready, he'll be there waiting."

"Remy wishes he was dead."

Faith was surprised Remy was talking about her feelings with Alex. "She's angry. Things will get better."

"Not for her they won't."

Faith had been worried enough about her children. Now the worry grew deeper. "Time takes care of—"

"It hasn't helped Grandmother, has it? She's still angry about Hope. And we're going to be living with her and with Grandfather. He's angry, too. Everybody's angry, and living with them is just going to make things worse! Why did you have to sell our house?"

The lump in Faith's throat grew larger. "Daddy's not working right now, and I don't have the experience to get a job with a salary large enough to pay the mortgage. We're only going to live with your grandparents until we can get back on our feet. It won't be forever."

Even as she said it, Faith wondered. She had looked at three-bedroom apartments, and the rents were astounding. Unless David was able to find a good job—unlikely, since he had closed one set of doors with his conservative rhetoric and the other with his recent announcement—they might be living with her parents until the children went to college.

"Everything I do is wrong." Alex looked uncharacteristically glum. "Whenever anyone's angry or sad, they take it out on me."

Faith had a glimpse of the future her son envisioned. Months of criticism stretching into years. Angry pleas to stop fidgeting. Constant prodding to do better, to be more like Remy, to fit himself into the Hustons' narrow mold. Faith would intervene when she could, but she would be sharply reminded that she and the children were living in the Hustons' house now, playing by their rules.

"We'll find a way to make this work," she said at last.

"Faith, are you coming?" Lydia leaned past the open front door. "I need help. Do you have a notepad? There's one in the car, but I didn't think to bring it. Alex, are you finished being rude?"

Alex looked at Faith, as if to say, *"Here's living proof I'm right, Mom."*

"We're coming," Faith said. "I have paper for notes."

"Well, I could certainly use a little assistance." Lydia vacated the doorway.

"Maybe we could buy a tent and camp until I'm a grown-up," Alex said. "Then I can take care of you."

She wasn't sure whether to laugh or cry.

 4

The row house had been designed for convenience. The first story held a spacious living area that flowed into a formal dining room, with a kitchen, powder room and small breakfast nook in the rear. The second had a narrow hallway, three bedrooms and a bath. The third story was a large attic used for storage.

Today the first two floors were enough to deal with. She found Lydia in the back bedroom on the second floor.

At sixty-six, Faith's mother was an attractive woman who routinely visited her gym, her image consultant, and her plastic surgeon for required nips and tucks. Her most recent face-lift had erased years but not the lingering traces of her cynical world view. Even when Lydia smiled, her blue eyes, so much like Faith's own, rarely warmed.

Lydia wasn't making any attempt to smile now.

"I'm sorry, Mother." Faith tried to put her arm around Lydia's shoulders, but her mother moved away.

Lydia didn't glance at her. "Sympathy is nice, but it doesn't help matters, does it?"

"Actually, some people believe it helps a lot."

"It won't fix what's wrong here."

"That's going to take a parade of workmen and some uncalculated amount of money." As she searched the house for her mother,

Faith had informally catalogued the problems. The wood floors were deeply scarred. Ceilings were stained from unrepaired leaks. All the exposed plaster needed patching and painting. Wallpaper had to be stripped—probably layers of it—right down to bare walls. The kitchen was filthy and so out-of-date that she doubted most of the appliances worked. The powder room toilet was missing a seat, and the sink had no faucet.

That was just for openers.

"It's my own fault." Lydia was so tight-lipped it was surprising sound emerged. "I pretended the house wasn't here."

She faced Faith, clearly preferring her daughter's face to the sight of exposed electrical outlets and frayed extension cords. Two bare mattresses lined one wall, and the air here was worse than stale. The unmistakable scent of urine added a pathetic top note. "This was your sister's room."

"I know."

"How could anyone deface it this way?"

"What are you going to do?"

"Hire a contractor. Pay what needs to be paid. Do what needs to be done."

Faith wondered if "doing what needs to be done" was her mother's mantra. She tried to point out the problems as gently as possible. "Do you have time? The job's going to require a lot of supervision, even if you can schedule a good contractor—which is tough, because they're all so busy. And when the work's finished, you could end up with the same problems all over again. Students aren't necessarily the best—"

"Then I'll find professionals to rent it this time. If the house is renovated, that shouldn't be hard." Lydia crumpled a little. "And no, I don't have the time. Of course I don't. This is an election year. My appointment book is as thick as the Yellow Pages even if your father's not up for reelection. But what choice do I have?"

The answer, when it came to her, was so simple, so perfect. Faith was amazed neither of them had seen it from the beginning.

She eased into it. "You said in the car that the house is going to be mine one day?"

"Don't tell me you're just going to sell it when it's yours. I don't want to hear it."

"Give it to me *now*. Let me take over."

Lydia frowned. "Look around, Faith. I can't imagine what renovations will cost. You don't have the means. You can't even afford to rent a place to live on your own."

"I could afford to own this house. The children and I can live here while the repairs are under way. I can do some of them myself to save money."

She was getting excited now. Eight months had passed since she'd felt anything like enthusiasm; now she held on to it. "I can paint and wallpaper. I can refinish cabinets and maybe even floors. And I can be on the spot to supervise everything else and make sure it's done right."

"Live in Georgetown? With the children?" Lydia sounded as if Faith had just proposed a move to Outer Mongolia.

Faith was still thinking out loud. "I wouldn't even have to buy a car right away. The bus system is adequate. This way I won't have to find a job immediately. If we don't have to pay rent, we can live on the money I got from the sale of the house and cottage for at least a year, and I'll still have enough to invest for college. I can help the children settle in and adjust. They—"

"How would you get them to school?" Lydia paused. "You're not talking about taking them out of the academy?"

Remy and Alex attended a private academy with a small student body and a traditional approach to education. There, with children from nearly identical family backgrounds, the values and religious beliefs they'd grown up with were strictly reinforced. Until David's announcement, Remy had flourished in the regimented environment. Alex never had.

When Faith didn't answer, Lydia crossed the room to run a finger along a peeling window ledge. Beyond the narrow, overgrown backyard, Faith could see the Whitehurst Freeway, but not far away the Potomac glimmered, and at night the lights of Rosslyn, Virginia, were undoubtedly spectacular.

"I can't believe you'd consider taking them away from their friends and teachers. They've already lost their father and their home."

"They haven't lost David." Faith hurried on before her mother could object. "And it was hard for them to stay at the academy for the rest of last year, to be whispered about and pitied. Anywhere else what happened would have been overlooked or forgotten quickly, but not there, not—"

"People move on. Things will be better—"

"Maybe, but maybe it's time Remy and Alex discovered that the world isn't the little nest we made for them. Maybe overprotecting them was as bad as exposing them to everything that came along. They had no resources to face what happened with David. *I* had no resources."

"Surely you, of all people, know that bad things can happen when you least expect them. You grew up knowing that."

For once Faith chose not to be cautious. "After Hope was kidnapped, you built a fortress around your life and raised me inside it. I grew up being afraid of the big, bad world. I married a man who could give me the life I was already accustomed to. I didn't ever question anything. And now the walls are tumbling and the gate's open. But if the children and I move in with you and Dad, the walls will go up again. Even higher."

Lydia's voice was even colder than usual. "I'm sorry you see our offer to help as a prison."

"That's not what I'm saying." Faith joined her mother at the windows. "Look, be honest. You don't want us living with you. The children drive you crazy, and it's only going to get worse until they're through adolescence. On top of that, you don't want the responsibility of this house. Let me take over."

"I don't want my grandchildren living here. You know what happened in this house."

"The house isn't cursed. The house is a disaster, but it isn't haunted. A terrible thing happened, but that was a long time ago. Life has to go on."

Lydia crossed her arms. "Right after... Before I had to face the fact Hope was gone for good, I wanted to raze everything. Tear it to the ground and build another in its place. A different house. Any house. But, of course, I couldn't. Even in those days, the preservationists would have had my head if I'd tried. I thought about selling it. We needed the money to buy our property in Virginia. But in those days, nobody wanted to live at the site of the infamous Huston kidnapping."

Faith remembered that O. J. Simpson's house had been demolished after its sale. And Nicole Simpson hadn't even been murdered there.

Lydia faced her daughter. "So I held on to it. Despite the tour companies that brought people to stand on the sidewalk and stare twice a day. Despite only being able to rent to students. And eventually, when I knew Hope wasn't coming back, I no longer wanted to sell."

"Maybe the house needs family in it again. I know living in the city would be a big change for Remy and Alex. They wouldn't be happy at first. And maybe it would be a mistake to bring them here. But what's one more change among so many? We'd be independent, and we'd be doing you a favor. You don't have to give me the house now, if you don't want to make it final. Just let us live here until we're back on our feet."

"There might be tax consequences for you if I hand it over before I die. I'll have to talk to my attorney."

Despite a host of misgivings, Faith was becoming more excited. "That's a good idea."

"Your father won't approve. I would have taken a mortgage to put it back in shape, then used what rent I got to pay it off. I can guarantee he won't do a thing to help you fix it up."

"I don't need his help," Faith said.

"Joe doesn't have any say over whether you move in or not." Lydia smiled grimly. "This is my house. His name isn't on the deed. If I decide to give it to you, he'll have no choice but to go along."

"I don't want to come between you."

Lydia didn't answer.

Faith scanned the room that had once been Hope's nursery. "This house deserves another chance. It's been punished enough. It deserves better than beer bashes and screaming stereos. I can turn it into a home again, if you'll let me."

"I can probably live with the fallout if you can." Lydia almost sounded as if the thought of Joe's disapproval pleased her.

"It looks like we might have a deal."

Faith felt her mother's hand on her shoulder. Briefly. Lightly. But the touch, possibly even meant to be comforting, surprised her more than any other event of the day.

5

Remy's room in the McLean house was nearly as large as an entire floor of the house on Prospect. She had her own bathroom and a closet big enough to stable a horse. Faith wasn't sure what she and David had been thinking when they agreed to the architect's plans. Perhaps they had hoped if they made the house perfect for the children, their lives would be perfect, as well. She remembered that she had wanted the house to be so welcoming, so accommodating, that the children would never want to leave. Unfortunately, she had been successful.

Now, hours after the trip to Georgetown, the McLean house was oddly silent. At the moment Faith stood in the doorway of Remy's room and waited for her solemn-faced daughter to invite her in. Remy, sitting cross-legged in the center of her white canopy bed, didn't say the words.

"Megan couldn't make it, huh?" Faith said.

"She's sleeping over at Jennifer's." Remy flopped down on her back and stared at her canopy.

"May I come in?"

"If you have to."

Faith crossed the room, passing a wall of built-in shelves neatly displaying fourteen years of Christmas and birthday gifts, an historical exhibit of Remy's life. She lowered herself to the edge of her daughter's bed. "You're upset."

"No I'm not."

Faith tried to figure out how to get to her through a back door. "If I were you—and I know I'm not—I'd feel like my life was ending. Everything is changing, and you have no power to stop it."

"So?"

"Well, being powerless sucks."

"You don't have to talk like a kid so I'll listen."

Faith waited.

"Everybody knows about Daddy. At school, here on the street. How come you didn't know right away? You were married to him."

Faith knew Remy was particularly hurt by David's absence. Of the two children, she had been closer to her father. Remy and David had always had a bond that sustained them through any ruffling of peaceful family waters. But not this time.

Faith drew a deep breath before she spoke. "I can tell you honestly that this never crossed my mind. It was a very deep secret, one even your father didn't want to face."

"Yeah, well, he's done a pretty good job of facing it now, hasn't he? He's living with a man. They have sex. That's so sick I can't even think about it."

"You don't have to think about it, honey. But no matter what the rest of his life is about now, he's still your father."

"He shouldn't be anybody's father. He'll never be mine again. I never want to see him."

Faith knew better than to explain that, eventually, Remy would have to see David. Ironically, the very man who believed anti-discrimination legislation was unnecessary would have the court on his side if things came to that.

"Let's talk about you right now," she said. "Look, what can I do to help you through this?"

"I want to go to boarding school."

Faith reached for Remy's hand, but Remy shook her off, punching the next words for emphasis. "I don't want to live with Grandmother. I won't. And Grandfather's impossible. I'll never be allowed to have friends over or listen to music. I want to go far away and never come back."

Faith wondered how many times she could be stabbed in the heart without bleeding to death. "You can't go to boarding school, Remy. We don't have the money for it."

"You keep talking about money!"

"Unfortunately, I have to. You don't have to worry about being put out on the street, about not having enough food or nice clothes to wear. We're not in any danger. But extras like boarding school aren't possible."

"We would be out on the street if Grandmother and Grandfather didn't take us in."

"Things will get better soon. I'm going to get a job. Your dad's trying to find a good one, too, so he can pay child support."

"Like anyone would want him now. Who wants a queer telling people what to think?"

"Remy, you will not use that word!"

"It's true."

"It's a derogatory term, and this is your father, who's loved and cared for you since the day you were born."

Remy turned on her side, away from Faith. "We're going to be poor forever. You've never even had a job, and he won't find one. I'll have to live with Grandmother until I graduate."

Faith's prospects were few. She had a degree in European history and no significant work experience. She'd been destined to go on to graduate school and eventually teach—until she met David. She had always planned to go back someday, when the children were older, but she hadn't felt a burning need for a career. She had the perfect marriage and husband. What was the hurry?

Had David simply died, there would have been a huge network of political and social contacts she could call on. Now, though, most of them would be embarrassed and probably reluctant to hire her. She might be Joe Huston's daughter, but the senator's conservative allies would remember more clearly that she was David Bronson's clueless ex-wife.

She tried to reassure Remy. "I'm going to take some word processing classes and look for a civil service job. I'm not a total loss, you know. I'm actually pretty smart."

"Not smart enough to figure out you were married to a homosexual."

Faith flinched. This was an entirely new side to the child she'd believed she was raising. Now she remembered her conversation with Lydia. Here was living proof that she and David had raised offspring with no ability to cope. Remy was a delight when things went her way, but life wasn't always like that.

Unfortunately, Faith had forgotten to tell her daughter.

Faith got to her feet. Empathy hadn't worked any miracles. It was time for the truth. "Here's the plan, Remy. We've sold the house. There was no way around it. Your father and I are getting a divorce, and there's no way around that, either. You're fourteen and have to live with me, but there are some things we can control. I've thought of a way to keep us from moving to Great Falls with your grandparents."

As she had guessed, Remy reluctantly let curiosity take the reins. "How?"

"If your grandmother says yes, we're going to move into the house on Prospect Street."

Remy sat up. The sullen expression was replaced by incredulity. "You've got to be kidding. That house smells like someone went to the bathroom in the halls. And I saw something moving in the kitchen, maybe a rat, and there was a homeless man down the street picking cans out of somebody's trash. How would I get to school?" She paused, the reality dawning. "I wouldn't, would I?"

Faith considered how best to answer that. She was still making decisions, still proceeding with caution. "None of this is certain yet. As for the academy, the tuition is too much for me if I'm going to save for college, too. I have to invest whatever I can now, so you can go to a good university."

"Let Grandfather pay for college. He will."

"And if he pays, you'll have no choice about where you go or what you major in. Those are the hard facts." Faith knew from experience.

"Then let him pay for the academy. He will."

Faith wasn't sure her father *would* pay the academy fees, even if she begged. He was still so angry at his son-in-law's humiliating "defection" that he wasn't above punishing the children just to make David squirm.

But even if he did, she didn't want to be beholden to Joe Huston. He was a rigid man, and leverage was a senator's stock in trade. If he helped Faith pay tuition, he would exact repayment in a thousand different ways, none of them endearing.

Faith looked down at her daughter. "Here's a big dose of reality, because you're old enough to handle it. The last half of the year at the academy was tough for you, and it's always been tough for your brother. I think you need a new school, one that doesn't pretend everybody in the world thinks the same way. You need a larger view."

"I'm not going to public school."

"Maybe you need to start over. Not boarding school, but somewhere with a different outlook. Public school could be the place."

"You just don't want to spend your precious savings on me. You don't care."

The telephone rang, and when Remy made no attempt to answer, Faith reached for it. Her mother was on the other end of the line.

Faith hung up a few moments later.

"You're really going to move us to that slum, aren't you?" Remy said. "No matter what I say."

Faith wondered what she had just agreed to. She had given up the security of Great Falls and a lifestyle that was, at the very least, familiar. She had traded that known quantity for a wreck of a house on Prospect Street and the dubious joys of city life.

She gave a short nod. "Georgetown is nobody's idea of a slum. If you think it is, then you really do need a larger view of the world. So you're about to get one. Your grandmother has decided to let us move into the house."

"I'm not going."

Remy had no choice. Faith only hoped that in the not too distant future her daughter would understand why this move and everything that came with it were necessary.

An hour after her conversation with Remy, Faith lay in the tub in the master bathroom. She had capped off her session with her daughter by breaking the news to her son. Alex, heavily involved in trying to bypass the strict controls David had set up on his computer, looked up when she finished.

"Can I live in the attic? I don't want to go unless I get to live in the attic."

"What are you, kiddo, a bat?"

"I bet it's neat up there. And that's where the ghost lives, right?"

"There's no such thing as a ghost."

"Mrs. Garfield said there was. She said ghosts are spirits who get kicked out of heaven for not doing what they're told."

Faith suspected this was just another way for the eternally creative Mrs. Garfield—Alex's fifth-grade teacher—to ride herd on her son. She ruffled Alex's wild red curls. His hair—both color and texture—was only one way he was different from everyone else in the family. Faith didn't believe in ghosts, but a changeling sat right in front of her.

"Listen, maybe you can make the attic a workshop right off the bat. A place to invent."

"Off the bat?" Alex chortled. "Off real bats? Do you think the attic really has 'em?" The thought seemed to please him.

She hoped that bats were one problem they wouldn't face.

Alex's face brightened even more. "Can I go to a different school?"

"You're okay with the idea?"

"Awesome." He looked as if he was trying to decide whether to say anything else. "Maybe someplace where they like me better?"

Now, soaking in the whirlpool tub that she would be giving up in a little over a week, Faith wondered why she had ever agreed to enroll Alex in a school where he felt rebuffed. In her present state of mind she wanted to blame it on David, but she couldn't. She had bought an entire way of life, an entire way to think, when she had married David Bronson. And it wasn't as if she hadn't known.

Her father had been the one to introduce her to her future husband, touting the quiet young man as an up-and-coming force in conservative politics. Late bloomer Faith was just beginning to feel her own way through life, but she was so enamored of David, so thoroughly and instantly smitten, that she willingly traded her fledgling independence to become his wife.

She knew what came with the package. She had watched her own mother build her life around her father's career, so instinctively she did the same. For fifteen years she worked side by side with her husband to create a perfect family, and she learned to see it as her calling.

And she had done her job well. Time and time again she had been asked to speak on the subject of making a Christian home, an honor she avoided by claiming she was too busy making one to lecture on the subject.

On the other hand, David never missed a chance to speak on the subjects he held dear. He was soft-spoken and modest, a rarity in political and religious circles. He abstained from criticism of differing views, and stated his own succinctly and compassionately. Had he used the master of divinity degree he earned at Harvard to become the next pastor of his evangelist father's mega-church, the theme of every sermon would have been "Love thy neighbor as thyself."

But on Arnold Bronson's death, David hadn't ascended to his father's ministry. Now Faith wondered if even then her soon-to-be ex-husband had been wrestling with his personal demons. For in keeping with his father's commandments, he would have been called on to forcefully revile the sin of homosexuality. And surely some part of him had questioned the wisdom of that.

With her eyes closed and the soothing fragrance of chamomile and citrus surrounding her, Faith could almost feel sorry for David. He had lied; he had used her to perpetuate a myth about who he was. But she knew he had never wanted to cause her pain.

She opened her eyes and looked down at her body stretched languidly in the herbal-scented water. She was never pleased at what she saw. She had a runway model's small breasts and narrow hips, but not the long legs to go with them.

She wondered if her very lack of feminine attributes had made her neutral enough for David to continue the farce of their marriage.

The thought hadn't yet lost the power to torment her. She shuddered and scrutinized herself more closely. Yes, she was ordinary, but weren't most women, and men still found them sexy? Did her dissatisfaction with her body and her lack of confidence come from a fifteen-year relationship with a man who couldn't, by his very nature, find her sexually appealing?

Had she unconsciously picked up David's disinterest and taken responsibility for it? Just the way she had taken responsibility for every single thing in their obscenely perfect lives?

Furious, she swept her towels, the tube of bath gel and an unlit candle to the tile floor before she realized what she was doing. The cordless telephone teetered on the edge and clanged to the bath mat before she could catch it.

"Damn!" The word was relatively untested on her tongue, but tonight she liked the feel of it. She was determined to begin a new life for the sake of her children, but was there anything left inside her to work with?

The telephone rang. She snatched it off the floor and heard her father's voice. After she said goodbye, she stepped out of the tub and reached for her robe.

One of the longest days of her life wasn't over yet.

David stood outside the house he had helped design and gazed up at the second-floor windows. Remy's bedroom light was off, but Faith's window was softly lit.

He imagined she wasn't sleeping well. Faith never slept well when he wasn't in the house. She wasn't a woman who jumped at every noise or imagined the rambler rose slapping against the trellis was a burglar. She'd told him once that she simply felt incomplete when he was away.

She had told him so much, and he had told her so little.

As a child, his father had taught him not to cry. Isaac hadn't cried as *his* father prepared to sacrifice him. Who was David to cry when a child at such terrible risk had remained silent?

He wanted to cry now. For who and what he was. For who and what he had become. For falling prey to an attraction so powerful it had exposed the lies he'd told himself.

And right now for the woman he had left behind.

The moon was nearly full tonight, and it shone softly on the two story colonial. A magnolia he'd planted was nearly as high as the roof. A sycamore he'd spent a thousand dollars to protect when the lot was cleared towered over the garage. The house had been his retreat and refuge, but for the last few years it had seemed like a prison.

Faith wouldn't welcome this visit. She had arranged to be away one afternoon several months ago so he could retrieve his personal belongings. They had agreed through their attorneys on what furniture and possessions he could remove, but he had forgotten about several boxes of books Faith would have no use for.

He had parked on the street like a stranger. Now he trudged up the long brick sidewalk and rapped lightly on the front door. His hands were cold, though the night was sultry. He was nervous about walking through the door of a house he had owned until today. And he was more nervous about encountering the woman who was still his wife.

He was surprised when she answered right away. She was barefooted, wearing denim shorts and a bright yellow T-shirt, and her hair was damp.

"Dad, I—" Her eyes widened when she saw David. "What are you doing here?"

"Faith, don't close the door. Please."

She stood solidly in the middle of the doorway. "Didn't we say enough this afternoon?"

"I'm sorry."

"You already said that."

"No, I'm sorry that I'm bothering you tonight. But on the way ho—after I left the settlement, I remembered I never looked through the books in the family room. I got the ones from my study, but I didn't—"

"I'll pack them up and have them sent. What do you want?"

"I'm not sure, exactly. I'd like to look through them. You can check to be sure you don't want—"

"I don't want any of your books, David."

"Then may I come in and get them? I waited as late as I could."

She raked her hair over her ears. "Your timing couldn't be worse. My father's on his way over here to lecture me. Unless you want some of what he's dishing out, you might want to leave."

"What's he lecturing you about?"

She raised a brow, clearly questioning his right to ask.

He managed half a smile. "I could take the heat for you. Lord knows you've been taking it for me for months, haven't you?"

She didn't smile in return. "In ways you can't even imagine."

The woman blocking his access seemed both familiar and unfamiliar. They had shared so much, memories that would forever haunt him. But he wondered how well he had really known her. He suspected he had underestimated Faith. He had been so afraid to tell her the truth; he had expected her to dissolve. Now the evidence was clear. She was getting on with her life. Oddly enough, that disconcerted him.

"I'm moving into the house on Prospect Street," she said at last.

For a moment he thought he hadn't heard her correctly. "Prospect?"

"Mother's house in Georgetown. It'll be mine eventually, so she's giving it to me now, a tax-free chunk at a time, until it's in my name. But for all practical purposes she's turning it over to me this week. It solves a lot of problems, not the least of which was giving the children a home of their own. I won't have to buy a car right away. I can look for a job in the city." She shrugged.

He felt a flash of anger. "Don't you think you should have consulted me?"

Her blue eyes widened. "Excuse me?"

"They're my children, too. Shouldn't I have a say in where they live?"

"Not when that decision affects me personally. What would you have said, David? Faith, you have to live with your parents? I insist?"

He felt as if he were navigating through a whirlpool. "Of course not. I'd just like to be part of things. I'm their—"

Her voice, when she found it again, shook with anger. She stepped outside and pulled the door closed behind her. "Yes, you are their father. But what gives you the right to make decisions about the way I'll live the rest of *my* life? I did everything you expected me to do for fifteen years, and look where it got me. Now it's my turn to make decisions. And I'm moving the children to Georgetown."

He had never seen her so angry. "Without telling me."

"I *did* tell you. The decision was made tonight, and I just told the children. You've lost the right to be at the top of my list."

He took a deep breath. He needed it. "Can we talk about this without a fight?"

"There's nothing to talk about."

"If we talk about everything that affects Alex and Remy, it's easier for me to help. I didn't know you had given up the Volvo until yesterday, when I got the paperwork from the car dealer. Why didn't you tell me? I'm leaving the Accord with you. That's the other reason I came. It's yours. I'm signing it over. I don't want you depending on your mother for transportation. You should have told me."

"Why? Maybe you'd still like me to be dependent on you? You don't want *me,* but you want to control me? Well, guess what? I can make it without you, David."

"I don't want to run your life."

"Of course you do. You've been running it for years, and I let you. But not anymore."

"I don't want to run your life," he repeated. "I just want to make it tolerable." He turned up his hands in unconscious supplication. "Will you please take the Accord?"

Her answer was cut off by the sound of a car turning into the driveway.

"Oh great." Faith rested her forehead against her palms for a moment. "Are you going to gang up?" She looked up. "That would be something, wouldn't it? You and the senator in league again. Deciding together what I should do and where I should do it."

"For the record, I don't know whether I'm against the move or not. I only wanted—"

She cut him off with a vicious swipe of her hand. "You still have time to leave. Do it."

"That's what Joe expects. A sissy runs. A real man stays and fights."

"He will never see you as a real man again, no matter what you do."

She was deliberately trying to be cruel, he knew, so unlike herself that she felt like a stranger to him. Belatedly he realized she was also trying to warn him. But David didn't need a warning. He knew Joe Huston as well as he knew himself. He knew how easy it was to condemn and how soothing it was to bask in self-righteousness. He had done both, and he had been struck down. Joe was still in his prime.

When he didn't leave, Faith stepped forward. "Wait a minute. How do you plan to get...wherever, if you're leaving the car here?"

He met her eyes, and she saw the answer.

"I see," she said. "Mr. Stein followed you. He's out there waiting?"

He inclined his head.

"That's accommodating," she said.

"I'm sorry, but I had to have a ride home."

"Home..." She straightened as her father's footsteps became audible. "We've talked all around it, but there it is, huh? Well, you have one, and I deserve one. So there's nothing left for us to discuss about this move. We are done. Finished."

Joe Huston appeared. He stopped when he noticed David, clearly disturbed by his son-in-law's presence. At sixty-eight the senator was still a large man, solid and formidable. His thinning hair was cropped military-style, and his stance was a soldier's at attention.

Faith's father was a veteran of the Korean War, a genuine military hero who had parlayed his stellar youthful service in the marines into a reputation for unflinching devotion to country, and success in the toughest campaigns. If Joe ever felt tired, no one was the wiser. Two years ago he'd checked himself into George Washington University Hospital for bypass surgery, and until that moment no one had even known he suffered from chest pain.

"What is he doing here?" Joe demanded of Faith, as if David had lost his right to speak.

David spoke anyway. "I came to leave Faith the car. And to get some books."

Joe didn't even glance at him. "You planned to let him in the house?" he asked Faith.

"I didn't plan anything." Faith stood taller. "But he's welcome to his books. David, get whatever you want off the shelves. My father and I will talk out here."

"No, I think he should hear this," Joe said. "I can't believe he'll approve of this move to Georgetown any more than I do."

"I appreciate your opinion, Dad," Faith said evenly. "But when it comes right down to it, this is my decision. Not yours, and not David's. I have to do what I think best."

Joe stared through narrowed eyes, as if she were a particularly recalcitrant defendant at an impeachment hearing. He had never been handsome, even in his youth. He was too coarse-featured and beetle-browed, and he hadn't grown more distinguished with age. But the senator had considerable presence. His voice boomed; his eyes blazed, and his intensity, once unleashed, drove away all thoughts of physical beauty. Liberals and moderates of both parties disliked Senator Joe Huston, but nobody underestimated him.

Joe finally shook his head. "Well, you're wrong. Dead wrong. And I won't have it. I took a look at the house this evening. How can you imagine that's an appropriate place to raise my grandchildren? It's a hovel."

She sighed. "It's *my* hovel. And with some hard work and elbow grease, it'll be a home."

"What's wrong with the house?" David turned to Joe, since it seemed clear Faith wasn't going to tell him.

David watched Joe balance ignoring him against using him as an ally. "There's nothing right about it," Joe said, reaching a compromise. He addressed David, but he didn't look at him. "It's unfit to live in."

"The house has been neglected," Faith explained. "It needs work. I can do some of it, and I'll hire people to do the rest. The first thing I'll do is clean it from top to bottom. It may not be pretty when I'm finished, but it'll be livable."

"And what about school?" Joe demanded. "Have you considered how many hours a day the children will have to commute?"

Faith didn't quite look at her father. "I'm putting them in public school. I can't afford the academy anymore, and I don't think it's good for Alex."

David couldn't remain silent. "You were going to change their school without telling me?"

"And why should she tell you anything?" Joe said, fully addressing him for the first time. "You have lost all rights to parent those children. There ought to be laws to protect children from people like you. If I had my way, there would be."

"Dad!" Faith stepped forward. "Enough." She turned to David. "I told you this just happened."

"And when would you have told me? After they were registered?"

"How did you think I was going to manage the tuition?"

That stopped him. Had he really expected her to move in with her parents so she could continue to send the children to a school he had chosen for them?

"I can take care of my grandchildren." Joe didn't smile, but clearly, the idea that he could provide for them when their gay father couldn't, pleased him.

Faith shook her head. "Thanks, but *I* can take care of my children, Dad. They're my responsibility."

"The responsibility is ours, not yours," David said.

Joe made a sound of disbelief. "It's too bad, isn't it, that you didn't think about that before you decided you couldn't live without Abraham Stein? I suppose it never occurred to you that falling into homosexual ways would affect your relationship with your children."

Faith held up her hands. "I'm going inside. David, get your books tomorrow. I'm taking the children to Prospect Street in the morning to start cleaning the house. Take anything you want, because most of what we have won't fit in the row house, anyway. Dad, you can't talk me out of this. My mind is made up. But we'll talk again when everyone is calmer."

Before either man could speak, Faith slipped inside and closed the door. David heard the sound of the bolt being thrown. For the moment Faith had locked them out of her life.

"How does it feel," Joe asked, "to know you destroyed her?"

David couldn't answer. There were no words to describe it.

"I will see that you never work at anything meaningful again," Joe said. "That you never have the tiniest bit of influence. That you are never called on for an opinion, even a passing thought. No persons of faith will want you within ten miles of their churches. Even the mainline denominations don't know what to do with your kind, David, much less the religious right."

"Does this give you pleasure, Joe?"

"You had the world at your fingertips, and you threw it away. For what? Another man? A Jew and a reporter, at that! And you brought my daughter down with you. You'll never be forgiven."

David faced him. "For what? For hurting your daughter or for damaging your career? Isn't that where all this self-righteous fury's coming from? This has been tough to explain. You were grooming me to replace you, even though I always told you I wasn't interested. Now, suddenly, you have a gay son-in-law—"

"Not for long, I don't."

"Well then, the father of your grandchildren is a gay man. That's not going to change with the divorce. Newt had to explain his lesbian sister. During your next campaign you'll have to explain me. And that's what's killing you. You didn't see it coming. You can't hide that."

"Oh, I can explain about you, all right. You and your kind are everywhere. Hiding behind decent women. Sneaking into positions of power. I'll tell people even I was fooled, that they should look closer at everybody they know and root out the sinners!"

David was appalled. Joe's stance against homosexuality was well-known, but David had never heard this kind of hate-filled rhetoric from his father-in-law. "You've gone off the deep end. That could cost you an election, but maybe that's a good thing."

"Stay away from my daughter, and stay away from my grandchildren! If they need anything, I'll see that they're taken care of."

"I will see my children," David said. "Soon. There's not a court in this nation that will prevent that from happening. And I'll find a job and help support them. Meantime, I'd advise you to take a good look at Faith. She's determined to do this her way, and she isn't going to let either of us stop her. So ease up."

"May I be struck dead on the day I take advice from you."

Continuing was pointless. David left the senator gazing at the door that separated him from his daughter.

Out on the street, he opened the front door of Ham's sedan and slid into the passenger seat. He didn't speak.

"Are you going to leave the Accord parked on the road?" Ham asked.

David nodded.

"It didn't go well, did it?"

David glanced at him. Ham wore a tattered blue sports shirt and khaki shorts. He owned two ties, which he alternated when he had to, one sportscoat and an expensive tuxedo for the occasional White House dinner. His Dupont Circle apartment—which David shared—was furnished in Danish modern, contemporary art and whatever papers and books Ham dropped in piles on the floor.

Ham had announced he was gay in junior high school, lived through his parents' dismay and settled back into a loving relationship with them. The Steins had no qualms about David's sex, only that he was a Christian and a conservative.

David's heart still sped up whenever Ham caught his eye.

"It's never going to go well," David said.

"Did you see your children?"

"I didn't even get inside."

"You have the right to see them. If you continue to avoid it, the reunion's going to be even harder." Ham started the engine and pulled out, turning around at the end of the cul-de-sac to get back to the main road.

David wondered if the day would ever come when he could share his children's lives again, a day when he could even introduce them to Ham.

He remembered the expression on Joe Huston's face and knew that if the senator had anything to say about it, David himself would become a stranger.

"I'm going to arrange a visit." David leaned back against the seat and closed his eyes. "But I can guarantee they won't be ready for it."

"You're in a tough position, David. I imagine they believe everything you told them all those years."

David wondered how he had ever thought he had the right to tell anyone else how to live.

 6

Hating David would have been simplest, but the next morning, when Faith began to pack the Accord with cleaning supplies, gratitude was higher on the list. Despite what she'd said about saving on gas and insurance, having the Accord was going to make her life and the children's twice as easy.

"I don't see why I have to go." Remy, in modest shorts and a T-shirt of the same blue-gray as her eyes, had been repeating the same sentence from the moment she'd discovered she was going to spend the day in Georgetown.

Faith was already tired, and the day had barely started. "When did I tell you that whining was a good way to get what you want?"

"I don't want to go there. I hate it!"

Faith lifted a box of clean rags into the trunk. "You'll hate it less when it's clean."

Remy moved directly in front of her mother, just in case Faith hadn't gotten the point. "I'll never hate it less. I'll just hate you for making me live there."

Faith snapped to attention. "Listen carefully, Remy. You're entitled to your feelings. I want you to be aware of them. I really do. But you won't take them out on me."

"You don't care how I feel."

"You're going to have to face facts. This is our best shot, and we're taking it. Now go inside and get Alex. We're leaving."

Remy didn't have to go inside. Alex came flying out of the house. "Can I sit up front?"

"*I* don't want to, that's for sure." Remy slid into the back seat and slammed the door hard enough to rock the car.

Alex took advantage of his sister's bad temper and chatted all the way into D.C. Faith realized how rare it was for Alex to be the child who was "in tune." He seemed thrilled by the possibilities.

"Do you think there'll be any kids in the neighborhood?" He unlocked, then relocked, his door for the fifteenth time in as many minutes.

Faith crossed Key Bridge and turned uphill onto a side street that would take her to the house. "Just plenty of college kids, and maybe some politicians—who'll be too immature for you. But we'll have plenty of room for your friends to visit."

"Like anybody would want to come," Remy said.

Faith searched for parking. "Even though you don't want to live here, Georgetown's a major attraction. The shopping and restaurants are fabulous."

"You can stop making it sound like fun."

Since the tour guide routine wasn't working, Faith got down to business. "One of the things you have to do today is figure out which bedrooms you want. I'm taking the one at the front, so I can keep an eye on things. The other two are the same size. If you can't decide, we'll flip a coin."

"I want the attic," Alex reminded her.

"We'll check it out."

In the rearview mirror Faith watched Remy roll her eyes. Scenes from *The Exorcist* had been filmed on Prospect Street. Faith wondered if there was a convenient priest who could rid *her* daughter of the bad spirits that seemed to have taken over her slender body.

They parked two blocks away, and Faith made a mental note to get a residential parking permit. She unlocked the trunk and began to remove the boxes of cleaning supplies, handing one to Alex and another to a reluctant Remy.

"This isn't going to be fun," she admitted, as they trudged toward the house. "We're just going to get the worst of it today.

There's a crew coming in to refinish the floors next week. They'll be finished just in time for us to clean up again and move in." Somewhere Lydia had found the money for the floors, insisting that the floors and broken slate on the roof were her duty.

Remy halted in front of the house. "I hope they plan to do more than that."

"There's no time, but you'll be amazed how much better the place will look once we patch and paint. And once we put new appliances in the kitchen."

"Can we bring our refrigerator?" Alex loved the side-by-side they had installed in the McLean house. He had nearly worn out the ice chute on the front door trying to figure out how it worked.

"Afraid not. It would take up the whole kitchen."

"Don't worry, Alex." Remy mimicked her mother's voice. "We can always eat at one of Georgetown's fab-u-lous restaurants if our new refrigerator can't hold any food."

Faith laughed, not the effect Remy had intended. "Listen, I've cooked so many meals in my life that eating out every night would be a dream come true."

"You like to cook," Alex said. "You like all that stuff."

Faith wondered if that was true. She had never given cooking much thought. She'd simply seen three attractive and nutritious meals a day as her life's calling. "Well, I also like pizza, and once I start working, we'll be having it more often. Unless you guys learn to cook."

She paused on the stoop. She wasn't even sure why, except that she'd seen movement out of the corner of her eye. She turned and gazed at the house next door, where the old woman with the turban had been standing when they had come here with Lydia.

The woman was there again, dressed much the same, although this time her outfit was dazzling fuschia. Faith waved. Despite her mother's warning, this woman was going to be her neighbor. She introduced herself. "Hi, I'm Faith Bronson. And these are my children, Remy and Alex. We're moving in next week."

"It's not fit for habitation. Your mother abandoned it to the contempt of strangers."

Faith realized the woman must know who she was. "I'm afraid my mother didn't tell me your name."

The woman disappeared. A moment later Faith heard the sound of the window closing.

Remy moved aside so her mother could unlock the door. "Oh great. Nutty neighbors, too."

Faith couldn't help but smile. "I'll just bet there's a story there."

Remy swept inside the moment the door was open. "Alex, you go next," Faith said. "In case we have an infestation of dragons."

She joined her brood of two after she locked the door behind her. They were standing together in the middle of the living room, staring at their new home. For a moment Faith gave in to the despair she saw in her daughter's eyes. She couldn't imagine the house as anything other than what it was right now. A filthy, dilapidated wreck, haunted by the ghosts of better times—and worse.

"Sometimes..." Faith knew she had to say something. "Sometimes you really have to see things at their worst to appreciate them at their best."

Remy dropped the box of rags with a resounding thump. "Do you have a stupid saying for every occasion?" Before Faith could answer, Remy burst into tears and fled up the stairs.

Alex moved close enough that Faith could put her arm around his shoulders. "Remy doesn't know how to look at things and see what they can be," he said. "That's what inventors do."

"Uh-huh." Faith fought back her own tears. "Do you think you could invent something fast to fix this place up?"

"It's already been invented."

"Fire?"

He dug his elbow into her side. "Hard work. That's what you told us, remember?"

She took comfort in the fact that if she hadn't done anything else of worth in her life, she had given birth to this young man. "Let's get to it, shall we? We might as well start in the kitchen."

"That's where Remy saw the rat." He didn't sound worried.

"I called an exterminator this morning. He's coming sometime this century."

"If I catch him first, can I put him in a cage in my room?"

"Not a chance."

* * *

Remy didn't care which room Alex wanted. She chose the one in the back because it had windows. She'd need them to escape.

She couldn't believe her mother was going to make her live here. For months Remy had awakened every morning hoping she had dreamed this whole disaster. She was sure she would get up, go downstairs and find her father in a fresh white shirt, eating his traditional bowl of shredded wheat at the dining room table. She would kiss his cheek, and he would ask her how she'd slept.

Then he would go back to his newspaper, and she would find her mother in the kitchen baking cinnamon rolls or squeezing orange juice, like some old show on Nickelodeon. Her mom would tell her she looked nice in whatever color she was wearing and ask if she had any activities after school.

Remy wouldn't think twice about any of it. Because that was the way things were supposed to be. That was the way God meant for things to continue.

But she hadn't dreamed the bad things. They were real. This house was real. Her father's sin was real, and so was everything that had come afterward.

None of it was fair. She had lived a good life. She didn't smoke or swear. She studied when she needed to and made straight A's without half trying. The one time a friend stole a can of beer and asked her to share it, Remy told Faith. She wasn't messy, like Alex, and until this terrible thing with her father, she hadn't even been rude.

What was the point of all that goodness if things like this still happened? She couldn't think of one thing she had done wrong, or rather, the things she could think of, like locking Alex out of the house when her mother went grocery shopping, didn't seem big enough for something like this. She could only conclude that being good didn't really matter. Because other people could bring down the wrath of God. Right on your head.

She wondered, as she had for months, if she was being punished because she hadn't been a good enough daughter. If her father had loved her more or been prouder of her, wouldn't he have stayed out of Satan's grasp?

If her mother had been a better, more loving wife, wouldn't her father have stayed at home where he belonged?

She wished there was something to sit on, because she had no intention of cleaning, no matter what Faith said. She wandered the small space, wondering where she could put her things. She had dopey furniture. She'd picked it out when she was little and dopey herself. Now she tried to imagine how it would look in this awful, awful room. She didn't need a tape measure to figure out that the furniture was too large. Her bed might fit all right, because the ceiling was tall. But the dresser and chest that went with it would take up all the wall space. She was too old for the toys and dolls she kept on her special shelves, but she still needed a bookshelf and a desk, in case her new school required minimal reading skills and homework.

Remy wiped her eyes with the hem of her T-shirt. She had expected her mother to come up, but she could hear Faith and Alex talking downstairs. Sound carried through the empty rooms. She just bet Alex was taking advantage of this opportunity to make her look bad.

She kicked a wad of paper and sent it flying across the room to land at the edge of one of the mattresses. She followed it, kicking the mattress with her toe to see if anything was living in it. When nothing appeared she tried again. She walked to the end and shoved it out from the wall with her toes. Nothing emerged.

The mattresses stank, and she was going to be hiding out until lunchtime. She didn't want them here. She sure couldn't sit on them. She dragged them into the hallway, and when she returned to the room the cobwebs gave her the creeps. She didn't want spiders—or worse—falling on her when she walked around.

She went in search of rags and a broom.

By the time she had spent an hour cleaning, Faith had expanded her pizza fantasy to three meals a day. Even with new appliances, she couldn't imagine cooking in the kitchen. Shelves were missing in the closeout-sale cabinets. The sink was chipped, and the pipes under it leaked. Alex's rat friend had made a nest in one corner of the pantry, eating a portion of the electrical wiring leading toward the stove as an encore.

Alex joined her, and she straightened slowly after unsuccessfully trying to clean a stain off the most recent layer of vinyl flooring. "We need a list."

Alex had been washing windows in the front of the house. He had contented himself by devising shortcuts. "What kind of list?"

"Of what needs to be done."

"What's wrong with it?"

She shook her head. "Pretty much everything."

"I like it."

She wondered if he was just trying to make her feel better. She wasn't sure if she was ready yet for this poignant role reversal.

"The floor's still pretty yucky." He went to a corner where nothing anchored the vinyl flooring and pried it loose with a putty knife Faith had used to scrape off a wad of gum. "There's more floors under here."

"I know."

"What's at the bottom?"

She wasn't sure. She watched him tug back the vinyl and didn't stop him. Alex in exploration mode was at his best. "Anything interesting?"

"Just wood. Like the rest of the house."

That was exactly what she'd hoped. "Terrific. We'll get the contractors to cart away the vinyl and refinish this floor, too." She felt a little better.

"What else is wrong?"

"It needs everything. Wiring, plumbing, countertops, new cabinets."

"What's wrong with these? Can't we paint them?" Alex thumped the side of the cabinet closest to the breakfast nook, which was a windowless space just large enough for a table. Beyond it were a closed-off stairwell and a small utility room, blocking any potential for a view.

She supposed a lumberyard could cut new shelves. "Maybe a nice coat of white paint—"

"White? Red!"

"Red cabinets?" She thought longingly of their Shaker-style kitchen in McLean, with its natural maple and vanilla Corian.

"It's not like anybody else's kitchen, and it's ours, right? So we get to pick."

A pounding started at their front door. Faith wondered who had arrived and what bad news they'd brought with them. "Better let me get that."

"Sure. I'll be looking for Lefty."

Great. Her son was naming the resident vermin.

She peered out the sidelight and saw an unfamiliar woman standing on her doorstep. Faith unlocked the door. Turbanless and dressed in black crepe, the woman from the house next door looked very different, but Faith recognized her by the graceful length of her neck and her extraordinary cheekbones.

"Oh, hi. It's nice to—" She stopped. She didn't know what to say. As it turned out, it didn't matter.

"I've brought you a bottle of Scotch. Glenfiddich, to be exact. It's a good single malt. There's no point in any other kind under the circumstances. Bad Scotch will merely make you drunk— which might not be a bad idea, considering what you're facing here. But good Scotch will make you think all things are possible— which they aren't, of course, but I can guarantee you won't care one little bit." She held out the bottle.

Faith, who didn't drink, reached for it. "Yes, well..."

"I'd like to come in and see exactly what's been going on."

Faith stepped aside. "You're very welcome to come in, but the house is a true disaster."

"No one knows that better than I." The woman hesitated, then stepped forward. Her hair was wispy white and shoulder-length, and her skin, although deeply wrinkled, was beautifully cared for. "I can tell you exactly how it came to be such a disaster, but that's a story for another day."

"I'm sorry, but I still don't know your name."

"I can't understand why not. I'm Dottie Lee Fairbanks. I've lived in the house next door for eighty-one years, and they will have to carry me out on a stretcher. As cold and rigid as my doorknob."

"How do you do, Mrs. Fairbanks?"

"Never Mrs. Only Dottie Lee, and please don't forget the Lee."

"I'll remember." Faith set the Glenfiddich on the bottom step of the staircase and trailed behind the woman, who walked with the gait of a much younger one. "And I'm Faith."

"Yes, I know who you are. I've seen your husband on talk shows."

Faith lowered her voice. "Ex-husband. Very soon."

"Yes, well, he seemed nice enough, even if he's on the wrong side of every political debate. David Bronson is the perfect example of how an intelligent human being can be misled."

"Misled?"

"He's against everything he should be for. Turn his politics backward and you have a perfect party platform. Your father, on the other hand, needs more than a 180-degree shift. He needs a lobotomy, does Joe Huston. I hope you've inherited your mother's level head, girl. Think for yourself. Think for yourself."

Faith was too intrigued to be annoyed. "How well do you know my parents?"

"Better than I want to, particularly your father. Your mother?" In the middle of the dining room she stopped and grimaced. "Your mother is not the woman she was."

Dottie Lee started forward, heading straight for Alex. "And who do we have here? Alex Bronson. Favors Joe a little, but better looking. Quite."

Alex looked intrigued. "You're the lady next door."

Dottie Lee laughed. "Oh, never that, young man. Never a lady. What a boring thing to be."

Alex glanced at his mother, as if to ask what he should say next.

"And what do you think about living in this house, Alex Bronson?" Dottie Lee said. "What exactly do you think?"

"Well, I think it's better than living with my grandfather."

"Joe? Of course it is. I see you wash windows, Alex Bronson. I've been watching you from outside. Would you like to come and wash mine once you're finished here?"

Alex looked at his mother. Faith shrugged.

"Sure," he said. "But not for a while. There's a lot to do here. Not for weeks, maybe."

"And you're helping your mother?"

"Uh-huh."

"Yes, ma'am," Faith prompted him.

Dottie Lee shook her head. "Never a ma'am, either, although this is a Southern city, even if people sometimes forget it. You may call me Dottie Lee," she told Alex.

"Okay, Dottie Lee."

Faith held her tongue.

"And now I must be going. I'll save the upstairs for my next visit. This is quite enough for one day." She pivoted and started quickly back through the house. Faith trailed her.

"I have tea every Wednesday afternoon at four," Dottie Lee said. "It's a civilized custom, even if it is associated with the English. You'll be ready for a break about then. I'll expect you and the children." She opened the door.

"I'm not sure we can—"

Dottie Lee turned. "Faith, there are few rules for life on Prospect Street. One of them is never to turn down my invitations." Then she smiled.

Faith was sure the room had brightened fifty kilowatts. The smile was magnificent. "We'll be there. Or Alex and I will be. I don't know if my daughter will be coaxed out of her room."

"How old is she?"

"Fourteen."

"Unfortunate." Dottie Lee nodded, then she turned and started down the steps.

Faith watched her go and wondered about the other rules for life on Prospect Street.

 7

Lunch didn't go well. Remy found nothing to tempt her appetite at Booeymonger, a small Prospect Street deli several blocks away. She sipped bottled water while Faith and Alex dove into sandwiches the size of paperback dictionaries. On the way back, Faith tried unsuccessfully to point out landmarks. Cafe Milano, one of the city's talked-about restaurants. The lovely and gracious Prospect House, once used to house foreign dignitaries. Remy was unimpressed.

A block from their house, Remy finally spoke. "There's that man again." She froze midstep and pointed. "He's digging through the trash. That's sick."

Despite the hot weather, the man in question was dressed in overalls and a sweatshirt. He was bearded, with grizzled hair that straggled past his chin, but even though he was old enough to be spending his waning years on a Florida golf course, he appeared— at least from a distance—to be a healthy weight for his large frame.

Faith and David had struggled to instill compassion and sensitivity to the plight of others in their children. As a family they had always celebrated Thanksgiving by preparing dinner at a local shelter. Remy and Alex had grown up fashioning table decorations from construction paper, and serving turkey and dressing to people just like this.

Now she realized that seeing the homeless in a warm, safe environment had made them more palatable. The children had probably gone away every year believing that one good meal had almost cured the problem.

"The only sick part," she said carefully, "is that he has no other way to take care of himself."

"He could get a job."

Since Faith had heard that sentiment from older and more influential people, she couldn't fault Remy. "Not easily."

Alex reached for his mother's arm. "Do you think he's looking for food?"

"Probably something he can sell."

"He might be hungry."

"He might be." Faith waited to see what her son would do.

"He *ought* to get a job." Remy had progressed in her thinking.

"He has one, Remy," Faith pointed out. "Whether you approve or not. He's doing what he can to support himself."

"I'm going to see if he's hungry," Alex said. "He might want a sandwich. I'll tell him how good the sub is."

The homeless were not stray dogs to be fed in back alleys and petted if they came close enough. They deserved respect and sometimes, like all human beings, caution. But Alex also deserved a chance to feed a hungry stranger. Faith was torn.

"We'll go with you," she said.

"Not me." Remy stepped back. "No way."

"Fine. Here's the key. We'll meet you at home."

"What's wrong with you? He might be dangerous."

"We'll meet you at home."

"It's not my home!" Remy grabbed the key and crossed the street, giving the homeless man a wide berth.

"Come on." Alex started toward the man, and Faith followed close behind.

He stopped just before he reached the can where the man continued to sort the trash. "Hi," Alex said. "Find anything neat in there?"

It wasn't the way Faith would have opened the conversation. The man straightened, frowning. He stared at Alex for a long time before he spoke. "This is my can."

"Oh, I don't want anything. I just wondered."

The man's gaze flicked to Faith. "He's yours?"

She nodded. "No question."

He looked surprised at her smile; then his frown faded a little. "Then you tell him I'm busy."

"I would, but he's incorrigible. He wants to ask you something."

Alex moved closer. "I just ate this great sandwich from the deli." He pointed. "I thought you might like one. Would you let me buy it? We're new here, and I saw you the other day and I thought—"

The man took a step closer. "You thought what?"

"Well, I thought you might be hungry. I'm always hungry."

Faith put her hand on her son's shoulder. "We don't want to bother you. Really. Alex just thought—"

"Alex? Your name's Alex?"

Alex nodded. "Uh-huh. What's yours?"

"Alec."

Alex grinned. "That's going to make things hard. People are going to get us mixed up. Cool."

Alec looked up at Faith as if he couldn't believe she had given birth to this child. "He always like this?"

"Pretty nearly."

He turned his attention back to her son. "What kind of sandwich?"

"Whatever you want. I had the sub, and it was this big." He spread his hands to demonstrate.

"Now, that's funny, because the sub is my favorite, too."

"No way. On a roll?"

"No other kind, to my way of thinking."

"Would you like a Coke, too?"

"You're reading my mind."

Faith wondered if Alec was really hungry, or if he just wanted to make her son happy. She had the uncomfortable feeling that he was helping *them*. "Can we get you anything else?"

"That'll do."

"We'll be right back." Alex started back toward the deli. Faith lingered a moment.

"Thanks," she said softly.

Their eyes met. He shrugged a little. "Some things ought to be encouraged." Then he went back to digging and sorting.

By four o'clock Faith was ready to quit. They had done what they could, and the rest would have to wait until the floors were finished. She had been sorely tempted to begin removing wallpaper, but a few forays in that direction had been fruitless. Despite being decades thick, even the top layers didn't peel off. She was going to have to read up on the process, and the job was going to require the patience of Job.

Alex was grumpy, too. They had made a tentative attempt at investigating the attic, but the absence of lightbulbs, a midafternoon thunderstorm that had robbed them of sunshine, and a flashlight low on power had meant little progress. Faith had seen enough to know they had their work cut out for them. Just removing the trash could take days.

"We won't give up on it," she promised, as they washed faces and hands and tried to make themselves presentable for afternoon tea. "I promise we'll get to it as soon as we can. I need to put some boxes up there myself."

"How many boxes?"

Faith was determined not to hang on to all the minutiae of her life with David, but there were things the children might want someday. She hugged him hard as he continued to grumble. "I don't know. But it's a big attic. We can work it out."

She decided to make one more attempt to get Remy, who had already said no, to accompany them next door. Upstairs, Faith knocked on Remy's door, counted to five and opened it. She was surprised to see that her daughter had cleaned and swept and washed the two windows that looked toward the river. The thunderstorm had passed, and sunlight glistened through the panes.

"Hey, it's looking better. Did you make a stab at removing the wallpaper?"

"Like I care."

"It's pretty awful." Faith traced a peeling seam. She wondered who had chosen the floral print. It wasn't old enough to be charming or new enough to brighten the room. Sad sprigs of tulips dotted corridors of wide black lines. There was evidence of masking tape and thumbtacks all over the walls, as if someone had tried to cover as much of it as he could with posters.

"This was my sister's nursery," she said, when Remy didn't answer. "There's probably a baby pattern under this somewhere. Old-fashioned storks, or teddy bears..."

"You mean this is the room where the kidnapping happened?"

Faith wished she'd thought before she spoke. "That was a long time ago."

"I don't want to live in here."

"I'm sure Alex will trade. This is a nicer room, and he was generous to let you have it."

"His room has the entrance to the attic. That's the only reason he took it."

Faith waited.

"I don't want those stairs anywhere near my room. Who knows what's up there?"

"Then you'll have to stay here, I guess."

"You think this is funny, don't you?"

Faith leaned against the wall. "I think you've had a tough break. We all have, and it's not going to be funny at any point along the way. But that doesn't mean that eventually we can't be happy here. We're allowed."

"I'm never going to be happy again." For once Remy's tone was something other than defiant. She sounded genuinely sad.

Faith was touched and worried, but she knew better than to put her arms around her daughter. "I know that's the way it feels right now."

"How can you think it's going to be any different?"

"Because the things that are most important in your life haven't changed. You still have a family that loves you—"

"I don't have a father."

"Yes, you do, and he loves you every bit as much as he did when he was living with us."

"I don't want to see him again. Not ever."

Faith moved on. "I had the strangest feeling today when I was cleaning downstairs. This house belonged to generations of women in our family. They lived here, loved here." She didn't add that some had probably died here, although she suspected as much. Lydia had never acquainted Faith with family history.

Remy looked dubious as Faith continued. "I was thinking that other women, women who helped make us what we are, probably began new lives here, too. We know one terrible thing happened in this house, but we don't know anything else. And this is our heritage, yours and mine. We should find out, and we should make this a happy house again."

"That's so lame."

Faith had to smile. "Okay, it sounds lame. I'll tell you the truth. Sometimes I feel like I'm just hanging on by my fingernails, and I'll dig them into anything that gives me hope."

Remy focused on the last word. "How could somebody just carry off a baby that way? The windows are so high…."

"Nobody knows how it happened. But not through your windows. Certainly not in broad daylight."

"They aren't *my* windows."

"Are you sure you don't want to go next door with us?"

"Just leave me alone."

Faith resisted the urge to smooth her daughter's hair.

Dottie Lee Fairbanks liked red, brilliant Oriental-red, and brassy, eye-torturing gold. She liked mahogany and rosewood carved into fanciful dragons and serpents, and furniture so massive it dwarfed the rooms of her house. She liked anything that gleamed or menaced, and apparently despised the ordinary. Because there was nothing ordinary in her house. Nothing at all.

"Do you like dogs?" she asked Alex, as he stepped through the doorway.

"Sure. Everybody likes dogs."

"Well, you might not like mine." She thrust two fingers between her lips and gave such a piercing whistle that it was all Faith could do not to cover her ears.

A pint-sized Chihuahua arrived on cue and proceeded to bare its seed-pearl teeth at Alex. He ignored the warning growls, got down on all fours before Faith could stop him and barked back. The dog backed up a foot—which considering its size took a few moments—then dropped to its mini-haunches and eyed the boy.

"A sensible child," Dottie Lee said. "I see I didn't misjudge you."

"Here, boy," Alex said, holding out his hand. The Chihuahua frowned, an expression Faith wouldn't have believed if she hadn't seen it herself.

"Girl," Dottie Lee informed him. "Nefirtiti. Titi for short."

"Here, Titi."

Titi considered, then launched her three pounds in Alex's direction. He caught her, tucked the dog under his arm and got to his feet. "Have you met Alec, Dottie Lee?"

"If you mean Alec, the Can Man, yes, of course I have."

"Alec, the Can Man?" Faith followed Dottie Lee through several centuries of priceless Chinese antiques to the back of her house. Dottie Lee's dining room stretched along the back, illuminated by floor to ceiling windows. She had a clear view of the Kennedy Center and the Watergate, as well as a stunning view of Key Bridge. The table was imposing, too, but now that the storm had passed, natural light streaming into the room tamed it like a lion snoozing in the sunshine.

"That's what he calls himself. He used to sleep in your basement, you know."

"He did?" Alex joined them. Titi's eyes were closed, as if she had already fallen asleep.

"Until he found a better one."

"Where?"

"I believe he sleeps in mine," Dottie Lee said. "When it's cold, that is. He prefers sleeping outdoors when the weather allows for it."

"How does he get in?" Alex said.

"I leave a window unlocked. We don't discuss it, of course."

Faith was still coming to terms with the fact that her own basement hadn't been nice enough. "It's a difficult life. He's not a young man."

"He eats well. Some of the restaurants on the street give him leftovers at the end of the day. He gets clothes at the end of the school term, when the students are moving out. He's still strong as a bull."

"Why does he live that way?" Alex plopped into a dining room chair after Dottie Lee pointed to one.

"He drinks." Dottie Lee motioned Faith to a seat across the table. "A lot."

"Oh." Alex rubbed Titi's ears. "Can't he just stop?"

"Have you tried it, boy?"

Alex shook his head. "Does he know how bad it is for him?"

"Who would know better?"

Alex considered that. "I'm going to fix up our basement."

Faith moved on quickly. "Did you pick up all this extraordinary furniture on your travels, Dottie Lee?"

"Not a stick of it. I was never much for travel. There's very little of the world I can't find right here on Prospect Street. But I knew men who did, of course. And they knew what I liked."

Faith imagined that was one story Alex could do without. "Is there anything I can do to help with tea?"

"Mariana will bring it to us." Dottie Lee lowered herself slowly to a seat at the head of the table. She rang a tiny crystal bell. Titi awoke with a start and yapped in the same tinkling key.

A connecting door opened, and a woman who appeared to be only slightly younger than Dottie Lee came through the doorway carrying a bamboo tray. She was stooped and wrinkled, but she walked with a firm step.

"Mariana used to do all our baking." Dottie Lee removed a black china teapot from the tray and set it on a trivet. "But now we simply buy what we need. Mariana likes a daily walk."

"I don't like to walk at all," Mariana said with just the hint of an Hispanic accent. She wore her steel-gray hair like Buster Brown, and the bangs skimmed lovely chocolate-brown eyes. "This one, she likes to get rid of me."

"Mariana has strong views on every subject," Dottie Lee said, as if she herself didn't.

Faith had expected tea and perhaps some cookies. She hadn't expected the feast Mariana set on the table. Tiny sandwiches, scones with jam and cream, cookies. "This looks wonderful. Aren't we lucky?"

"Your mother used to join me for tea." Dottie Lee took a tray of fancifully cut sandwiches and passed them to Alex. "In the days when she still knew who she was."

Faith wasn't sure how to respond to that. Lydia Huston knew exactly who she was. She was the wife of Joe Huston, powerful Virginia senator.

"How can somebody forget who she is? Unless she has amnesia." Alex started to reach for a sandwich, but Faith barred him from the tray.

"You need to put Titi on the floor and wash your hands."

He protested. "She's not dirty."

"She certainly isn't," Dottie Lee agreed. "But perhaps a hand washing would be in order to please your sadly mistaken mother."

Mariana led him from the room. Titi waited silently by his chair.

"How *is* Lydia?" Dottie Lee asked.

Faith had the uncomfortable feeling that Dottie Lee already knew the answer. "Busy. She does fund-raising in what spare time she has."

"For missing children, presumably?"

"No. For my father. For the party." Faith took several sandwiches from the platter.

Dottie Lee passed a plate of scones. "Odd, I think. Don't you?"

"She's interested in many things." But none of them passionately. Faith doubted there was a passionate bone in her mother's body. She took a scone bursting with currants and set it on her plate.

"Let's talk about you, instead," Dottie Lee said. "You have plans for the house?"

Faith decided to be honest. "The first order of business is making it livable. Beyond that, we'll have to take it a little at a time. You know how neglected it's been."

"Your grandmother would turn your mother over her knee if she was alive to do it."

Faith realized they were back to Lydia again. "Did you know my grandmother?"

"Yes, very well. You didn't, of course."

"No. She died before I was born."

"Millicent died too young. Malaria, I believe."

"I think so." Faith was surprised she wasn't sure. The past had never been a prime topic in the Huston household.

"You might ask your mother about her," Dottie Lee said. "She was a woman of many talents."

Alex returned to be served.

"You will not feed Titi from your plate while your mother is watching." Dottie Lee passed him jam and butter.

Alex ladled enough jam on his plate to induce a diabetic coma. "Who are all those men on the walls in your hall? They look important. Maybe even famous."

"Friends."

Faith looked up. Dottie Lee was smiling her magnificent smile, and Faith suddenly understood what her mother had meant about Dottie Lee being the wrong kind of woman.

"Dottie Lee was just telling me about your great-grandmother," Faith said quickly.

"Did she live in our house?" Alex's mouth was full, but he didn't spew crumbs, for which Faith was grateful.

"She did for many years, but not as an adult. She was born there, several years before I was born in this house. In the very room your mother will undoubtedly take as her own. Millicent moved away after she married Harold, of course. Her parents continued to live next door until they died, and soon after that, your grandparents moved in."

Faith was curious now. "Then you must have known my great-grandparents, too. At least a little."

"My dear, I am a fountain of information. I sat on Violet's knee as a girl, and she taught me my ABC's. I spent many a happy hour on her mother's lap, too. Candace was like a grandmother to me."

Faith was surprised to find that the relatives she knew so little about were real people to Dottie Lee. "I hope you'll tell me about them."

"In good time." Dottie Lee bit into a cucumber sandwich and chewed thoughtfully. "I will tell you this, since you need a surprise in your life, and a mystery." She paused and frowned at Alex. "Alex Bronson, does your mother need a mystery?"

"Does her sister getting kidnapped count?"

"Yes, it surely does. But I was thinking of something a little more cheerful."

Mariana came into the room with another pot of tea. "Stop fussing and sit," Dottie Lee commanded.

Mariana muttered but did. Dottie Lee passed her the plates so she could help herself.

Faith was glad Mariana had joined them. She was always uncomfortable when others served her.

"I'm sorry, but right now the only mystery I want in my life is the kind that comes with an author's name on the front cover."

"You've grown up to think a mystery means an unpleasant surprise." Dottie Lee poured cream into Mariana's tea. "You've had your share, and no one's told you otherwise. But you aren't correct, you know. So here's proof I'm right. You see the move to Prospect Street as something of a comedown, I expect?"

Faith didn't deny it.

"Others have not felt that way," Dottie Lee said. "And at your house, hidden away from prying eyes, is the proof."

Alex's eyes were huge. He had sharpened his reading teeth on Encyclopedia Brown and the Hardy Boys, and he fancied himself something of a detective. "Can you give us more clues?"

"I can, but I won't. This way, Alex Bronson, you will have to come and visit me often. Perhaps something will just slip out when neither of us is expecting it. You'll be surprised at everything I know."

Faith watched as Alex and Dottie Lee continued their banter. She was delighted that her son had found someone else who saw him as the delightful young man he was. At the same time, she was sad that it hadn't happened sooner, and in his own family.

Dottie Lee looked up, almost as if she had heard Faith's thoughts. "Your daughter looks astonishingly like Lydia did at her age, but your son is the one who is very much like her, you know."

Faith must have looked surprised, but Dottie Lee gave a throaty laugh. "Another mystery? I'm delighted, dear. We can only hope I live long enough to tell you everything I know."

As if to tempt fate, Dottie Lee spread clotted cream on another scone and lifted it in a toast.

 8

Everybody liked Pavel Quinn. In the days before Communism took a tumble, a former lover explained that everybody liked him because nobody had to love him. Pavel, she claimed, knew exactly where the boundary between the two was drawn and marched the perimeter as heavily armed as an East Berlin border guard.

He'd reasoned patiently with her, of course. Pavel might be a Russian name, but not every Russian was a Communist, certainly no one in his family. And clearly no Quinn had ever tramped German borders. They were too busy throwing rocks in Belfast.

The lover threw up her hands and orchestrated her own march out Pavel's front door. He had watched her go with a mixture of sadness and relief. She was a Chilean beauty, the most inventive lover he'd ever invited into his bed, and a woman who loved good food almost as much as he did.

She was also possessive and temperamental. She had tried too hard to find things inside him that simply weren't there. Who would know better than he?

Since then, Pavel had taken other lovers. He loved women, the sounds they made when they were contented, the warmth they exuded sleeping next to him, the fragrance of their hair, the pillowy softness of their breasts. He wouldn't say he loved them all with the same intensity, but the experiences were remarkably similar. Women came into his life. He enjoyed them immensely. They left.

Today he was helping one of them pack.

"You are the most exasperating man!" Odette threw the contents of one dresser drawer into a shopping bag. Since the drawer in question was filled with neatly folded lingerie, there was room once she finished. She topped it with knit shirts and the sexiest shorts south of the Mason-Dixon line.

"Well, I know I'm not easy to live with." Pavel, who was helpfully folding a lavender cotton sweater, felt obligated to take his share of the blame.

"That goes without saying, but that's not what I'm talking about." Odette jerked open the final drawer and scooped out socks and a bag of cosmetics.

"What are you talking about?"

"You're a radar screen without any blips."

He supposed that was what came of making love to an air traffic controller. "You wanted blips?"

She straightened and frowned. "That's what every woman wants, Pavel. You're old enough to have discovered this on your own."

He was forty-one, fast approaching the old-dog-immune-to-new-tricks phase of his life. Especially where women were concerned. "You wanted fights? Make up sex? What, Odette?"

Odette sighed. She wasn't a particularly emotional woman. "No, I don't like fights, either. Maybe knowing I made blips on *your* radar screen would have done it."

"You did. Of course."

She looked up. "I need another bag. And no, I didn't. By next week you'll have forgotten I was living here."

"I'm going to miss you."

"Give it up, Pavel." She was a leggy brunette with hair that swung halfway down her back and the figure of a bomber squadron pinup girl. Her features were too pronounced, even coarse, perhaps, but that had made her more appealing. Pavel hated perfection.

Having run out of things to say, he left for the kitchen, fishing under detergent bottles, cleaning supplies and dirty dishcloths to come up with another paper bag. She took it when he returned and piled what was left of her things inside. "Well, that's it. I'm gone."

"Do you want me to call? We could have dinner next weekend."

"If you have to ask, the answer is no." Odette looked up. "The answer is no anyway, so don't bother." A half smile twisted her lips. "I guess we had some fun, big guy. Have a nice life."

Since he fully expected to, he smiled back. Then, before she could resist, he gathered her to his chest for the ultimate bear hug.

"I might miss that," she said, after he stepped away. "But not much else about this place. Hire somebody who knows what he's doing to finish the renovations. The place is a dump." Odette lifted the bags, one in each arm, shaking her head when he tried to take one for the trip to the car. "I'm out of here."

He walked her to the front door and opened it solicitously. Then he stood on the threshold and watched her navigate the front steps. Once she was safely in the driver's seat with the bags tucked in the back, he headed inside, realizing at the kitchen refrigerator that he should have stayed to watch her drive away.

He closed the refrigerator and twisted the cap of a Heineken. His new sink stared up at him from the middle of the checkerboard tile floor. He wasn't sure how long it had been there.

"There's a difference between a dump and a challenge," he said to no one.

The beer slid down a throat that hadn't had time to parch. Mockingbirds had only just started to sing on his magnolia tree. Unfortunately, Odette had been of that species called "dreaded early riser," and now he had an entire day ahead of him.

He capped the Heineken and put it back inside the refrigerator door. He didn't need alcohol at this hour. He needed food and coffee, both of which were in short supply in his kitchen. Next on his wish list was the business section of the *Post,* and as usual someone had swiped his copy off the sidewalk before he could get to it.

He lived in Georgetown, and there were dozens of places to go for breakfast. But there was only one he considered. He raked his fingers through uncombed dark curls and went in search of his Birkenstocks.

Faith awakened on moving day with dread like a clenched fist pressing against her chest. In the days since she had decided on the move to Georgetown, she'd had little time to question her decision and less to prepare for it. She had packed and sorted and tagged boxes until she was so exhausted she was probably ignoring essentials simply to avoid packing them.

On Tuesday a local auction house would hold an estate sale, and everything Faith didn't move today would disappear into the arms of collectors and scavengers. Although the rooms were filled with furniture and items she wasn't taking, she wondered how she was going to fit everything she *was* keeping into the row house.

She took her final shower in the master bathroom, chucked her towel and the few toiletries she hadn't already packed into a box, then changed into the jeans and shirt she'd left out last night. Finally she went to wake Remy.

She found her daughter sitting on the window seat, staring at the same view she'd looked out on nearly every day of their lives in this house. She was surrounded by boxes. In the end there had been little except furniture that Remy was willing to part with.

"The movers will be here in a half hour." Faith joined her at the window. "If you take a quick shower you'll still have time to eat."

"I'm not hungry."

Faith knew this wasn't the moment to sympathize out loud. Neither of them had the emotional resources for it. "I'm going to check on Alex. I think I heard him stirring."

"He's already dressed. He's excited, like this is some sort of adventure."

"Then he's the lucky one, isn't he?"

Faith found her son clearing a bookshelf. She had asked him repeatedly to pack his books. "You only have half an hour before they come," she warned.

"I'm almost done."

He looked up and grinned, and she had to smile back. "I'll meet you downstairs when you're finished. We have juice and cereal."

In the kitchen she poured juice for everybody and got the milk from the fridge. She had cleared away everything else and scrubbed the shelves clean. The smaller refrigerator she had ordered for the row house hadn't been delivered. For a few days, at least, they were going to make do without one.

The doorbell rang before she could pour the cereal. She knew the movers hadn't arrived because the neighborhood dogs would be sure to announce their presence. She sipped her juice as she walked to the front door, throwing it open to stare at David.

The juice pooled in her throat until she thought to swallow. "What are *you* doing here?"

He held up a McDonald's bag. "I brought breakfast." He stepped closer. "Faith, I know how hard this is. I wanted to help."

"You think coming today will help?"

"Let me take the kids somewhere and get them out of the way. They don't need to watch their life being dismantled."

She didn't know what to say. Until now he hadn't pushed, and she had respected Remy and Alex's own timetable for spending time with their father. But neither child had gotten closer to wanting a visit.

"They won't get used to the idea that things have changed unless they spend time with me," David said. "Patience is well and good, but it's not working. They need to know I love them as much as I ever did."

Reluctantly she stepped aside and made room for him to pass.

"I brought sausage biscuits. Alex can never get enough."

"He'll be down in a minute. Remy will take longer. This is harder on her."

"She's always been so well-adjusted. I know it's hard now—"

"She's never been tested. That's why. We've kept our children in a bubble. Alex is resilient, but Remy has no defenses against a world that isn't picture-perfect."

He didn't try to point out a brighter side, which surprised her. If Faith had worn sunglasses against the glare of reality, he had worn blinders.

In the kitchen he put the bag on the counter and began to take out the food, setting it in neatly spaced piles. "Do you have any pointers?"

"You're asking my advice?"

"I am." He smiled, but it didn't touch the pain in his eyes. "I'm afraid. Afraid of my own kids." He shook his head, and the smile faded.

For once she refused to play diplomat. "If I had any advice I'd take it myself. I'm flying blind here."

"You're coping."

"You seem to be coping, too."

"I wake up every morning and wish I were somebody else. Then I remember I was somebody else for years and years, and in the end I couldn't handle it."

"Please don't try to make me feel anything except anger toward you, okay? I can't handle compassion yet. I don't have it in me."

"We'll put it on hold for a while."

"Don't hold your breath."

Their eyes met and held. "Do you know what I want more than anything?" he said.

"No. And I don't want to know."

"I want to have a real conversation with you again someday."

"What are the chances, David?" The voice that emerged was Lydia's, sarcastic and bitter.

He shook his head. "I don't know."

"We have the kids to think about. That's all I can handle. More, at times." She turned away to collect herself. Footsteps sounded on the stairs, and when she turned back, Alex was standing in the doorway.

"Dad." He froze in place, as if the man standing at the counter had come to rob them.

"Alex." David smiled. "I brought breakfast. I knew you'd be hungry."

"What are you doing here?"

"I just told you."

"You don't come for months and you come today?"

"Timing doesn't seem to be my strong point."

"Go away," Alex said. "Don't you think you've hurt Mom enough?"

Faith couldn't let that pass. "Alex, your dad's not trying to hurt me. He's here to see you and Remy. He misses you."

"Well, he *has* hurt you. I know. I hear you crying at night, even if you think I don't."

"Nothing I did was meant to hurt anybody," David said. "You need to understand that. I care how your mother feels, and I always will."

"Oh? As much as you care about some man?"

"Alex..." Faith went to her son's side. "I can take care of myself. Let me, okay?"

Alex looked straight at his father. "I don't want to see you."

"I want you and Remy to spend the day with me."

Alex turned and ran back up the stairs.

"Well, that went well," David said.

Faith was fighting tears. "Neither of them is going anywhere with you if Ham's there."

"Give me credit for some sense."

"That's going to be a condition of all your visits."

"In other words, you don't want them to face who I really am?"

"I don't want you flaunting it in their faces."

He stood a little straighter. "I'm going up to see Remy. If she's as resistant as Alex, I'll leave. But once you're settled, I'm going to visit regularly. Even if it takes a court order."

He didn't wait for an answer. She heard his footsteps on the stairs and his repeated knocking. Remy's door was locked. She didn't answer, and she refused to let her father in.

Faith drove ahead of the first load to Prospect Street, leaving a grumpy Lydia in charge of the children and the neglected contents of Alex's closet. Faith had discovered her son's clothes hanging in place when she went to check on him after David's departure. Alex himself was sitting on the closet floor, pants legs and shirttails hiding his tears.

A local company, surprisingly cheap, was doing the work. The two men had managed to pack the truck without consequence, but now she wondered how they would lift the rosewood spinet up four narrow steps and maneuver it through the front door.

The spinet had belonged to Faith's great-grandmother Violet, and once upon a time it had graced the row house. Lydia had given it to Faith many years before.

Faith knew that bringing the piano back to Prospect Street was foolish. She was leaving more useful pieces to make room for an instrument that was seldom played. But even though she had never known her great-grandmother, she felt a kinship that transcended common sense. The spinet belonged to the house in a way that the walnut entertainment center never could. She had abandoned one to make room for the other.

Once the truck arrived, she supervised the placement of beds, dressers and area rugs, then boxes in the kitchen. Finally she stood to one side with arms folded and watched the men prepare to unload the spinet.

"You're sure you don't need another man to help?"

The driver grinned at her. She estimated he was two hundred and fifty pounds of solid muscle. "This bitty thing? I can carry it in the palm of one hand."

"Please don't."

"I'll play you a tune when it's all tucked in pretty."

Faith heard a door slam and looked over her shoulder to see that Dottie Lee was standing on her lawn. Dottie Lee was arrayed in scarlet gauze harem pants and a matching tunic embroidered in silver. She seemed excited by all the commotion.

"Violet's piano," Dottie Lee said. "She taught me my first C scale on that very instrument."

Faith exchanged quick greetings. "Did she play well?"

"Goodness, Faith, she was a gifted musician. Her husband gave her that piano as a wedding present. You know so little it's shameful. Does your mother still play? She inherited Violet's talent."

"My mother?" Faith couldn't remember her mother touching the piano. She'd never realized Lydia knew one key from another. Despite a plethora of classes in every womanly art, Faith herself had never been offered lessons.

"I take it Lydia gave up her music along with her spirit," Dottie Lee said.

"My daughter played when she was a little girl." Faith wondered where Remy's fascination with music had gone. The academy was too small to offer more than the most basic music curriculum, but Remy had never complained. Instead she had taken up gymnastics and soccer to be with neighborhood friends.

"Nobody plays the piano now," Faith said. "But it wanted to come home."

"Of course it did. I'm pleased to see you listened." Dottie Lee disappeared back inside.

The movers were on the first step now, and so far they weren't breaking a sweat. Faith wasn't sure who to feel sorrier for. The driver at the bottom, who had to bear most of the weight, or the man at the top, who had to bend over to stay in the proper position.

She wished the spinet was a full-sized upright. Then the movers would have an extra helper. She was afraid to watch and afraid not to.

The men made it to the top step with a minimum of grunting and groaning. Passersby had gawked all morning. Students, mostly, who streamed toward Wisconsin Avenue from Georgetown University. Now a small crowd gathered, as if the piano was better entertainment than the shops.

"Five bucks says the guy at the bottom drops it," one male voice said.

Faith looked around and watched two young men in Hoya T-shirts slapping palms. Her stomach knotted.

When she focused on the movers again, they were frozen in position. Then, slowly, the driver slid his hands lower so he could lift higher. The spinet began to tilt, and the driver cursed sharply. Faith gasped in horror.

A man broke free of the crowd and sprinted to the steps. He was large and muscular, and before either of the movers could respond, he steadied the piano with his chest and knees. Then he reached beneath it, stooping carefully as he did, to give the extra boost the movers needed. The driver positioned his hands and lifted, moving up a step as he did. With one more step the piano was level with the landing, and the men eased it through the doorway.

"Well, he would have dropped it if that guy hadn't come along," the gambler told his friend.

"You owe me five bucks."

Faith didn't stay around long enough to see if the gambler paid his debt. She started up the steps and reached her living room as the three men set the piano against the appropriate wall. She waited until the stranger straightened before she spoke.

"I can't thank you enough." She held out her hand. "I'm Faith Bronson, and that's my great-grandmother's piano."

The man wiped his palms on the legs of his ragged cutoffs and took her hand. "Pavel Quinn. I live on O Street."

He was a giant, broad-shouldered and big-boned enough to hire on permanently with the movers. His hair was a chocolate-brown mop of curls that fell over his forehead and ears, and his eyes were the same color. He clearly hadn't shaved for days—possibly even a week—and his T-shirt was speckled with paint. But at the moment he looked like a hero to her.

"I'm glad you happened by," she said.

"We wouldn't have dropped it," the driver assured her. "Never have dropped no piano, not in all my years." The movers left to unpack the rest of the truck so they could drive back to McLean for the final load.

Pavel Quinn took in the interior of the row house. "Your landlord ought to be shot."

She was too relieved to take offense. "It's my house. A work in progress. Not much progress, though."

"Your house?" He frowned. "The Hustons sold it after all these years?"

She wasn't surprised Pavel Quinn knew the story. Everybody knew the story. "I'm a Bronson by marriage. A Huston by birth." She hadn't decided whether to resume her maiden name, but she was leaning toward it. "Soon to be a Huston again, I guess."

His gaze warmed and focused on her. "Divorce?"

"Yeah."

"I'm sorry." He continued to stare at her. She could almost see the bits of information she'd given click into place. Her shoulders drooped. She was exhausted. The move was taking more than a physical toll, and the elation at saving the piano was gone. "My life's an open book, isn't it? Is there anybody in Washington who doesn't know my shoe size?"

He winced. "I'm sorry. I really am. It's just that local history fascinates me. It's something of a hobby. And this house..."

He didn't have to say more. "I know. It's a landmark."

"Mine is, too. In the nineteenth century a Secretary of State died at a dinner party there. Fame's a consequence of life in Georgetown. You'll get used to it."

He was trying to be nice, but she was too tired to pretend he had succeeded. "Did *your* wife leave you for another woman?"

"No wife."

"Then you don't know what my life is like."

"How many times have I put my foot in it since I stepped through the doorway?"

She took a long, slow breath. "I'm sorry. You've been nothing but kind. It's me. I—"

"Do you always take responsibility for other people's rudeness?"

"Always."

"We'll make a pact. You don't have to take responsibility for mine."

Ashamed of herself, she started toward the door to show him out. "Thank you for being in the right place at the right time."

"I was having breakfast at Booeymonger."

"And you came to watch the fun. We seem to be the neighborhood circus today."

"You'll find we're all curious about each other here. We're a small town in a big city."

"You should meet my next-door neighbor."

"Dottie Lee?" He grinned. He had a smile that shone through every pore, nothing polite or restrained about it. "I know Dottie Lee. Everybody knows her. You've moved next door to the neighborhood historian."

The movers came in with a sofa and plunked it across from the spinet. "That's everything," the driver said. "We'll be getting back to Virginia now." They took off down the steps.

Faith had to lock the house and go. "Well, thanks for your curiosity," she told Pavel. "You saved a piece of history."

"I'm sure we'll run into each other again. If you're on O Street, stop by. My house is the Stick style Victorian on the corner of 31st. But don't expect the inside to match the outside. Mine's a work in progress, too." He held out his hand.

She took it, and hers disappeared inside. Nothing about the man wasn't generous.

After Pavel left she trailed her fingers over the spinet keys. The sound was sadly discordant. For years the little piano had simply been a piece of furniture. Now it was the centerpiece of the room. The spinet needed a good tuning.

Very much like Faith's own life.

 9

Remy wasn't sure she liked her grandmother. When her friends talked about their "nanas" sewing Halloween costumes or putting together scrapbooks, she always felt different, because there was no way in the world Lydia would ever do those things for her.

Lydia didn't ignore her, of course. She gave presents on special occasions, extravagant presents like real sapphire ear studs and a pink cashmere twin set. But even though her friends were envious, Remy wished that just once her grandmother had asked what she wanted. Then she would have known that Remy never wore pink, and that instead of sapphires, she'd really wanted rubies, her birthstone.

Although Megan could talk to her grandmother about everything, Remy had never talked to Lydia about anything important. So today she was doubly surprised when Lydia came into her room while her mother was in Georgetown with the movers and lowered herself to the edge of Remy's desk chair.

"Are you doing all right, Remy?"

Remy, who was sitting cross-legged on her carpet, knew better than to say no. No one wanted to know how she was really doing, most particularly her grandmother.

"I'm okay." She cleared her throat and tried to remember the kind of stuff she used to say to make an impression, the stuff she'd been so good at once upon a time. "Did Alex get his closet packed?"

"It's unlikely he'll ever be able to wear any of his clothes again, but yes, he did."

Remy thought maybe Alex really wasn't as happy about leaving their house as he pretended. He was trying to be the man of the house now that her father had flipped out, but she thought that not packing his stuff was the same thing as chaining himself to a front porch pillar.

Lydia, who looked as if she would like to be anywhere else, got stiffly to her feet and went to the window. "How old were you when you moved here? Do you remember?"

"I don't know."

"I think you were four. Alex must have been almost two. Nobody could keep up with him."

"Who wanted to?" Remy wished her grandmother would leave before her limited store of small talk gave out.

"You were a pretty little girl. Quiet. Well behaved." Lydia crossed her arms over her chest and turned. She was frowning. "Like your mother."

"I'm tired of people telling me I'm like her. I'm like *me*." The words left her lips, and Remy's heart sank immediately. She knew better than to cross her grandmother. She was in for it now.

Lydia didn't miss a beat. "You're angry at her, aren't you?"

For a moment Remy couldn't believe she'd heard her grandmother right. "What?"

"You're angry at *her*. Don't pretend you're not. You think this move is her fault."

"She married my father, didn't she? Nobody twisted her arm."

"And you think she should have seen into the future." Lydia shook her head, but maybe not in anger, as Remy had expected. For a moment she almost looked sad.

"Yeah, that's what I think." Remy wove her fingers together. "I think if she'd looked down the road a little, it would have helped."

"You probably think I don't understand."

Remy knew better than to answer that. Even now.

Lydia grimaced. "I can see you do, Remy. You probably don't

think I understand anything. Like how much you want to blame somebody."

"It doesn't matter."

"Of course it does." Lydia's tone hardened. "I wish I knew how to make you believe that."

"I don't want to talk about it."

Lydia turned back to the window. "I used to talk to my grandmother all the time. For years she was my best friend."

Lydia as *anybody's* best friend was hard to imagine. "Did she look like us?"

Lydia perched on the edge of the window seat and faced her granddaughter again. "Like us?"

"Like my mother and me. Everybody says we look like you. Did you look like her?"

"Oh, no." Lydia nearly smiled. For a moment she almost looked like a girl. "Not at all. She had red hair. Bright red, almost orange, even when she was a grandmother. Her name was Violet, but my grandfather called her Carrot Top. Not very original, I suppose, but he meant well. She was small, like we are, but very round. And freckled. I have pictures."

"That's where Alex gets his red hair."

"I'm sure."

"Nobody ever tells me anything."

Lydia raised a brow. "Somebody just did."

"I don't want to move to Georgetown. I don't want to live in that house."

"I know."

"Mom's acting like it's a good thing, like it doesn't matter if I hate it or not."

"It matters. You just don't want to see that right now."

"If she cared how *I* feel, she'd find another way."

Lydia didn't tell her that was childish, the way Remy had expected. "When I visited the house on Prospect as a little girl, it was a very different place." She got to her feet again, as restless as her grandson. "I'll tell you about it someday when you're ready to listen."

Remy doubted that moment would ever come.

"In the meantime," Lydia said, "I want you to understand something. Your mother has been through a great deal these last months. I don't want to see her hurt any more. Do what you can to prevent it."

Remy glared at her grandmother. "You're worried about her but not about me? Fine. I can take care of myself."

"You still need your mother, and she needs you. Don't shut her out."

Before Remy could say anything the golden retriever next door began to howl. Lydia leaned forward and peered out the window. "The moving truck is here. Time to finish up."

Remy wanted to scream, but she was sure if she did, no one would hear her.

By the time the movers left, Faith felt like an item the men had flattened in transit. By the time evening approached, her head throbbed and her back ached from moving boxes and unpacking essentials. Had she been childless, she would have made her bed and crawled under the covers.

But she wasn't. "Who's up for pizza?" She stood in the hallway between Alex and Remy's bedrooms. She'd pumped a liter of false cheer into her question, and the effort nearly finished her off.

Alex opened his and stuck his head through the doorway. "Pepperoni?"

"Any kind you want. We're celebrating."

"Remy hates pepperoni."

"Remy can have something else." When her daughter appeared, Faith informed her they were going out as a family and no protests were allowed.

They waited until a sullen Remy put on her sneakers, then locked up and started toward Wisconsin. Faith wasn't sure where they were going. She just wanted to get away from boxes and peeling wallpaper. On Wisconsin she took a right toward M Street, where there were dozens of restaurants. On M Faith selected a bistro that looked less like a bar than some of its neighbors and ordered a vegetarian pizza for Remy and a pepperoni for Alex. She ordered a salad for herself, which she picked at once it arrived, too tired to eat.

Remy hadn't said a word since leaving the house, and Alex fell silent in the middle of his second slice, worn down by the day's events. Faith didn't know what to say, either. She wanted to talk to them about David's visit and the need for forgiveness. But at the moment she had no forgiveness in her soul. She was one hundred percent exhausted, with no room to spare for the man who was the cause of it.

Instead of talking, she watched her children. The bistro was cheap enough to attract a wide variety of diners. Students made up about half the population, but the rest was decidedly mixed. The four corners of the world were well represented. A Sikh family in traditional clothing sat at the next table, and their small, dark-eyed daughter gaped at Alex as if she had never seen red hair. Just beyond them, half a dozen young adults from Southeast Asia laughed and spoke in their native language, and beyond *them,* an African-American couple, obviously on a date, were killing a bottle of wine and a platter of calamari with their heads close together and eyes focused on each other.

Alex was fascinated, but Remy seemed uncomfortable. She shifted in her seat, and her gaze swept the room as if she was afraid to let it linger. Faith realized that she wasn't one hundred percent exhausted after all. There was still room for some percentage of shame. Despite living their entire lives just minutes from the capital, her relentlessly suburban children were acting like visitors to the National Zoo.

And she and David had let that happen, perhaps even encouraged it.

For the first time since their lives had been turned topsy-turvy, Faith saw glimmers of a silver lining.

When they got back home, the street lamps were on. Remy took a shower without being asked, and Alex took one under protest. Afterward they disappeared into their rooms, too exhausted to complain about the tepid water temperature.

In the kitchen, Faith tried unpacking boxes, but half a box later she realized she couldn't go on.

As one last gesture she opened a cabinet to put away the glasses she'd set on the counter and saw the bottle of Scotch Dottie Lee had given her. Dottie Lee claimed good Scotch made a person believe all things were possible. That sounded suspiciously like a prescription for what ailed Faith.

She stared at the bottle. Before David, in between living with her parents and marrying her husband, she had been a social drinker. A glass of wine with dinner. A mixed drink at parties. Budweiser at an Orioles game. Nevertheless, she had abandoned drinking without a qualm when David came into her life.

After all, they'd had their image to think about.

That struck her funny. Maybe because she was exhausted. Maybe because laughter was better than the alternative.

"Oh, David..." She shook her head as big gulps of laughter shook her. For a moment, just a moment, she wished he were there to share the joke.

The cap came off the Scotch without effort, and she poured an inch into a glass. She doubted that after fifteen years as a teetotaler she could handle it straight, so she compromised by turning on the faucet and letting the water run for a full minute. Then she stuck the glass under it and added another inch of liquid.

"Scotch and water. Hold the rocks 'til we have a refrigerator." She held up the glass in toast, lifting it toward the ceiling. "To all the women who've lived here, and to my sister Hope, who should have."

That small measure of contentment—along with a second helping of the eighteen-year-old Glenfiddich—helped her fall asleep immediately. Although the windows were shut and the ancient air conditioner labored away, she was vaguely aware of noise in the street, students talking as they wandered toward Wisconsin or back home again, tires on pavement, laughter and, once, something that sounded like an argument.

Although it was a stark contrast to McLean, the noise was oddly comforting. The streets grew quieter as the deepest part of night descended, and she slept fitfully, waking once to find the lamplight tracing patterns among the faded cabbage roses of her wallpaper.

She had only just fallen asleep again when she felt the warmth of a body in her bed. Half-conscious, she thought it was David trying to shake her awake.

Then she realized where she was. She jerked upright, pulling the sheet to her breasts. "What—"

"Mom." Alex sounded terrified. "Mom!"

She was awake now, jolted back to reality. "What?"

"Listen!"

She sat perfectly still until she heard a high-pitched keening, like an infant in sharp distress. She hoped she was still dreaming.

"Do you hear it?" Alex wiggled under her arm and laid his head on her shoulder. "Mom?"

Her door creaked. It was a D.C. summer night, hot and humid enough for tropical fish to flop merrily through the streets, but Faith's skin was as cold as January. A figure flew across the room and leapt on her bed, and Faith threw open her arms to let Remy into the circle.

"Mom, did you hear it?" Remy could barely choke out the words.

"Uh-huh." Faith pulled them closer. "Can you tell where it's coming from?"

Two arms shot up, fingers pointed toward the ceiling.

Faith looked above her, at dark stains where plaster had cracked. "The attic?" She whispered, as they had.

The keening began again, and every nerve of her body vibrated in answer. The sound was clearly coming from somewhere above them.

"Is it Hope?" Alex sounded terrified. Apparently his interest in ghosts had vanished with the first cries.

"No, of course not." Faith sounded more certain than she felt. She didn't believe in ghosts, never had, and didn't intend to make an exception. But at the moment, no other possibilities occurred to her.

"Then what?" Remy demanded. "You're the mom."

"I'm the mom" was Faith's final response to every argument, and now it was coming back to haunt her. Haunt her. She closed her eyes. "I am, aren't I?"

"What are you going to do?" Remy demanded.

"Well, I guess I'm going to go up to the attic and give that noise a piece of my mind."

Both children grabbed her arms. Alex whimpered. "No."

"There's something perfectly natural and normal making noise up there, and if we don't find out what it is, we won't get any sleep." Faith gently shook off both children.

"Let's call the police!" Alex grabbed her arm again.

"I would if I thought it was a burglar. It's not."

Remy refused to move out of her way. "There are windows up there. You can see them from the street. Maybe somebody climbed in."

Faith wished she had investigated the attic the way she had promised Alex. But there hadn't been time to do anything except cast out the worst of the trash to make sure there was room for storage. The movers knew more about the attic than she did.

"That would have to be one stupid burglar." She edged past Remy and shook Alex off again. "There are a lot better ways to enter the house."

"What?"

She cursed her words. "I mean if someone wanted to break in, he wouldn't do it from the roof. But nobody's going to break in. Nobody did. Nobody will."

"Oh, right." Remy flung herself to the middle of the bed and grabbed Alex. The two sworn enemies clung to each other like Velcro strips.

"I can see I'm not going to have any company." Faith pulled on her robe, one of the few personal items she'd unpacked. Slippers were only a dream. She slipped on the flats she'd worn all day and tied her belt. She was halfway to the door when the keening began again.

"Mom!"

She held up her hand to silence Alex and waited until the noise ended; then she opened her door all the way and peered into the hall. A night-light in the lone hallway wall socket lit a sea of boxes and a narrow path between them. She was glad she'd thought to put it there.

She needed a flashlight. She tried to remember where she'd put hers. She had left it behind on the day of the cleanup and replaced the batteries on her next trip so it would function.

"The kitchen pantry." She debated the journey. Down the stairs in the dark, into the kitchen, into the pantry, where a rat named Lefty had his hideout. McLean seemed a thousand miles away.

The keening began again. She took off down the stairs, turning on the dining room light when she got there. When she flicked the kitchen switch the bulb sputtered, then popped and went dark. She searched the pantry by feel.

"I swear, Lefty, if you show yourself right now, you're dead rat meat," she whispered fiercely.

If Lefty was there, he lay low. Faith grabbed the flashlight and snapped it on. The light flickered, then died. She shook it and tried again. This time it stayed on.

"New flashlight. New flashlight." She chanted the words as if there was some chance she might forget them by tomorrow morning. She climbed the stairs and peeked in Alex's room. Boxes crowded every corner. There was a path to his bed.

And a path to the attic door.

One of the movers had told Faith how lucky she was to have a spacious attic. Right now she would gladly give him every single square foot. The keening began again, rising in pitch, falling, then rising until it ended in a terrified scream.

Silence fell.

Faith reconsidered. Her hands were shaking. If she waited until tomorrow morning, she might have better luck.

If she waited until tomorrow morning it was perfectly possible the children would never set foot in the house again.

She turned on Alex's light, then opened the attic door and reached for that light switch. Nothing happened when she flicked it on. She remembered that she hadn't replaced the lightbulbs. There had been plenty of daylight for the movers to see.

"Lightbulbs. Lightbulbs." The chant gave her no courage.

She shone the flashlight on the steps, which looked clear of boxes. She took the first few with an eye toward her escape route. The attic was silent now.

She moved a little faster, waving the flashlight back and forth to make sure there were no surprises. On the top step, just before she entered the attic proper, she paused. The flashlight was woefully inadequate, She could only illuminate a small section of the room at one time. But from her vantage point, nothing looked amiss. The attic had a solid floor, and boxes were piled everywhere. The space was tall enough in the middle for an adult to stand up straight, the roof sloping gradually to the floor at the edges.

She stood poised for flight and continued to wave the flashlight around the room. At one point it flickered, and she shook it hard. It stayed on.

"Okay, what's going on up here?" she said into the darkness. Had someone answered, she probably would have tumbled down the steps.

Nothing moved. Nothing screeched, keened or wailed. And no ghost baby materialized to solve a mystery that was older than Faith herself.

"Personally, I don't believe in ghosts," she said into the darkness. "And this wouldn't be my favorite time to have my mind changed."

"Mom?"

She jumped, and instinctively her hand covered her pounding heart before she realized Alex was calling from the bottom of the steps. "It's okay, honey."

"Who are you talking to?"

"Myself. Go back in my room."

"You might need me...."

"I'm fine. Go take care of Remy."

"I'm right here. I'm older than he is, remember?" Remy sounded a little less scared, a little more disgusted. Things were looking up.

"Okay, stay there, both of you." Faith stepped into the attic, waving her flashlight as she moved between boxes.

"Mom?" Alex sounded worried.

"Nothing so far," she shouted down to him. "Except a very messy attic."

Suddenly something gray flew through the air in front of her. Faith shrieked. The specter shrieked, then disappeared behind boxes.

She didn't know a heart could beat so fast, and she was gulping air even faster. She was so relieved she felt faint.

"Cat!" She turned and made tracks for the stairs. "Cat. There's a cat up here. That's what we heard. Just a cat!"

She heard footsteps on the stairs and trained her flashlight in that direction so Alex could find his way. Remy was right behind him.

"Cat?" He sounded excited.

"Well, somebody should have been smart enough to figure that out." Clearly Remy thought that someone was Faith.

Faith waited until the children joined her. "I don't know how it got in here, but this house is so old it probably had plenty of choices."

"What's a cat doing here?" Alex was dancing from foot to foot in excitement now.

Faith tried to remember if cats could contract rabies. Surely a wild cat when cornered could do some serious damage even if it didn't harbor deadly diseases. "I don't know. Maybe it's a nice place to live."

"Look!" Alex pointed as the cat darted between boxes and disappeared again. "He's gray."

The cat, or what Faith had seen of it so far, looked to be pale gray and long-haired. Alex started past her before she could stop him. "Maybe he can't get outside. Maybe the movers blocked him in."

Faith grabbed her son's arm. "Alex, don't go near him. I'm sure he's wild. If you get too close you could get torn to bits."

"By a cat?" Remy edged past Faith. "It's just a little cat."

"Not so little." Faith barred her daughter's way. "I think we'd better leave well enough alone."

"Mom, we have to look around. If the way out is blocked, it's going to keep yowling all night long."

That prospect didn't appeal to Faith, either. She debated. Tomorrow morning they could check more thoroughly, perhaps even call the animal warden. But morning wouldn't arrive for hours.

"Just stay behind me," she cautioned. She trained her light along the rafters leading down to the floor. The space where they met was, in most places, seamless, carefully planked so that no gaps existed. But in one spot a plank appeared to be missing. At least that was her best guess, judging from a small gap. A pile of boxes had been shoved over the rest of it.

She started in that direction, and the kids followed her. "Okay, let's check this out." She shone the flashlight on that area and saw she'd been right.

"Here, kitty, kitty," Remy said. "Nice kitty."

Faith wasn't so sure about that. "It looks like the movers might have covered the cat's exit. This was the direction he came from when I first saw him."

"Why didn't the movers tell us there was a cat up here?"

"It was probably hiding. Hold the light." Faith held it out to Remy. "We'll move the boxes and see if there's a cat exit."

"Maybe that's not a good idea." Remy couldn't resist the urge to pass the flashlight beam over everything within twenty feet. "Then anything can get in, right?"

"Right now I just want something to get out."

Remy shrugged, and the flashlight beam bobbed. "You're the mom."

"Very funny." Faith lifted the top box, one marked "Remy's winter clothing," off the pile. It was lightweight and moved easily. By the time she set it down, Alex had the next one. They worked in silence, straining together over the box on the bottom marked "kitchen miscellaneous."

The plank was missing, just as she'd thought. A space one plank wide ran along the edge of the roofline. "Shine the light in there, would you?" she asked Remy. "Let's see if we can see through to the outside.

"Mom!" Alex was on his knees peering into the gap already. "Listen..."

Faith squatted beside him and waited. The faintest whimpers greeted her. Her skin prickled in response.

"Mom!"

Faith turned just in time to see a streak of gray leap past Remy and into the gap. The cat disappeared in a flash.

"Our he's a she. With kittens," Faith said. "Give me the light. Alex, stand back."

She got to her knees and leaned down. She could just see a spot of gray under the plank that should have connected to the one that was missing. As she watched, the cat shifted, and Faith glimpsed movement beneath it.

Faith got to her feet. "Kittens. More than one, I think. She wasn't trying to get out. She's probably got another way outside and in. She was trying to get to her babies. Poor thing. They've been separated all day."

"Kittens?" Remy sounded interested. She had wanted a cat from the time she was old enough to say the word. But David was allergic to animal dander.

"Wild kittens, honey," Faith warned.

"That's why she was making all that noise," Alex said. "She did sound like a ghost. Hey! Ghost! We can call her Ghost."

Faith figured that things were quickly getting back to normal. "Come on, you two. We need to leave Ghost alone. She's been away from her babies, and she needs to take care of them without worrying about us. I'll put some water out for her."

Reluctantly, Remy got to her feet. "You're not going to do anything to the kittens, are you? Like trap them, or have somebody come and take them away?"

Of course those would be sensible alternatives, but Faith was utterly incapable of being sensible when it came to small animals. "We'll figure out what's best for them."

"Ghost belongs here," Alex said. "She's lived in this house longer than we have."

Remy stood, but she wasn't as careful as Faith. She knocked her head on a rafter as she straightened. "Ouch! Damn!"

Faith was surprised at the expletive, but it seemed fitting after the night they'd had. "I'll bet that hurt." She put her arm around Remy's shoulder and shone the light on her head. "Let me see if it's bleeding."

There wasn't any blood, but the flashlight beam caught something odd on the rafter. Faith leaned closer, shining the light directly on it. "Remy, are you okay?"

"I just want to go back to bed."

Faith's own exhaustion had fled at the first yowl. She guessed she had a year's worth of adrenaline still running through her veins. "Look at this."

Alex joined her. "What?"

"I'm not sure. Something carved into the rafter. Can you see?" Faith ran her fingertips over the wood, brushing aside years of cobwebs and dust. "I need something better to clean it with. Find me something."

Alex ripped the tape off a box labeled towels that he had shoved out of the way. He handed her a monogrammed hand towel from her former master bath. "Here."

"I want to go to bed." Remy was beginning to sound like her new self again. "Who cares who carved what where?"

"Just wait one minute, okay?" Faith passed the towel over the rafter. Back and forth, until it was as clean as she could get it. Then she stepped closer and aimed the light directly on the carving.

"Oh, look!" Faith traced letters connected in beautiful old-fashioned cursive. "Millicent Charles." She turned to her children. "Millicent was my grandmother. She carved her name here."

"Awesome." Alex sounded genuinely intrigued.

"So? What's the big deal?" Remy sounded less so.

"Well, it's not a big deal. It's just, well, nice. Don't you think?"

"I'm going to bed."

"I put my name in wet cement once down the street from our house, but somebody came along and smoothed it out before the cement got hard," Alex said.

Faith draped her arm over his shoulder, glad she was only hearing that particular story now. "Wood carvings are harder to erase. It's been here for years."

"Hey, Mom, Dottie Lee said there was a surprise in the house. A mystery. Maybe that's it." Alex stopped at the top of the steps. "I'm coming up here tomorrow to look around some more."

"Well, you'll have company. Just stay out of Ghost's way." Faith thought about that name. "We can't call the cat Ghost. Your grandmother won't understand."

"Guest." Remy pushed past Alex and started down the stairs. "It sounds like Ghost."

"I like Ghost," Alex said.

"Ghost Guest then. But Guest for short."

"We're the guests." Alex followed her. "She was here first."

Faith waited until both children were back in their rooms with their doors closed before she found a bowl and filled it with water for the last attic trip. She doubted they would hear more noise tonight. Guest had gotten what she wanted.

Back in her own bed, she couldn't sleep, though all was quiet now. Her mind whirled in a thousand directions. She thought about the woman who had carved her name in the rafter, about David, who had been turned away by his own children, about her own mother, who had experienced tragedy here. About Dottie Lee, who had made her feel welcome, and the man from O Street who had saved the spinet from destruction.

Just months ago her life had been predictable, perhaps even boring.

She squeezed her eyelids tightly shut.

Well, no one could say her life was boring now.

 10

Lydia and Joe hadn't slept in the same bedroom since moving to
Great Falls ten years ago. When engaging the architect, Lydia had
insisted on separate bedroom suites and vetoed a design that placed
them in the same wing. She wanted open spaces, soaring ceilings,
and Joe as far from her bedroom as possible.

Separate suites had made little difference in their relationship.
Long ago the Hustons had come to an understanding. Whatever
tender emotions they'd felt at the beginning of their marriage had
melted in the crucible of Hope's kidnapping. But if they couldn't
have a fulfilling marriage, they could at least have one that appeared fulfilling to the world at large.

Every Sunday after church the Hustons compared calendars at
the Old Ebbitt Grill, a power breakfast favorite where they could
be seen and remarked on. Over waffles or eggs Benedict they penciled in time with Faith and her family, along with state dinners,
and Joe's committee meetings and responsibilities to his constituents, including overnight trips to his three Virginia offices. Joe,
for all his faults, was almost fanatically devoted to his job and the
people he served.

This morning Lydia had insisted they skip church and have
breakfast at home. She wasn't certain Joe could act the part of senator while discussing his daughter and her new living arrange-

ments. Lydia had expected him to be angry when she turned over the Prospect Street house to Faith, but he had moved beyond anger to brutal sarcasm. She didn't want to chance being overheard.

She was still setting pastries and scrambled eggs on the buffet when Joe came into the breakfast room. Without a word of greeting he poured a cup of coffee, then slammed it on the table so that drops sprayed over the brand-new French country tablecloth. Lydia watched the coffee bridge what had been a snowy space between rose and lavender bouquets and wondered if she'd been mistaken not to meet with Joe on neutral turf.

"Marley's in the kitchen," she pointed out. "Let's be civilized, shall we?"

"Marley knows which side her bread is buttered on, and who pays for it."

"She pays for every slice with hard work." Marley, their housekeeper, ran the Hustons' lives with calm efficiency.

Joe dropped into his chair. "Lydia, I have no stomach for rhetoric this hour of the morning, and I'm in a hurry. I'm going into the office."

"Marley made some of the cinnamon rolls you like so much."

"I'll take one with me."

"We need a few minutes to go over next week's calendar so neither of us misses anything important."

"Genevieve can call you about mine tomorrow." Joe, who believed that women belonged in the home, nevertheless surrounded himself with them at work. Genevieve, his personal secretary, was another model of female efficiency.

Lydia served herself a croissant before she took a seat across from her husband. "I don't want to talk to Genevieve. If I did, I would have invited her to breakfast."

"What's the problem? Do you suddenly have more nasty revelations for me? Faith is going to live in that Georgetown rat trap where her baby sister was kidnapped. What's next?"

"We lived there. Remember?"

His eyes blazed. "Oh yes, I remember."

She paused for a moment, hoping to give her words more weight. "I don't have any new revelations. I simply want to talk this through. I don't want you taking out your bad temper on Faith and the children."

"Try this on. She brought it on herself."

Lydia was used to Joe's narrow take on the world, but this time he surprised her. "I'm sorry?"

"If Faith had been woman enough for David, David would have been man enough for her."

Lydia hadn't realized Joe could still shock her. "That's ridiculous."

"If our daughter was a better wife, she would still have a husband."

"If that's what you planned to say to her every day, I'm glad they didn't move in with us."

"Do you have any idea how much ribbing I've gotten about this?"

She leaned forward to make sure he was paying attention. "This isn't about you."

He dropped his fist on the table, and the coffee sprayed again. "And now she's dragged my grandchildren to Prospect Street. Tell me, just tell me, how that's going to help anything."

"Well, for one thing, there's nobody in the row house to bully her."

"You really ought to be more careful about the things you say."

"Why?" Lydia picked up her own cup, but she lowered her voice. "Your threats haven't worked for a long time. I know too much about you, and you know too much about me. So here's what we're going to do. Marley and I are driving to Prospect Street this morning to help Faith clean and unpack. About noon, Faith will get a delivery from a Capitol Hill florist. The card reads 'Happy Housewarming, Dad.' The order's already been placed."

"If you think that's going to change anything, you're dead wrong. Faith knows how much I disapprove."

"Maybe, because she lived with you all those years, and she knows you never forget or forgive even the slightest prick. But your grandchildren haven't quite caught on."

"Has it occurred to you, Lydia, that by living on Prospect Street, Faith might discover a thing or two you don't want her to know?"

Lydia's gaze traveled beyond her husband to two adult deer

standing like statues at the edge of the woods behind their house. Ten years ago, when she found this land, she believed the move to Great Falls would finally bring her peace. But she had been naive, even foolish, to think that trees and windows and wildlife would solve the problems of her life.

She turned back to her husband and carefully set down her cup. "The row house has always held secrets, hasn't it, Joe? I guess you and I will have to trust that it gives up only the best."

The spinet man was sitting at one of two outdoor tables with his newspaper when Faith and the children made their way to Booey-mongers for breakfast. The morning was nearly perfect, sunny, but mild enough to make outside dining a pleasure. One glance at the line and Faith knew she and the children wouldn't be sitting anywhere inside or out. It was going to be takeout breakfast among the boxes.

The man—whose name she couldn't recall—looked up, saw them and grinned. "Hey there. How's the unpacking?"

Faith made a detour to his table. "I'm sorry, I've already forgotten your name."

He lumbered to his feet, shoving the table a foot forward as he did. "Pavel. Pavel Quinn."

He looked expectantly toward the children, and she made the introductions, struggling to pronounce his name as he had. "Pah-vyel," with the stress on the first syllable. Remy clearly couldn't have cared less, but Alex looked interested.

"What kind of name is Pavel?" He pronounced it perfectly. "It sounds like a last name."

"Russian." Pavel said the word with relish—and an exaggerated accent.

"Cool." Alex was clearly impressed.

"It's a zoo here on Sundays," Pavel said. "Would you like to join me?"

"Oh, no, I—" Faith was interrupted by her son's whoop.

"Cool," Alex finished. "Then we can watch people go by."

"I'll be here waiting." Pavel picked up his paper, and Faith knew she'd been bested.

By the time they returned, Pavel was feeding bits of toast to two pigeons who'd made themselves at home under the table. He was dressed much as he'd been yesterday, shorts, a rumpled T-shirt—although this one, at least, wasn't splattered. He'd shaved and combed his hair, and he looked at the very least presentable.

"Pigeons carry germs." Remy plunked her tray on the table across from him.

"These pigeons come with the Surgeon General's seal of approval." Pavel finished crumbling his toast and dusted off his hands. "Meet Laurel and Hardy."

"They have names?" Alex took the seat on Pavel's right.

"All God's creatures have names. You just have to concentrate hard to hear them."

Remy snorted. "Who are you, Doctor Doolittle?"

"God named them Laurel and Hardy?" Faith took the last chair, uncomfortably close to Pavel, who seemed to take up more than his share of space. "God has a sense of humor?"

"You only have to look around to see what a sense of humor she has."

"She?" Remy looked disgusted. "You're calling God a she?"

He gave a loose-limbed shrug.

"God is a man," Remy said.

Faith tried to head off Pavel. "People all over the world see God in different ways."

"Then they're wrong."

Pavel smiled at Remy, as if he remembered a time when he had known everything, too. "So, do you think you're going to like living in Georgetown?"

"No way." Remy ducked her head and started on her bagel.

Faith shook her head, and this time Pavel smiled at her. "How about you?"

"Do you?"

He sprawled in his chair, making himself comfortable. "I do."

"Did you grow up here?"

"California." He turned to Alex. "How about you, champ? Your sister's certain, and your mom is undecided. Do you think you'll like it here?"

"Oh, sure."

"Good. What are you going to like about it?"

Alex considered. "I think it's a place where you can be different if you want."

Faith's heart squeezed in her chest. "You can be different anywhere, can't you?"

"Not when you're eleven."

Pavel leaned forward, dropping his forearms on the table to look right at Alex. "You are a very different eleven-year-old. I can see that already."

"I'm an inventor."

"If you'd given me another minute, I would have guessed that."

"Really?"

Faith watched Pavel enchant her son. Despite his casual, almost sloppy appearance, he was a born charmer. His eyes were wide-set, slightly tilted and darkly lashed, and he knew how to focus them so the person he talked to felt bathed in their warmth. He had the strongly defined bone structure of a Slav and an Irishman's knack for using all his assets without seeming to be aware of any of them.

"You have an interesting boy here, Faith."

Faith pulled herself out of her reverie. "I've always thought so."

"Every family needs an inventor."

Alex's inventions were one of the few things Faith and David had disagreed about. David wanted to use "invention time" as a reward to make their son finish homework and chores. Faith believed Alex should have more control over when and how he worked.

Now the choice was hers alone.

"Is there an inventor in your family?" Alex asked Pavel.

"I'm my own family, so I have to be a jack-of-all-trades."

Faith was surprised he wasn't married with children of his own. Perhaps he had a partner or lover. She wondered what Dottie Lee could tell her.

She searched for a safer subject. "Didn't you tell me your house was a work in progress? Does that mean you're in the midst of renovations?"

"Eternally. I'm doing the work myself."

Faith was sure her eyes brightened noticeably. "Are you?"

"Do I detect a note of special interest? One renovator to another?"

"Honestly? I don't know how to do a blessed thing except wield a paintbrush. But I'm going to learn."

"I saw the inside of that house, remember? You're biting off a lot."

"I'm not going to rewire the house myself and burn it down. You don't happen to have a list of contractors, do you?"

"Around here, that's like asking for the keys to somebody's safety deposit box."

"No kidding?"

"I have a list. I might share in exchange for a home-cooked meal. We barter here, too."

She laughed, and she wasn't even sure why. She was in no mood to entertain. In fact she might never be in the mood to entertain a man again.

Entertain a man. She sobered quickly. Until that moment, Pavel had seemed like nothing more than a neighborhood find with shoulders wide enough to hold up a piano and hands that could plaster or plumb.

She was getting a divorce. She was almost in the position to entertain a man. She had never expected to be in that position again.

"Is your cooking that bad?" Pavel's eyes sparkled.

"No, but apparently my social skills are. I'm sorry, I'd invite you in a minute, but you haven't seen my kitchen."

"That bad?"

"Abysmal."

"Would you like me to give it the once-over? One renovator to another?"

She wasn't sure how to refuse. The offer was nothing more than friendly, and she needed all the advice he could give. "Right now the path's blocked with boxes, but maybe by day's end. Why don't you just stop by next time you're on the street?"

"I'll do that."

Faith became aware of Remy's stare. She met her daughter's eyes and saw more hostility than usual.

"Maybe when you come over I could show you what I'm doing to my computer," Alex said. "Do you like computers?"

"Absolutely." Pavel pushed back his chair. "I'd better be off. I've got a sink to install this morning. I haven't had running water in my kitchen for..." He counted on his fingers. "Five months."

Faith groaned. He nodded in sympathy. "Prepare yourself for the long haul," he warned.

Pavel got to his feet, towering over the table for a moment. He stuck out his hand, and Alex took it, man to man. "I'll look forward to seeing your inventions." He nodded to Faith and Remy; then he was gone.

Remy threw her napkin on the table. "Mother, who is that man?"

"He's a neighbor. Remember I told you about a man who helped the movers when the piano—"

"You don't know him? All you know is he can move a piano? And you invited him to our house?"

Faith felt anger flare. "I haven't heard of a single serial killer on the loose here, Remy. He's a neighbor, not Jack the Ripper."

"How would you know? You lived with a man for fifteen years and didn't know anything about *him!*"

"Well, I've lived with you for fourteen, and I know I won't tolerate your blatant rudeness to other people."

Remy glared at her. Then she got up and started back down the street toward their house.

Silence fell over the table. Faith realized she hadn't eaten more than a bite or two of her egg sandwich, and now she'd lost her appetite.

"I'm not mad at you, Mom," Alex said at last.

She squeezed his hand, but she didn't trust herself to speak.

Remy passed the row house and kept walking. She was too angry to go home and unpack. A wild animal was loose in her body, and she could feel it clawing and struggling to get out. If it escaped while she was in her room, she wasn't sure what she would do.

She was headed for Georgetown University. Her mother had insisted on a driving tour of the neighborhood, and she had recited facts about the university as if Remy might possibly be interested. She wasn't, of course. It was just one more way her mother was trying to make the move "fun." As if living near a university could possibly make life more endurable.

If they still lived in the house in McLean, she would probably just be waking up from a sleepover with Megan and her other friends. She supposed she might still be invited to sleepovers in McLean, but she wasn't going. All those girls knew about her life. About her awful father, and her mother, who thought public school in the District would toughen Remy so she could face the cold, cruel world.

Well, she was tough enough already to face anything. She had even thought about running away, just to show Faith what was what, but she really didn't know where to go. The only place she wanted to be was back home, and that was out of the question.

She needed a time machine. Maybe Alex, the new light of Faith's life, would invent one so he could send Remy away. He would like that.

She walked several blocks before she started to pay attention to where she was. Prospect Street was one row house after another. All old. All small. All completely different from the house she'd grown up in. She came to a corner and thought about turning downhill toward M Street, but turning required energy, and climbing back up the hill when she got good and ready to come home would require more. So she kept walking toward the university.

Two young men exercising a dog were coming toward her. The dog was huge, the size of the wardrobe boxes she'd used to pack her hanging clothes, a box with black curly fur and a lolling pink tongue. The dog made her think about Guest and the kittens, and she remembered with a pang that she had planned to check on them after breakfast. Faith had promised to buy cat food.

The dog seemed perfectly tame and friendly, but the moment he got close enough to lunge at her, he did. Paws on her shoulders, he shoved her backward until she tumbled to the ground, where he proceeded to lick her face with big, nasty swipes of his tongue.

She screeched, more from surprise than fear, covering her face. "Get this thing off me!"

By now one of the young men was hauling hard on the leash. The other had thrown himself between Remy and the dog and was trying to pry the dog loose.

"Whoa, Bear. Cut it out, stupid!"

Bear sank to his haunches, and Remy scrambled away. "He attacked me!"

"Nah. He's just too friendly for his own good." The man without the leash offered his hand to help her to her feet, but Remy refused it. She stood on shaking legs.

"If you can't control him, you shouldn't have him on the street."

"He didn't hurt you, did he?"

She did a quick assessment of body parts. "No..."

"I'm sorry." The young man grinned. He had blond hair and big brown eyes, and the grin was picture-perfect. "I should have figured he'd do that. He likes pretty girls."

She was momentarily tongue-tied. She smiled to cover up the lapse.

"I'm taking him home," the other man said. He was dark-haired and dark-eyed, and unlike his friend, he wasn't smiling. "I'm tired of hauling him off people. We ought to take him back to the pound." He turned and started in the opposite direction.

Remy found her voice. "Pound?"

"Yeah. Selim's sister works there. They were going to put Bear down, and she grabbed him before they could. Then she gave him to Selim."

"That was lucky." Remy wasn't sure why she'd said that. She wasn't sure it was lucky at all. She was covered with dog slobber in front of the cutest guy she'd ever seen.

Except that if it hadn't been for Bear, she wouldn't even be talking to him.

"You don't have to feed that monster. That's the worst part about him. You at Georgetown?"

Remy was surprised, then absurdly pleased he'd mistaken her for a coed. She considered lying, but she knew if she did, the joke could only last so long. "No, we just moved in." She hiked her thumb behind her.

"We live a few houses that way." He hiked his thumb behind him.

She looked over his shoulder and saw Bear and Selim going inside a row house like her own. "You're at Georgetown?"

"I start again in a couple of weeks. Where do you go to school?"

"Nowhere right now." Which was true enough.

"You ought to give Georgetown a try."

"I might." She didn't point out that even high school was still in her future.

"Heading anywhere interesting?"

Remy shook her head. "Just out looking around."

He stuck out his hand. "I'm Colin Fitzpatrick."

His hand was large and warm, wrapping around hers just hard enough to make itself felt.

"Remy Bronson."

"Would you like to see the campus? I don't have to be anywhere for a while. I could show you around."

Remy knew exactly how her mother would feel about *that*. Colin was a stranger, and her mother didn't know she wasn't at home.

She smiled her most adult smile. "I just bet you could."

He laughed. "Would you like to see our house first? Since we're neighbors."

"Okay." Remy figured if Faith could invite a complete stranger to their house, she had every right to see Colin's.

"We had a party last night, so don't expect much. It's never very clean, but this morning's it's worse than usual."

They started toward the house. Remy wasn't sure which part of this was better. Being with the most exciting man she'd ever met, or wondering what Faith would say when she realized her daughter wasn't home.

She was just sorry she wouldn't be around to see her mother's face.

11

Lydia and Marley arrived before noon, at the same moment the flowers did. When Faith opened the front door, Lydia wasn't sure which surprised her daughter more.

Faith took the flowers, an extravagant fall bouquet in a silver-plated vase, greeted Marley, and finally leaned over to kiss her mother's cheek. Lydia tipped the deliveryman and sent him on his way.

"They're gorgeous." Faith scanned the card and gave her mother a knowing smile. "Dad has such terrific taste. Almost as good as yours."

"He hasn't been at his best. I believe the flowers are an apology." Lydia wasn't sure why she bothered with the charade. Faith knew Joe had never apologized for anything in his life.

"I'm going to put them on the kitchen table. I think there's actually a spot without junk on it."

Faith left, and Marley wandered the first floor, surveying the damage. Lydia wasn't sure how old her housekeeper was. Nearly fifty, she supposed. Slender and tall, Marley was a woman of boundless energy. Being with her exhausted Lydia even more.

Marley aimed her words at Lydia so Faith wouldn't hear them. "This isn't a house, it's a fifteen-year plan. The floors are nice." Marley had grown up in Jamaica, and her voice still held an unmistakable lilt. Her real name was Mary Louise, but a lifelong love affair with reggae had earned her the nickname.

"I had them redone. They *are* nice, aren't they?"

"Make everything else look worse."

"Marley, that's not helpful."

Marley shrugged. She rarely spoke to Joe, but she said anything she liked to Lydia, knowing full well Lydia wouldn't survive without her.

Faith came back into the room and stood at the bottom of the stairs to call the children. A door opened upstairs, and from the clumping of footsteps, Lydia knew her grandson was on his way down. She wondered what to say to him. Alex always put her at a loss for anything except criticism.

He stopped just shy of the bottom. "Hello, Grandmother." He caught sight of Marley and gave a big whoop. "Marley. Hi."

"You getting so big, I don't think I recognize you anymore." Marley went to stand at the bottom of the steps. "See, you bigger than me now."

"We've got kittens upstairs." Alex addressed the revelation to Marley. "Do you want to see?"

"Kittens?"

"Kittens?" Lydia echoed. "Faith, are you out of your mind? You don't have enough to do here?"

"The kittens came with the house, Mother." Faith joined Marley at the bottom of the steps. "Alex, go get Remy, would you? What's she doing?"

"I don't know. Her door's been closed since we got home."

"Well, run up and get her, please." Faith faced her mother. "There's a cat living in the attic, and she has kittens. The kids and I discovered them in the middle of the night."

"What were you doing in the attic in the middle of the night?"

"Trying to find out what was screeching like a banshee."

"Oh." Lydia understood everything Faith hadn't said. *The ghost baby, come back to haunt them all.*

Shoes sounded on the stairs again, and Alex appeared. "She's not there. And she's not in the bathroom or up in the attic. She would have come through my room."

"Maybe she went up there when you came down." Faith shook her head. "Mother, I'd better check this out. I'll be right back."

Lydia wondered how Faith could lose a child Remy's size, but, wisely, she didn't say so. "Let's get organized," she told Marley. "Alex, would you like Marley to help you unpack?"

"Sure."

Faith returned, looking troubled. "She's not there."

"The basement?" Lydia knew there was no place else.

"No reason for her to be down there."

"Maybe she didn't come home," Alex said.

Lydia didn't like the expression in Faith's eyes. "Come home from where?"

Faith silenced Alex, who started to explain, then did it herself. "We went out to breakfast, and she got angry. She left before we did, walking in this direction. She has a key. I just assumed..."

Lydia bit her lip. She didn't remind her daughter that they were in a city now, and Remy needed protection. She didn't remind her that thirty-eight years ago another child had disappeared on Prospect Street.

"How long ago?" Lydia glanced at her watch.

"We've been home for two hours or so."

"And you say she was angry?"

"Remy hasn't adjusted well."

"Could she be lost? Does she know the streets well enough to find her way back home?"

"She knows our address. Prospect's a short street. All she'd have to do is ask someone if she got turned around."

"There are three of us who can comb the streets."

"Four!" Alex jumped off his step to the floor. "What about me?"

Lydia stared at her grandson, aware of him in a way she really hadn't been before. As usual, her first impulse had been to silence him. But the boy staring back at her looked disturbingly adult. For the first time she glimpsed the man Alex was going to be.

She tried to enlist his cooperation. "Alex, somebody has to stay here in case Remy comes back. Frankly, I think she'd rather come home to you than to any of us. If she sees us waiting, she might pass right by. And you can call us on our cell phones to let us know. Will you do that?"

He frowned, aware, she supposed, that he was being cajoled. "I guess."

Lydia touched his shoulder in thanks. He looked puzzled, as if he hadn't known she had that in her repertoire.

"I'm sure we can count on you." She turned away and wondered if she'd done anything in her sixty-six years to be proud of.

The university tour never transpired. Somehow, after a look at the downstairs of Colin's house and a roughhouse session with Bear, they never got any farther. Selim's father owned an electronics store, and Selim had brought half of the inventory to college, including a big-screen television tuned, at the moment, to a comedy Remy's father had undoubtedly held up as an example of American immorality. At least in the old days.

She was slouched on a beat-up sofa with Colin, watching two college-age men on the screen, who were trying, yet again, to get a woman into bed after a night of drinking and near-miss seductions.

"You haven't seen this?" Colin asked. "It's practically a classic."

"Don't think so." Remy was fascinated. She had watched R-rated movies with her friends. She wasn't a complete goody-goody. But this one, which made fun of everything she'd been taught to believe, was in a different league.

And she was watching it with a guy; she was sitting right next to a guy watching guys in a movie trying to have sex. Colin seemed oblivious to the implications.

"How old are you?" He turned in the middle of a scene in a strip club that had her mouth hanging open.

"Seventeen." She glanced at him. The lie felt as natural as repeating her name.

"Oh, I thought you were older. You're in high school?"

The next lie was every bit as easy. "Uh-huh."

"I guess you'll be a senior."

"Uh-huh." Someday.

"You want a Coke or something?" When she nodded, Colin got up and stretched, then disappeared into the kitchen. He was cute, really cute. Megan would never believe Remy had captured the attention of a college man. She couldn't wait to tell her. Then she remembered Megan wasn't just down the street anymore.

Colin was just down the street.

She was distracted by a noise behind her. She shifted and saw a new man coming downstairs. Colin had told her that four of them shared the house. Besides Selim there was another student named Paul, and a fourth man named Enzio, who was a Georgetown dropout. Enzio sold clothes at one of the shops on Wisconsin, and sometimes he got everybody discounts.

The guy coming down was wearing leather pants with more zippers than a Levi's outlet and a tight gray T-shirt. He lit a cigarette on the landing, but he didn't put it between his lips.

"Who are you?"

"Remy."

"You a friend of somebody's?"

"I live down the street. Colin and I are watching a movie."

"Yeah." He stretched and smoke twirled in the air over his head. "Colin will watch anything."

Remy was fascinated. Colin looked like an older version of the boys she knew. Scrubbed clean, hair cut short, clothes from Abercrombie or Banana Republic. But this guy was a different story. His jet-black hair hung halfway to his shoulders, and she could see, even at this distance, that one ear was pierced. He hadn't smiled. He probably wasn't any older than Colin, but he looked as if he was already tired of living. She wondered what had happened to make him so cynical. She could relate.

"Are you Enzio?" She could picture this roommate dropping out of school.

"Yeah."

The training of a lifetime kicked in. "It's nice to meet you."

"Don't kid yourself."

She could feel her cheeks growing warm. She felt thoroughly fourteen. He made his way down the steps and lowered himself to the sofa beside her, taking a drag from the cigarette as he did. Then he offered it to her.

She shook her head. Her cheeks were on fire now. The offer to put her lips where his had been seemed unbelievably intimate.

"You a student?" Enzio looked around for an ashtray and settled on a dirty plate that was probably left over from last night's party.

"High school."

"Jailbait, huh?"

"I'm seventeen." She wished.

"How'd you meet Colin?"

"Bear knocked me down on the sidewalk."

"That's original." Enzio picked up the remote and started channel surfing just as Colin came back in the room.

"Hey, we're watching something." Colin handed a can of Coke to Remy and swiped the remote from Enzio. "Move it, Castellano."

"How come?"

Colin smiled at Remy. "I saw her first."

Enzio got to his feet and reached for his cigarette. "Anything to eat in this dump?"

"Cold pizza." Colin took his place beside Remy.

Enzio started toward the front door instead of the kitchen, and Remy turned to watch him go. Centered in the middle of the window, looking over the street, was her grandmother. Lydia was peering from one side of the street to the other, as if she was searching for something.

Or someone.

Enzio disappeared out the door, and it banged shut behind him. Upstairs, Bear marked his passing with thunderous barks. Slouched down on the sofa, Remy continued to watch out the window as unobtrusively as she could. After Lydia had been gone long enough, she got to her feet.

She forced herself to sound nonchalant. "You know, I hate to do it, but I'd better get home. My mom will wonder what happened to me."

"You can call her. The phone's here someplace."

"I'm supposed to unpack today. I'd better get to it."

"I never showed you around the university."

"I'm right up the street. I'll see you around."

Colin's gaze flicked back to the screen. One of the guys in the movie had finally gotten lucky. "Yeah, okay. Want me to walk you home?"

That was a no-brainer. Besides, as long as Colin didn't know which house was hers, he wouldn't come knocking at her door. "No. Finish the movie."

"Next time we have a party, come on down."

"Yeah. Sure." She got to the door and peered outside. Lydia was a couple of blocks away. The other direction looked clear for the moment. She knew she was going to be in trouble no matter what she did, but she was absolutely certain that if anyone saw her coming out of this house, trouble would be too mild a word.

She slipped outside and started down the sidewalk toward her house. She had just been out for a walk. If she was going to have to live in this place, she deserved to know what the neighborhood was like. She hadn't done anything wrong. She wasn't a baby.

She practiced her responses, knowing she would be called on to use them. And as she did, she wondered when she would see Colin Fitzpatrick and Enzio Castellano again.

Remy had been gone for more than two hours. Faith told herself there was no reason to be concerned. Remy would find her way home when she got good and ready. She was angry, trying to prove she could hurt Faith the way she'd been hurt.

And all the time Faith was telling herself this, a louder voice insisted that Remy was alone in Georgetown without an ounce of street smarts. Too upset to pay attention to her surroundings, Remy was easy pickings for any pervert.

Faith stopped near M Street and 33rd, and pulled out her cell phone. Alex had promised to call when Remy got home, but she didn't want to wait. She leaned against a display window so she would be out of the way of pedestrian traffic and dialed their new number.

"Any news?" she asked when Alex picked up.

"No. Marley came back. She says Remy'll come home when she gets hungry."

Faith wanted to believe her. "Just call me as soon as you hear something, okay?"

"Sure. I will."

Faith considered what to do next. She'd already called Sally, Megan's mother, in case Remy had asked them to pick her up and take her back to McLean. Sally said they hadn't heard anything but she would be sure to call if they did. Faith had tried two other friends of Remy's with no luck.

She hadn't tried David.

Remy would not call her father for help. Faith was certain of that. No matter how much she disliked her mother right now, Remy clearly disliked David more. But David was Remy's father, and, as such, he deserved to know she was missing. What if something really had happened to her?

Now Faith debated calling him. She had the number of Ham's apartment. David no longer had a cell phone; in fact, she was holding what had been his phone—a lemon in the competitive world of cellular technology—in her hand. But she could call him at Ham's, and even if he wasn't there, she could leave a message. She knew it was the right thing to do.

With a heavy heart she looked through her purse for her address book and found the number. She punched it in and waited. She was greeted by an earsplitting buzz. The second time she connected.

The voice that answered wasn't David's. The pitch was higher, a shade more nasal. She knew she was talking to the man who had seduced her husband out of the closet.

"I'd like to speak to David Bronson, please." Faith didn't identify herself.

"I'm sorry, he's not in right now. May I take a message?"

She considered hanging up. That sort of display went against everything she'd been taught. Of course, this whole situation did. No one had ever taught her how to communicate with the man who was her husband's lover.

"Still there?" Ham said.

She attempted to sound businesslike. "This is Faith Bronson. I called to tell David Remy's missing. She's only been gone a little while, but I knew he'd want to know."

"Missing?" Ham's voice rose a key.

She didn't want to explain the situation to him. He wasn't part of their family, no matter how David viewed him. "Please, just tell David to call me when he gets back. By then she might be home."

"I'll track him down."

"No, you don't have to do that. It's not an emergency. She—"

"Faith, please. David's her father. He'll want to know right away."

She didn't know when she and Ham had ascended to a first-name basis, but she didn't like it. She wanted to tell him to call her Mrs. Bronson, but that name no longer seemed to belong to her.

"Do whatever you like," she said after a long pause. "He can call me on the cell phone."

"I know this is no consolation, but I'm sorry to be part of your pain, Faith. I hope someday we can be friends."

A million sarcastic replies occurred to her. She took the politest route and simply hung up. She closed her eyes, the phone cradled against her chest. When it rang, she viewed the buttons through a mist.

Static crackled, but through the interference she heard Alex on the other end. Remy was home.

 12

Faith, who had just heard a string of excuses from her daughter, was attempting to sound calm, even though she had enough adrenaline washing through her system to fuel a filibuster.

"You just walked around? That's all? You didn't think I would be worried when I discovered you weren't here?"

Remy glanced down at her fingernails. "I didn't think you'd go ballistic. What's the big deal? You're making me live here. I might as well see what Georgetown looks like."

"You're fourteen, not forty. And even if you were older, I'd still expect you to keep me in the loop. That's what people who live together do."

Remy looked up. "Oh? You're saying Dad kept *you* in the loop? You knew where he was every minute? Not!"

"Go to your room, please. Plan to stay."

"Wow, I don't have to listen to your lame lectures anymore. Real punishment." Remy ran up the stairs, and her door slammed loud enough to rock a less sturdy house.

"You're putting up with too much from that child," said Lydia, who had witnessed the entire scene. Wisely, Marley had disappeared into Alex's room to keep him out of the furor.

Faith sank to the sofa and put her head in trembling hands. "How would you know?"

"What?"

"I said how would you know? You don't have any experience with this kind of behavior, Mother. I did whatever I was told. Right now I wouldn't say the results are something I want to pass on to Remy."

Lydia dropped down beside her. "Are you somehow blaming your daughter's abysmal behavior on me?"

"I don't like the way she's acting. Do you think I do?"

"Of course not, but—"

"But I will *not* tell my daughter she has to keep every little thought and feeling inside her out of respect for God, country and apple pie. That's the way you raised me, and I will not repeat your mistakes."

Lydia's nostrils flared in anger. "I'm sorry, I didn't know you felt so abused."

"I felt like I couldn't say a word. I still do."

"Well, you're doing a fine job of saying a few right now."

"How did this get to be about you and me? As if I don't have enough going on?"

Faith felt her mother's narrowed gaze all the way to her toes, but she refused to apologize.

"Did you really feel like you had to be perfect?" Lydia asked at last.

"Think about it. I was the daughter of a man who campaigned for family values before anyone even knew what that meant. *I* was the one who wasn't stolen from her crib. I had to be good enough for both Hope and me."

Lydia sat back and stared at the opposite wall. "Maybe you wish Hope hadn't been kidnapped so somebody else could share the burden of being my daughter."

"No, I wish Hope hadn't been kidnapped so you wouldn't be so distant."

"Distant?"

"This isn't getting us anywhere."

"I was distant?"

"You *are* distant. Don't pretend you don't know it, either. You don't want to be any closer than you have to."

"I don't know how you survived such an intolerable childhood."

"Mother, what would you have done if I'd behaved the way Remy did this afternoon?" Lydia was silent. Faith suspected she really didn't know. Faith lowered her voice. "I'm feeling my way with Remy. I know I'm putting up with a lot, but I feel so bad for both kids. Remy's a mess, and Alex is trying to take David's place in the family. But he's not even twelve. He shouldn't be worried about me. Worrying is my job."

"Well, even from my extreme distance, I can see you're underestimating Alex."

Faith supposed that one silver lining to her current situation was that Lydia was trying to be helpful. For once there was more to her mother's advice than simply saying the expected. And maybe both of thcm were saying things that should have been said years ago.

Lydia continued. "As for your daughter, maybe she does need to get a few things off her chest. That's to be expected, I suppose. But that's no reason for letting her talk to you that way. It shows a lack of respect."

"I'm not worried about respect right now. Deep down she—"

"I'm not talking about Remy. I'm talking about you, Faith. Self-respect. You've shown a mountain of it since you found out about David. But not with your daughter."

Faith was still too shaken by Remy's disappearance to have a handle on anything. So she wasn't quite sure, but she thought that maybe, just maybe, hidden in Lydia's criticism was something close to a compliment.

She told her something she hadn't intended to. "I called David to tell him Remy was missing. I got Ham instead."

"Lovely. Did you tell him how much fabric softener David likes in his jockey shorts?"

Faith couldn't help herself. She started to laugh.

Lydia actually smiled. "I can be wicked. You don't know me half as well as you think."

Faith put her hand on her mother's. "Not because I didn't try."

Lydia didn't return the squeeze, but she didn't withdraw her hand, either. "I was friends with my mother. You and Remy will be friends again one day." Unspoken was the third side of that triangle. *Maybe the two of us will be friends one day, too.*

Faith knew they'd gone as far as they could. "Ham said he was going to track David down. He gave me a little lecture about David being Remy's father. As if I didn't know."

"Well, at least we'll be spared that visit now that she's back home."

Like a cue in a Neil Simon play, a knock sounded on the front door. "You did call him back, didn't you?" Lydia said.

"I got his voice mail. Ham was probably on the phone trying to find him." Faith stood. "I hope he got my message."

She peeked outside and knew David hadn't. She opened the door and stood stiffly in front of him, blocking his entrance. "You should have checked your voice mail. She's home."

The lines of strain in his forehead eased. "Where was she?"

"She claims she was walking around, but she was gone from breakfast until just a little while ago. That's a long walk."

"That's a long time for you to be out scouring the streets alone. Why didn't you call me sooner?"

"We didn't know she was gone until almost noon."

"You didn't know she was gone?"

Faith heard dismay in his voice, and something more. Accusation. She bristled. "No, I didn't, David. I haven't resorted to electronic monitoring quite yet."

"I'm not blaming you, Faith, but where did you think she was?"

"Upstairs in her bedroom with the door closed. Where teenagers spend most of their lives."

"And you didn't check on her?"

"I've never had any reason to check on her. I'm hoping I won't in the future."

"This is a pretty big lapse. There must have been some sign she was going to act out—"

"If you want an explanation for why your daughter is acting out, you can just march into my powder room and look in the mirror."

"You can hardly blame this one on me."

She held on to her temper by a thread. "David, you've lost the right to tell me how to parent Remy. You stepped out of this family of your own accord, and I won't have you ordering me around from a safe distance. You don't know what it's like to parent a teenager." She didn't add that he might never have the chance. He knew that better than anyone.

For a long moment he didn't speak, and when he did, his tone was gentler. "You must have been frantic. I was frantic, too, and I feel helpless. I guess it's showing."

She released one shaky breath, and in the time that took, she realized what she had to do next. "Would you like to come in?"

David looked past her to Lydia, sitting on the sofa. "Maybe another time." He started to turn away, but she touched his arm just long enough to stop him.

"Alex is upstairs. Why don't you go up and see him? Marley's helping him unpack. Maybe he'd like to go out for ice cream." She glanced at her watch. "Better make that lunch, I guess. It hasn't been much fun around here today."

Hope sparked in his eyes. "What about Remy?"

"Remy's grounded for the rest of the afternoon."

"Good call."

She should have repeated that she didn't need his blessing, but the words wouldn't come. She wasn't quite sure they were true, anyway. He might soon be her ex-husband, but despite everything she'd said, she had a suspicion that David's opinion was going to continue to matter to her.

She lowered her voice. "I wish you'd just abused me, David. You know, locked me in the basement or drunk up my inheritance. Then I could hate you."

"I don't think you have it in you."

"Maybe I'm as good at hiding things as you were."

"You can't compete."

Maybe comfort was called for, but she didn't yet have it in her. Instead, she stepped aside to let him in. "Alex's room is at the top of the stairs."

He glanced around, nodding to Lydia but wisely not speaking to her. "The bones of this old place are good, Faith."

"That and an endless supply of cash will make a showplace out of it."

"I have a lead on a job."

"What are the chances?"

He shrugged. "About one in a hundred."

"Things are looking up."

"I'm trying hard. I'll be able to give you more money soon.

Maybe soon enough so you can get this place in shape without killing yourself."

She didn't doubt he was trying, or that he wanted to help. But she questioned whether the political world he'd known so well would forgive him. "Run up and get Alex. Unless you'd rather I did?"

"No, I'd like to see his room."

"Get him to show you the kittens."

"Kittens?"

"He'll tell you the story." Faith watched David disappear up the stairs. She heard Alex's door open and low voices. In a moment Marley joined her at the bottom. Faith waited.

"You want him to go out with Mr. David, don't you?" Marley said.

Faith hoped she did. She hoped she wanted what was best for her son.

"A boy needs his father."

She heard another door open and steps moving farther away. Alex was taking his father to see the kittens.

David took Alex to Johnny Rocket's, one of a chain designed for fifties nostalgia buffs. He figured they couldn't go wrong with hamburgers and milk shakes. Alex might be living in ethnic food central now, but he doubted his son had lost his taste for all-American.

"Would you like the Rocket Double?" David sounded as if he were addressing a stranger. He would never have asked Alex what he wanted before. Alex would have been tugging at his sleeve or waving his hand in front of David's face.

Alex barely glanced at the menu. "I don't know. What is it?"

"A double burger with cheese. I can tell them to leave off the tomato."

"I guess."

David put down his menu. "A chocolate shake?"

"Uh-huh."

"I'm getting the same thing." He felt vaguely guilty. Ham was a strict vegetarian, and David had been secretly craving beef for weeks.

Alex was gazing around the room now. David watched him take in the polished chrome, red padded seats and white soda jerk uniforms. Alex couldn't remember a time when diners were commonplace. For that matter, David hardly could himself. But he remembered going to one very much like this with his dad after a revival in a tiny Georgia town. Arnold Bronson had saved enough souls to engage in a little celebration that night.

Celebrations during his childhood were rare, which was why David remembered that one. His father spent many more hours worrying about the souls he couldn't save than the ones he could. His standards for David were high, but his standards for himself were higher. He wanted to prepare the world for the Second Coming, to banish all sin. On his deathbed, he had begged David to take over his ministry.

Arnold was surely spinning in his grave.

David signaled the server and gave her their order, adding a bowl of chili fries in hopes of sparking Alex's interest.

Once the waitress was gone, he cast around for a safe subject. "What are you planning to do to your room?"

"I don't know."

David tried again. "The attic looks big enough to do something with."

"Yeah."

"This is hard for you, isn't it?"

Alex looked up. "What?"

"Everything. All of it. Me. Your mom. Remy. Living on Prospect Street. Changing schools."

"I guess."

They sat in silence, not quite looking at each other. Finally David sighed. "Alex, everything that happened is difficult to explain."

"I don't want you to explain it."

They sat in silence again.

"Well, I'm going to have to," David said. "Whether you want me to, or I can find the words, or any of that. There are some things you need to know."

"No." Alex looked up. Anger flickered in his eyes. "It's sick. I don't want to hear about it."

David wondered if he could have chosen a worse time in his children's lives to declare his sexual preference. At this age, kids with heterosexual parents were conflicted enough about sex. How much harder to have a gay father who'd made up his mind so late in life.

"I'm not going to explain anything you don't want to hear, but you have to know this isn't something I chose, Alex. I only chose not to be honest with myself and everybody else. But I'm still me. I'm the dad you've always had, only I'm telling the truth for the first time."

"Maybe you just should have stayed quiet and lied."

"That might have been easier in some ways."

"Why didn't you?"

Why hadn't he covered his tracks? Lived a lie? Told Faith one thing and done something else when she wasn't around? He sighed. "Really? I guess I thought it was more important to tell the truth."

"You hurt Mom. You lived with her all those years, and you didn't love her."

"I always loved her. I still do, but in a different kind of way, I guess. That part's hard for you to understand, I know. But you will someday."

"Me? I'm not like you!" Alex slid across the booth as if he was planning to get out.

David grabbed his arm. "Alex, that's not what I meant. Having a gay father doesn't mean you're gay, son. One has nothing to do with the other. You don't have to worry about that. I just meant that someday, when you fall in love with some lucky girl, you'll understand."

Alex shook off David's hand, but he didn't complete his exit. "I don't want to talk about this anymore."

That was fine with David. He suspected the most important things had already been said. "Come back here and tell me what you're doing with your computer. It looks like you're making modifications."

Alex slid back into the booth. "You won't like it."

"Try me."

"I got rid of the controls."

"You're right, I don't like it." And he particularly didn't like the fact that Faith had allowed it.

"What are you going to do about it?" Alex challenged.

In the old days David would have ordered Alex to reinstall the controls or give up his computer. In the old days, just months ago, when he'd been sure he knew what was best.

David shrugged. "I guess I'm going to ask you to be reasonable and remember a computer is just a machine. There's a whole big world out there you have to get to know, and you can't do it if you're sitting in front of a computer screen all day."

"I can surf the whole Internet now. Not just the places you want me to go."

"Can you be trusted not to go places you shouldn't?"

Alex made a face. "Nobody's ever bothered to ask me before. Like nobody thought I was smart enough to know what's good to see and what's not."

David thought about all the things he'd tried so hard to protect his children from. And the things they'd had to face anyway. "Just be careful." David cleared his throat. "Just use the good sense God gave you."

For the first time since their reunion, Alex smiled.

 13

With Marley and Lydia's help, boxes were unpacked and carted away, and the row house began to assume some semblance of order. Alex returned from lunch silent and downcast, but he did tell Faith he and David were going out again on Friday to the movies. Remy was invited, too. Faith was sure that was one ticket sale the theater would never see.

By late afternoon they were ready to quit. Marley's daughter picked her up, and Lydia got ready for the drive home.

Faith had tried out the stovetop by making a pot of tea, since iced tea was out of the question. Two of the four burners worked marginally well.

"I want to show you something before you go, Mother." She handed Lydia a cup of oolong and poured one for herself. "Something in the attic. And you haven't seen the kittens."

"All these comings and goings haven't scared away the mother?"

"She doesn't seem very wild. I'm wondering if your last tenants just left her here."

"I wouldn't be surprised, though they weren't supposed to have pets. Of course they weren't supposed to destroy the place, either."

On the second floor Remy poked her head out of her doorway. "I'm sorry I worried you. Can I come out now?"

"*May* I come out now," Lydia said.

"You're already out."

"You may." Faith thought the smile, although not terribly genuine, seemed like a hopeful sign. "Would you like to see the kittens with us?"

"I guess."

Faith knocked on Alex's door, and they went through his room to the attic stairs. The four of them tiptoed to the side of the attic where the kittens were hidden, and Faith motioned for her mother to stoop down for a view.

Lydia leaned over farther. "Can you tell how many?"

"Two, maybe three. The mother's always on top of them when we visit."

"Thank goodness the fan is working or the poor things would be cooked. The fan's fairly new. I remember paying the bill."

"It looks like a lot of houses on the street use their third stories for living space. Some insulation, an air conditioner and we might have something here."

"My mother didn't live in this house after she married, but she told me that my grandfather talked about converting the attic into a barracks for all the sons he planned. No sons, no attic renovation."

"And when you lived here with Dad?"

"I don't think Joe planned to live here long enough to need the room." Lydia stood. "He was never fond of this house."

"And you?"

Lydia didn't smile. "Inordinately fond, until..."

She didn't have to go on. Faith knew.

"I wanted to show you what we found last night." Faith moved to one side and pointed to the rafter where Millicent had carved her name. "Did you know this was here?"

Lydia traced the letters with a fingertip. "I hadn't thought about it for years."

"Dottie Lee didn't forget." Alex joined them after his own pointed feline investigation resulted in a hiss. "She told us there was a mystery here."

"A good one," Faith hurried to add. "I think she was trying to make us feel better."

"I suppose you have no choice but to talk to Dottie Lee since

she's your neighbor now. But really, Faith, you don't need to frat-
ernize. She is a woman with a reputation." Lydia's expression told
the rest of that story.

"I like her, and she seems to know a lot about this house."

"She'd know about the carving. My mother was only four or five
years older than Dottie Lee. Dottie Lee was like a younger sister."
Lydia dropped her hand. "But you've only discovered part of the
mystery, if this is the one she's talking about."

"What other parts are there?" Alex said.

"It's too hot to go into it up here."

Faith saw that even Remy looked interested. "Do you want to
finish your tea and tell us?"

"Maybe."

They trooped downstairs to more comfortable climes and tea that
had cooled enough to drink. Lydia took full advantage of their attention, showing a flair for the dramatic Faith hadn't known she
possessed. She refused to say a word until she was comfortable,
recovered from the higher temperatures and half finished with her
tea.

"I'm not sure exactly when the house was built. There's a lot I've
forgotten. I do know that counting you, Faith, five generations of
women in our family have lived here. I did the math on the way
downstairs."

Faith had never felt any real connection to her relatives. What
was left of her father's family lived in southwestern Virginia, and
family gatherings had dwindled through the years, although Joe
still made full use of all the connections he had during election
years. Her mother's family was even more remote. Faith's grandparents and great-grandparents had died before she was born. She
knew of no relatives on Lydia's side, even distant ones.

"That makes Remy the sixth generation," Faith said, trying to
include her daughter.

Remy sniffed. "Don't count me. I'm a prisoner."

Wisely Lydia only sent her granddaughter a warning glance.
"Some of us lived here longer than others. I never lived in the house
until I was married, and then my stay was brief. My mother only
lived here *until* she married. But my grandmother Violet was born

in this house and died here. All eighty years of her life were spent under this roof."

"She died here? Where?" Alex, who had only been half listening, stopped playing with the fireplace tools.

"Your mother's room. She refused to go to the hospital. My grandfather passed away the year before she did, and she was ready to get things over with. She was a very organized, strong-willed woman." Lydia smiled a little, as if reviewing a private memory. "She was a talented pianist. As a child I would come here to spend the night and wake up to the sound of music."

Although they had gotten off the subject of the mystery, Faith saw the right moment for another question. "Dottie Lee told me that you were a talented musician, Mother. But I don't remember ever hearing you play the piano."

"I never did. Not since before you were born."

"Why did you stop?"

For a moment Lydia seemed to weigh a response. Then she met Faith's eyes. "I put Hope to bed on the afternoon I brought her home from the hospital, and once she went to sleep, I came down here to rest. In those days there were glass doors between this room and the dining room. I pulled them to, so not to wake her. Then I sat down at the piano and began to play. Playing always relaxed me. To this day, I'm still not sure how much time passed—not a lot, I think—before your father came home from a meeting. But when he arrived and I went to check on Hope...she was gone."

Lydia nodded at the realization in Faith's eyes. "If I hadn't been at the piano that afternoon, I would have heard the intruder, and Hope might be sitting here with us now."

Pavel stood outside the house on Prospect Street and gazed up at the roofline. The house was fairly ordinary by Georgetown standards, built for a working-class family sometime before the turn of the twentieth century. He knew local history. Although some of the houses on Prospect were nothing less than mansions, built by shipbuilders and tobacco merchants, the row houses on this block had been built for the laborers they employed.

Still, by today's less exacting standards, the row house was a graceful architectural gem on a picturesque street.

On the way over he'd stopped on Wisconsin to buy Faith Bronson a bouquet of asters from a flower vendor and dinner from his favorite hole-in-the-wall takeout. Since it was already past nine, he supposed she had eaten earlier. But no one with a soul could refuse green chicken curry. The flavors danced across the tongue. Even the aroma was enough to send him into ecstasy.

He was a connoisseur of Georgetown, and he knew this house well, the way a shutter at a first-floor window buckled and curved away from the brick, the rust nibbling at the iron porch railing, the narrow, virtually abandoned flower bed beside the sidewalk. In the years he'd lived here he had watched the house deteriorate.

On the porch he knocked softly, hoping he would find her awake. He imagined that after a day of unpacking, Faith was exhausted. He had just decided to head home when she opened the door.

"Pavel." She ran a hand through her hair, as if hoping to undo serious damage.

Faith's hair looked neat enough to him, but grooming was not an issue he dwelled on. On the whole she just looked a little blurred around the edges.

"Too late to look around the kitchen?" he asked.

She slumped against the door frame. "You're a man of your word."

"I just finished a conference call, but I didn't forget."

"Alex has already gone to bed."

He was sorry. Faith's son was an interesting kid. He knew enough about David Bronson's buttoned-down ethics and Joe Huston's retro-patriotism to wonder where a free spirit like Alex had come from.

"I can come back, but this won't keep." He held up the takeout bag.

Her gaze drifted down to the flowers in his other hand, then back up to his face. "I warn you, being nice to me could have side effects."

"What and how many?"

"I might start babbling."

"Or you might fall asleep in the curry."

"Curry?" Her eyes lit up.

"If I tell you where I bought it, you'll become an addict. It's dangerous. If you've had dinner already, you can put this in the fridge for tomorrow."

She laughed. The sound wasn't what he'd expected. She had the face of a cheerleader and the low, sexy laugh of a Marlene Dietrich.

Faith stepped aside to let him in. "We have to eat it tonight. The refrigerator doesn't come until next week. Will you share?"

That was no hardship. Pavel was always hungry. "I bought a bottle of white wine to go with it." She didn't respond immediately, and he remembered what he knew about her. "I bet you don't drink."

"Wine sounds lovely, but we'll have to drink it out of water tumblers."

Wisely he kept silent. Obviously Faith didn't need to be reminded that her life was an open book. And maybe David Bronson's stand on temperance hadn't appealed to his wife anyway.

She marched through the house, with him at her heels. With furniture and fewer boxes, it was starting to be a friendlier place. "The flowers are lovely. You've been very kind."

In the back of the house he spotted an extravagant display on the kitchen table. "I'm not the first." He nodded toward the arrangement.

"Those are from my mother, although she's pretending my father sent them." She held out her hand for Pavel's bouquet. "I've actually got a vase unpacked. And these are perfect. Very fresh and natural. My favorite."

He turned over the asters; then he set the takeout on the counter. One brief glance around the room and he saw what she was up against. "Nice floors."

Faith, who was filling a cut-glass vase with water, glanced at him, then apparently saw the larger truth in his eyes. She laughed. "Pavel, you'd better stop right there or your nose is going to grow."

He lifted his hand to his face. "If it does, I'd better move to another room."

"The kitchen's not that small. There's room for a lie or two."

"The floors *are* nice."

"They are, aren't they? Heart of pine. But the rest of the room? Heartbreaking."

"If you like to cook, I'm afraid you're right."

Faith set the vase on the counter and began to rummage through one of the three wall cabinets, victoriously pulling out two glasses after a skirmish with a set of white pottery. "I'm surprised Betty Crocker never sued me for copyright infringement. From the moment I said 'I do,' I never served a meal that wasn't perfectly balanced."

"Sounds deadly."

She stopped fussing with the glasses. "Look where it got me. Not that anything would have changed, but at least I would have had a few moments of real pleasure along the way."

Pavel realized how much he liked looking at Faith. She was not his usual type. His women were more exotic, less American Standard. She was too fresh-faced to be beautiful, with features a discerning eye might pass over in its search for a more interesting place to rest.

Despite that, his own gaze was resting squarely on her. He supposed it was something in her face, not of it, particularly. One part honesty, two parts modesty, three parts intelligence. All exceedingly easy to miss and vitally important.

"You're still young." He pulled the wine from the bag. "Lots of pleasure to come."

A smile, genuine and unhurried, lit her face. "I forget sometimes."

"Consider tonight a turning point."

She tilted her head to one side, as if weighing his comment. They had been talking about food. Simply talking about food. And now they seemed to be talking about something else entirely.

"You know, I don't know anything about you except that you like to be helpful and you live nearby. Tell me more."

"First tell me if you have a corkscrew?"

She continued to stare at him. "Got me, didn't you?"

"I had a feeling you never had a lot of need for one."

"Let me see if I have anything that'll do the job." She dug through a drawer of utensils, coming up with a bottle opener. "Voila." She handed it over to him. Embedded in the side was a corkscrew, the implement at its most primitive.

"I can make it work."

"I'm going to check with my daughter and see if she wants to join us."

He already knew the answer to that. Remy Bronson had disliked him on sight.

While she was gone, he managed to insert the corkscrew without shredding the cork. He was carefully wiggling it loose when Faith returned. "Remy just turned off her light, and Alex went to sleep half an hour ago. The move's bled both of them dry."

"Unpacking can only interest anybody for so many hours a day."

"I'm sure you picked up Remy's antagonism. She doesn't want to be here."

Since he made a habit of getting out of relationships before they progressed toward antagonism, he had nothing personal to offer. "Kids get over things like this, don't they?"

"Do you have children?"

"I've never been married." He caught a new look of assessment in her eyes and realized what she must be thinking. "Not because I don't like women, Faith. Let's put that one to rest."

She had pale skin that turned pink with very little provocation. "Well, let's just say that no one would accuse me of being a good judge on that point."

He freed the cork and nearly filled the glasses she'd set out. It was a Pinot Grigio he'd enjoyed before, aged to perfection and definitely not a bargain vintage. He handed her a glass and watched her eyes grow rounder at the size.

"What do I know? But it strikes me you should never have had to judge. Everything should have been out in the open. Right?"

She made a face that took ten years off her age. "You'd think so. But people can lie to themselves as well as to the ones they're supposed to love."

He decided that if that was true, David Bronson must have been the grandmaster of repression. "You asked about me."

"Thank you. I did." She held up the wine in toast.

He gave her the CliffsNotes version. "I work with computers. Grew up in California, went to school in Chicago, moved here in my twenties to seek my fortune. The capital's been good to me."

"Why here?"

"I was born here, and I'd never been back. So I came to sightsee and stayed. The computer field wasn't as crowded here as it was in the Silicon Valley, and I thought I had a better chance to make my way."

"Did you?"

"I'm my own boss, which is what I hoped for."

"Tell me about your house."

He could feel himself relaxing, which was the first warning he'd been tense. "It's a real beaut. The first time I saw it, I knew it was waiting for me. The market wasn't as active then as it is now. At that point plenty of people had seen the potential, but no one wanted to do the work or spend the money."

"And you did?" Faith took the takeout cartons from the bag and set them on the stove. "This is more than curry, Pavel."

He shrugged. "A little rice. A little dahl. A little chutney. Naan to scoop it up."

"I'm overwhelmed. Thank you."

"Is it still hot?"

She checked. "Lukewarm, and I'm afraid I don't have a microwave."

"I eat it cold." He could see that didn't appeal to her. "Does the oven work?"

"We'll find out." She set the dial. "I'll warm up the bread in here and heat the curry on top. There's only one good burner and one that could serve as a slow cooker. The rice and lentils will be all right the way they are."

"My home-cooked meal will have to wait, huh?"

She laughed. "So you bought your house knowing you had to renovate?"

"What you're facing here is daunting, but at least you don't have to tear out a century's worth of bad renovations."

She scooped the rice into a casserole dish and put the bread on a cookie sheet. Then she poured the curry into a saucepan and set it on the stove before she picked up her wine again. "What kind of problems did you face?"

"Rooms reconfigured and subdivided with cheap paneling. Ceilings lowered. Fireplaces plastered over. The outside was the worst. Somebody decided they liked Arts and Crafts better than Queen Anne and tried to convert. Someone else layered asbestos siding over the exterior. I've never been quite sure how they got that past the city."

Fixed pupils were the usual reaction to his renovation stories, but Faith looked interested. He decided not to push his luck. "Anyway, I started with the outside. Most people question that, since I had to live with the interior the way it was. But maybe you'll understand when you see what I've done."

"You didn't do the work yourself? Not all of it?"

"Most of it, actually, except for removing the siding. If you get to know me better, you'll see what a high tolerance I have for chaos."

She no longer looked merely interested; she looked fascinated. Faith Bronson was a princess among women. "Enough," he promised. "I'm done."

"Spoilsport." She checked the oven and seemed happy with what she saw. "I'm going to clear off the dining room table. This one is hopeless." She nodded toward the table by the window, which was piled with dishes and pans.

"Why don't I look around a little while you do? That's what I came for."

"Terrific. It sounds like I'm in good hands." Their eyes met, and she laughed a little, her cheeks coloring again. "I guess I should say my kitchen's in good hands, huh?"

He realized he was watching a woman's transformation from "married" to "single." Obviously Faith was feeling her way.

"Don't worry, both you and the kitchen can trust me."

"Let me clear that table."

He poked around while she was gone, although there wasn't much to see. One glance at the wiring in the pantry and his hair stood on end. Something had chewed through the insulation around a makeshift splice, and disaster was imminent.

"You've had rats or mice," he called in to her. "And this wiring is lethal."

She came back into the room. "Should we evacuate?"

He was busy tracing the wiring to its source. "No, just don't use this outlet for anything." He pointed to one just to the right of the stove. "In fact, if you have some duct tape I'll cover it as a reminder."

"Let me see what I can find."

She came back a few minutes later with a roll in hand. By then he was under the sink, peering up at the plumbing.

"I'll cover the outlet," she told him.

"You're going to need an electrician, Faith. This room is a time bomb. Once you get a refrigerator and plug it in, the whole place could blow. Nothing's been done here for a long, long time."

"My mother couldn't face dealing with the house."

"The scene of the crime? The kidnapping must have affected all of you in countless ways."

"The house was almost never mentioned, for one. For that matter, the kidnapping was never mentioned. What facts I know I learned from other people. And what *they* know they probably learned from newspaper accounts."

"That surprises me."

"It wouldn't if you knew my parents."

That last sentence was muted. He wasn't sure he'd heard it right. "Politicians know how to keep secrets better than anyone else."

She changed the subject. "I guess this isn't a job I ought to tackle by myself."

He slid out from under the sink one vertebrae at a time. "Not unless you're an engineer."

"It's fixable, right?"

"Oh sure." He was sitting on the floor now, looking up at her. "And so is the plumbing."

"Give it to me straight."

"Good news? The plumbing isn't going to set the house on fire. Bad news? You might need an ark."

"How much time do I have to build one?"

"A while. Take care of the wiring first. But before you call a pro, you'll need to know exactly what you want. Are you planning to add a dishwasher? Garbage disposal? Change the floor plan in here?"

She looked overwhelmed. "I'm not even unpacked yet."

"I wouldn't unpack too much if I were you. Just the essentials. Once they start the renovations—"

"I can't afford anything big. Plumbing and wiring, but I think I have to keep the cabinets I have and go from there."

Pavel liked looking up at her. Angles changed everything. From this one he had a better view of the subtle curves under a shapeless blouse and slacks. "Let's just pass a few ideas back and forth over dinner." He got reluctantly to his feet. "Let me wash up."

She was in the dining room dishing out two equal portions of everything when he emerged from the bathroom. He drew a deep breath and his mouth began to water. "I ate at six, and I'm ready to eat again."

"It's heavenly. I had to sample some to be sure it was hot enough."

"I'll make a list of all the best takeouts. You'll need it until the kitchen's in shape." He took the seat she didn't and picked up his fork.

"You know, this is awfully nice of you. All of it. You don't know me from Adam."

"I think I can tell the difference."

She laughed that sultry Dietrich laugh again. "I know we have a rat, by the way. Remy saw one."

"Do you have traps out?"

"No, but we have a call in to the exterminator, and a cat."

He looked up. "Think that'll do it?"

"I don't know. But I'm afraid I might catch the cat in a trap if I put one out. She's small and wild."

"You have a wild cat living in your house?"

"In the attic, but for all I know she finds her way around while we're sleeping. She has to feed her kittens."

"Kittens?"

"Funny, huh? When I was married, David wouldn't let the children have pets. Now they have a houseful. Cats, rats, kittens..."

"Your husband didn't let the kids have pets?" He was predisposed to dislike David Bronson for any number of reasons. Bronson's sanctimonious attempts to make the world over in his own image. A marriage filled with lies, and a wife who must have been devastated by them. But this seemed worse, somehow. The act of a tyrant.

She must have read his thoughts, because she laughed again. "Pavel, David had allergies. Whatever he did or didn't tell me, he's a terrific father. He even tried shots so they could have a dog. They just didn't help."

"Are you always that good at telling what other people are thinking?"

She finished most of her curry before she answered. "It comes from being the only child of impatient parents. I always had to determine which way the wind blew."

"That's a pretty good insight."

"I'm just full of insight. More than you'll ever want to hear. All gleaned in the last few months."

"I know how your children feel about living here. How about you? You were vague this morning."

She sipped her wine, as if gathering her thoughts. "You said you work with computers. You're not a journalist by some chance, are you?"

"Am I doing research for an article on the Bronson family crisis?"

"Something like that."

"No." He sat back, the dinner a memory. "Our business is with the Internet. And any writing that gets done in my office is done by somebody else."

She relaxed visibly. "No book in this, I guess."

"Not unless you've invented a new computer language or virus. I'm just a neighbor." He felt badly putting it that way. It left out more than it said. If he were just a neighbor, he wouldn't be sitting here now. He wouldn't have made Booeymongers a second home over the years, or happened by the house when Faith's piano needed rescuing, or brought her flowers and dinner.

If he was simply any old neighbor he wouldn't be sitting in the house where Hope Huston had been kidnapped.

"A good neighbor." She started to smile; then she turned her head, peering into the kitchen. In a moment she was on her feet, sprinting through the doorway.

He was only one step behind.

The kitchen was rapidly filling with smoke. Faith jerked open the oven door, and flames shot from the bottom heating element. Pavel shoved her forward and the door snapped shut.

"Don't open it." He pinned her to the range with his body as he leaned forward to turn the oven dial to the off position. Then he pulled her away.

Faith looked shaken. "I had it on warm. There's nothing in there but the leftover bread. How could it have caught on fire?"

Pavel was watching the flames die to nothing through the window on the oven door. "It wasn't the bread. The element just went. And the thermostat's probably shot. That thing must be thirty years old, at least."

"I don't believe this!"

He still had his hands on her arms. She was shaking, but her eyes blazed. "It's okay," he said. "It's burning itself out. Nobody's in any danger unless you turn it on again."

"Well, that's too bad. I have more insurance than I have money."

He tried not to laugh, but he couldn't help himself. He couldn't help his next response, either. He pulled her close for a bear hug. "Faith, it's okay. Stoves aren't that expensive. I'll go shopping with you if you need a hand." He set her away from him. "Okay?"

She looked dazed. Only then did he realize what he'd done. They were practically strangers, even if he did know everything about her, and he'd pulled her into his arms like an old friend. Or lover.

"I'm sorry," he said, without one trace of real regret. "You just looked like you needed a hug. Hugs are a failing of mine."

"You're sure the oven's all right?"

"I promise. I can unplug it if that'll make you feel better." He didn't wait for permission. He put both hands on the oven and wiggled it forward until he could reach the electrical cord. One glance behind the stove and he shook his head. "Call the electrician tomorrow, Faith. I'll come back with a list of contractors in the morning. You'll need somebody who knows how to secure the needed permits fast."

"Maybe I really shouldn't have brought my children here."

"Deal with the safety issues right away, then you can take everything else one step at a time."

"It gets better, doesn't it? Somewhere along the way?"

He wasn't sure exactly what she was asking, but he didn't think she was simply talking about renovations. "Everything takes time. You have to enjoy the journey."

"So far, Pavel, it hasn't been much fun."

He wasn't a man who paid attention to emotions or personal philosophy, but his response came easily. "The world's going to open up to you in all kinds of new ways."

"Some of which I won't like."

"I'm sure. But more you will."

"You're an optimist, aren't you?"

"I don't dig deeply enough to classify myself as anything in particular. I'm at most an inch deep."

"The inch you show others, maybe."

That surprised him. It seemed to surprise her, too. She covered quickly. "Thank you again for dinner. For the flowers. For keeping the house from burning down."

It was time to leave. He held out his hand. "I'll come by in the morning with those names I mentioned."

She took it for a brief handshake. "Then thanks for that, too."

They walked to the front door in silence. He didn't speak again until he was standing on her porch. "Sleep well. Save all your worries for daylight."

"Sleep well, Pavel." She closed the door behind him.

Pavel took the steps to the sidewalk.

"Pavel Quinn?"

He looked up to the second story of the house next door. Dottie Lee Fairbanks stood outlined in the open window. They didn't exchange a word. She slowly shook her head before she disappeared inside.

 14

Pavel didn't sleep well that night. Every time he closed his eyes he visualized Faith as her oven died in a blaze of glory. This latest loss certainly wouldn't do her in, but somewhere in the rising panic he'd seen an expression he recognized. An "oh-sure-kick-me-while-I'm-down" look that continued to tug at him as the night unfolded.

Finally he gave up on sleep and went to his computer. An hour later he had several kitchen plans laid out for her using the original footprint of the house so that the preservation inspector wouldn't nab her. She might not be able to do all the work now, but she could show the electrician a master plan and work from there. He printed out lists of reputable contractors, Web sites that might be helpful, and businesses that had fair prices and good service. Then, finally, he was able to sleep.

He was on Faith's doorstep early the next morning, double-parked in front of her house, dressed for work and already late for a meeting. But no one expected Pavel to be on time. Punctuality was not one of his vices.

She opened the door, and he held out the folder to forestall chitchat. "I did some designs for you." He explained about the printouts, the wiring, the lists, then raised his hand in farewell.

"Uh, good morning, Pavel." Faith looked as if she'd slept better than he had.

He watched her gaze travel quickly down to his hiking boots, then out to his car, a six-year-old Subaru with all of D.C.'s requisite traffic dents. "Friday casual on Monday?"

"Friday casual is dressy at our office."

"That's a job I'd love. No panty hose."

He took a moment he didn't have. "Are you looking for a job? What do you have a background in?"

"European history. Seventeenth century, mostly, and we both know there's a terrific market for that." She clutched the folder to her chest. "This is so nice of you. You've gone to a lot of trouble. Thank you."

"Anytime." He would have checked his watch for effect, only he probably wasn't wearing one. He had several, including a Rolex his board of directors had given him one Christmas, but the last time he'd worn it, he had forgotten to take it off when he plastered a wall, and now the lens was spattered.

"Good luck with the electrician. Tell him I recommended him, and, oh, I almost forgot." He took off down the steps and opened the back door of his car, returning with a wire cage.

"It's a live trap. You can catch the rat without hurting him. That way, if you get the cat instead, you can just let her back out again."

"What do I do with Lefty once he's in here?"

"Faith, you're in trouble if you've named the rat."

"This from the man who names pigeons?"

He offered it. "Let's just say you have a variety of choices, most of which your children shouldn't watch."

Faith held the trap by her fingertips, as if she was afraid it might spring any moment. "How does it work?"

"Alex will figure it out in a heartbeat."

"You'd better get going. You're late, aren't you?"

"It's expected." He raised a hand in farewell. She was still standing there, trap under her arm, the folder to her chest, when he drove away.

Faith expected to wait days for the electrician, but when she mentioned Pavel's name he promised to come right away. Portly and mustachioed, he arrived just after lunch, investigated, made menacing noises under his breath, said words that had never echoed through a Bronson house, and looked over Pavel's plans with a practiced eye. He made a few swipes with his pen and handed them back to Faith. "I'll get you an estimate."

"This is an emergency, isn't it?"

"I'll drop it off on my way home tonight. I can have somebody out here to start on Wednesday."

"Start?"

"There's no Band-Aid to make this better. If we do it right, it's going to take some time, but you don't have a choice. Not if you want to use your kitchen again, and not if you want to be sure the rest of the house is up to code."

Faith was glad the students had moved out before disaster struck.

After the electrician left, she studied Pavel's plans more closely. He had printed out three. The most ambitious called for extending the kitchen into the eating area to enlarge it, knocking out the wall that hid an unused rear stairwell as well as the utility room, then putting in a breakfast nook with French doors looking over a small deck leading down to the back garden.

Since moving to Georgetown, Faith had only been in the garden briefly. It was narrow and surprisingly long, walled in stone and rotting timbers, and vaguely terraced, since it sloped toward M Street. The only entry was through the basement.

At the moment the garden was a wilderness of weeds, deadwood and English ivy that made topiaries of everything in its path. Entire trees were lost under its broad reaching canopy, and what the English ivy hadn't claimed, Virginia creeper and poison ivy had taken as their own. Luckily kudzu was still foreign to the area.

The yard had been swallowed and digested. Before anything else could be done, any planning or planting or nurturing, Faith's job was simply to uproot and remove everything that was still green.

She hadn't given much thought to the exterior, but she saw the merits of Pavel's design. Right now the view of the river and city beyond was wasted. If she changed the constellation of the kitchen and built a deck, she and the children could take full advantage. And if they had easy access to the yard, they could fix it up. David had always been the gardener in their family, but Faith thought she might like the challenges of this smaller space.

Roses and dogwoods. Azaleas and flowering bulbs.

"I'm hungry." Alex wandered in. He had already eaten an apple and two granola bars, the best she could provide without refrigeration or a stove.

"Remy's still asleep. Go wake her up and get dressed. We'll go out for breakfast."

But Remy had gone out on her own.

Remy knew she wouldn't be able to sneak out of the row house on a regular basis. Her mother might be blind when it came to the people she loved, but Faith wasn't exactly stupid. She would be watching Remy from now on, unless she was convinced her daughter was repentant.

So Remy planned to stop on the way home from Colin's house to buy muffins at Booeymongers. She would simply tell Faith she'd wanted to make up for yesterday's disappearance. She even left a note on her bed, in case anyone discovered she was gone. If they went to Booeymongers looking for her before she got there, she would tell them she'd decided to check a couple of other places first.

When she arrived at Colin's house, the door was ajar. She stuck her head inside and shouted "hello," but nobody answered. Inside, she called out again. A bare-chested, bleary-eyed Enzio drifted out of the kitchen. Remy's fourteen-year-old heart hammered faster at the sight of bronzed skin and threadbare jeans low on his hips. It was way cool, like watching MTV live.

"What're you doing here?" He yawned. "What time is it?"

"Almost ten. Nobody else is up?"

"Selim's gone somewhere. Colin spent the night out. Paul..." He shrugged.

She wondered if this meant they were alone. Being alone with Enzio felt very adult. "I just dropped by to say hi."

He didn't blink. He looked bored.

"Hi," she repeated.

"Hi yourself." He took a cigarette pack out of his back pocket. "Are you always this cheerful?"

She couldn't remember what it felt like to be cheerful. "I guess I'd better go."

"What's your hurry?"

"Things to do. You know."

"Want some coffee?"

Faith never offered her coffee at home. "You got some made?"

"Yeah. Ready in a minute." He dropped to the sofa. She realized she was probably supposed to join him there. She considered, weighing the possibilities of discovery against the delicious rewards of spending time with him.

"You have a job?" he asked.

She lowered herself to the sofa, sitting forward, because she really couldn't stay more than a few minutes. "No. Do you like yours?"

"It's okay."

She didn't know how to talk to him. With boys her own age, she knew exactly where she stood. Most of them were thrilled to have her attention. But Enzio was a different story.

"I sell a lot," he said. "I can sell anything, because I don't really care if people buy that shit or not. You know?"

She didn't, but she nodded anyway.

"They come to me because they know I don't care," he said.

She was beginning to get worried. It was late enough that someone at home might just knock on her bedroom door. "Do they pay you more if you sell more?"

"Yeah. Crazy, huh? I sell more because I don't care, and the store pays me more because they do."

That sounded very perceptive to her. "Want me to check on the coffee?"

"Yeah. I take sugar. Lots."

The mess in the kitchen was worse than at home, and Colin and his friends hadn't just moved in. She washed two dirty cups in the sink, then looked in the cabinet, where she found a bag of sugar spilling over into a stream of tiny red ants. She scooped ant-free spoonfuls into the mugs, then filled them with coffee. The milk in the refrigerator smelled okay, so she added a slug to hers. Back in the living room, she handed Enzio his mug. He nodded for her to join him on the sofa again.

"Why don't you have a job? Your mommy and daddy won't let you?"

She heard the sneer in his voice, but she couldn't tell him girls of fourteen were lucky to get baby-sitting or dog walking gigs. "Oh, they think I need to spend my time studying." She sipped the coffee and nearly gagged. It was like drinking melted ice cream.

"Aren't you any good in school?"

"They want me to go to a great college."

"College?" He made a derisive sound. "It's not what it's cracked up to be. The professors are off doing their own thing. You're lucky to see them at a lecture. Nobody thinks." He tapped the side of his head. "I think."

She was impressed. Enzio was so different from the boys she knew that he seemed like another species. "You're not going back?" She looked for a place to set her cup. She couldn't stomach another swallow.

"I'm going to open my own store. I know what sells and what doesn't. I'm going to get enough money to start my own business."

"How?" She didn't know anything about clothing stores, but anyone could figure out that starting one would be expensive.

"I have my ways. Clothes aren't the only thing I sell." He lifted one heavy black brow in emphasis.

For a moment she didn't know what he meant. A long moment. Then she realized he was talking about drugs. Enzio sold drugs.

She started to get to her feet, but he held her back, his fingers wrapped around her wrist. "Don't worry. I don't sell anything they'll really bust you for. How old did you say you were?"

"Old enough to wonder why you'd sell drugs when you could get caught."

"Because the money's great." He shook his head, as if he couldn't believe she was that stupid.

"So what? You could be a hit man, too, but would you?"

"What planet are you from? Nobody's hurt by what I do. They smoke a little weed and feel a little better. I offer a service, like a doctor. Better than Prozac. Not so expensive, either."

She had grown up believing that drugs in any form were the devil's work. Both at school and at home she had been taught to "just say no" to anything that ran contrary to her parents' teachings. But other things she had believed were being tested faster than she could draw conclusions. These days her "What Would Jesus Do" bracelet resided at the bottom of her T-shirt drawer, because the answer to that question now seemed hopelessly out of reach.

Enzio looked intrigued. "Don't tell me you've never tried any."

She got to her feet, and this time he let her. "Do the others know what you do? Colin? Selim?"

"Like they'd care. You don't think they'd sell their own grand-mas if they needed the cash? Just lucky for them they don't. Colin's dad owns the biggest car dealership in New Jersey. Selim's has three electronics stores. The only reason Selim and his sister work is because the old man thinks they need the experience."

"I'd better go."

He laughed. "Hey, was it something I said?"

"No, but I have to get back home."

"You're a baby. Go back to Mama."

She was hurt; but too smart to show him. "Yeah, I think I will. At least I won't get arrested there."

"Nobody's going to arrest me. I know what to sell and how to sell it. You think D.C. cops care about a little chronic? They're after the guys who sell to the cokeheads and the addicts."

She supposed there was something to be said for that. Excite-ment seeped into the hollow space left by her father's desertion. Maybe everything she'd been taught was a total lie. Maybe she ought to listen to other people and start thinking for herself. At the moment, though, she needed to think about how to get home with-out getting into trouble.

She lifted her hand in a flirtatious wave. "Well, I'm out of here. Just don't get arrested today."

His face lit up in a smile, and she held her breath in wonder. She hadn't been sure Enzio could smile, and she really hadn't imag-ined anything could be this stunning. She felt herself growing warm all over.

"I won't, little girl."

She took off for the door, remembering to look both ways for her mother before she inched outside to the sidewalk. She crossed the street and headed toward Booeymongers, hoping no one would glance out the front window of her house.

God hadn't punished her after all. Her family wasn't waiting at the deli when she arrived. She bought muffins for everyone and a latte for her mother before she started home.

By early afternoon most of what the family needed was in reach and a number of boxes had been repacked, marked and stored. With their furniture in place and most rugs down, the house was homier than Faith had expected.

Upstairs, Alex was trying to "build a better mousetrap." Before she could stop him he'd disassembled the cage that Pavel had loaned them and set to work on making the trigger more sensitive. Someday the world might beat a path to Alex's door.

Remy was on the telephone with Megan and had been for most of an hour. Faith knew better than to quibble over small things like too much time on the phone. Besides, after Remy's generosity that morning, Faith was feeling hopeful. One muffin and she had almost convinced herself Remy had returned to her sweet, uncomplicated self. Faith was well practiced in the art of denial.

She was standing at the front window trying to talk herself into a break before she tackled the kitchen when she saw a familiar figure gliding between houses. Dottie Lee had come to call.

She opened the door and greeted her warmly. Dottie Lee stood on the stoop and got immediately to the point.

"I see you've met Pavel Quinn."

"Dottie Lee, don't you want to come in?"

Dottie Lee shook her head. She seemed vaguely agitated. "I can only stay a moment."

Faith figured that since the subject had been broached, she ought to milk it a little before Dottie Lee disappeared. "I met him on moving day. What do you know about Pavel? He seems nice, but I could use a warning if one's needed."

"Warning?" Dottie Lee pulled a purple chiffon shawl embroidered with scenes of an elephant safari around her frail shoulders. "What should I warn you about?"

Faith wondered. What could one person warn another about? Would she have believed anyone's assertions that her husband was gay?

Dottie Lee elaborated. "Pavel is perfectly safe to spend time with, if what you're talking about is safety. I've known him for years. No one has a bad word to say." She paused. "Of course, no one knows him well."

Faith wasn't certain she liked the sound of that. "A lot of serial killers could be described the same way."

"Murder isn't in Pavel's repertoire. You of all people know that anyone of his stature is under constant, informal surveillance."

"Stature?"

Dottie Lee raised her penciled brows. "You don't know who he is, do you?"

"He said he works with computers. The Internet, I think." Faith remembered that early in last night's conversation he'd also said something about working for himself. "Does he own some sort of company?"

"My dear, not just any company. He's the president and founder of Scavenger."

Even Faith, who was hardly computer literate, knew about Scavenger. It was a worldwide search engine, one of the more popular, with offices in Northern Virginia just around the corner from America Online.

The man who had given her lists of bargain-basement contractors, who had stayed up late creating new plans for her kitchen, the man who had crawled under her sink, was most certainly a millionaire many times over.

She didn't know what to say. "He told me he did all the renovations on his house himself."

Dottie Lee peered over her shoulder toward her own house, as if she needed to get back home. "He's certifiably eccentric, our Pavel. A populist at heart. A more informal man doesn't walk the face of this earth."

"But he drives a Subaru. An old one."

"Pavel has no patience with status symbols or the people who care about them."

"Then what's he doing in this town?"

"I think I know why he never married," Dottie Lee said, ignoring the question.

Faith hated to admit to that much interest.

"I can see you're curious," Dottie Lee said.

"Oh, all right. Why not?"

"At heart he's the most private man you'll ever meet."

"Pavel?"

"Yes, surprising, isn't it? But under that St. Bernard exterior beats a heart that keeps to itself. He'll deny it, of course, but it's true."

"Do you know why?"

"Only theories. Lots of theories, and not worth the time it takes to share them."

Before Faith could question her further, Dottie Lee raised a hand in farewell and headed back home. Faith wasn't sure which had been more extraordinary, Dottie Lee's information or the way it had been dropped on her doorstep.

Pavel Quinn, not just a successful businessman but an icon in the computer world. Dottie Lee Fairbanks, mysterious consort of the rich and powerful. Faith thought that after blocks and blocks of soccer moms, Georgetown was going to take some getting used to.

By six the only boxes in the kitchen were small ones that held dishes and cutlery they might need in the coming weeks. Faith had taken Pavel's advice, emptying the cabinets of the few things she had put away and moving almost everything into a corner of the dining room. Once the electrician began his work, the kitchen would be history.

She was just about to call the children to make dinner plans when she saw a Lincoln Town Car scrambling for a place to park in front of the house. The car and the driver were too familiar.

Joe Huston had come to call.

Faith's hands went to her hair, and she smoothed it as she watched her father emerge and come around to the curb. She hadn't spoken to him since the night he had come to McLean to talk her out of the move, and she doubted the intervening days had brought about a change of heart. As a father and a senator he was implacable.

She greeted him, and once inside, Joe leaned over to brush her cheek with his lips. He had never been affectionate. An arm around her shoulders and a brief squeeze were a monumental sign of approval. Now the simple kiss indicated a skirmish ahead. Her father was in rare diplomatic mode.

"You look tired, Faith. Thin."

She didn't correct him, although she wasn't a pound thinner. She had eaten more, not less, since David's departure, her own response to depression. "Moving's a bear. I'm glad the worst is over."

He didn't answer. His eyes roamed the room, and his expression said it all. In Joe's opinion, the worst had just begun.

She trotted out her best manners. "I can't offer much, but we do have some cold drinks in the cooler. Would you like a Pepsi?"

"The cooler?"

"We've ordered a refrigerator." She started toward the kitchen, and he followed. In the doorway he made a sound low in his throat. She remembered that sound too well from her childhood. Clearly once again she had not lived up to Joe's expectations. One disapproving gargle and she was five again, silly and loud and relentlessly imperfect.

She didn't apologize for the state of the kitchen, and she didn't ask what he thought. She took a glass from a box, opened the cooler and popped the tab on a can of Pepsi. She handed him both without a word.

He took the glass and poured his drink, but he didn't raise it to his lips. "You can't live like this. What are you thinking?"

"I'm thinking things will get better quickly. I already have plans for redoing the kitchen. Would you like to see them?" She held up Pavel's designs.

He waved them away. "Independence is one thing. This is something else entirely."

"I don't want to argue with you."

"Because you know I'm right."

"No, because I plan to do what I think is best. Not because I'm stubborn or stupid, but because I need to learn to trust myself again."

Joe assessed her. He was looking for the woman she had been, the one who had lived to please everyone else and thought she was happy doing it. He was trying to find that woman again, some tiny piece of her he could appeal to.

"You've been through a difficult time," he began.

She smiled to soften her words. "And I'm not out of the woods. But they're *my* woods, and I'm beginning to make friends with them."

"I haven't been as much help as I should have been."

She was instantly wary, too long his daughter and too old to be fooled by crumbs of regret. "You've done everything you could. Now it's up to me."

"In the long run, perhaps, but I have a solution for the short haul." He smiled. "Will you listen and not make up your mind right away?"

"I'll certainly listen."

It wasn't the answer he wanted, and the smile wavered. "I know you need to be independent. I don't know why I didn't realize it before this. You need a job and a place of your own."

"I have the second."

"You said you would listen. I've just lost one of my aides, and I need to replace her immediately."

She nearly laughed. She respected her father's devotion to his job and his constituents. A million things could be said about Joe Huston, but never that he didn't take the trust placed in him seriously. Still, she would go into partnership with Alec the Can Man before she worked for Joe. He'd been hard to please as a father. As a boss he would be impossible.

"The job pays well enough," Joe was saying. "And there's room for advancement."

"You'll be accused of nepotism."

"A clear case can be made for hiring you. You're intelligent, knowledgeable—"

She folded her arms. "I can't believe you want me that close to you every day. I know this whole situation with David is difficult. We aren't a model family anymore, and I'll be a reminder to your colleagues, the press—"

"The press doesn't need any reminders."

"What do you mean?"

"You didn't see yesterday's paper?"

Faith had been a little busy for a leisurely go at the Sunday *Washington Post,* daunting under any circumstances. "What did I miss?"

"Abraham Stein is writing a series on gay rights. Your husband's lover is making waves that could lap at the foundation of Capitol Hill. There were some unattributed quotes that probably came from David."

She knew the rest. Abraham Stein had never kept his sexual orientation a secret, but new notoriety was bound to stir up more talk about David's outing and their relationship.

"I don't understand," Faith said. "This will probably revive talk about David and me, at least for a little while, and you want me sitting in your office where any reporter who stops by can get to me?"

"The vacancy is in Roanoke." He held up his hand to stop her. "In my office there. You'll be handling problems my constituents bring you. You're a good listener, and you've watched me long enough to know how to get things done. You know how the system works. You'll be a natural."

She would be a natural, all right, a natural living more than two hundred miles away. Out of sight, in a strange city where D.C. gossip was comfortably muted.

Before she could protest, Joe ticked off the benefits. "Living expenses in Roanoke are half what they are here, and it's a lovely part of Virginia. You'll be secure. Your mother and I will loan you the down payment for a house in a section of town where the schools are good. I get down there frequently, and your mother can visit whenever she has time. You can make a new start."

Joe wanted to wave his magic wand and render her invisible; Faith was as sure of that as of anything in her life. Her father did not want her living in Georgetown, where so many of his colleagues had homes. He didn't want the scandal of his daughter's marriage to merge with the scandal of Hope's kidnapping. And he didn't want David to have easy access to his children. By offering this job, Joe could tuck Faith, Remy and Alex safely out of sight and still look like a good guy.

Faith was angry, but she knew better than to say so. The tenuous ties that bound her to her parents could easily be severed, and she had already lost too much.

She chose her reply carefully. "No matter what you think of him, the children need to be close enough that David can visit. And this area's their home. They need at least something familiar in their lives. We're going to stick it out right here and take whatever comes. I appreciate the offer, but I'll find a job once we're settled in."

"Just like that? You're turning me down without even giving the idea a chance?"

"I've just made the *only* move I intend to make for a long time."

"Have you thought about what it does to your mother to have you living here? To be forced to face the past every time she visits?"

Faith didn't point out that Lydia actually seemed warmer and more relaxed in this house. She didn't understand it herself, and she doubted Joe would believe her.

"I can't do what you want," she said. "Please trust me to know what's best for the children and me."

He was clearly furious. "Why should I? Your track record is abysmal."

He was a master at twisting the knife, so she had been on guard. But his words still hurt. She lifted her chin, much as he often did. "No, *my* track record is impeccable. I can't be blamed for something David hid from all of us. You included."

"*I* wasn't sleeping with him."

"I certainly hope not. That would have been a real scandal."

His eyes narrowed, but she forced a conciliatory tone. "You'd better go before one of us says something that really can't be taken back."

"You're not going to think about this?"

She took his arm to propel him out of the room. "I hope you find someone perfect for the Roanoke job."

He reined himself in enough that they got through their goodbyes without another scene. But the moment he backed out of his parking space, Faith fell apart.

"Damn it!" She kicked a small area rug that was still rolled up in the corner, then kicked it again for good measure. It was too soft. She looked around for something else, but nothing presented itself. She stormed into the kitchen, her depressing, outdated, fire hazard of a kitchen, and slammed her palm against the farthest wall. Since it was only thin drywall that had been added to partition off the back stairwell, it shook noticeably. When she hit it again—her palm stinging from the abuse—it shook harder.

The electrician had said the wall wasn't load bearing, and that if she went with Pavel's most extensive plan, the wall could be removed without problem. She was too angry to question what had been a casual remark. She stood back and kicked it with all her might, using the heel of her ankle boot as the driving point.

The kick jolted through her and she nearly fell, but she righted herself and did it again. A hole opened, jagged, small and ugly, but to her, it looked like a tunnel toward freedom. She never lost her temper this way. Adrenaline and something like elation surged through her.

"I—am—nobody's—good—little—girl!" She slammed her foot against the side of the hole, opening it farther.

She tried to remember when she had given up on Joe, when she had realized he would never be the kind of father she needed. She had been young, too young for that kind of revelation, so she had taken the blame. She had been certain there was something wrong with *her*. She wasn't good enough, pretty enough, smart enough. If she had been any of those things, Joe would have been a better father.

Only later, when she was old enough to rationalize the behavior of others, had she begun to let herself off the hook. She'd told herself that Hope's kidnapping had been too traumatic to bear. The tragedy of losing his first daughter had closed Joe off to the rest of the world. He had been afraid to love his second.

She kicked the wall again, and it crumbled under the force of her heel. No, *age* hadn't helped her reevaluate her relationship with Joe. Who was she trying to fool? David was responsible. She'd watched her husband with their children, and for the first time she'd seen a good father up close. David adored his kids. He took parenting seriously, and he liked nothing better than listening to Remy's and Alex's problems. Not because they were particularly exceptional—although they were—but simply because he was their dad.

After several years of marriage she had realized that none of the fault in her relationship with Joe was hers. Joe's role as a parent was to love her and accept her as she was. For a man who prided himself on getting a job done, he had fallen down miserably on that one.

She kicked the wall again, with less force, but she hadn't gauged this new spot well, and her heel slipped too far into the ragged opening, catching and capturing her foot.

She bounced, trying to free herself, but in the end, she went down anyway.

From her vantage point on the floor she stared at the mess she had made. Her leg throbbed; her hands tingled. She felt cleansed, as if she had kicked something out of her life—at least temporarily.

"Have a cow, Mom. Jeez!"

Faith turned to see Remy standing in the doorway. For once she hadn't thought about the children. She hadn't even considered that they would wonder what had possessed her to kick a hole in the kitchen wall.

"I imagine this looks strange." Faith twisted her foot, trying to free it.

"Yeah, well."

"We're going to take out this wall. I guess I got ahead of myself."

"Chill, would you? If I started kicking in walls you'd ground me for life."

"I seem to be stuck." Faith twisted her foot the other way.

Remy crossed the kitchen and grabbed her mother's ankle, giving one sharp tug. Faith was free again. She scooted away from the wall, but Remy stayed put.

"The wall's really gotta come down?"

Faith was testing the heel of her boot, which seemed to have a new wiggle. "Uh-huh."

"Good!" Remy slammed the heel of her sneaker against the wall beside the hole. "Hey, look at that."

The wall had crumbled a little more. Remy kicked again and the hole got larger as her effort merged with Faith's.

Faith wondered exactly which part of Remy's life the wall represented. Whatever it was, she seemed to find as much satisfaction in destroying it as Faith had.

"Be careful, or you'll get stuck, too." Faith joined her daughter at the hole, and between them they made a sizeable increase in it, taking turns wordlessly until they were both panting with exertion.

Faith dropped to the floor—gracefully, this time—as Remy stepped back. She felt the way she used to when she and Remy made cookies or sewed doll clothes together. Mother-daughter bonding.

"Awesome," Remy said. "Now the kitchen looks even worse. Like that's possible."

Faith knew she should apologize and point out that there were better, more mature ways to handle anger. But she didn't feel one bit sorry for kicking in the wall. For once she had done something simply because it felt good.

Instead of apologizing, she scooted closer to the hole and peered inside. She couldn't see much, but Pavel had been right. By removing this wall and the one leading into the utility room, they would open up enough space to substantially expand the kitchen.

"By the look of it, this has been closed off for years."

"Where did it go?" Remy asked.

"I think there must have been a sleeping porch or maybe just a platform of some kind outside your windows. This was probably built as a fire escape, although not a very effective one. Or maybe backstairs for the servants. When this house was built even people without a lot of money had domestic help."

"Is that how Hope was kidnapped? Somebody took these stairs up to the platform and opened my windows? You said nobody could get in them."

"I'm sure this was closed off well before Hope was born." Faith scooted closer. Something lay just in reach. A piece of paper, yellowed with age. She stuck her hand through the hole and felt around, just contacting it with her fingertips. Gently she scooted the paper closer until she could almost lift it through the hole.

"What's that?"

"A genuine antique piece of trash." Faith grasped the paper between her fingertips and sat back, bringing it through the hole with her. The paper wasn't old enough to crumble, but as she unfolded it, it tore along one crease. She smoothed it carefully.

"What is it?"

"A note." Handwritten with what looked to be a fountain pen on lined school paper. The script was faded but legible. The letters were well formed, as if the writer had learned penmanship during a time when it was faithfully taught in school.

"What does it say?" Remy lowered herself to the floor beside her mother. Faith could smell her daughter's citrus shampoo and feel the soft cotton of Remy's T-shirt brush against her forearm.

She dragged out the moment. Not too many months ago she'd had a daughter, not a teenager, and she deeply missed the child who had shared every thought and valued her mother's opinion. She believed she and Remy would be friends again someday, but for now she would settle for the illusion.

"It's hard to make out," Faith said. She lifted it higher. "Dear Mrs. Huston..."

"Grandmother? Maybe it's a ransom note."

"I doubt it's anything that exciting." Remy's head was next to Faith's now, and Faith had the unforgivable desire to hug her. But Remy and Guest had too much in common. Grab either of them and the claws were immediately unsheathed.

"Let me see it." Remy paused. "Okay?"

"Be careful or it will tear even more." Faith handed the letter to her daughter. "Read it out loud."

Remy puzzled over the faded script, reading slowly. "There is much to do, and I only made a small beginning. Just as you ask, I begin in the kitchen and removed the wallpaper." Remy looked up. "Whoever wrote this doesn't spell very well. There aren't enough *n*'s in *beginning*. And the grammar's funny."

"What else does it say?"

Remy finished reading. "When I come again I will prepare the walls for painting. Sincerely, Dominik Du...Du?" She looked up. "The rest of it's smudged."

Faith had been following over Remy's shoulder. Now she sat back. "Dubrov. Dominik Dubrov."

"How do you know? You can't make it out any better than I can."

Faith's mind was whirling. "Because before I was born a man named Dominik Dubrov worked on a number of houses in this neighborhood."

"That was what, like a hundred years ago? How do you know that?"

Faith put a hand on Remy's knee. "Because Dominik Dubrov was the prime suspect in Hope's kidnapping. Even today, most people who know anything about the case think he was the one who took my sister."

 15

Summer turned into fall without asking for permission. Faith thought the change of seasons might be the only thing she hadn't been forced to organize and execute. Even though the family was more or less settled, she was still working so hard she was bleary-eyed with exhaustion. There were moments, though, when she looked at what she had accomplished and felt a surge of pride.

She had agonized over the expense, but in the end she'd opted to go with Pavel's most extensive redesign. She hired a contractor to add French doors to the back of the house, even though they would lead to empty space until she could afford a deck. For the price of a crowbar and sledgehammer—plus a new heel on her boot—she and the children took out the necessary dividing walls. The tools were cheaper than a psychiatrist.

The idea to use the Can Man to help clear the back garden was Dottie Lee's. She told Faith she used Alec as a gardener herself, and that he worked at a reasonable rate. When Faith hesitated, Dottie Lee reassured her that he never drank on the job. According to Dottie Lee, he didn't even curse.

Qualms satisfied, Faith hired the Can Man on the next trash day. Alex, who always needed money for more computer equipment, volunteered to help when he learned he could earn minimum wage in his own backyard. He liked working with the Can Man, and the results were encouraging.

The electrician rewired; the plumber ran lines for a new sink and dishwasher, and the contractor removed all the old cabinets and helped her order new ones. She chose inexpensive oak from the home improvement center, planning to refinish them herself, and basic laminate counters in a deep red—to please her son.

While everyone else labored, Faith removed all the downstairs wallpaper, fighting the good fight with a sprayer, putty knives, industrial-size sponges and 80-grit sandpaper. She primed the walls, spackling the smaller holes so the plasterer could concentrate on the bigger jobs. When he finished, she primed the ceilings, too, then went to look for paint.

That was when she had realized how little she knew about the house.

For five generations the house had been a womb, nurturing and sheltering a matrilineal succession of her ancestors, who had watched Georgetown grow from a quiet tobacco port into a pricey neighborhood at the edge of a bustling metropolis. Hope's kidnapping had separated Faith from that heritage, but now, in the wake of her own personal drama, the artery to that past had been reconnected.

She knew far too little about the women who had come before her to blithely renovate their house. She knew too little about their hopes and dreams, their habits, their desires. For that matter, she knew too little about the history they had lived through, and the styles and tastes that had developed as a result.

She knew too little about almost everything. And so did Lydia.

Lydia, who had always scheduled her visits to Faith the way she scheduled appointments with her hairdresser, had taken to dropping by the Prospect Street house every time she was in the city. If Faith was involved in a project, more often than not Lydia rolled up her sleeves to help. Faith was wary of this new mother, the one who bit back criticism and took a genuine interest in the renovations. But she was seduced by the intimacy, too.

This afternoon Lydia had dropped by again, though the two women weren't working. They had boiled water in an electric kettle for tea, and they were sitting in the back garden, gazing out over the space that Alec the Can Man and Alex—under Faith's supervision—had slowly reclaimed.

Faith hoped that bringing Lydia outside might jog her memory, but so far the effort had been unsuccessful. "Doesn't sitting out here remind you of anything about your childhood?"

"I really can't tell you much more about the history of the house than I have already." Lydia was repeating a familiar refrain.

"Mother, you must know more than you've let on. The day we showed you the kittens, you were going to tell us about *your* mother, but you got sidetracked."

"I really don't remember much. When I left the house, I shut away everything connected to it. I'm ashamed."

Faith had never heard her mother admit to any such emotion. It was cause for alarm. "We all forget more than we remember."

"Not all of us forget on purpose."

"You had good reason not to think about anything connected to Prospect Street."

"I blamed a house for something that happened inside its walls. Doesn't that strike you as the ultimate shifting of responsibility?"

Faith was feeling her way along unfamiliar paths. "You seem to be more at peace with it now."

"I like what you're doing here. You're sweeping out the cobwebs in the house the way you're sweeping them out of your life."

"David was more than a cobweb."

"You still miss him?"

Faith was so surprised that she had to scurry in a different direction. "I... At times. I miss talking to him at the end of the day. That's when we were at our best together."

"I gather he hasn't found a job?"

"No." Or reconnected with his daughter.

"David's a good man."

Faith wondered how many more revelations the next few minutes could sustain. "Where did that come from?"

"I do occasionally think for myself. As angry as I am, I can still see a certain nobility in his decision to admit who he was."

"Well, he got caught. He didn't really admit it, did he?" Faith made a face. "But he would have, I guess. The big revelation was coming. Lying was eating him up."

The door behind them slammed, and Alex ran out to the table where they were sitting. "Remy's on her way."

"You're supposed to walk together," Faith reminded him.

"She walks too slow. She's somewhere down the street."

With September's arrival Remy and Alex had begun attending middle school at Georgetown's western edge—Alex with a certain degree of optimism, Remy because she had no choice.

The school, as underfunded as so many of its urban counterparts, was a far cry from the academy in which they'd spent the bulk of their educational years. But there were definite compensations. The student body was integrated and multicultural, a more accurate slice of life than they'd encountered in the past. Alex, once considered the scourge of the classroom, was finding teachers who knew how to deal kindly with him. Remy was absorbing a different view of the world.

"Shouldn't you check on her?" Lydia asked Faith.

"She'll be fine. She's never in a hurry to get home...or to leave in the morning, for that matter."

"She failed a science quiz." Alex was incapable of keeping anything to himself.

Faith filed that away. If it was true, it was a first. "I was telling your grandmother how much you've done back here."

"Me and the Can Man."

Lydia looked disapproving but didn't say anything. She had already lectured Faith about letting a homeless man work side by side with her grandson.

"He hasn't been back this week," Alex said.

Faith was afraid that Alec was off on a drinking binge and hoped it wasn't something worse like illness or injury...or incarceration.

"He'll be back," she assured him.

Alex glanced at his grandmother, but his expression said it all. The afternoon was going to be a bust if he stayed out here.

"Your mother was just asking me if I remember anything about the history of the house," Lydia said. "Are you interested, Alex?"

Alex looked as if he knew his future happiness—immediate, anyway—depended on his answer.

Lydia didn't wait. "There's a secret back here which you apparently haven't discovered. I could tell you what to look for, but only if I hear a little enthusiasm."

"Awesome!"

"Much better. But we'll wait for your sister."

His face fell. "She might take a while. She's walking with somebody."

"Somebody from school?" Faith thought this could be a good sign.

"Some girl in her science class."

Faith hoped it was somebody her daughter could study with. "There's lemonade in the ice chest. Get yourself a bottle, and one for Remy, too."

Alex disappeared back inside.

"When do the new appliances come?" Lydia said. "Aren't you tearing your hair out with no refrigerator?"

With the new kitchen constellation Faith had been able to change her special-order refrigerator for a larger model. She had a stove on order, too, and a dishwasher. All dependable, low-end appliances that would serve them well.

"They come next week, and now that the wiring's safe, we can plug them in and use them even without the cabinets and counters, although we probably won't."

"You must be tired of eating out and heating soup on a hot plate."

"I love it. I'm a new woman, Mother. I'll be thrilled to have a kitchen, but I'm never going to see cooking and attending committee meetings as my life again."

"You seemed happy at the time."

"Maybe I was. I don't know anymore. But even if I had reliable alimony and child support, I would still want something different in my life now."

"Like another man?"

Mysteriously, a picture of Pavel Quinn leapt to mind. Pavel had come by several times in the past weeks to monitor her progress. Once they had shared a pizza over kitchen plans, and another time he'd spent an hour with Alex making modifications to his computer. Whatever the two had done had been too technical for Faith to understand, but Alex had been thrilled.

"My divorce won't be final until December," Faith said. "Isn't that question a little premature?"

"The marriage is well and truly over. A piece of paper won't change that."

"You're surprising me today."

"Life is much too short to wait for the courts to end something that's already finished."

Alex arrived with the lemonade. "Remy called. She went to Billie's house. Is that okay?"

"Did you get a number?"

"She said she'd be home in an hour."

Faith didn't scold Alex. She would have to talk to both of them again about checking in. She didn't want them to feel they were in prison, but the crime rate in the city was high enough for caution.

"Does this mean you're not going to tell me what to look for out here?" Alex asked his grandmother.

"I'll tell you part of it. It's another name."

Alex looked disappointed.

"Like the one in the attic?" Faith was intrigued.

"Exactly like that." Lydia smiled slyly. "Only different."

"Whose?"

"I think Alex should find out for himself. Or maybe you'll discover it when you start to bring order to this chaos."

Alex wandered off to check around the bases of the nearby trees.

"What do you remember about the garden, Mother? I'd like to restore as much of it as I can. At least some of the basics."

"Truthfully? Very little." Lydia considered. "But...you know, I haven't thought of this in years."

"What?"

"I think my grandmother won a prize in a local garden contest. There was a tour, a garden tour of Georgetown." Lydia seemed to be panning for nuggets from a forgotten past. "She was so thrilled. I do remember that. Her garden won an award."

"I wonder if I could track it down? Check out newspaper accounts? Can you remember when this happened? Maybe there's a description of the garden somewhere."

Lydia leaned forward, eyes shining. "There might well be. I

was young, too young to know whether it made the papers, I guess. But old enough to remember how excited she was."

"Make a guess about your age. Five? Ten?"

"Maybe seven? That would put the tour somewhere around the spring or early summer of 1941. Just before we entered the war. I doubt there was much time for garden tours once we started sending men overseas."

Faith moved beyond her great-grandmother's garden to the rest of the house. "I wonder what else I could find out? This *is* the capital. History is what we're about. We could fill in all those holes in your memory."

"You're interested enough?"

Not only was she interested, Faith realized, but this was something she could do for Lydia to thank her for turning over the keys. Lydia, so self-sufficient and aloof, would never look into this herself. This was a gift Faith could give her.

Alex returned. "If this was Violet's garden, then it must be Violet's name we're looking for. Right?"

Lydia smiled at him, and Faith thought it was the first time her mother had resembled a doting grandmother. "Aren't you smart?" Lydia said. "You do have a way of figuring things out, Alex."

Alex grinned back at her.

It wasn't exactly chocolate chip cookies, homemade baby quilts and trips to Disney World. But Faith thought Alex and her mother might be on to something at last.

She told Pavel about the garden tour that night when he dropped by with takeout again. This time the bag was filled with pad Thai, lemongrass soup and spring rolls.

He kissed her on the cheek in welcome, like an old, dear friend. Like Jesse Helms or Strom Thurmond, who had known her since childhood. Like the organizer of a campaign fund-raiser.

She felt a little hurt until she realized where her thoughts were leading. Then she simply felt embarrassed.

"This is my way of checking the kitchen's progress." Pavel wore a sky-blue sweater, and he stripped it over his head as he spoke, revealing one more in a collection of paint-spattered, misshapen T-shirts.

Faith had never told Pavel what she'd learned about him from Dottie Lee. She assumed it would come out on its own, but so far he had been silent. Now she shook her head. "Look at you, Pavel. I'm on to you, you know. Dottie Lee told me all about you, so you don't have to dress like a roadie anymore."

He paused in the middle of folding the sweater over his arm and looked down at her. "Dottie Lee?"

"There are no secrets on Prospect Street."

His expression changed subtly. His easy smile hadn't quite achieved its usual width. She realized he wasn't happy that she knew his identity.

"It's nothing to be ashamed of," she pointed out. "Most people are proud of their successes."

"What successes are we talking about?"

"Scavenger."

He finished folding the sweater. She took it off his arm to lay it carefully on a coat closet shelf. "I'm not ashamed of it," he said. "It's just irrelevant. It's what I do, not who I am."

"I don't know. I bet a large part of Scavenger *is* who you are. How can you spend that much of your life on something and not have it define you, even a little?"

"I like to think of myself as the man on O Street with the house he's putting back together a room at a time."

She had taken a stroll to 31st and O several weeks before, just to sneak a peek at his house. It was a sprawling, turreted ode to Stick style splendor, painted in maroon, burnished gold and pale gray-blue, with a lot four times as large as her own. Next to its staid Colonial and Federal style neighbors, it was the chorus girl of the block.

She plunged in deeper. "Well, the mystery's solved about why it's taking so long. I've been by to peek, and the house is fabulous. But how many hours a week can you spend on it?"

He was clearly pleased at the compliment. "I'll have more if Scavenger is ever bought out."

"Wouldn't that be traumatic?"

"Not even slightly. I like starting projects. Next time I'll be careful not to be so successful."

She was used to the rich and powerful, so she knew better than to fuss. "Come see the kitchen."

"Where are the kids?"

"Upstairs doing homework."

"I bought enough for them, too."

She guided him around boxes. The cabinets had arrived late in the afternoon and now took up the entire living room. She planned to move them, one by one, into the kitchen to finish them. "They probably won't eat. My mother took them down the street for hamburgers before she left this evening."

"You, too?"

"I stayed home and swept up sawdust in the kitchen." She stopped in the kitchen doorway. "Voila." She flipped her hand in introduction.

"A wonderful empty space."

She turned and discovered he was closer than she'd thought. She nearly bumped his collarbone with her nose. "Can't you see it? Shiny white appliances in place? Cabinets all refinished and gleaming? Bright red countertops and a peninsula that stretches..." She turned around again and gestured. "To there?"

"I can definitely see it."

She stepped into the room, as empty as an echo chamber. "It's worth all the trouble. It's gorgeous."

He stood behind her and rested his hands on her shoulders. "You know what I think? I think you're obnoxiously proud of yourself."

"And well I should be."

The weight of his hands was welcome. His pinky fingers massaged the very tops of her arms while his palms pressed and released in a slow, nonthreatening rhythm. She had forgotten how good it felt to be touched casually by a man.

"Did you feel this much pride in the last house you lived in?" The kneading continued.

"All I had to do in that house was choose from samples and nod at the architect. This feels like mine." She paused, trying to focus on what she was saying. "Oh, and yours, too. After all, you're the one with the vision."

"Mine?" He laughed and dropped his hands. She felt a stab of regret. "Does this mean I'll get a meal or two out of it?"

"I bet by now you don't even think I *can* cook."

"Scrambled eggs with somebody you like is as good as a five-course meal."

She faced him. "You really were the catalyst. I'm so glad you thought of extending the room. Someday I'll build that deck, and we can sit out on it and watch the lights come on over the water."

"Something to look forward to."

They stood staring at each other. She suspected Pavel was rarely at a loss for words, and as a child she had learned to fill the many silences of her parents' marriage. Now, oddly, neither of them seemed to know what to say.

"Mom, I..." Remy stepped through the doorway and stopped, staring at Pavel. Faith hadn't heard her coming down the stairs.

Faith recovered. "Pavel brought Thai food for dinner."

"I don't want any." Remy glared at him.

"How's school going?" he asked. "Feel like you're settling in?"

"Oh yeah. That'll be the day." She made a point of dismissing him and turned toward her mother. "I need help with an English paper, but I can see you're too busy."

"When's the paper due?"

"Tomorrow."

"And how long have you known about it?"

Remy didn't answer.

"I *am* too busy," Faith said. "You'll have to finish it by yourself."

"You never used to be too busy." Remy eyed Pavel again. "I guess everything's changed." She stomped out of the room and back up the stairs.

Faith wilted, but Pavel squeezed her shoulder. "Come on, Faith. I'm impressed."

"By what?"

"By the way you didn't let all that guilt she was slinging weigh you down."

"She was, wasn't she?" Faith felt a little better that someone else had witnessed it.

"Tons. Megatons. I was shaking in my boots."

"You're wearing sandals."

"I was wearing boots when she started. This is all that's left." He smiled warmly. "She does this often, doesn't she?"

"She's having a bad time."

"Is it your fault?"

"In her eyes. I didn't hold the most important relationship in her life together."

"Underneath all that anger, she understands why. She knows it wasn't your doing."

For a moment Faith couldn't speak. After David's announcement, she had purposely shut herself off from the people who might have helped her. Women she'd known from the children's activities, friends she'd gone to school with. She had been too ashamed of her own failure. She had been afraid she would never pick herself back up again if she sank that low.

Now Pavel's support was particularly sweet.

"Thanks." Her voice was husky.

"Faith, you need a night out on the town. When was the last time you got away from all this angst and just had fun?"

Fun was a foreign notion. Fun was something you provided for your children, trips to amusement parks and pony rides.

He read the answer in her eyes. "You're going to need converting."

"What do you do for fun?" She really wanted to know.

"Good food. Good music. Any two-word combination with good at the beginning."

Good sex. She wasn't sure where that thought had come from, although she suspected that standing this intimately with Pavel had jolted it out of her. For Pavel, having sex was probably like indulging any healthy appetite. Apparently it had never come with strings attached, with bells and whistles and wedding rings.

A night's entertainment. Fun.

"I know you're not divorced yet. And I know you're pretty traditional." He held up his hand when she started to interrupt. "That's not slander. I'm telling the truth, but I think you're in danger of letting expectations get you down. Who could fault you for enjoying yourself a little after what you've been through? There's no reconciliation in the wings."

He was almost echoing her mother. "Are you asking me out?"

A smile hovered at the corner of his lips. "Yeah, I think I am. One friend to another."

"Like a practice date?"

"I wasn't thinking of it quite that way."

She wasn't sure of the wisdom of accepting. He was funny and kind and, yes, enormously sexy—if you went for teddy bears with bedroom eyes. When he showed up on her doorstep, her day was automatically better. She didn't want a date to spoil all that.

"Tell you what." She cleared her throat. "Here's the thing. What if we don't have fun? I mean, what if you find out I'm the most boring woman you've ever met? Then you'll stop coming over with takeout food and lists, and Alex will be angry with me."

"What if I promise ahead of time not to find you boring?"

"I don't think you can."

"Then what if I promise not to let that stop me? That we'll still be friends afterward, no matter how many times you trip over your own feet or chew with your mouth open."

That sentence was punctuated by more footsteps on the stairs. Alex appeared. "Pavel, hey!"

"My man." Pavel held up his palm and Alex slapped it. "Do you eat Thai food?"

"I eat everything. Do you want to see what else I did to the mousetrap?"

"Caught a rat in it?"

"Not yet. But he's hanging around my room. I found a nest of chewed-up newspaper in the corner."

Faith shuddered. This was the first she'd heard of it.

"You breathe on it and the door falls," Alex said. "Want to see?"

"Sure." Pavel turned to Faith. "Well?"

"I'll dish up for you guys while you're gone."

"That's not what I meant."

She smiled at him. "Sure. Okay."

"Friday? I can invite some friends along, and we'll start at my house so you can see the inside. We'll have fun."

"I'll have to see if I can work out something with the kids."

"Let me know." She watched him follow Alex out of the room and wondered what she'd just agreed to.

 16

In any family, life can change in a heartbeat. The next morning Faith rose early to make a trip to Wisconsin Avenue for bagels and fresh orange juice. By the time she returned, Remy was playing an hour-long variation of Chopin's "Minute Waltz."

"I haven't heard you play in years." Faith closed the door behind her. "I can't believe you remember that."

"So?" Remy stopped in the middle of a measure and pulled the top down over the keys.

"I always loved to hear you. I was sorry when you stopped taking lessons. So was your teacher. You were her most talented student."

"I was just killing time."

Faith knew that one more word from her and Remy would never touch the piano again. "I got cinnamon raisin for you and blueberry for Alex. They're right out of the oven."

"Mom!" Alex appeared at the bottom of the stairs. Faith wasn't even sure he'd taken the steps. "I got him!"

"Got who?" Then she realized what he meant. "The rat?"

"Lefty! Come see."

"This is so gross," Remy said. "This place is a shack."

Faith was getting very good at not reacting. "Alex, remember, you can't keep him. I warned you."

"You're going to be surprised. Big-time."

She followed him upstairs, and Remy trailed behind.

Alex's walls were still covered with fading panels of peasants harvesting wheat and spinning wool, but otherwise his room clearly belonged to a budding young scientist. His computer desk took up one wall. Adjacent to it a table held electronics he had scrounged from neighbors, a fish tank filled with Venus flytraps thriving under a fluorescent bulb, a basic chemistry set, and a trash heap of mismatched cables and batteries. Pavel's trap claimed the opposite corner.

"Look at this." He stooped beside the trap and, after exchanging grimaces with Remy, Faith did, too.

A white lab rat with eyes as pink as petunias stared back at her.

"Not just any rat," Alex said. "A *scientist's* rat."

"What's the big deal?" Remy joined them. "That's the rat I saw. So what?"

Faith got to her feet. "You've led a sheltered life. That's not your garden variety city rat. For that matter, it's not your typical trash dump rat, either. Alex is right. This is the kind they sell at pet stores and use in labs."

"The kind they do experiments on." Alex's eyes were as bright as Lefty's were pink.

Faith put her metaphorical foot down. "I hope you're not thinking about using the poor thing that way. Because you can't."

"Just to run through mazes. Fun stuff. It'll be like an amusement park." He sensed she was caving in. He pulled a long face. "I've never had a pet of my own, Mom."

"This is so sick." Remy abandoned the room. Faith heard her at the end of the hall gathering her things for the long walk to school. After the first week Faith had refused to drive them unless it rained. They were city kids now, and they needed the exercise.

"Let me make a call or two." Faith ruffled Alex's red curls.

He rolled his eyes. "I can take him to the vet for a checkup or something."

She was tamping down fantasies about escaped lab rats from Georgetown's medical school, fantasies that included bubonic plague and new strains of the Ebola virus. "Let me see if I can find one of the students who used to live here. I'll ask him if he knows anything about Lefty. Then we'll see."

He looked hopeful. "Don't do anything until I get home. Promise?"

She saw them off to school and watched as they strolled toward Wisconsin. She wondered what the two sworn enemies discussed every day as they trudged up, then back down, the sloping avenue. They hadn't spent this much time in each other's presence since the summer they'd both contracted chicken pox.

She managed to reach her mother before Lydia left on the day's errands. Lydia, annoyed by the interruption and the news of a rat in her ancestral home, located the number of one of her former tenants. Faith was sure she would be waking the young man but felt no remorse.

By the time she hung up she was certain Lefty posed no threat. One of the roommates had "liberated" him from a psychology lab before Lefty could be sent to that great mouse hole in the sky. Lefty had been given the run of the house. If Alex wanted a rat who could negotiate mazes, he'd gotten the best.

She was tidying up the kitchen—a question these days of simply throwing out the trash—when the telephone rang. Pavel was on the other end.

"We're all set for Friday. Still on?"

"Absolutely." She sounded a little too eager. Her dating skills had atrophied.

"Why don't you come here first for a tour? I can pick you up."

"Don't worry about it. I'll walk, but I'd love to see what you're doing."

"It might sour you on the process."

She really *did* need a night out when looking at someone else's half-finished restoration sounded like fun. They settled on a time, but Pavel didn't seem inclined to end the conversation. "What do you have planned for today?"

She had told him about Lydia's visit and the revelations about Violet. "I'm going to work on the cabinets this morning. Then I think I'm going to head for the library after lunch and see what I can find out about the garden." She paused. "Actually, about the house. I think I'm going to do a history for my mother. A thank-you present for letting us move in."

Pavel was silent for so long she wondered if the connection had been severed. When he spoke, he was clearly feeling his way. "There's a lot of history connected to the house. Are you sure you want to be the one who digs it up?"

"You mean my sister's kidnapping?" She had given this a lot of thought in the night, when she always had more time to think than she wanted. It didn't seem strange to be discussing it with Pavel. In the brief time they'd known each other, they'd moved quickly beyond the usual social conversation.

She tried to explain. "For my whole life, Hope's kidnapping has been a cloud blocking the sun. I don't want to live that way any-more, and I don't think it's good for my mother. I want to put our lives and this house in some kind of perspective."

She could almost picture Pavel considering. He squinted when something was on his mind, and he usually rubbed his fingertips along one stubbly cheek. Odd that she'd noticed and remembered.

"We all have things in our lives we tiptoe around," he said. "Sometimes we need someone to lead us right through the middle of them."

She changed the subject. "What's on your plate today?"

"If I told you, it wouldn't make any sense. It doesn't even make sense to me. Just don't tell our stockholders."

She was laughing softly when she hung up; and smiling for minutes afterward as she prepared for the morning's manual labor. She had taken steel wool to the cabinet that would hold her new sink before she realized just how much the simple exchange about the day's plans had warmed her.

The Georgetown Regional Library was, like everything else in the neighborhood, stately and imposing. In keeping with the area's fascination with history, the library housed the Peabody Room, a collection of documents relating to local houses, events and his-torical figures. Faith knew that was the place to begin her search.

Once she'd found her way around and settled at a table, she waited until the librarian was free. She was an African-American woman about Faith's own age, soft-spoken and well versed in the potential and limitations of the collection. Faith explained what she was looking for as succinctly as she could.

"And you said the address was…?" The librarian was too thin, but pretty, with eyes that were a shade darker than hazel and lips that formed a perfect heart.

Faith told her, and watched her perk up with interest.

"That's the Huston house?"

"I'm Faith Huston Bronson," Faith acknowledged.

"Dorothy Waylins." The librarian extended her hand, but she was either too tactful or experienced to make a fuss. "We have quite a bit about your house. But the documents that come to mind don't go back that far."

Faith cut to the chase. "You probably have a lot on my sister's kidnapping."

"We have an entire scrapbook the staff put together at the time. A driver's license, credit card and solemn oath on the oldest Bible in the collection will give you access."

Faith gave a perfunctory smile. "Today I'm going further back."

"Let's see what we can find. We have information on chain of title, assessment records, houses and buildings and the alterations that were done. We also have local maps, plats...." Dorothy shrugged. "You name it, it's here somewhere."

It all seemed too easy, but Faith could feel her excitement growing. "It looks like I'll be spending some time at that table."

Dorothy gave a regal nod. "Just let me warn you, this can become an addiction. You and I, we'll know each other pretty well before you're finished."

The next two days followed a pattern. Faith got the children off to school, then worked on the cabinets until her arms felt ripped from their sockets. Afterward she showered and wandered toward the library, stopping at Marvelous Market along the way for something to munch. Although she liked the physical labor, the library portion of each day was her favorite.

By three-thirty on Friday afternoon, Faith had roughed out a simple history of the house. It had been built in 1885 for a man named Jedediah Wheelwright, who was Faith's great-great-grandfather and the husband of Candace.

By Georgetown standards, the row house was a teenager. There had been other buildings on the site before it, the history of which Faith was still trying to track down. But she did know that Jedediah wasn't a rich man. He, like others in the neighborhood, worked on the canal, and purchasing the house, which was inexpensive even by the standards of its day, had probably sent him into an early grave.

Candace supported herself after Jedediah's death by making hats. Faith even found a small advertisement in a newspaper of the day claiming that Wheelwright Millinery was the only shop for "ladies of distinction."

After Candace's death the house passed to her only child, Violet Atkins, and her husband, James. Violet and James lived there until their deaths several years before granddaughter Lydia and her husband Joe moved in.

Although she had grown up in the house, Millicent, Lydia's mother, never lived there as an adult. She moved away after her marriage to Harold Charles, whose prestigious career with the State Department necessitated stays all over the globe. Millicent died of malaria contracted during a tour in the Congo. Harold, who was considerably older, died in a fatal car crash two years later.

And finally Lydia took the stage. Rudderless and alone, she fell in love with Joe Huston in the months after her father's death. Faith guessed that the brash politician with all the answers had appealed to a young woman adrift. The lovely debutante with the surname that opened all the right doors in Washington had appealed to a man trying to establish a political future for himself.

Faith felt as if she'd caught a glimpse of the stream that had washed her into the world. Names. Dates. Occupations. Every fact she discovered made her feel more a part of her own history. She wasn't researching a residence so much as the source of that stream. The house was merely a spring that had husbanded and nourished her ancestors.

And she had obviously been at the library too long.

"You look like you're enjoying yourself."

Faith looked up. An older woman, clad in a navy designer suit that even Lydia wouldn't have found fault with, was standing across the table from her. Her short hair was silver, and every strand was as disciplined as a private in a dictator's army.

"I am." Faith tried to place the stranger but couldn't.

"I can't imagine why. The books you've been looking through are even worse than the ones they gave me."

"Are you researching a house? Or a person?"

"House. I'm having my music club for a recital next week, and I know somebody's going to ask more than I know. They always do. This time I want to sound informed." She grimaced, an expression that was foreign to a face that had been rigidly schooled in wrinkle prevention. "I would much prefer to let someone else do it...." She wandered off.

"Who was that woman?" Faith asked Dorothy when she stopped by a few minutes later. She couldn't shake the thought that she ought to know her.

Dorothy smiled, as if to say that names were off-limits. But she did give a hint. "During the Reagan administration she and Nancy had lunch together whenever they could coordinate their calendars. She flies out to California at least once a month now to continue the tradition."

"I doubt she's in the Peabody Room too often."

"You'd be surprised the number of people like that. They want the facts, not the stacks."

Faith digested that. She couldn't imagine anyone not finding this look at the past as fascinating as she did.

Dorothy started to leave, but Faith stopped her. The look at her family history had led her to consider the portion that had affected her most deeply.

"You mentioned that you have a scrapbook on my sister's kidnapping?"

"I wondered how long it would take you to ask."

"I don't have time to go through it today, but I wonder if there are any articles I could copy, just to start?"

"Are you going to be around a little longer?"

Faith looked at her watch. Remy and Alex were due home from school at any moment, but they would be all right for a little while. Technically Remy was old enough to baby-sit. Faith could try using her cranky cell phone to leave a message.

"Another twenty minutes or so," she told Dorothy.
"I'll see what I can do for you."

David knew he might cause more trouble for himself and his children by showing up on their doorstep. But he had just completed a job interview nearby, and the longing to see both Alex and Remy had propelled him to their front steps. The house was locked tight, and he guessed that Faith had gone to pick them up from school. Gingerly, in his best suit, he settled himself on the stoop to wait.

David had spent the first forty-odd years of his life convinced that he knew what to do about everything. His father had never encouraged doubts. There was one way, the Lord Jesus Christ's, and nothing else was worth discussion. As an adult, of course, David had seen through Arnold Bronson's prejudices and convictions. He had formed his own instead, borrowing some from his father, some from other mentors, some from hours spent on his knees.

Now he was rudderless. Particularly where his children were concerned. He was establishing a new and tentative rapport with Alex, which gave him hope. The stilted conversations were gradually warming into old-fashioned father and son dialogues. He realized he had never really appreciated his son quite the way he should have. Alex had been Faith's child, and Remy had been David's. He had loved them both. He would have laid down his life for Alex without a second thought. But he had never really tried to understand him.

For the first time he saw what a unique and interesting child he had fathered. The time they spent together was doubly precious. He was making up both for the days he spent away from Alex now and the years when he had been too preoccupied to see his son for the boy he really was.

This new closeness to Alex made him miss Remy more.

He remembered so clearly the day he and Faith had brought their daughter home from the hospital. She was a small baby, so breakable and vulnerable. One look at his baby daughter and he had been transformed from just any man into Remy's dad.

In the years since, little had changed. He remembered every milestone, every recital, every soccer game. He treasured the hours they had spent together on school projects, the discussions of history, religion, morality.

He missed Faith's friendship, and he missed coming home to Alex every night. But he missed Remy the way he would miss an arm or a leg.

David shifted so he was sitting against the post. The railing was old and rusty, and he was careful not to put much weight against it. The house needed so much work. Their *lives* needed so much work. Like the railing, under any new stress their family might be destroyed beyond repair. He needed to reestablish ties with his daughter, and he needed to do it now. If he didn't, the rust could eat away everything that was left.

More minutes passed before he spotted Remy and Alex coming toward him from Wisconsin. He hadn't realized they walked to school, and he was annoyed with Faith for allowing it. He wondered what they found to talk about. Did they discuss the changes in their lives? Did Alex try to convince his sister to give David a chance?

In his wildest imaginings he had never considered that his son might someday be forced to plead his cause.

David knew the precise moment when Remy saw him. She and Alex were half a block away and in the midst of an animated conversation. Not a happy one, by the expressions on their faces, definitely an argument of some kind. Alex was taller than his sister now, despite the difference in their ages. Where once Remy could treat him like a pesky little brother, now she was forced to look up at him when they spoke. Just before she spotted David, her chin was stubbornly tilted, her fingers curled into fists. Her voice was raised—he could hear that much.

Then she saw her father.

David watched annoyance turn into something darker. His daughter's eyes narrowed, and even from that distance he knew they flashed dangerously. She stopped midstep, rocking back on her heels. Suddenly, with a twist of her body and another change in posture, she was poised for flight.

David's first impulse was to go after her if she ran. His second and saner was to do nothing. He had to consider Alex. He had to consider Remy's humiliation if he chased her like a rebellious two-year-old.

He held his breath, praying silently that she would approach. His prayer was answered. Alex said something to her, something so low that David could barely hear the murmur of his son's voice. Remy tossed her head, her bright blond hair spilling over the shoulders of a wrinkled green shirt. She looked tired, upset and bedraggled, as if she no longer cared what she wore to school or what anyone thought of her.

She said something to Alex, again too low for David to hear. Then, as if she'd made up her mind, she marched toward him.

"Hello, Daddy." The words were an epithet. He had been called a number of things since emerging from the closet. None of them had been said with more venom.

David got to his feet. "I was hoping you and Alex would go out for ice cream with me."

"Like we used to do in McLean, right? Like the good old days?"

"I miss you, Remy. I know you're angry at—"

"Angry? Me?" She forced a laugh. "Why should I be angry?"

"Remy," Alex said, "Dad's just trying to—"

"Shut up!" She turned on her brother, fire in her eyes. "Just shut up, Alex. Like you have any idea how I feel!"

Alex shot David a worried glance, and David's heart went out to his son. Alex so badly wanted to play peacemaker, but he was out of his league. Madeline Albright would be out of her league here.

"Alex, son, it's okay," David said. "Remy and I have to work this out."

"Right, Alex." Remy faced her brother. "You can't fix everything, you know? You're just a kid. And what do kids know?"

"This is Daddy," Alex said, pulling himself up to tower two scant inches over her. "You gotta hear what he has to say. Honor thy father and—"

She exploded, shoving Alex so hard that despite outweighing her, he stumbled backward.

David had seen enough. He grabbed Remy's arm to stop her, and she rounded on him. Before he understood her intent, she slammed her right fist into his stomach, and as he bent from the impact, she did it again.

"I hate you!" She screamed the words. "I hate you! I don't want to see you. I don't want to hear you. I don't want to ever, ever talk to you again! I hate you. You ruined my life! You ruined Alex's and Mom's. You're a fag! A queer! You should never have had kids! People like you don't have kids!"

She broke away from him, stepping backward, and held both fists in the air in front of her like a shield.

Alex lunged for her, but David quickly stepped between them. He caught his breath. A slender fourteen-year-old girl couldn't pack much of a punch, but it had been enough to knock the wind out of him for a moment.

The impact on all their lives was far more devastating.

"Alex, go inside," he said. "Do you have a key?"

Alex was sobbing. "Yes, but—"

"Use it, son. We'll talk later."

Alex stumbled up the steps. In a moment the old door swung inward and Alex disappeared.

David stared at his daughter. She still held her fists in the air, but the rage in her eyes had dimmed. She looked marginally more like the child he had sired and raised. But she wasn't the same child. Not anymore. And he didn't know how to relate to this new incarnation.

"It doesn't matter how angry you are," David said carefully. "You will never take your fists to me or anyone else in this family again."

"Really?"

"Really."

She lowered her fists an inch, no more. "I meant every word. I want you to leave me alone. Stay away from me!"

He didn't know what to do. Nothing in all his years had prepared him for this. He could continue to force his way into Remy's life, even insist that the courts back him up. Or he could do as she asked and step out of it. Not forever, but until she gained enough maturity to have a better understanding of the things that had happened.

His gaze dropped to the ground at her feet. "While I was waiting for you, I sat here and remembered all the wonderful times we've had together, Remy. Being your father and Alex's is the best part of my life." He looked up again. Her expression hadn't changed. Bravado might be a mask, but it was an effective, impenetrable one.

"I don't want to destroy that," he said quietly. "So I'll wait for you to find me again. And I'll be there waiting, whenever you're ready. You don't have to worry that I'll hate you for what happened today, or that I'll move on to something else and forget about you. I'm your father. I'll be here until the day I die, even if you don't want me to be."

"I don't and I won't."

"You made your point."

"Did I? That's a nice change."

He heard the sadness behind the sarcasm, as well as the insecurity and the fury. He had told her one thing for thirteen years and something altogether different since. She had no way of judging who he was anymore, and she was too frightened to give him another chance to explain.

He understood all that. He saw it all clearly. But the pain in his gut wasn't from his daughter's fists. It came from witnessing her shattered heart.

"Do you have my phone number?" he asked.

"I don't need it."

"Alex has it. Your mother has it."

"That's their problem."

He stepped aside. She swept past him and through the unlocked door, closing it with a bang behind her.

David was still standing there, unable to move or even think, when he heard a voice behind him.

"David?"

He turned and saw Faith coming toward him, just as their children had a few minutes before.

"What are you doing here?" She didn't smile, but she didn't seem upset to see him, either. "Anything wrong?"

"Anything wrong?" He gave a bitter laugh. "Our daughter hates me. That's what's wrong."

She glanced toward the house, then back at him. "You spoke to Remy?"

"I tried." He could feel emotion welling where a moment before there had been dark desolation. "She told me she hates me. She shoved Alex. She hit me."

Faith sucked in air, as if her lungs were empty. "David, no, I—"

"What are you telling her, Faith? Are you feeding this? Are you talking about how lonely you are, how financially insecure, how sad you are that your life has changed?"

She looked startled. "What are you talking about?"

"This is Remy! My daughter. My daughter who adored me! This has to be coming from somewhere." He combed his fingers through his hair and realized his hands were shaking.

"Are you saying this is *my* fault?" Faith was clearly angry now. "How dare you! I love Remy. I wouldn't do that to her. I've tried to smooth the waters for you, although God knows that will take a miracle. But how can you think I'd make her unhappier than she is? There's only one person at fault for all the changes in her life, and it isn't me!"

"*You're* the parent in charge. You're living with her every day. What do you think is happening here? You think this kind of anger is normal? You think it'll just blow over? Why haven't you gotten her any help?"

"I think she's adjusting to a million things at once. I think she needs time, and apparently so do you. But don't you ever, *ever*, come here again and accuse me of making things worse. How much room did you leave us, David? How much room was there for things to be worse?"

They were both out of breath, staring at each other. He crumpled first, but only a little.

"I'm sorry." He barely shoved the words out.

"You damn well should be."

"She needs help, Faith."

"We all need help, David."

"I told her I won't contact her again until she wants me to."

"We're both flying blind. I don't know what to tell you, and frankly, you're at the bottom of my worry list. I'm getting through this one minute at a time."

"What about professional help?"

She took a deep breath, as if she needed the time it took. "If I tell her she needs to see a therapist, she'll go over the edge. Our rapport is fragile. You're not the only one she hates."

"You think you can handle this alone?"

"What choice have you given me?"

"The choice of consulting a professional."

"If things get any worse, I'll broach seeing a counselor. In the meantime, I'll do what seems best. I'm the one who has to pick up the pieces of the lives you cracked wide open."

He considered what to say or do next. But that, like everything else in his life, was a question mark. In the end, he simply nodded curtly and walked away.

 17

Remy waited for her mother to punish her. Alone in her room after the encounter with her father, she sobbed out her frustration, pounding her pillow until one side split and wispy tufts of batting floated in the air. She heard Faith come inside a few minutes later, and she fully expected her to arrive at the bedroom door. But her mother surprised her.

Sometime later, when she was armored again, Remy made her way downstairs for the confrontation. Faith was sitting in the living room, staring into space. Remy could hear voices in the backyard, and she supposed that Alex and that awful homeless man were wrestling with more ivy. The man's presence was just more proof that her mother had gone crazy right along with her father.

Faith looked up as Remy approached. She didn't smile. "How could you? He's your father. Nothing changes that. How could you ever believe you had the right to hit him?"

"He grabbed me first."

"Yes, I know. After you shoved your brother. I heard the whole sordid story from Alex."

"Alex is a tattletale."

"Alex struggled very hard to be fair to you. There wasn't much he could say, though. There is no excuse for your bad behavior. None. Period."

Remy felt a hundred more important questions trying to squeeze their way out, but she only had courage for the most mundane. "So, are you going to ground me?"

Faith patted the sofa. At first Remy had no intention of yielding, but as Faith's expression darkened, Remy saw what was in store if she didn't make this concession. She sat on the edge, as far from her mother as possible.

"I don't know what to do with you or for you," Faith said. "I know you're in a lot of pain. I know you're angry at everyone. But I wonder how it came to this, Remy? Did somebody in our family teach you it was okay to abuse the people who love you? Is that what you've witnessed in your own home?"

Despite everything, Remy felt a shudder of remorse. She hadn't missed the expression in her father's eyes when she punched him. He'd looked like someone watching a pileup on the Beltway. And she'd wanted to be glad. Some part of her *had* been glad. But the rest of her had felt sick.

In that moment she had remembered, for no good reason, all the times David had held her on his lap when she was sick or afraid.

"Are you sorry?" Faith asked.

Remy knew her immediate future depended on her answer. She wanted to lie and say yes, just to get herself off the hook. Maybe it wasn't even a lie; she didn't know. But every lie she told weighed her down a little more, even when the freedom they bought made her stinking life a little more tolerable.

"I'm sorry I hit him," Remy said at last. "I was just so mad. I don't want to see him, and I don't want to talk to him, and I couldn't get past him to get inside. I felt trapped. I always feel trapped now, like I'm in a cage. Like that stupid rat Alex caught."

"He misses you. He just wanted to see you, not trap you."

"I don't miss him!"

"Yes, you do."

"You think you know everything about me."

"I wish I did. I wish I knew the girl I raised was still in that teenage body somewhere. The one who didn't hit people or call them terrible names. The one who understood how to forgive others for their mistakes."

"That was one frigging mistake, wouldn't you say?"

"It's time to look beyond your own pain. You're not alone in this. You're one of four people in our family."

"He's not in our family anymore. You're getting a divorce."

"David Bronson will always be your father. And your dad and I will always be connected by you and Alex, even by the things we shared when we were married. Our family changed, but we're still tied to each other."

"You have an answer for everything. It's like you're always reading some stupid book about teenagers and divorce and reciting what you learned."

Faith's lips twisted into some indefinable expression between a smile and a frown. "You know, honey, I wish somebody would write that book. I could use some help."

Remy could feel herself deflating. Despite her attempts to pump up her anger, it wasn't bottomless, and she had used up the day's supply. Just as she'd had a moment of empathy for her father, she now had a full minute for her mother.

At last Remy shook her head. "I was just so angry. I didn't mean to hit him. But he grabbed me, and I freaked. I don't want to make things worse for you or Alex."

Faith looked relieved. Remy supposed that this time she had said the magic words with enough sincerity to please her mother.

"I'm not going to ground you," Faith said. "But, Remy, this can't happen again."

"He said he's going to leave me alone from now on."

"It's costing him everything to give you more time. He needs his daughter. This is a very bad moment in your father's life."

"Yeah, well? Maybe he should have given this whole homosexual thing some thought."

"I suspect he gave it quite a bit."

"I want to go out for a while." Remy got to her feet. "Maybe I'll walk over to Billie's."

"I don't know, I—"

"Look, am I in prison here? Just tell me and I'll go crawl in the cage with Alex's stupid rat. At least then I'll have some company. In McLean I could go for a walk whenever I wanted. But if that's changed like everything else, let me know, okay?"

Faith looked torn. She was never good at hiding her thoughts, and now Remy was glad, because she pressed her advantage. "If Georgetown is that dangerous, we shouldn't live here, should we?"

"Please don't be gone long. Okay?"

Remy had given her mother Billie's phone number. In fact, a few weeks ago Faith had talked to Billie's mother to be sure it was all right for Remy to spend time there in the afternoons. Billie's mom, who worked two jobs, had apparently satisfied Faith, even though Remy had never met the woman.

"If I'm at Billie's house, can I be gone an hour?"

"I guess so."

"Good." Remy started toward the door.

"I'll get chicken for dinner and that bean salad you like. But be sure you're home by 5:30. Don't forget, I'm going out. Your grandmother's coming to get you at 6:00."

David wanted to buy her ice cream. Now Faith was trying to bribe her with bean salad. Remy couldn't imagine any human beings lamer than her parents.

Outside, she turned toward Wisconsin, and once there, she turned left, heading toward Lawford's, the clothing store where Enzio worked. She knew he had an afternoon shift on Fridays because she'd visited him at the store last week.

Billie Wolfgard did go to Remy's school, and they were in the same science class. She was older than Remy by two years, because she had been held back twice. Billie didn't like to do homework, which was part of the reason she was still in eighth grade. Remy wasn't doing much herself this year, but it was a small sacrifice to do the science assignments, then stop by Billie's every morning so she could copy them. Remy had made Alex promise he wouldn't tell Faith about her daily detour.

Remy didn't really like Billie, who was loud and hyper, but in exchange for copying Remy's homework, Billie had agreed to pretend Remy was at her house in the bathroom or some other place where she couldn't come to the telephone if Faith called. Then Billie would call Remy at Enzio's house or at the store. She might not be good in school, but she was smart enough to remember where she kept those numbers.

Billie was the closest thing to a school friend that Remy had. The rest of the kids looked at her as if she had two heads, and even the ones who tried to be nice disappeared the moment she let them know she didn't want their charity. She was Remy Bronson. Last year she'd been picked to lead the academy's Easter parade. The cutest boy in the school had asked her to be his lab partner. Every single day she had eaten lunch with the popular kids.

Now her only friend was a delinquent with a nasty laugh and plans to drop out of school the moment she was old enough. Welcome to Georgetown.

Remy walked along Wisconsin, paying little attention to the people pushing past her. The shops and restaurants were sandwiched together in old buildings, not like the mall where everything was bright, spacious and easy to find. She didn't know what her mother found so charming about Wisconsin Avenue. The sidewalks were crowded; the stores were narrow and often dark inside. Sure, they sold good stuff, but nobody could afford it, especially her.

Once she spotted Lawford's she slowed her pace. She wasn't sure what Enzio would say when she showed up again, but she didn't have any other place to go. Last time he'd been cool about it, but he'd treated her like his sister. One of the other salesclerks had snickered because she was so surprised at the prices. She'd felt like the country mouse in the story her father used to read to her. That thought made her sad.

At Lawford's she peered in the window for a while before she went inside. Hip-hop pulsed from speakers cradling the doorway. She couldn't understand all the lyrics, but the beat cheered her a little. The walls were painted black, and stark steel chandeliers lit the room. The clothes, lots of leather and spandex and shiny lizard skin fabrics, glowed like jewels under the fluorescent bulbs.

She searched for Enzio but didn't see him immediately. Half a dozen customers stood at the racks, combing through the clothing. One bored salesclerk, with a bleached buzz cut and two nose rings, stood watching them, arms folded over a pumpkin-colored bustier.

Remy pretended to look at jewelry while she waited for Enzio. Most of it looked like restraints or shackles from an ancient Roman slave galley. She thought that one gold bracelet, snapped just right, might secure Alex to his bed frame.

"Hey, gorgeous."

Remy's heart did a flip. She looked up just in time to see Enzio's face hovering inches from hers. He lowered it the necessary distance and gave her a proprietary kiss, right on the lips; then he stepped back. "What's happening?"

Her entire afternoon shifted focus. She smiled shyly, glad she'd graduated from sister to something more intimate. She tried to be cool. "I'm just hanging."

"I found something that will look good on you."

"I didn't bring any money with me."

He shrugged and disappeared to return with a lime-green skirt and jacket with a rhinestone encrusted zipper. He held it against her, the back of his hand brushing one breast. The skirt was barely long enough to cover her panties. "Just try it on."

She knew what her parents would say if they ever saw her in an outfit like this one. Her mother's clothes were like leftovers from a ladies' club yard sale, expensive clothes that were so discreet they faded into every background. Faith picked out clothes like that for Remy, too, and until now Remy hadn't thought much about it. "You're sure?"

"Hey, you're with me. You can do anything you fuckin' please."

You're with me. She was with someone. She was with Enzio. Feeling about ten years older and ten pounds lighter, she grasped the hanger and went off to find the dressing room.

From the moment Pavel invited her to dinner, Faith wondered what she should wear. She had never been a clotheshorse. She was too petite for excesses, too blond for bright colors, too traditional to expose much skin. Early in adulthood she had settled on pastels, grayed tones and classic design, but there was a fine line between classic and dowdy. She empathized with Queen Elizabeth, although at least she knew better than to wear flowered hats.

Now, after a shower that didn't quite wash away the afternoon's traumas, she stood at her closet surveying the two candidates that were battling for first place. The more conservative was a navy dress with red piping that outlined princess style panels. She had good red shoes, a matching purse and her grandmother Millicent's pearls. She could carry a red linen jacket in case the restaurant had the air-conditioning turned too high.

The other possibility was a salmon-colored camisole worn under a gray knit suit. The suit had subtle stripes of the same salmon, and she had gray sandals to wear with it. The camisole seemed a little risque. She had no undergarment that worked with the thin straps and, frankly, no need for one. But what kind of message did that send? She wouldn't pick up much business wearing it on a street corner, but still, what exactly did baring her shoulders communicate?

She was a thirty-seven-year-old fuddy-duddy.

She decided to wear it and keep the jacket on, no matter what the temperature.

Remy came home, called up a halfhearted greeting and went into the dining room to eat her dinner. Alex had eaten earlier. He wasn't excited about going to his grandparents' house for the evening, but Lydia had promised he could pick out a DVD on the way to Great Falls. He had already decided on *X-Men,* which, with a story line about mutant adolescents learning to cope with their extraordinary powers, always fascinated him. If Lydia survived the viewing experience, she would grow a full notch in Alex's estimation.

Lydia arrived and came upstairs to greet her. Faith was just fastening gold studs in her earlobes, and Lydia sat on the bed to watch.

"You should cut your hair," she said. "Not short. Just have it shaped and layered."

"I look like yesterday's *Vogue,* huh?"

"Not even yesterday's."

Faith looked at her mother and saw the smile on her face. "Well, thanks. You're good for my confidence."

"You're not even forty yet. And you're lovely and thin." She paused for effect. "And you don't have to represent all the evangelical Christian women of America anymore, or the right wing of the Democratic party, for that matter. You can just be you."

Faith paused in the act of slipping the second stud in place. "I can be me, huh?"

"Exactly."

"The problem is, that *was* me."

"You'll figure out the new you."

After her mother left, Faith brushed her unstylish pageboy and wondered if Lydia knew something she didn't. Maybe tonight was the first step on the road to a new and better Faith.

She left for Pavel's house at six-thirty. She wore comfortable shoes and carried the sandals, along with some vegetable paté she'd picked up at Dean and Deluca on M Street. She took her time, enjoying the marginally cooler temperature of evening, and the sights and sounds of her new neighborhood. Despite temperatures in the eighties, brightly colored chrysanthemums graced porches and yards, and harvest wreaths were beginning to appear on front doors.

Finally she arrived at Pavel's house, the painted lady grinning among its dowager neighbors. Wisely, he had chosen colors that were appropriate for the historical period but not among the gaudier possibilities. She wondered if this was the way Pavel saw himself. A little different from his neighbors, more creative, more flamboyant and less apt to follow tradition but still—if just barely—in the mainstream.

If she played that game, what would her house say about her? Hemmed in by tradition? Narrow perspective with limited views? She hoped not. She preferred another choice. Integral part of family, neighborhood and history. A keeper of the flame. Now *that* she could live with.

Pavel came out to greet her as if he'd been watching from a window. He stood on his porch, master of all he surveyed, and grinned. "Hey there, lady. Can I interest you in a tour?"

She played along, resting an index finger against her cheek. "I don't know. Does it come with spooky organ music?"

"Only if you want it to."

She opened a low iron gate and let herself in, climbing the steps to his porch. "I'll want the full-scale production. Music, bats, ghosts."

"Tame ghost stories, as they go around here." He leaned over and kissed her cheek. "You put me to shame, Faith. Now I'll have to dig up my sportscoat."

Actually, Pavel looked pretty good the way he was. His pants were khaki, but they'd been pressed, and she bet his blue shirt had just come off a laundry hanger. He had shaved, and his hair was shorter, although still a tad unruly. She felt just the faintest stab of nostalgia for misshapen T-shirts.

He shepherded her inside. "Wow!" She stood back a little, trying to get the whole effect.

She took a deep breath and quoted: "'Spots or cracks at the windows do not disturb me; Tall and sufficient stand behind, and make signs to me; I read the promise, and patiently wait.'" She paused. "Walt Whitman. *Leaves of Grass.* I memorized the poem in high school for a contest. He must have been talking about this house."

"I'm impressed. I remember about half a dozen naughty limericks and that's it."

"Don't share."

"Not at the beginning of the date."

She was taking in the scenery. The house was asymmetrical, so although a curving staircase and hallway loomed in front of them, the rooms to each side were different in shape and size. To her left was a circular parlor, which was the ground floor of a turret that extended at least two stories. The parlor was almost empty of furniture except for an antique pump organ flanked by a pair of spade-footed candle stands.

Pavel pointed. "Your organ music."

"Do you play?"

"Not a note."

To their right was a larger, rectangular room with a fireplace and comfortable masculine furniture of leather and dark walnut. An Oriental carpet of dark reds and golds defined the space. This room looked complete. The wallpaper was an elegant, subtle gold stripe. The mahogany wainscoting shone with a polished luster.

"I started in here," Pavel said, leading her into the room. "I knew I needed one place to retreat where nothing was left to do. The wainscoting and the rest of the trim were covered in six coats of white paint, but at least no one had removed the woodwork. I called it my 'board of the day' project."

She didn't count, but she figured refinishing had taken months.

"There was a false ceiling. Somebody didn't like the height and lowered them all. The plaster was cracked, but the medallion and cornice mouldings were still intact."

She followed his finger to gaze at skillfully wrought grapevines held by winged cherubs, strangely not at odds with the masculine furnishings.

"The fireplace was boarded over and the mantel carted away, although the cast iron insert was still here. I studied similar houses and found this one on a trip to London. The stone is Derbyshire fossil. The mantel was taken from a house just a little older than this one. What do you think?"

"It's wonderful. The whole room is lovely. It's a place to relax and be yourself." And it was, but her eyes were already wandering.

"Okay, you've seen the future. We'll wander through the present into the past."

They spent the next half hour viewing everything that was left to do, ending in Pavel's kitchen. He had opted for the twenty-first century here, black granite countertops, stainless steel appliances, light cherry cabinetry. Windows looked over the wraparound porch, which descended to a yard with clipped, if unimaginative, shrubbery. Only a black-and-white tile floor, probably installed sometime in the 1950s, was jarring.

"So, what do you think?" Pavel spread his arms to encompass it. "I have running water now. I have appliances, counters."

"I'm pea-green."

"The floor's next, probably cherry and walnut parquet, then I'll be finished in here." He opened the refrigerator and pulled out a bottle of champagne as she seated herself on a stool at the center island. He held it up. "I thought we'd celebrate."

"What, exactly?"

"Friendship. Houses. Georgetown. There's always a good reason for champagne."

"I brought paté." She fished the plastic bag out of her purse and held it out to him. Their fingers touched as he reached for it, but he didn't withdraw.

"You know, this is probably the first time I've showed the house to a woman who hasn't asked me why I'm doing all the work myself."

"I know why. What would you do if somebody else came in and finished it? Sell the house? Start on another one? You want the thrill to last. You want the house to really be yours when you're done. Am I close?"

"You saw some of the mistakes I've made. Some of the problems I've uncovered that I don't have a clue how to fix yet."

She was aware that their fingers were still touching, and that neither one of them seemed inclined to end the contact. "I saw some skilled detail work, as well. Was your father handy? Did you learn what you know as a boy?"

"I never knew my father, and my mother never remarried."

"I'm sorry."

He shrugged. "She's gone now, too. That was one of the reasons I left the West Coast. No family to worry about, and I knew I could make friends anywhere I went."

"Not the kind of friends you grow up with, though. The kind who stand behind you through thick and thin."

"You have friends like that?"

"I didn't let them stand anywhere near me when David left."

"Too personal?" He took the paté and got plates out of the cupboard. She watched him dump crackers on a tray, along with the paté carton. He went back to pop the cork on the champagne, and she resisted the urge to place the crackers in neat little rows.

"I was raised to keep everything to myself," she said, when he was standing in front of her again. She brightened a little. "Hey, I could work for the CIA. I have all the right credentials. I never thought of that."

Pavel's nostrils flared, and she laughed. "I'm kidding. Besides, David's outing probably destroyed my security clearance."

"You can laugh about that?"

"Not at David's situation. He's never going to get a job like the one he had. In political circles, once the mighty have fallen, their so-called friends tend to step over the body."

"You've come a long way if you can worry about him."

"And I'm talking about this with a virtual stranger. I guess I'm not my father's daughter anymore."

Pavel poured champagne into two crystal flutes. "Say a little more. I dare you."

"About what?"

"About your father. Something tells me you're just getting started."

She took her glass and cradled it between her palms. "Do you know why he named me Faith?"

"No, but the world probably expected a little Charity to come down the line after you."

"I was at the Georgetown library today, and I asked the librarian to copy some of the articles on Hope's kidnapping. And you know what the headline of the first one was?" She lifted her glass in toast. "Hope Is Lost."

"Ouch."

"My father named me Faith to make a statement. When Hope is lost, you must have Faith."

"He didn't."

"He certainly never admitted it out loud, but the message was there. He was a man the voters could count on. Nothing could strike Joe Huston down. A man with faith. A righteous man."

"Hard to love, though."

She couldn't deny it. "There wasn't much chance Charity was next in line. Charity of any kind was never my father's greatest priority." She sipped, then added, "Frankly, neither was having more children. My father tried it twice, failed flamboyantly the first time, found it messy and inconvenient the second, and passed on the chance to do it again."

"I can't imagine you were ever messy or inconvenient."

"Imagine what the senator would have thought if he'd had a normal daughter? One with a mind of her own?"

"You have a mind of your own, Faith."

"Not one I've exercised very often." She smiled, to let him know this wasn't a pity party.

"So where does that leave you?"

"Sitting in a stranger's kitchen, reciting my life story."

He leaned across the island and propped his elbows in front of her. "Can you be happy again?"

She wanted to smile, to say something flippant or sophisticated. But she couldn't. His brown eyes were troubled, and even though she didn't know him well, she thought that was unusual.

He was digging deeper now. She could feel him reaching toward her, even though he didn't move. Her answer seemed important to him. It was important to her, as well.

She leaned across the island and inclined her head, kissing him softly on the lips, a kiss that lasted longer than she'd expected, a kiss that was meant to be reassuring and turned into a question of its own.

His lips were warm and tasted of champagne, and the only thing wrong with kissing Pavel here, now, was that a granite island kept them from touching more intimately.

She settled back on her stool and smiled. "I can be happy again."

 18

Faith arrived home just a little before Remy and Alex were due. She and Pavel had joined his friends at Sea Catch on the C & O Canal, where they'd settled on a narrow, tree-shaded balcony to eat some of the best seafood in the District. Joan and Carter Melvin were nearly as laid-back as Pavel, accepting her into their circle immediately with a warm, casual welcome.

She was surprised by how much she had enjoyed sampling crab-cakes and chatting. Joan and Carter had recently bought a house in Glover Park, just over the Georgetown border. They, too, were in the midst of renovations, as, it seemed, was half the city. They were also interested in history.

"You're actually doing a history of your house?" Joan, an attractive brunette in her late forties, seemed fascinated. "From the ground up?"

Faith was delighted to talk about it. "I have all sorts of ideas. Photos, blueprints, copies of documents, maybe even a watercolor or charcoal drawing for the front cover."

"You're turning a simple history into a book," Pavel said.

"I guess. I want it to be a keepsake, something to pass down through generations. Each new crop of owners shouldn't have to dig up the history all over again."

Joan sat back, pushing away a plate still heaped with seafood linguine. "Will you do my house next?"

Faith hoped she was joking. "I'll make notes on how to find answers and help you when you're ready."

"I'm not kidding. Would you consider doing the history for our new house?" Joan hurried on, before Faith could find a tactful excuse. "I'm not asking as a favor. You obviously love this, and you said you were going to be looking for a job. Why not offer your services at a price?"

Carter Melvin worked in public relations at Scavenger and was only a shade more buttoned-down than his boss. "Every upwardly mobile public servant wants to be able to brag about who lived or died in his row house. Georgetown alone could keep you busy for years. Hell, Jack Kennedy lived in half the houses—and visited the other half."

Faith thought about Nancy Reagan's friend, who'd confessed to wishing somebody else would do her research. Nancy's friend, who would probably pay almost anything Faith asked to have that annoying burden lifted, who would display the history prominently and tell her friends where to find the author. And there were many more just like her.

"*I'd* hire you, too," Pavel said. "And not to help you. I'd love to know what you can find out."

"I'm beginning to see how Scavenger got off the ground," Faith said.

The others had laughed good-naturedly and gone on to another topic.

But Faith wasn't laughing. The idea had nibbled at her for the rest of the evening. She needed a job, preferably one that could make use of her extensive contacts in the city. She had a degree in history, and, yes, it was European history, but what did that matter? She had learned how to research, how to dig deeper and proceed with caution. Perhaps the scope had been larger, but the methodology was similar.

And how wonderful to be able to work at home, to be there when the children arrived from school, to take time off when they needed her. They were growing up, but they still needed supervision and support.

Of course, she had a lot to learn. She knew she was hooked when the thought of all that work only excited her.

By the time the children walked in, followed by her mother, she was flying high. Good food. New friends. A possible career solution. And, of course, Pavel Quinn, who didn't belong at the end of the list.

"You look like you had a good evening," Lydia said.

Faith saw Remy watching her. Remy was clearly not excited that her mother had enjoyed herself. "We had a nice time." Faith settled for describing their meal.

The children trooped upstairs, bickering about who needed to use the bathroom first, and Lydia left for her drive back to Great Falls. Faith turned off the lights and made sure doors and windows were locked, then went up to get ready for bed.

An hour later, when the children closed their bedroom doors for the last time and the house was finally argument free, she still lay awake, staring at the ceiling.

In just a few months she would be divorced. After she'd discovered David with Abraham Stein, she'd been sure she never wanted another man in her life. She still couldn't imagine being married to anyone else—she had already spent too many years as someone's underappreciated wife. This was the time to find out who she was.

But now, for the first time since her life had changed so dramatically, she realized that she had been thinking in absolutes. She wasn't Joe Huston's child for nothing. Her role had changed. She had changed. The world had changed, and she was free, for the very first time, to make the decisions that would affect her most. Like whether she should sleep with Pavel Quinn.

She smiled in the darkness. Pavel hadn't invited her into his bed. He seemed comfortable with a casual relationship. She remembered what a come-on felt like, and not because she'd experienced one recently. Pavel was polite, informal, friendly.

But Pavel wanted her.

Their fingers had touched. Their bodies had brushed. She had kissed him across a black granite island. Tonight he had hugged her at her front door. Quickly, but she'd had the distinct impression that the speed of the embrace had had more to do with not giving away his state of arousal than with disinterest.

She wasn't sure she was ready for sex. She wasn't even sure she was very good at it. But she *was* sure that having a man want her was the most powerful aphrodisiac out there.

She had no time to savor that thought. A yowl sounded from the attic. Her heart stopped, then made up for the pause with an extra beat. She sat up and grabbed her robe. "Stupid cat." She felt better the moment she said it. It wasn't Guest's fault that she sounded like a baby crying.

"What's going on?" Remy stumbled into the hall at the same moment her mother did. "Why's she crying?" Alex came out, too.

The cat had made it clear she didn't want their interference. Food was good. Water and litter were fine. But any time they'd tried to extend the relationship, Guest hissed and spat. Faith was determined to take the whole feline family in to the vet to be checked and immunized, but so far she hadn't had the nerve to attempt the capture.

"We have to go up in the attic and see," Faith told them.

"What if something's wrong with the kittens?" Remy didn't sound tough now.

"Let's not borrow trouble." Faith went into Alex's room and opened the attic door.

Guest stood at the bottom, a gray carbon copy of herself hanging from her jaws. As they jumped back, Guest trotted past them, the kitten mewling and waving tiny paws in protest. The felines started down the hall toward Remy's room.

"Mom, it's hot as heck up there!" Alex was waving his hand as a wave of heat hit him.

Faith climbed two steps to the fan switch and flipped it. Nothing happened. "The fan's not working. Maybe we blew a fuse."

"The kittens were getting cooked," Alex said.

"There's an image." Faith was watching Remy, who had tiptoed after Guest. Now Remy stood in her own bedroom doorway. Faith joined her.

Guest emerged from an open drawer in Remy's dresser and hopped to the floor. She paused until they moved aside, then started back down the hallway and up the stairs.

"Is she going to bring them all down here?" Remy whispered, as if Guest might not like conversation.

"I'd say so." Faith watched her daughter's expression. She hadn't seen Remy this excited in months. She looked as if she'd just been given a pony or a new bicycle, the way she had looked so often before her young life fell to pieces.

"Why did she choose my room?" Remy asked.

Faith hoped Alex would understand. After all, he had Lefty, who was now at home in a real cage, with an exercise wheel and the latest in mouse care technology. "She knows a friend when she sees one."

"You are so bogus."

"I know," Faith said modestly.

Guest passed with another kitten, this one white and feistier than its sibling. Eventually two more, a black-and-white and what might be a tortoiseshell, made the journey before Guest settled into the drawer for the night. That was one more kitten than they'd guessed.

"Thus endeth the saga of the ghost baby in the attic," Faith said. "Tomorrow they go to the vet." She dashed upstairs to grab the litter, food and water, before the heat immobilized her.

The children disappeared again into their rooms, Remy with the supplies and more enthusiasm than usual.

Faith was smiling when she got back into bed after snapping the circuit breaker and restarting the fan. She was positive that she wouldn't sleep for a while. She focused on a neat stack of papers she'd set beside her bed and debated whether to look through the articles Dorothy had copied for her.

In the end she propped herself up on a pillow and paged through them. The house gradually fell silent as she set the copies in chronological order. This was only a portion of what was available, but Dorothy had tried to give her a taste of what had been written over the weeks when Hope's kidnapping was front page news.

"Hope is lost." She shook her head. She wondered what her life would have been like if Hope hadn't been lost, if she had grown up with a sister to confide in and fight with and stand beside when the going got rough in the Huston home. Maybe she would have developed more backbone.

"On July 18th, the newborn daughter of Congressman Joe Huston and his wife Lydia, nee Charles, was kidnapped from the family's Georgetown home."

Faith looked up, and her gaze circled the room. She sighed and glanced back at the article. One paragraph later, she put it aside for daylight hours and got up to find her favorite collection of Dave Barry's columns. She knew if she didn't find something to laugh about, she wouldn't sleep at all.

Lydia rearmed the security system and called down to the guest cottage to reassure Samuel, the young man who watched over the Great Falls property, that she had arrived home safely. She was sure he already knew. In exchange for the cottage and a salary, he kept watch over all the Hustons' comings and goings and served as a chauffeur when Joe didn't want to drive himself to the Senate office building or to meetings around the city. If Lydia hadn't arrived home in time, he would have tracked her down with the help of the global positioning system in her Mercedes or notified the authorities. She and Joe had learned the hard way about the importance of personal safety precautions.

She turned off everything but the hall light and started toward the wing where her bedroom was located. Joe was probably hard at work in the other wing. He was known to routinely attend parties and leave before the serious drinking could begin. He worked the room; then, business completed, he departed for home before the real party animals got started.

Alex and Remy hadn't seen much of him tonight. Joe came home from a reception at the National Archives, made one obligatory foray into the family room where the remarkable X-Men soared and oozed over the screen, asked how the children were doing in school, told Alex to get his feet off the coffee table; and left muttering under his breath about Hollywood violence. She saw the look that passed between her grandchildren and wondered how often she had been a cause of it herself.

In her room she changed into a long cotton gown, then sat at her dressing table to remove her jewelry and makeup. She wasn't pleased at her reflection. No matter how hard a woman fought, eventually the years took their toll. No surgery, diet or fitness regime could turn back the clock. She was sixty-six and felt every year of it.

In bed at last, she lay on her side with her eyes squeezed shut and wondered if she would have the dream again tonight. Oddly enough, she'd had it less frequently since Faith moved to Prospect Street. She wasn't sure, but she thought it had to do with the improvements Faith was making. She loved watching the house come alive again, although she hadn't expected to feel this way. She had expected the house to be a painful reminder of the worst moment in her life. Instead, as she watched Faith cope with the renovations, she found herself remembering the excitement she'd felt as a young wife fixing up her first home.

That had been long ago, of course. She wasn't usually given to reminiscences, because most often they were shackled with guilt. Now she thought of a time when the house was newly hers and Joe was newly hers, as well. She hadn't been sixty-six forever. Once she had been twenty-six, filled with energy and confidence, a young woman who had chosen her husband from an impressive list of suitors. She had been enthusiastic about life and sure of love.

How long ago that had been.

Lydia chose slender pink tapers to grace the table where she and Joe would eat their first meal together since their return from a brief honeymoon in Bermuda. She polished the sterling candlesticks, despite the fact that they hadn't had time to tarnish since the April wedding. She had visited a flower vendor on Wisconsin Avenue and carefully chosen six pink-and-white peonies, and now she arranged them in a Czech crystal vase with greenery from what remained of her grandmother's garden.

Their wedding china, creamy white with thin borders of silver and gold, rested on a pale avocado linen tablecloth her college roommate had given them, and the new silver place settings with the delicate shell-shaped handles rested on cream-colored napkins from one of Joe's aunts.

Early June in Georgetown was definitely summer. Today the temperature had soared unexpectedly to ninety and the air practically sizzled. She had almost forgotten about summers here, how they could wilt even the most stalwart. As a child she had lived in

Bombay and later in Samoa. She knew heat and humidity intimately, but she'd forgotten that sometimes Washington felt like the tropics, too.

The old row house was used to the heat. The walls were thick enough to shield the inhabitants from some of it. Architects knew how to design houses in the nineteenth century. High ceilings, so the heat had somewhere to go. Windows that mirrored each other to encourage drafts.

She wanted to install air-conditioning, but there hadn't been time to find contractors and get bids. As soon as she and Joe had returned from Bermuda, Joe had flown off on a fact-finding mission to Cuba. He hadn't been in Congress long enough to be chosen for an important mission like this one, but Joe was a bona fide war hero, a man who had risked his own life at Inchon and proved his stake in a strong, Communist-free America. So of course he had to go, because the Cuban trip was such a feather in his cap.

Lydia was so proud of him, but she had been lonely as she set up housekeeping. From Cuba Joe had flown to Norfolk, then on to Roanoke and Richmond on a short speaking tour of his home state. Travel and campaigning were part of his job, and Lydia understood that. She was just thrilled he was finally coming home tonight.

In the weeks while her new husband was away, she'd struggled to ready the house. She knew Joe didn't really like the row house, despite the fact that some people considered Georgetown to be the fashionable place for politicians. She supposed he appreciated the windfall. The house had been presented to Lydia on a silver platter after her grandmother's death. How many young congressmen started careers without the normal worries of where to live and how to afford it? Still, Joe was simple and straightforward, and the narrow tree-shaded streets of Georgetown, with their quirky charm, seemed foolish to him.

She smiled fondly. Joe was the kind of man who would prefer to see efficient modern high-rises on this spot, like the ones going up across the river. If he had his way, he would bulldoze Georgetown to the ground, although he was much too good a politician ever to say so.

She moved her plate one-tenth of an inch to the right and went into the kitchen to finish the dinner preparations. On their honeymoon she'd discovered that Joe's tastes in food were simple, too. He'd been raised on country ham, corn bread and beans, like most of his Southern Virginia constituents. What was good enough for the people who elected him was good enough for Joe. She found his food choices amusing, but she'd set about to reform him.

Tonight, for their reunion dinner, she'd fixed beef stroganoff, using the finest cut the local butcher offered. What was stroganoff, after all, except steak and gravy? She had cooked green beans— longer than she liked—but now she made a sauce of butter and blanched almonds to serve over them. She had Parker House rolls, and for dessert, slices of pound cake to serve with fresh strawberries.

Joe would be impressed.

She was also certain he would be impressed by everything she'd done to the house. She had culled her grandmother's antiques, saving the things that were valuable or that she just couldn't part with. Then she had mixed in the best pieces from the apartment she lived in before marrying Joe, and a few good pieces that Joe possessed from his family home.

She had stripped away Violet's heavy, faded drapes and bought inexpensive substitutes right off the shelf at Woody's. Maybe the bachelor Jack Kennedy had arrived at his first Georgetown house with the Kennedy family cook, but not everyone serving in Congress had a family retainer and a bottomless checking account.

Lydia had hoped to finish repapering the kitchen before Joe arrived home, but the job was harder than she'd expected. She was almost ready to strip off what she'd managed to put up and paint the kitchen a bright lemon-yellow. She would enjoy that riotous splash of color every time she walked through the door.

When everything was ready in the kitchen, she ran upstairs to change into her favorite blue sheath and stick a few more hairpins in the French twist her hairdresser had crafted that afternoon. Like everything else in the capital, her hair was wilting, despite heavy clouds of hair spray, but she still looked cool and unruffled. On the event of her engagement to Joe, the *Post* society columnist had compared Lydia's blond, patrician looks to Princess Grace. Life was wonderful.

The front door opened while she was still upstairs. She smiled, glad that she could make an entrance on the stairwell. Before she went to meet her husband, she straightened her skirt and adjusted the gold chain with the teardrop pearl that Joe had given her on their wedding day.

Joe was standing at the bottom of the steps when she made her appearance. His shaggy brows shot nearly to his hairline when he saw her coming toward him. He wasn't a man who smiled much—that was one of the first things she'd noticed about him. But his scowl had grown on her over the months of their courtship. When he did smile, the effect was startling.

"Congressman Joseph Huston, I presume?" She stopped to pose a few steps above him. "To what do I owe this pleasure?"

"You look lovely, Lydia. Good enough to eat."

Since that was the way she planned to end the evening, the comment was promising. "And you look like a man who needs some iced tea and a kiss."

He held out his arms, and she gave up her pose and leapt into them.

Minutes later, he stepped away from her. "I've ruined your makeup."

"I don't care. You go up and change, and I'll fix it. I'll have your tea ready when you come down."

The glasses were sweating by the time he returned. He looked okay in a suit, but better in casual clothing, since he was built like his farmer ancestors. He had changed into a striped Oxford shirt and neatly pleated gray pants and loafers. He had combed his hair, but his cowlick had already regathered the troops for another assault.

Joe wasn't handsome. No one would ever dare accuse him of such a thing. But he had strong features that announced he was a man to rely on, and the broad shoulders and stocky physique to second the nomination. In just a few short years she had lost her mother and father and her grandparents, but in her hour of need, Lydia had found Joe.

With a pert smile, Lydia handed him his tea. "I put lots of sugar and lemon in it, and some mint from my grandmother's garden. Maybe I can put it back to rights before it's hopeless."

He took three large swallows before he responded. "I hope that's not your first priority."

"No, there's more to do inside. This wallpaper, for instance." She grimaced. "I'm sorry about it. It's harder than I expected. I may take it down and paint."

He looked as if he was biting back a comment, unusual enough to make her curious. "Joe? You haven't said a thing about the changes I've made so far."

"I haven't really had time, have I?"

She lifted the lid off the stroganoff. "You look around while I get dinner on the table. Tell me what you think."

When he left the kitchen, she added the sour cream, then ladled the stroganoff into a serving dish. The noodles were just tender enough, and she drained them and put them in another. The string beans went into a third; then she carried the dishes into the dining room.

"I expected you to get rid of this old table." Joe was squinting at her table setting.

"It's mahogany. Once I've done a little refinishing it'll be gorgeous."

"I don't like these old things. This is the twentieth century."

She was surprised at the edge to his voice, but she put it off as exhaustion. "Darling, this is Georgetown. It's chock-full of history. The antiques blend with the house and neighborhood. Chrome and Naugahyde would hardly do here, would they?"

She was disappointed he hadn't noticed how lovely the table looked, but she was philosophical. Men went out in the world to slay dragons, and when they returned, they were still wielding their little swords. A woman's job was to calm and domesticate them again. Some days it took longer than others.

She tried to tease away some of his bad mood. "Besides, Joe, you're always talking about the way things are moving too fast, the way we need to take stock and remember the values of previous generations. Just think of the antiques that way."

"I suppose if *you* like them…."

"Me? I like my husband, and I just want him to be happy."

That seemed to soften him a little. When everything was on the table, he pulled out her chair and seated her. She passed him each serving dish first, only taking her share when he'd finished. From under her eyelashes she watched him take his first bite of the stroganoff. And she saw the distaste flicker across his features. He chewed and swallowed, but he didn't take another bite. He moved on to the green beans.

"You don't like the stroganoff?" She couldn't imagine such a thing. Her father had wheedled the recipe out of a chef at the Mayflower Hotel. Harold Charles had complained it was harder to get the recipe than to get concessions from Joseph Stalin after World War II.

Joe looked pained. "I don't like mushrooms. I despise them."

"My goodness. I had no idea. You never told me."

"It's not exactly a conversational opener, Lydia."

"Well, we're married now, Joe. I have to know these things. Maybe you'd better make a list."

He held up a fork of green beans and glowered. "I don't like nuts in my vegetables."

"That's just a few almonds, darling. For flavor."

"The string beans have plenty of flavor, thanks."

Her joy in the meal, in the table setting, in his return, was fast disappearing. "Well, can you pick out the things you don't like?"

He set down his fork. "That would be about everything."

Tears sprang to her eyes. "I worked hard on this meal. I wanted to make it special."

He seemed to think better of his behavior. He took a deep breath and picked up his fork. "I know you worked hard. Maybe I just need to work a little harder learning to eat something different."

She blinked away the tears and concentrated on finishing the food on her plate, which now seemed to have as much flavor as cardboard.

"So, what happened to the drapes?" Joe took a big gulp of iced water. He was taking a gulp after every bite.

"They were old and faded. That heavy fabric didn't let in any light, and I like to watch the world go by. Besides, these row houses can be so gloomy."

"The whole world can see us now."

"At most they'll see shadows moving behind the curtains."

"I'm in Congress. I don't want anyone knowing what I do and whom I do it with."

She looked up. "Joe, if anyone important comes here to see you, they'll have to get out of a car and walk to the front door. They'll be in plain view. Once they're inside, a shadow behind a curtain is nothing."

"What if somebody wants to harm me or a visitor? They'll know exactly where we are every minute."

She pushed her chair back and threw her napkin on the table. "Then *you* choose curtains. Okay? You go to the store and choose them or, better yet, get some World War II blackout curtains at the Army-Navy surplus store. And buy some new furniture you like while you're at it. Nothing I've done so far has pleased you. What's the point of continuing?"

"Don't get hysterical. For heaven's sake, I was merely making a comment about security."

"And about mushrooms and mahogany and nuts in your vegetables. Well, nuts to you!" She got up, grabbed her plate and stormed into the kitchen.

At the sink, she stood with her head bowed. A rotating fan on the counter ruffled tendrils of hair languishing at her neckline. One flap of loose wallpaper scraped the wall every time the fan spun in its direction, keeping time as her tears splashed against the porcelain.

She straightened when the worst was over and began to scour the pots and pans. She worked so ferociously that she didn't hear Joe until he was right behind her.

"You're overreacting."

She supposed that was his idea of an apology. "You haven't said one nice thing about the work I did."

"I'm a congressman. I live in the public eye. We're not just any young couple setting up housekeeping. There are standards we have to adhere to."

She faced him. She didn't even care that her mascara was probably running down her cheeks. "I am the daughter of an ambassador, Joe. Don't you think I learned about standards? Two of the first things Daddy taught me were never to be cruel to other people, and

never, never, to believe that my way was the only way to do anything."

"Then you'll agree that this time, your way isn't working."

She couldn't believe he had turned her words back on her, that
he had entirely missed her point. "What would you like me to do?"

"You need to consult a professional. Find someone to do the
work and make the decisions about what's proper here. I'll talk to
some of my colleagues and see if they have suggestions."

"A decorator? You want to spend money on a decorator?"

"Just for ideas. To put things to rights."

"I don't need anyone to tell me what's right. I have taste. I have
style."

"I want you to."

She considered saying no. What would he do then? How would
he punish her?

"Please?" He managed a smile. "It's a big job for a little woman.
You're going to have other things on your mind. We need to start
our family. I don't want you refinishing furniture and inhaling
paint fumes and climbing on ladders when you're pregnant."

At the moment she didn't want his children. She was too angry
and, worse, too hurt. She turned around and stared at the wall over
the sink.

Joe put his hands on her shoulders. "You've already done so
much to make the place nicer. Why not get a little help? You'll have
more time to do other things, socialize with some of the other
wives."

The house was hers. Hers! And she loved it in a way that no decorator ever would. She bit back the words. "I'll get some names,
and I'll consult. But only a consultation, Joe. The final decisions
about this house are mine. Are we agreed?"

"If you promise not to do the work yourself. You have more important things to think about. You do want a baby, don't you?"

She wondered why *he* did. Did he need someone in his home
who would be forced by sheer inferior size to obey his every command?

That thought scared her. She was blowing this out of proportion.
Joe was tired, and the house was hot. She had made a mistake

choosing stroganoff for dinner, so he was also hungry. But this was the man she'd chosen. This was the man she loved.

"I promise," she said tightly. "And yes, of course I want a baby. But maybe not right away. I want to feel settled first."

He rubbed the tops of her arms. "Then let's get settled. Make some calls tomorrow, okay?" He forced her to turn around. "Do I see strawberries?"

"And pound cake." She lifted her chin. "You probably don't like that, either."

"Two of my favorite things. I can't wait." He leaned over and kissed her.

She let him, but the joy in it was gone.

 19

On Monday evening, with thunder booming in the distance and raindrops splattering the sidewalks, Faith placed the telephone receiver in its cradle and stared blankly ahead.

Alex came into the room and tapped her on the shoulder to remind her where she was. "What are you looking at? There's nothing on that wall."

"Not even a decent paint job." Faith snaked an arm around her son's waist and captured him for a hug. "How would you like to spend a little time showing me how to buzz around the Web? It's not storming hard enough to turn off the computer, is it?"

"You?"

She couldn't blame him. Within the family, she was notorious for her disinterest in technology. She had an e-mail address she never checked, but only because David had insisted.

"Do you know what people will pay for a history of their house? Hundreds, sometimes even thousands, of dollars."

Alex scrunched up his nose. "That's a lot more than I make pulling ivy."

She supposed the day was coming when her son would permanently scrunch his nose at the thought of minimum wage. "I'm thinking maybe I ought to consider getting into the house-history business instead of looking for a clerical job. I've called four firms across the country to find out what they charge. If I was good at it, eventually I could probably support us."

"That's why you want to check out the Web?"

"Exactly, you brilliant boy." She squeezed one final time and released him. "I don't know even a tenth what I need to, but I can learn. Do you have time now?"

Alex looked as if she'd handed him a personal key to the pearly gates.

As the storm drew closer, she made a brief acquaintance with the Internet. With Alex and Scavenger's help, she swept from one historical site to another, discovered and ordered books on research, and perused the archives of list servers and bulletin boards.

An hour later she pushed her chair away from Alex's desk. "This is amazing. Where have I been?"

"Cooking."

She glanced at him, hoping he was kidding, but he wasn't. "I guess not having a kitchen's been a good thing, huh?"

"Are we ever going to have one again?" He sounded as nostalgic as an eleven-year-old could.

"We're getting close. The cabinets are almost ready to install." She saw skepticism in the twist of his lips. "Really."

"Maybe you could make chicken and dumplings someday."

"First thing on my list." She got to her feet. "I'm going to have to buy a computer, but I guess I can deduct it as a business expense. And I'll need one with some zip."

"You mean a zip drive?"

She had no idea what she meant. "Something that moves fast, like yours. The last time I used a computer everything took forever. I didn't have the patience for it."

"If we get DSL or cable modem, I can network our computers so I can use it, too. And if you buy the biggest computer available, it won't go out of date for at least a few months."

He made that sound like a good thing. *She* made a face.

"I could make a list of what you need." His stubby fingers flexed, then flexed again, over the keyboard. Nostalgia was gone. He was looking toward the future.

"Can you buy computers online?" When he nodded, she put him

in charge of getting prices. He went to work. Faith figured she wouldn't hear from him again until bedtime.

Downstairs in the kitchen, she surveyed the work she'd done. The carpenter would arrive later in the week to install the cabinets. Chicken and dumplings were on the way.

"And so am I." Faith had made valuable contacts since the days when she was a tow-headed campaign asset. She had presented bouquets of black-eyed Susans and purple coneflowers to Lady Bird Johnson. She had watched *The Cat From Outer Space* and *Superman* with Amy Carter in the White House movie theater. Perhaps she was no longer on the important party lists, but the same people who might not want an everyday reminder of the so-called scandal in her life would be happy to quietly hire her for research. All she had to do was reach for the brass ring.

Her arm extended. She smiled; she could feel the ring's cool, hard surface against her fingertips. But even if the ring had been real, she couldn't have seen it, because the lights had gone out.

"Mo-om!"

She heard the screech from upstairs and the sound of her son's bedroom door opening. "Mom, the power's off. Flip a switch!"

She doubted the sudden darkness had anything to do with circuit breakers. "Go in my room and look outside," she called up to him. "I bet the lights are off all up and down the street."

From her own vantage point she could see that the street lamp outside their window was dark. The storm hadn't seemed that close, but obviously it had caused damage somewhere in the capital.

Another door opened. Remy had been listening to music, and now the silence from her room was notable, but it didn't last long. "I can't do anything up here without electricity! This sucks."

"Come on down and we'll light candles. But be careful on the stairs." Faith went back into the pantry and rummaged until she found two cinnamon scented candles in apothecary jars that Alex and Remy had given her on her last birthday. She lit them and carried them out to the dining room table. The old house looked better. The fact that she hadn't yet settled on colors for the walls was less noticeable. Scarred woodwork was hardly worth mentioning.

Alex joined her. "Hey, this is neat."

"I'm sorry you couldn't finish what you were doing."

"I got some information. I printed up one page. I can finish later. Can I light some more candles?"

Alex located a box of tea lights, and Faith found juice glasses to shelter them. In five minutes shadows danced along the walls. Faith settled herself on the sofa, feet tucked up for the long haul.

"You're going to burn this shack to the ground." Remy descended the stairs to sit dejectedly on a bottom step.

Faith could almost feel her daughter's struggle. Remy had nothing to do except talk to her family, but it was an awful price to pay for entertainment.

Alex flopped down beside his mother. "Let's play charades, like we used to when Daddy—" He stopped himself, but not in time.

"Charades are stupid," Remy said. "Trying to make people guess what you're doing when you could just tell them."

"You don't know everything," Alex said.

In the days when the children had depended on her to entertain them, Faith would have pulled out board games or read to them from one of the classics, candlelight flickering across the pages like it must have when Candace and Jedediah Wheelwright moved into this house.

That inspired her. "Your great-great-great-grandmother lived in this house when it was brand-new, and she probably never had electricity. She made hats. Did I tell you that before? She had a little shop on Wisconsin. I bet in the evenings, when she closed up, she came home with boxes of feathers and tulle and beads, and all the other things good milliners needed, and sat in this very room making hats for wealthy ladies to wear. All with the help of candles and kerosene lamps."

"Hats?" Remy's tone made it clear what she thought. Hats were something you wore in winter, and only under duress.

"In those days no self-respecting lady went outside with her head uncovered. Women had yards of hair they piled under hats with a mountain of decorations on top."

"What kind of decorations?" Alex asked.

"Flowers and feathers. They used real birds—"

"Live ones?"

Faith was in her element. She told them how the Audubon Society had been formed to put a stop to the wholesale slaughter of herons and egrets.

"How do you know all this?" Despite herself, Remy sounded interested.

"I found a magazine article at the library."

Alex formed birds with his hands, and the shadows fluttered along the wall. "How come she made hats? Didn't her husband work? Did everybody work in those days?"

Faith was glad to share what she was learning. The strength and resourcefulness of her ancestors made her proud of a past she had never even glimpsed. Until now, she hadn't realized she was a descendant of strong, even remarkable, women.

"Well, I'd guess she started working so they could afford to build this house. Jedediah died young. They only had one child, your great-great-grandmother Violet, so I imagine Violet had to help her mother in the shop."

"I—" Alex's next question was cut off by knocking at the front door.

Reluctantly Faith uncurled her legs. "I hope Dottie Lee's all right. Maybe they need candles."

"Dottie Lee has candles everywhere," Alex said. "It set the right atmosphere when men came to visit her."

Faith wondered if Alex might just be spending too much unsupervised time with their neighbor.

By now the storm seemed to be centered right over them, and rain was gusting in iron-gray sheets across the road. She peeked through the sidelight to see her mother standing under an umbrella.

She flung open the door and ushered her inside. "What are you doing out in this?" She didn't give her mother time to answer. "Alex," Faith called, "come get your grandmother's umbrella and put it in the powder room sink."

He did, getting a brief wet hug from his grandmother. From the staircase Remy muttered a grudging hello. Obviously she thought things had been better before Lydia arrived. Faith had to agree. For a few minutes, at least, she and her children had almost seemed like a family again.

"There's a cold front coming through. We're going to have

storms for the rest of the week." Lydia handed her raincoat to Faith and kicked off Ferragamo pumps as if they were Dollar Store mules. She was wearing a dressy green knit skirt and shell with discreet beading along the neckline.

Faith hung the raincoat in the closet. "You're all dressed up. Were you on your way to a party?"

"I was *imprisoned* at a campaign party over on Dumbarton Street. The most boring affair I've ever been to. Your father's still there, shoring up support for his assignment to the finance committee."

"You sneaked out?"

Lydia smiled. "The lights went out and so did I. I told the hostess I had to come and see if you and the children were all right. I'd much rather spend the storm with my family."

Faith was surprised and touched. "Does Dad know you're gone?"

"He expects me to work one half of the room while he works the other. We rarely see each other. Maybe he won't even notice."

Faith doubted that. Joe Huston noticed everything.

"So what did I interrupt?" Lydia sounded interested.

Faith led her mother to the most comfortable armchair in the living room. "We were just talking about Candace Wheelwright. I was telling the children about her millinery shop."

Faith expected Lydia to change the subject, as she usually did at any mention of the past, but her mother surprised her. "How do you know about that?"

Faith was stuck. She didn't want to tell her mother about her research, because the history was a surprise. She settled on a half-truth. "I was looking up that garden tour you mentioned."

"My grandmother used to tell me stories about the hats she helped her mother make."

"Can you remember any of them?"

Lydia curled her stockinged legs under her, much the way Faith was recurling hers on the sofa. She looked younger in the candlelight. Or maybe it was simply that she looked at home, as if she really belonged here. "I do remember one story."

"Mom says they used real birds on the hats." Alex hadn't moved beyond this indignity.

"The story I remember's about fruit. My grandmother was about your age, Remy, when her mother came down with some illness. Unfortunately, Candace had promised a hat to the vice president's wife."

"Who was the vice president?" For the moment, at least, Remy forgot to sound disgruntled.

"Lord knows. We'd have to look that up. Wasn't McKinley president about then?"

"I could find out in a few seconds on the computer," Alex said. "If we had electricity."

Faith knew she was watching something unusual unfold here. Her mother had settled in as if she were a real part of their family life. She hadn't intruded, after all. She was enhancing what they had begun. "So what did Candace do?" Faith encouraged her.

"She told my grandmother she would have to make the hat. The vice president's wife planned to wear it at a garden party celebrating some new trade agreement with South America. I can't remember the details. I just remember that bananas were involved, and the vice president's wife wanted a fruit salad sitting on her head."

Remy giggled, a sound Faith hadn't heard in months. "So Violet had to design a fruit salad for her very first solo experience?" Faith said.

"Exactly. Only she was much too enthusiastic. Her mother had ordered a large selection of wax fruit, but Violet couldn't choose. So she used a little of everything. When she finished, the hat was so heavy the brim couldn't hold the weight. The vice president's wife came in for a fitting and the hat collapsed, raining fruit on her lap and poor Violet's feet."

"That's too funny." Remy was laughing out loud now. "I know how I'd feel."

Lydia smiled, obviously pleased. "Of course Violet burst into tears, but after the shock wore off, the woman started to laugh. She was still laughing when she left, but she told poor Violet she would be back the next day to try on the hat again, only this time, she wanted half a helping."

"That's wonderful." Faith was delighted her mother had remembered the anecdote. After a little research into vice presidential wives, it would go into the history. "And the hat was finished and Candace recovered?"

"Candace lived another twenty years or so. And the hat was a success, although Violet claimed the owner was annoyed by bees every time she wore it."

After everyone had another laugh, the room fell into a comfortable silence. Faith only broke it when Alex began to squirm. "I did discover a little about that garden tour."

Lydia settled deeper into her chair. "Well, tell us. I need an excuse not to go back out in that rain."

"Nobody elected *you*. Let Dad earn the family income by himself for a change."

Lydia smiled a little. "I like the sound of that."

"You were right about the tour. I found two brief mentions in old Georgetown papers, as well as a mention in the *Post*."

"I didn't realize you were going to do so much work."

Faith backpedaled. "It just took a visit to the library, that's all. One day in April of 1941, some percentage of Washington D.C. came tramping through our house, down the basement steps and out into our garden."

"Just to see somebody's yard?" Remy clearly found that hard to believe.

Lydia tried to put it in perspective. "It must have been quite an honor. My grandmother was an ordinary woman, from ordinary working people. Although she did have an extraordinary romance with my grandfather."

When Remy looked interested, she continued. "Picture this. Violet, who has no father, no brothers and very little contact with men, goes into the millinery shop to open up one day when she's only seventeen. She's behind the counter when this fabulously handsome man comes inside with an equally beautiful woman on his arm."

Remy leaned forward. "How do you know he was fabulously handsome?"

"I've seen photographs. I probably have them packed away somewhere."

"Mother, you know what a shame that is, don't you?" Faith said.

Lydia waved her hand. "I'll find them and give them to you. They would look nice in the stairwell, wouldn't they? Anyway, the handsome man was there to buy a hat for his fiancée, a woman from one of Georgetown's finest families. He was a scholar and teacher named James Atkins, already known at that time for a biography of Lincoln. There was nothing scholarly about his reaction to my grandmother. He fell madly in love with her right then and there, broke off his engagement, and married Violet six months later. Quite a scandal."

"This part's boring," Alex said.

Lydia reached over and patted his knee. "Okay, we'll skip ahead to the guts and glory. Do you know anything about World War I?"

"It came before World War II."

"Brilliant," Remy said. "And I liked the other part."

Lydia shot her a smile. "James, my grandfather, enlisted and refused a job in administration. Unfortunately, he was gassed in France and nearly died. They sent him home, but even though he lived many years, he was very frail. He became something of a recluse. In the meantime, my grandmother was worried about going out to work and leaving him alone, so she turned to the only skill she had. She taught piano in this living room on that piano."

"That wasn't her only marketable skill." Faith had been taking notes in her head. Now she added her piece of the puzzle. "Not quite."

"No?"

"Violet grew potted flowers in her garden to sell. Potted bulbs in the spring. Annuals in the fall. She became well-known in Georgetown's west end. That's how she got on the garden tour. The little snippets I found called her Violet Green Thumb. The local society ladies came to this house for their plants."

"Grandmother worked all the time," Lydia said. "I don't remember the plants. Maybe she stopped selling them once the country went to war, but I do remember she was never still."

"There are a lot of role models in our family." Faith addressed Lydia, but she hoped Remy was still listening. "Including your mother, who traveled all over the world and helped your father represent the government."

Lydia didn't respond. Faith wondered what her mother was

thinking. Was she wondering how her own descendants would see her? She'd survived her daughter's kidnapping, but at what price?

And what would Remy's children and grandchildren say about Faith herself? That she had let herself grow bitter after a divorce? That she had retreated into self-pity, or that she had picked up the pieces, like her ancestors, and gone on to find happiness? She had never quite realized just how much she wanted it to be the latter.

"I think this discussion calls for a field trip," Lydia said at last, rising from her chair and picking up a candle. "Would you like to see something Candace left behind?"

"Another signature?" Alex was already on his feet. "I haven't found the one in the garden yet."

"I can't surprise you no matter how hard I try." Lydia started up the steps past Remy, and in a moment there was a parade of Bronsons behind her. She led them to Faith's room.

"After Jedediah passed away, Candace wouldn't sleep in this room anymore. Too many memories, I think. Instead she made it her workshop. This is where she worked on hats in the evenings and on Sundays. My grandmother told me that Candace sat right here." Lydia gestured to the center of the room. "At a table where she could see out the window. She was watching for Jedediah to come home."

"But he was dead." Alex was frowning. "Was she crazy?"

"No, but when he was alive, she would always change her clothing and fix her hair before he was due home in the evenings. So she was usually in this room, watching for him. She said that seeing Jedediah walk up Prospect Street was the best part of her day, and after he died, she tried to hold on to those moments. She said it made her feel close to him."

Faith realized she was about to cry. She cleared her throat. "I bet I know where she carved her name." She went to the window and knelt so she could look beneath the wide ledge. "Here it is."

Remy was the first to join her. She knelt beside Faith and looked up. "Because she spent so much time watching for her husband here?"

"I'm sure."

Remy traced the script with her fingertip, faded with time and never carved by an expert to begin with. Simple Victorian graffiti. A love poem.

Alex joined them, and Faith made room for him. "Is your name anywhere, Grandmother?"

"No, it's not."

Faith was glad when another knock sounded on the front door so that the silence didn't go on any longer. Where would Lydia have left her name? On the floor under the crib where her first daughter had been put for her only nap on Prospect Street?

"We don't have this many visitors when it's sunny." Alex leapt up to get the door and ran down the steps full tilt. "Hey, it's Pavel."

Faith glanced at her mother and saw that Lydia looked interested. The two hadn't met. Faith resisted the urge to finger comb her hair. She padded down the steps in her bare feet and arrived at the bottom just in time to watch Pavel shake like a water spaniel. Alex already had his umbrella and was on the way to the powder room to set it next to Lydia's.

"Hey there. Did you get lonely in the dark?" The moment she said the words, she realized how they could be construed.

He grinned, obviously construing them just that way. "I was worried about you and the kids. It looks like the power's going to be out for some time. Some major glitch. I wasn't sure you were prepared, so I brought candles and matches and an extra flashlight." He lifted a plastic grocery bag in testimony.

"That was thoughtful." She stepped aside so that Lydia could finish her descent. "I don't think you've met my mother." She made the introduction.

For a moment neither Pavel nor Lydia said a word. Lydia stood still, examining him. Pavel was the first to move. He came forward and stopped just in front of her. Lydia extended her hand, and they shook and murmured politely.

Pavel looked around the room. "These old houses were meant to be softly lit. It's lovely this way."

"Feel free to join us," Faith said. "But I warn you, we're telling old family stories."

"Thanks, but I have to get home. I'm charting a leak in one of the upstairs bedrooms."

"Pavel's restoring his house all by himself," Faith explained to Lydia. "You should see what he's done."

"Can I see?" Alex said. "Can I come over sometime?"

"You and Remy have a standing invitation," Pavel said.

Remy sniffed.

The door rattled again, the pounding even louder this time. Faith slipped past Pavel to answer it. Joe Huston glowered under a wide black umbrella. "Faith." He gave a short nod.

She motioned him inside, taking and shaking his umbrella as he stepped past her. She gave up on the powder room sink and set it against the wall.

Joe didn't move any farther than the entryway rug. "Lydia, our hostess told me I would find you here. I felt awkward staying, since you'd already taken off."

"I hardly 'took off.' I just wanted to be sure Faith and the children were all right."

Faith introduced Pavel, and the two men shook quickly. Joe managed a gruff hello to his grandchildren.

Faith took Joe's arm to propel him farther into the room. "I'm glad you're here. Now you can see what I've done since the last time you visited."

"Not tonight, Faith." He didn't shake her off, but she felt his whole body tense, and he didn't move. His feet were firmly planted. She dropped his arm, and he seemed to realize he had been abrupt. "Your mother and I need to get home. I'll come for a tour another time. When there's enough light to see."

"We drove separately," Lydia reminded him. "I'll be along in a little while, Joe, when the storm lessens."

"No, it's easier for Samuel if we come in together."

"You can tell him to expect me soon."

For a moment he looked as if he planned to continue the argument; then he shrugged. "I'll see you at home, then."

Lydia looked as if she doubted that very much.

Faith opened the door and handed her father his umbrella. He had destroyed the fragile warmth of family and memories. For too brief a time the house had glowed with both. She was outraged for herself and for the others.

"Come when you can stay," she said politely. She lowered her voice so the others couldn't hear. It shook with emotion. "And only if you're in a better mood. This is the second time you've been rude to me in my own house."

The moment she said it, she couldn't believe she had. He stiffened, but she didn't trust herself to say more. She stepped back inside and firmly closed the door.

 20

The Georgetown Regional Library opened every morning at ten, and for the next week Faith was waiting on the doorstep every day. There was no longer any point to working on the house after the children went to school. The contractor arrived early every morning to install cabinets and oversee deliveries. Faith was only in the way, so she escaped.

She had put off reading about her sister's kidnapping long enough. Now she knew more about distant ancestors than she did about the people closest to her. Candace and Violet were interesting enough, but Hope had affected her life most of all.

On Tuesday Faith asked Dorothy for the scrapbook. She read until noon, jotting questions and making notes. She was surprised by how much information was available. The scrapbook was a day-by-day account of the kidnapping and investigation. She knew the basics, but she discovered right away that there was much more to the story. She was drawn into the pace of the search, the suspects, the alibis, the theories, even the personalities of the reporters, who had obviously been required to turn out stories every day, whether there was news to report or not.

By Friday she had more questions than answers. She could have asked one of her parents for clarification, but both avoided the topic of Hope's kidnapping. Lydia shunned it because it was painful. Joe

shunned it because his daughter's disappearance was a sign of personal failure.

The kidnapping hadn't been Joe's finest hour. Even though
Hope's abduction had brought him untold publicity, a sympathetic
outpouring of votes in his next election and, eventually, a seat in
the Senate, Joe was still the man who had allowed his baby daughter to slip through his fingers. Besides, Joe was a man who nursed
grudges, and until she apologized for her comment during the
storm, Faith was persona non grata.

As she worked, Faith made lists of the investigators mentioned
in the scrapbook, and on Friday afternoon she called both the FBI
office and the District police to see if any of the men involved were
still on the payroll. The long shot didn't pay off. Everyone prominent in the case had retired, transferred or quit long ago. Even
though the case was technically still open, it was inactive. That left
ordinary people who might remember details the newspapers had
left out, people who weren't too emotional to talk.

And *that* boiled down to Dottie Lee Fairbanks.

Although Dottie Lee always found reasons to turn down invitations to their house, Faith and Alex went to hers for tea almost every
Wednesday. Faith had quickly grown fond of both Dottie Lee and
Mariana. She knew from tidbits fed to her with the scones and
lemon curd that a chosen number of Washington's elite had been
regular visitors of Dottie Lee's through the years. From a few more
well-placed hints Faith guessed that someday, perhaps after her
death, Washington was in store for another in a long series of scan-
dalous memoirs. Over the years Dottie Lee had collected stories
and information the way some women collected quilts or Fabergé
eggs.

Now Faith took scarlet roses she'd bought on her library trip and
knocked on Dottie Lee's door. Alex had joined a science club at
school and was taking a field trip to the Smithsonian. Remy had
permission to spend the afternoon with Billie. That gave Faith at
least an hour before either of them came home.

Dottie Lee answered, and the pleasure on her face was enough
to convince Faith that more impromptu visits were called for.

"I couldn't resist these." Faith held the roses out as Titi took a ceremonial nip at her ankles. "They're beautiful *and* they're fragrant. I thought they'd look lovely on your mantel."

Dottie Lee buried her nose inside the bouquet. "Hush, Titi. They're lovely. Simply lovely. Come in."

Faith stepped around the yapping Chihuahua. Once she was inside, the dog took off for parts unknown, her job completed.

"You didn't come simply to bring me roses. You came for some of my Earl Grey."

"I'd love a cup. The electricity is off at my house again. They're redoing something in the basement."

"Your kitchen will be ready soon?"

"With luck the countertops will be finished Monday morning." Faith lowered herself to a rosewood love seat with dragon-head arms while Dottie Lee asked Mariana to make tea. Then Dottie Lee joined her.

Faith knew better than to pretend this was strictly a social visit. Dottie Lee had too few years left to waste even a minute, and she'd said so numerous times.

"I've spent a lot of the week at the library reading about my sister's kidnapping. They have an entire scrapbook devoted to it."

Dottie Lee pulled her chair a little closer. "This is a town that relishes scandal and tragedy. It's something in the water."

Faith wasn't sure she was kidding. "My mother and father rarely talk about Hope's disappearance. They told me just enough so I wouldn't be surprised if I was asked about it."

"And you've never investigated on your own?"

Faith wondered how she could have been so apathetic. "I learned to avoid controversy, and nothing was more controversial than the kidnapping. It was the most important event in my parents' lives and the one thing they never spoke of."

"That makes it the most important event in your life, as well."

"You mean next to discovering the man I'd been sleeping with for fifteen years was gay?" Faith wondered if by not marrying and only taking lovers Dottie Lee had shown extraordinarily good sense. "I guess this is my way of explaining why I know so little."

"And why you're here?"

"I'm wondering what you can tell me."

"You're asking an old woman who hasn't spoken of this in years to dredge up memories?"

Faith leaned forward. "You don't fool me. You remember everything. And the kidnapping is going to be a chapter in your memoirs, isn't it?"

Dottie Lee's smile was flirtatious. "What memoirs would those be?"

"The ones you mentioned a couple of weeks ago. I have a feeling you could set the city on its ear if you chose."

"I don't choose to...in my lifetime." Dottie Lee inclined her head, attired this afternoon in a 1920s spray of rhinestones and jet to hold back her white hair.

"And after you're gone?"

"You might well be sorry you knew me. Not that you'll be mentioned. I've decided to leave you strictly out of it."

"You considered putting me in?"

"Boring old you, dear? Of course. Your story's as juicy as they come, getting juicier all the time."

"Dottie Lee!"

"I said I won't, and I won't." She paused for effect. "However, your parents are a different story, aren't they?"

Faith had been guessing about the book, using it to lead Dottie Lee back into her memories. Now she was appalled. "Are you going to destroy my father's career?"

"Will I need to, do you suppose? Or will Joe manage that on his own before I pass away? He's really not a very good senator. Oh, he's intelligent enough, and heaven knows he was the alpha male in his political litter. But he runs on vitriol, does our Joe. And eventually someone will notice and do away with him. Hopefully at the polling place."

Faith could think of a number of political leaders who seemed to run out of a desire to get even. She couldn't dismiss Dottie Lee's words, although she'd never thought of her father that way. "What could you say that would destroy his career?"

Dorothy lifted one penciled brow in what was obviously a question. "Why should I tell you?"

"Are you bluffing?" Faith asked.

"It's quite possible. I'm an old woman and need amusement."

Faith knew she'd hit a dead end on the topic of Joe. "Amuse yourself, then. Tell me what you remember about the kidnapping."

"Tell me what you find most interesting."

Mariana came into the room with a tea tray, and she and Faith chatted a moment. Faith waited until she left before she answered.

"All right, there were several things I've discovered that surprised me. I knew that a handyman, an immigrant named Dominik Dubrov, was questioned and released for lack of evidence. I knew that a lot of people thought he was probably the kidnapper, despite the fact that he had an alibi."

"So that's what you knew. What *didn't* you know?"

"I never realized he had actually worked in my parents' home. Not until recently." She told Dottie Lee about the note she and Remy had found.

"He certainly worked there," Dottie Lee said.

"The papers made that clear, and they claimed he had a key. Obviously that was important to the police, and that's why they questioned him."

"Of course it was important," Dottie Lee said. "The key is the reason Dominik was under suspicion. But then he had a key to my house, as well, and several of the other neighbors."

That was news. "To yours?"

"Dominik was a lovely man. Strong, intelligent—although woefully undereducated. He escaped the Soviet Union with his parents when he was a teenager, and they managed somehow to find their way here. By then he was too old for school, and his command of the English language was poor, but he was a master with his hands. I've never seen anyone do such fine work. An old-world craftsman." She shook her head sadly. "His ilk no longer exists."

"So he did work for you, as well?"

"Oh, yes, and for several other neighbors. That's how he made his living. He had a young friend, a cousin of sorts, named Sandor, who worked with him sometimes. Sandor's family escaped from Hungary during the revolution, and between them they could do anything. Plumbing. Wiring. Fine woodworking. Masonry."

Faith was less interested in a catalogue of Dominik Dubrov's assets than an explanation of how he fit into the kidnapping. "Did my parents recommend him to you?"

"No, I'll tell you how it happened." Dottie Lee searched for the right words. Finally, she shrugged. "This isn't possible without telling you the whole truth. Your father drove your mother to hire Dominik."

Faith was trying to follow this. "How did my father figure in?"

"After your parents were married, your father insisted your mother fix up the house. Joe felt he had an image to live up to, and he wasn't certain Lydia could manage the work on her own. Lydia came to me and asked for suggestions. I thought Dominik would be the perfect choice. He could do the hardest part, but Lydia would make the decisions. Everyone would be happy."

"And were they happy with his work?"

"That's hard to say now, isn't it? I can tell you what I saw and heard, but not what anybody felt."

Faith knew Dottie Lee was hedging. "Why did he become a suspect? Only because he had access to the house?"

"That's quite a bit, wouldn't you say? There was no sign of a break-in. Somebody simply entered through the backyard, climbed the steps and entered the house. Then whoever it was swooped upstairs and grabbed your sister." Dottie Lee shrugged. For her, it was ancient history.

"My mother told me she was playing the piano. She never heard a thing. Maybe if Hope had cried, things would have been different." She considered that. "Maybe she *couldn't* cry."

"I'm sure the police considered that possibility."

Faith fought against the mental picture of an infant being lifted from her crib and muffled, perhaps smothered, so that the kidnapper could make an undetected escape.

"Dottie Lee, do you think Dominik Dubrov was the kidnapper?"

She didn't answer directly. "Dominik was right here in my house at the time the kidnapping took place. I'd had a leak in my plumbing. He came to repair it."

"You were his alibi? He was here the entire time?"

Dottie Lee hesitated. "Not quite."

"What do you mean?"

"He went out for supplies. He wasn't gone long. I estimated twenty minutes. It may have been thirty."

"Twenty minutes was long enough to kidnap my sister. She was right next door."

"Yes, but he returned with supplies in hand. The receipt was dated that day, although it wasn't time stamped the way it might have been in this day and age. But a clerk at the hardware store thought he remembered Dominik buying the supplies that afternoon about the time he left my house. Then there was the question of what he would have done with the baby after he kidnapped her."

"Given her to someone he'd made arrangements with in advance? Someone who was waiting nearby?"

"I suppose. But the police felt the alibi was good enough. He had no motive for taking Hope."

"One article claimed money was the motive. He was poor, with large medical bills. He had a young son with asthma who had been in and out of the hospital frequently."

"Yes, but remember, there never was a ransom demand. Not even before Dominik became a suspect. It took days for the police to get around to him, because everyone liked him so much no one considered pointing a finger in his direction."

"And the response is that Hope probably died during the kidnapping and whoever kidnapped her lost his nerve."

"There are many, many maybes."

"There must have been other suspects. A child doesn't simply disappear."

"I believe you watch too many movies. There really aren't as many brilliant detectives as Hollywood and Agatha Christie would have us believe."

"What did you think of the investigation?"

"Flawed. The authorities descended on the house like a cloud of locusts. If any evidence existed, they destroyed it in the first ten minutes."

"That's terrible."

"Youthful enthusiasm, for the most part. They wanted to catch the kidnapper. They knew he had to be somewhere in the vicinity. In the heat of the moment they tore the house and neighborhood apart. There was nothing of interest left when they'd finished."

"Dominik Dubrov..."

"Still?" Dottie Lee shook her head. "You're not ready to move on to other possibilities?"

"He committed suicide six months later. Wasn't that practically an admission of guilt?"

"People kill themselves all the time, Faith. It's an epidemic. Did every one of them kidnap a child?"

"Of course not, but—"

"The scandal destroyed Dominik. He was a good, decent man, with old-fashioned values. Even though the police never arrested him, the newspapers and local television stations tried and convicted him. They had very little else to discuss, of course, and they needed stories. Dominik probably had what in those days we called a nervous breakdown. He hung himself."

"You don't think he did it. That's clear."

"Have I said as much?"

"Not exactly."

"If you're really interested in what happened, settling for the most likely scenario is counterproductive. The police tried that, and they were unsuccessful."

Faith leaned forward. "Dottie Lee, do you know who took my sister?"

Dottie Lee met her gaze. "I haven't been asked that question since a rude young police lieutenant came into this house, sat on that very love seat and shook his finger at me."

"What did you tell him?"

"I told him what I'll tell you. I wasn't there. I saw nothing and heard nothing, and nothing I believe could ever be used as evidence, so why go on record?"

"Then you have some ideas?"

Dottie Lee picked up her teacup. "Everyone has ideas, dear, unless their brains have shriveled beyond repair. I predict you'll have a few yourself before this search is over."

 21

Except for paint and put-away, the kitchen was finished. While Alex worried the new Formica countertop with his fingernail, Faith admired everything from floor to ceiling.

"Alex, this means we can cook." Faith kissed the top of his curly head on her way to the sink. She couldn't resist turning on the water again. Running water, in her kitchen. It seemed like years. She'd grown so accustomed to doing their few dishes in the powder room that the tiny sink felt natural now.

"Tonight?"

"Nothing fancy. We still have to put things away." She saw his mouth droop. "Omelets? With bacon and English muffins?"

"How? We don't have any food."

"You know, there's such a thing as a grocery store." She tried the faucet again. She felt like Granny of the Beverly Hillbillies.

"It's kinda late." These days Alex always seemed to be on the verge of starvation; it was only five o'clock.

"Look, I'll run to the Safeway. You see which of these boxes is hiding our frying pans. And see if you can find the toaster and plug it in..." She looked around the room. "There." She pointed to the counter to the right of the refrigerator. "I'll be home in a jiffy. Find some plates. Get Remy to help." She grabbed her purse and a light jacket, and headed for the car.

At the grocery store she wound her way between cars and shopping carts, enthusiastically grabbing one as she passed. The new kitchen and all its gleaming potential beckoned.

"Faith?"

She had been concentrating so hard on not running over the rush hour crowd that she hadn't really seen the man she'd been trying to pass. She came to a stop beside him. "Pete?"

"What are you doing here?" he asked.

Pete Conley was a representative from the Tidewater area of Virginia. He had everything a politician needed, intelligence, charisma and a profile that suggested the younger Ronald Reagan. Several years earlier, his wife of twenty years had died in an accident on the Potomac, and after a year of mourning, Pete had emerged as Washington's most prestigious catch.

"I live in Georgetown now," she told him. She remembered vaguely that he did, as well.

"Faith, I'm sorry about..." He shrugged, the intelligent ending to his condolences.

"Me, too. How are you?" She forced herself not to peek at her watch or picture her pathetic, ravenous son.

"I get by. You know how it is."

If the gossip mill had any validity at all, he more than got by. She had always liked Pete. He was witty and compassionate, although a trace too political for her taste. She was sure that other women—most women, in fact—liked him, too.

"Losing someone you love is hard under any circumstances." She smiled to let him know she wasn't going to break down right next to the display of glistening McIntosh apples.

"Are you dating yet? That helps a little."

Her smile warmed a degree. "I guess I've made a stab at it."

They chatted about their families; then he moved a little closer. "May I call you?"

For a moment she simply stood there. Pete Conley wanted to call her? She was in jeans, and she hadn't touched up her makeup all day, because there was nothing to touch up. She hadn't even combed her hair before she took off for the store. She knew they called this the "Social" Safeway because of the abundance of young singles who shopped here, but until now, she hadn't thought that had relevance for her.

She recovered quickly. "Of course you can, Pete." She wondered if he wanted to talk about his wife. If he thought she, of all people, would understand his loss?

He had already pulled out his Palm Pilot. "What's your new phone number?"

She gave him the relevant details. "I'd better go. Alex is waiting for me. He's always hungry these days."

Pete had two grown daughters, and he nodded sagely. "Look, there's a cocktail party this Friday night at the French embassy. I know it's short notice, but I was going to take my sister, only she was called out of town. Would you come in her place? We don't have to stay long. Then we can go out to dinner."

When she hesitated, he moved closer. "Please say yes."

"Well, yes, then."

His smile widened. "Good. I'll call to let you know the time."

A little dazed, she made the appropriate response and continued on her way. Half an aisle later she analyzed what had happened. Pete Conley had asked her on a date and she had accepted. Pete was a friend, of course, and had been for years. She was replacing his sister, for heaven's sake. But still, there had been more to it than that. Her self-esteem might be hanging by threads, but she had all her faculties. He seemed interested in *her,* not just any warm female body on his arm. Her, despite lank hair and a bare face and jeans that were just a tiny bit tight these days.

More interesting was why she'd said yes. The reasons presented themselves. One, she wasn't dead yet. This was promising. Two, maybe it was time to find out if her reaction to Pavel Quinn was generic. Three, the chance to hold up her head in a gathering of her peers was too good to pass up.

Four, she might well need some of those very people in her corner if she started her own business. It was time everyone in D.C. knew she was more than David Bronson's ex-wife and Joe Huston's daughter. It was time they thought of her as someone they could willingly hire, someone who had survived betrayal and come out on the other side.

And she had.

Faith stood in the dairy aisle and realized she was smiling.

* * *

Over omelets, English muffins and ceremonial grape juice, Faith broached the idea of a shopping trip to her daughter. "I've been invited to a party at the French embassy. I need a dress. What would you say to helping me find one on Friday?" Both Alex and Remy had the day off.

There was a stunned silence, as if neither child could imagine their mother being invited to a party. Then Remy looked pained. "Like you don't have a closet full of dresses? Wear one of them. They all look pretty much like anything new you'd pick out, anyway."

"What a charming vindication of my taste."

"Taste? You dress like somebody's mom. Megan's mom wears tighter shorts than *I* do."

"I don't think tight shorts would be quite the thing at the embassy."

"You can be so lame."

Faith tried again. "Remy, you need some new clothes, too. We could have fun."

Alex spoke through a mouthful of omelet. "How come you didn't ask me?"

"Because you're a boy," Remy told him. "He's not invited, is he, Mom?"

Things were looking up. Faith could count on sibling rivalry as one of the few constants in her life. "Not because you're a boy, Alex. Because you hate shopping. Besides, you're going off with your dad for the day."

"Oh, yeah." He was mollified.

"So, what do you say?" Faith asked Remy. "The party's Friday night. A Friday afternoon shopping trip?"

"I don't have anywhere else to go."

By Friday Faith had asked herself a dozen times why she was going to the embassy with Pete. She had never liked formal gatherings. Yes, some of the country's finest citizens happened to be politicians. But at parties she could never shake the feeling she was surrounded by schools of tuxedoed sharks and the nasty little fish who fed off their leftovers. She knew what went on behind the cocktail chatter. The deals that were made, the reputations that were altered.

By the time Remy finally got ready for their shopping trip, Faith was on pins and needles. She wanted to have fun, perhaps put aside their animosities for the afternoon and resume—if only temporarily—what had been a good relationship. She'd never had to think about what to say to her daughter. Now every word needed a rehearsal.

Remy finally showed up wearing a pleated skirt that was too short and a shirt that was even shorter. Faith chose not to comment. "I thought we'd start on Wisconsin."

"You won't find anything you like there."

"Am I as stodgy as all that? I want something fun."

"Who are you going with, anyway? Grandmother? She won't let you in the car in something fun."

She told Remy about meeting Pete at the Safeway. Remy frowned, clearly not happy that her mother was going out with a man again. In a way Faith was relieved it wasn't just Pavel she objected to.

"His wife died, remember?" Faith said. "We've always been friends. Don't make more out of this than there is."

"You're going to face all those people? Every one of them knows."

Faith knew they were getting off on the wrong foot, but she couldn't let that go. "Nobody needs to be ashamed except the people who refuse to understand."

"Are you done?"

"For all the good it did, yes."

The two stared at each other, then Faith put her hand on Remy's shoulder. "Let's start again. Want to go to Wisconsin first and look around? If we don't find anything wonderful we'll drive over to Tyson's."

"I don't have anything else to do."

They walked up to Wisconsin in silence. Faith wondered where Billie was that day, since the two girls seemed inseparable, but asking produced a shrug. Last week Faith had insisted Remy bring the other girl home so she could form an impression. Billie, who seemed older than Remy but even less mature, had stayed the requisite hour, then taken off for her own house with Remy in tow. Faith didn't know what the two girls did at Billie's that was so much fun, but she was beginning to worry.

An hour and one new sweater for Remy later, they had shopped their way to a boutique with brightly colored dresses in the window. Faith took one look and started to move on, but Remy grasped the hem of her mother's sweater. "The orange dress. Take a look at it."

Faith backed up and squinted. She had never worn orange in her life. Peach, yes. Coral when she felt daring. But this orange was the original, the mother of all oranges, clear and fresh, a Popsicle on a hot summer afternoon. The dress itself was simply cut from a fine, silky cotton, but on the right body, it would be stunning.

"Have you ever worn that color?" she asked Remy. "Your hair's lighter than mine, but our skin tones are the same."

Remy's voice lost its edge; for the moment, anyway, she had forgotten they were at war. "I think you should try it on. You said you wanted something different."

The dress was certainly different. Not understated, which was Faith's usual preference. Not really classic, and certainly not dowdy. It exuded confidence and a quirky wit. It was everything she'd told Remy she wanted, and she was petrified.

"Mom..."

Faith knew that taunting tone. "Just the thing," she said, flinging open the door. "I'll give it a try."

"What *did* the wind blow in now?" The man who greeted them was well over six feet, with narrow shoulders and a body that looked like it would just stuff a tube sock. He had spiky bleached hair and black-rimmed glasses. He also looked ridiculously thrilled to see them.

"We, umm, saw the dress in the window. I thought I'd like to try it on."

The man appraised her, one finger resting against full lips. "Oh, honey, it's you, yes it is. The 'you' you were meant to be. What is that rag you're wearing?" He shook his head. "Does your mother dress you, poor thing?"

Faith burst into laughter. She should have been insulted, but every word he said dripped flamboyant sincerity. "Maybe I'll turn the job over to you."

"Oh God, make my day!" He began to bustle around the store, grabbing items off strategically placed racks. Faith was glad no one else was in the shop, since clearly she was going to be the sole focus of attention.

Remy watched the whole proceeding with her chin drooping to the hollow of her throat. Obviously the clerk, who must have swaggered proudly out of the closet many years before, was an entirely new phenomenon in her sheltered life. He caught sight of her and piled clothes in her arms. "Here, sweet thing, make yourself useful."

Faith watched the pile in Remy's arms growing. A rainbow-colored silk shawl, another dress of brilliant turquoise. Still another that was flesh-toned but a mixture of sheer stripes and opaque. That one wasn't even going to get an audition.

"Okay, scat now," he said, pointing toward a dressing room curtained in hand painted fabric. "Sweet thing, you go with her and make sure she tries them all on. Every single one, and my name is Ralph. Ask for me."

Remy found her voice. "You're the only person in the store." She took off for the dressing room as if propelled by hurricane force winds.

"Boo," Ralph said to Faith.

"Please. You don't scare *me*. The prices scare me."

"We sell second mortgages. Just try on the clothes for Uncle Ralphie."

An hour later Faith was still modeling dresses for Ralph, who tugged at hems and straightened zippers and unbuttoned the top two buttons of every garment that had them.

"What do you think, Remy?" he asked at last. By now the two were old friends, united in a desire to change Faith's image.

"The orange. Definitely the orange."

"Faithful?"

"The orange it is, then."

He rested his finger against his lips, where it most liked to reside. "Now the hair. You can't have the dress, darling, if you don't do something with the hair. It's the flaw in the ointment."

"Fly."

He looked down at his pants and pretended to zip them up. Then he looked up and winked. "Gotcha!"

Faith couldn't help smiling. "Well, I made an appointment to get it trimmed at five. I know it's a little long. I—"

"Where?"

"A place over near the Capitol where my mother goes. I—"

He wrapped his hands around his throat and began to choke.

"Bad idea?" she said.

"I'll call Mitch. I'll tell him he has to get you in this afternoon or I'll have to steal back my dress. Do you understand? You can't have it. You simply can't..." He was already dialing frantically.

Remy's eyes were wide. Faith imagined that confusion and continual reassessment on the part of his audience were part of Ralph's life drama.

Ralph began arguing with someone, then louder with the great Mitch himself. The phone call was abusive. Mitch's parentage was questioned, and finally Ralph hung up. "He had a sudden cancellation. He'll see you both right away. Remy, you have to go and show your mother how to be brave. You'll start to take after her if you don't."

Remy wrapped her hands around her throat the way Ralph had. He nodded sagely.

Faith was a little worried. If Mitch cut Ralph's hair, she was in trouble. "This Mitch, he's good? I don't want to look like a plucked chicken."

"Buy the dress, cut the hair, bite the bullet." He saluted. Then he went around the counter and started to ring up the dress.

Faith glanced at her daughter. Remy's eyes were shining. Faith realized that she didn't care what the afternoon was going to cost. For the moment, anyway, she had her daughter back.

They found their way to Mitch's salon, which was just down a side street. The interior was white on white. Only Mitch himself wasn't. He was as beefy as a football player with coal-black skin and one gold earring that dangled halfway to his shoulder. As two other stylists worked on customers behind him, he assessed Remy and Faith much as Ralph had.

"Highlights," he said without preface. "Don't you know you

need to go lighter? Highlights. Sweet Mother Mary, woman, why do you think you were born blond?" He came around the counter and lifted her hair unceremoniously in his hands. "Too much of this. Why so much? Little face, long hair. Bad idea." He dropped her hair and turned to Remy. "Better." He nodded. "Ready for something radical?"

"Me? Like what?"

He looked around the room, then strode across it to a display of pictures, poking a stubby index finger at one. "This."

Remy joined him. The haircut was short. Very short and just feathered over the nape, forehead and tops of the model's ears. Her eyes looked twice as big in contrast, and her cheekbones looked sharp enough to slice bread.

"Here's what you ought to know," he told Remy. "You'll always be pretty, which is nothing. Nothing! It's better to be striking. This will do it."

Remy was frowning. Faith knew better than to intervene. "Won't I look like a boy?" Remy asked.

"Trust me, darling, that won't be a problem."

Remy smiled. "Let's do it."

Two hours later, Remy and Faith stared at each other. The difference was striking. Faith's hair was blonder, shorter and layered so it swirled around her chin when she moved. Her bangs were spiky and emphasized her eyes. She looked younger and sexier, and she felt like a million bucks.

Remy's transformation was even greater. The short cut emphasized every lovely feature. Unlike her mother, the new haircut made her look older, more the woman and less the child. She could easily pass for a college student. Faith wondered what she would need to do in the coming years to protect her daughter.

"Wow," Faith said. "I've got to say, Mitch made a believer out of me. You look fantastic."

Remy glanced in the mirror again. "You think so? Really?"

"It's a big change, but a good one."

"You look good, too." Remy didn't even sound grudging.

"You think Ralph will let me keep the dress now?"

Remy giggled. "He wanted to wear it himself."

Faith laughed, too, sure Ralph would have joined them. She paid

Mitch, adding a big tip she couldn't afford, and followed her daughter out into the sunlight. She felt lighter, younger and carefree. "Let's walk a little more before we head home."

Remy scanned the sidewalk ahead of them before she nodded, almost as if she were looking for someone.

"Do your friends hang out here?" Faith asked.

"What friends?"

"Kids from school?"

"I don't know."

"Do you and Billie come up here to window-shop?"

"Aren't I allowed?"

Faith backpedaled instantly. "I thought you might know if there's any other place we should look."

At Wisconsin, Remy stopped about halfway to the corner. Faith had never paid much attention to the shops on this side of the street. When she walked to the library she usually walked on the other side. These shops were too trendy for her, geared to a younger clientele that might just include her daughter.

"Would you like to look around a little more before we go home?"

"Let's just go back."

"Are you sure? I told you we'd look for some things for you, too." Music blared from speakers perched above the open doorway of the next store. Faith peeked inside. Black walls, stainless steel fixtures. The clothes were like something out of a science fiction movie with a low budget.

An intense-looking young man with long black hair stood smoking a cigarette in the doorway. He caught sight of Remy and tossed it to the ground, grinding it under the heel of a snakeskin boot.

"Hey there."

"Hey." Remy darted a glance at her mother.

"Nice haircut."

Remy self-consciously lifted her hand to her shorn head. "Yeah?"

"Yeah." He smirked, then turned around and went back inside.

"Remy, who's that?" Faith said. "Do you know him?"

"I don't *know* him. He's just somebody who works there, that's all."

"He seemed to recognize you."

"So?" Remy turned around and started toward home.

"I just wondered." Faith tried not to worry.

"Billie and I looked around in there a couple of times. I think she knows him."

The man was considerably older than either Billie or Remy. Faith didn't like the idea of her daughter hanging around the shop after school, even if she was only making conversation. Despite allowances for different tastes, there was something about the young man that made Faith uncomfortable.

She was afraid it was the way he had looked at her daughter.

"Look, I know you don't want to hear this, but be careful. Okay? You might give this guy the wrong idea. He might not realize how young you are."

"Like I'm stupid? Like I don't know the score?"

"Honey, you're fourteen. You need to take it easy. You need to be careful. That's all."

"Are we home yet?"

Faith fell silent. She hated to spoil the good time they'd had together, but she couldn't think of a change of subject.

"I love you," she said at last. "I hope you realize that's why I worry."

Remy didn't bother to reply.

When Faith left for her date with Pete, Marley was happily ensconced in Faith's living room with Alex and a pile of board games. Remy, angry that Faith had asked Marley to "baby-sit," had locked herself in her bedroom and turned on the kind of music that inspired Tipper Gore to lobby for warning labels.

When Faith returned from the embassy, Lydia was sitting in the living room watching television and Marley was gone.

Lydia got to her feet, waving away the obvious before Faith could ask. "I left another party early tonight and came over so Marley could go home."

Faith, who was removing earrings and jewelry, paused, her watch hanging open at her wrist. "You're making a habit of leaving parties, Mother." She hoped this time Joe wouldn't come looking for his wife.

"Such a waste of valuable time." Lydia looked exhausted. She reminded Faith of a greyhound. Too thin, too fast, running in circles after a counterfeit, unattainable goal. The pace seemed to be catching up with her.

"Are you feeling all right?" Faith closed the distance between them.

Lydia snapped off the television. "I don't sleep well. I haven't in years. It takes its toll."

"Have you spoken to your doctor?"

"What, so he can medicate me and make it harder to function by day? I'll take my chances with insomnia."

"He might find some underlying cause."

"I know the underlying cause. My life took a wrong turn before you were born. The reality of that keeps me awake at night."

When a woman never talked about feelings, it was easy to assume she had none. Now Faith realized she had been wrong about that, as well as so many other things. "Do you mean Hope's kidnapping?"

Lydia seemed to think better of her lapse. "Some women have the capacity to find a new route when the old one's closed off. Is that what the date tonight was about? A new route for you?"

"With Pete Conley?" Faith finished removing her watch. It was a Piaget, not one of the more expensive models, but still an extravagant gift from David on her thirtieth birthday. Tonight was the first night that she'd worn it since encountering him at the cottage.

"Did the date go well?" Lydia probed.

"Pete's one of the good guys. The embassy is always stunning." With its fabulous contemporary art and sculpture, the French embassy never failed to please. But tonight, even though there had been circus performers to delight them, Faith had still been bored for most of the evening.

"There are a number of women in the capital who would describe Pete in more glowing terms than 'one of the good guys.'"

"And they would be right."

"But not right for you?"

Lydia hadn't questioned her this closely when a much younger Faith had announced her engagement to David. "He's charming, sophisticated, intelligent, and we have as much chemistry as an underfunded public high school."

"I can guarantee it's not because you don't look fabulous. I like what you've done with your hair. And the dress is spectacular on you."

Faith dropped into the seat beside Lydia's, and after a second's hesitation, Lydia sat, too.

"Maybe I'm crazy to want more this time around," Faith said, "but I do. I spent a lot of years with David assuming I was at fault for the lack of sparkle in our marriage. I don't want to go through that again, not for any reason. I'd rather stay single."

"The chance lightning would strike twice in the same place is pretty poor, isn't it?"

"There are a lot of reasons for ho-hum sex besides a partner who's lying to himself."

"Weren't we supposed to have this conversation a long time ago?"

Faith laughed. "I can't believe we're having it now."

"I noticed you have a bottle of Scotch in the kitchen. Why don't you fix us both a drink?"

"If talking about sex doesn't kill me, that should finish me off." Faith got up and went for the bottle. She returned with two glasses filled with ice and Dottie Lee's Glenfiddich. "So why *didn't* we have this conversation before? What were you keeping from me?"

"How disappointed you might be in the long run. How mundane it all is. Marriage. Sex. Love." Lydia took a long sip from her glass.

"I'd been watching you and Dad all those years. I had your viewpoint figured out." Faith was feeling brave. Lydia seemed to be feeling receptive. "Why did you stay with somebody you didn't love?"

"You're certain I don't love him?"

Faith considered. There were many kinds of love. Maybe she and David had shared one kind. But it hadn't been enough for him, and she had survived his sexual rejection by taking the blame on herself. Her image of herself as a woman had been worn away, one lonely night at a time.

"I'm certain you don't love him," she said at last. "And I think you stayed with him because it's all you knew how to do."

Lydia didn't deny it. "The lure of the familiar."

Faith rested a hand on her mother's shoulder. "What if the papers hadn't gotten wind of David's affair? David felt so guilty that if I had begged him to stay with me, he might have done it. But would that have been enough?"

"It's not the same thing. Your father's sexual preference has never been in question."

"But his passion and his dedication to you have."

"Faith, Joe Huston's your father. Whatever else he is, he is that."

Faith knew she couldn't push any harder. Besides, she wasn't sure what she was pushing for. Lydia and Joe had worked out their relationship long ago, probably before Faith herself was born. She had no right to interfere.

"I will tell you this," Lydia continued. "Of the many reasons a woman should choose a man, passion is the key. I wish I'd told you that when you were about to marry David, because there's nothing more important. Respect matters. Passion without respect is nothing. But in the end, it's passion that keeps a relationship alive. And if you don't feel it with Pete Conley, there's no point trying."

Faith thought of the one man in her life who did inspire passion. Pavel Quinn, as different from David or Pete as an intelligent, red-blooded American male could be. This evening had taught her that her attraction to Pavel was more than sexual starvation. Because Pete had made it clear she could have any and all needs met tonight, and she hadn't felt a flicker of interest.

"I was a hit," Faith said. "That was part of the reason I went. I needed to see if people would be kind or cut me dead."

"You weren't giving your friends much credit. Most people have been waiting diplomatically for you to finish licking your wounds."

"I'm back to having a life." Faith smiled. "It feels odd."

"And good." It wasn't a question.

"And good."

"Just don't sell yourself short. Find the life you deserve. Find the man you deserve."

"Or do without."

Lydia swallowed the rest of her drink, then set her glass on the side table and stood. "An alternative my generation equated with failure. We were wrong."

Faith walked her mother to the door. "You're easier to talk to here, Mother. I know this house holds terrible memories, but when you're here, I feel like I know you better and better."

"One terrible memory and many good ones. They don't balance, but maybe I'm coming to terms with all of them." Lydia leaned over and kissed Faith's cheek, a gesture that was, in itself, unusual.

Faith stood in the doorway watching until her mother drove away. And when she was gone, Faith continued to stand there, thinking about the woman who had traded passion for familiarity and now, at sixty-six, clearly wished that she hadn't.

Faith wondered what Pavel was doing that night.

 22

Alec the Can Man still showed up intermittently to help Alex, and between them they had nearly cleared the backyard. Over the weeks Faith had grown fond of the older man. He arrived sober, worked hard, and guided her son with humor and tact. The Can Man had chosen a life on the streets, but he hadn't been destroyed by it.

On Wednesday afternoon he'd arrived just as Alex got home from school, and the two were already outside. Usually Faith went down to pull her own token sprigs of ivy, but this time she was delayed by a phone call from a counselor at the middle school.

It was some time before she joined the gardeners, and by then she was feeling anything but festive. Not only had the phone call been sobering, it had pointed out her isolation. She should have been able to pick up the receiver again to ask somebody for help, but in the end, she hadn't been able to think of a single person who could answer her distress call.

"One more hour," the Can Man told her when Faith finally made her way through the door, "and every last scrap'll be gone. You wait and see."

The garden already looked denuded. The ivy had held it together. Without it weaving tree to tree, bush to bush, nothing much remained.

Faith had looked unsuccessfully for a description of her grand-mother's garden. Now she was going to have to use her own best guesses to replant. "Can you identify any of the dead trees? Or is that impossible?"

"Try a nursery."

"I guess I'll have to."

"What will you do?"

Faith looked over to see Dottie Lee standing at her usual gap in the hedge. Faith beckoned her to join them. "Call somebody to identify the dead trees. I'd like to incorporate some of what Violet planted. It's just so sad that it's all so..." Faith shrugged.

"Dead, I believe." Dottie Lee picked her way carefully through the shrubbery and over what remained of a stone wall. "Dead is the word."

"Dreary. Depressed."

"Devastated." Dottie Lee nodded. "Definitely."

Faith laughed. "You don't remember anything, do you?"

"My dear, this garden is as clear to me as a summer's day. A sum-mer's day in a cooler city, of course, not here in Georgetown, where the heat fogs everything."

If her life had depended on it, Faith wouldn't have been able to describe her McLean backyard in any detail. She was amazed at Dottie Lee's memory.

The Can Man started down to the bottom of the yard. "C'mon, kid. We've got ivy to pull."

Faith watched the two head toward the back of the lot. It was a downhill slope, but evidence of clever terracing was still visible. The bottom plateau was the only one left to weed. She watched them don heavy gloves. Poison ivy was a threat, but so far they had avoided direct contact.

"Let me get a pen and tablet," Faith said. "Will you wait here a moment? I want to sketch what you remember."

Dottie Lee was still waiting when Faith returned. Before the trip back, Faith had tried a quick call to Billie's house, but no one had answered. That morning Remy had asked if she could go to Bil-lie's after school, and Faith had agreed to it, but the rules had changed while Remy was away.

Dottie Lee was watching the two males down below. "I believe they're about to have an epiphany."

Faith had experienced one too many epiphanies that day. "I'm not sure I can use any more surprises."

"I hear your doorbell."

Faith realized it was true. "I'm sorry. I'll be back. Will you wait?"

"I'm not going anywhere."

Faith raced up the stairs again. Pavel was just retreating down the sidewalk when she flung open the door, panting from exertion. "Hey there. I was out back."

He turned. She watched his eyes light, and her body warmed instantly in response. "I thought you weren't home," he said.

"Me? I'm almost always home."

"Not last Friday night."

That surprised her. "How do you know?"

"I stopped by. I guess Alex forgot to tell you. He remembered to tell me you were on a date." He didn't sound jealous, but there was a definite hint of disappointment in his voice.

"Party at the French embassy with an old friend," she explained.

"Your hair looks great."

She raised her hand without thinking, finger combing it into place. "Thanks."

"I just wondered if you and the kids wanted to go out for spaghetti tonight."

"I can't. I have to have a heart-to-heart with Remy. No one will be in the mood to eat afterward."

He was up on the stoop now, and she motioned him inside. She felt pleasantly flustered.

"Troubles? Want to tell me about it?"

For a moment she wasn't sure what he meant. Then she realized he was talking about Remy. "You don't want to hear." She started past him, but he held her still, one large hand cupping her arm.

"Try me."

His hand was warm, just a little rough. A workingman's hand, she thought, although he was probably worth more money than King Midas. A hand that rubbed along her nerve endings even when it was perfectly still.

She looked up at him. The kindness in his eyes was mixed with something steamier, something related to the way they were standing and not to anything she'd said.

"Remy's failing school. Her counselor called me. She's *failing*. She's not doing homework. She doesn't have any friends. Billie, the one friend she does have, is a bad influence. I think that about covers it." She paused. "Oh, and her chorus teacher says she's a musical genius. She has perfect pitch. I nearly forgot."

His hand slid along her arm to her shoulder, then to her nape. He began to squeeze. Release. Squeeze. "Not many people have perfect pitch, Faith."

She stared at him for a moment; then she laughed, and it rumbled from her chest, smoky and dark. She couldn't help herself. "Thanks. Silver linings, huh?"

"What are you going to do?"

She was going to stand there and let him rub her neck until she died of old age. She was going to stand there until she dissolved into a warm puddle of contentment, into a warm, flowing stream of pure sexual delight.

"Will talking help?" he asked, when she didn't answer.

"I can't think while you're doing that."

"I'm sorry." He dropped his hand.

She took it before he could pull away and threaded her fingers through his. "Because it felt so good, Pavel. I was just thinking a little while ago that there wasn't *anybody* who could make me feel better."

"Comfort, huh? I guess I'm good at comfort."

She suspected he was good at other things, as well. Pavel was a man who loved to touch and be touched. Even when she brushed his body by accident, the way he unconsciously moved in reaction, the slow undulation of his muscles, the contraction of his skin, seemed a sure indication that he was a man who expressed himself best physically.

That was the wrong subject to dwell on. "Dottie Lee is waiting for me in back. Come with me and say hello."

"I don't want to interrupt."

She refused to let go of his hand, even though holding it made a statement. "Please don't go. She'd love to see you. She likes you."

He didn't seem convinced. "On one condition." He tugged her toward him. She came easily. "You go out with *me* this weekend. No kids. No friends. Just you and me." He leaned down until they were face-to-face. It seemed to take him a long time. He rubbed his nose lightly against hers, a feathery touch that promised more if she wanted it. She lifted her lips and closed her eyes.

His lips were warm and not at all casual. He dropped her hand and pressed against her waist to bring her closer. Resistance seemed inhospitable, so she swayed against him. Since her hand was free now and needed a place to rest, she rested both hands on his shoulders, her fingertips lightly brushing his neck.

For a moment, just the briefest moment, she forgot to hold up the world. She let him hold it up for her, let him warm the hollow spaces in her heart, let the bulk of his body cradle hers.

The door slammed behind him, and, startled, she stepped back. So did Pavel. Right into Remy's path.

"Great," Remy said. "You can't do that somewhere else?"

Faith took a much needed breath. She had nothing to apologize for. Even now, with Remy glaring at her and her heart pounding madly, she knew it. "I've been calling you at Billie's."

"Well, I wasn't there. We were walking around. I just came home to get something."

"You're not going anywhere." Faith looked at Pavel. "Dottie Lee's waiting for me downstairs. Would you mind entertaining her for a minute?"

He nodded without a word and started toward the kitchen and the basement door.

"Too bad entertaining old Dottie Lee's not as much fun as entertaining my mother, huh, Pavel?" Remy called after him.

Faith watched him struggle briefly, clearly trying to decide between a response and silence. "You know, Remy," he said after a pause, "this is a hard time for you. I can understand that. But I'm tired of watching you browbeat your mom. I happen to think she doesn't deserve it. Lay off her."

"You don't have anything to say about anything around here. You're not my father!"

"For which I'm relieved, because if I were, I might turn you over my knee. And I don't really believe in child abuse."

Remy's eyes widened. Pavel disappeared down the basement steps.

"Did you hear what he said?" Remy demanded.

Faith was trembling. She'd wondered how she should deal with her daughter. Now there was no question. "I heard what *you* said! How dare you treat a guest in our house that way?"

"A guest? He was kissing you! That makes him more than a guest!"

"Remy, we aren't going to talk about me. This time we're going to talk about you. About the fact that you're failing school, talking back to teachers. You seem to think that just because your life's changed, everything you learned before doesn't matter. But there is never any excuse to quit trying, to be rude, to lie."

"What do you mean lie?"

"I ask you every night if you've done your homework, and every night you say yes. I got a call from your counselor today. According to her, that's a lie."

Relief flicked across Remy's face so quickly that Faith wasn't even sure she'd seen it. "The homework's stupid. I know that stuff backward and forward. I'm not doing busy work."

"If you know it backward and forward, why are you failing tests? Do you think you're too good for public school? Is that it? Or are you trying to prove how awful your life is? Are you trying to make your daddy and me feel even worse than we already do?"

"I don't care how you feel! I hate school. I hate the kids, and I hate the teachers. Nothing's the same as it was. Nobody there likes me."

"Because you're not trying."

"Why should I bother? I had friends. They're all gone now."

"You haven't made an attempt to get together with your old friends. When they invite you to visit, you refuse. You won't have them here."

"They know! They know everything."

"If they're your friends, they'll still love you."

"I don't need friends. I had friends, and what good did it do? There's nothing they could do to make this better. Daddy was your friend, and look what he did to you!"

"He hurt me. I'm not pretending he didn't. But friends forgive each other. Someday, when the worst of this is over, maybe I'll be able to forgive him, too."

"Bullshit! I don't believe that. That's just something you're saying. It's all lies. Everything is lies."

Faith didn't know how to reply to that. She and David had raised Remy and Alex in a black-and-white world, not realizing that at the first sign of gray, their daughter wouldn't know where to turn.

"You're on restriction until further notice," Faith said. "I have to be sure you're studying and doing your homework before I'm going to let you out of my sight. Until I am, I'll be picking you up and bringing you home every afternoon."

"You can't keep me in prison."

"I can sure try."

"What'll I tell...Billie? You want me to have friends, but you're keeping me away from the only friend I have."

"I have some concerns about Billie. For the time being, if you want to see her, you can see her here, in this house."

"She won't come. She says you're weird, that you hang around too much and won't leave us alone."

"Well, if she thought it was bad before, she's going to be really unhappy the next time."

"I hate you! And I hate that man! Keep him away from me. Kiss him somewhere else!" Remy turned and ran up the stairs.

"I found it!" Alex shouted when Faith had recovered enough to join everyone in the garden.

There was only one thing Alex had been looking for. "Violet's autograph?"

Dottie Lee was still waiting. "He'll show you."

Pavel gave Faith a sympathetic smile. "Things go okay after I left?" he asked.

"I don't think they'll go okay until she's twenty-one." She started toward the bottom of the garden, where Alex was kneeling in what looked like a depression in the ground.

"Look, Mom!" He pointed.

Pavel joined Faith, and together they stooped beside the boy. "Where?" Faith asked.

The Can Man was still clearing ivy at the bottom of the lot. Alex pointed. "Right there."

What looked like a stone patio covered the ground in a section about ten feet square. The rectangular, moss-covered stones had been carefully sunk without gaps between them, and even now they were almost perfectly level. In the center, though, was an old mill stone, and in the gap between the round mill stone and the rectangular pavers, tall weeds had taken hold. Alex had pulled enough of them to make a path for her to see the millstone clearly. Violet had carefully chiseled her name over the square hole where an ancient axle had powered the wheel.

"Well. Wow." She leaned over and traced it, much as Remy had traced Candace's name on the windowsill.

"What's it doing way down here?" Alex rubbed the sole of his shoe back and forth over one of the stones. "It's like the floor of something."

"A greenhouse," Dottie Lee said. She joined them.

Faith touched the signature again. "This is where Violet must have raised plants to sell before the war. I should have realized she'd need a greenhouse for that."

"James built it for her. He was too sick to do it all at once, of course. He did a little at a time. A stone here, a piece of the frame there. Then he'd have to rest for days. They used windows they found in the rubbish and set them back-to-back to trap layers of air for insulation."

"Recyclers. Like the Can Man," Alex said proudly.

"Quite the same, yes. James was good with his hands. He carved the trim himself. Garlands of ivy, I think. It was a thing of beauty once it was complete. No electric heat, of course, but a little coal stove in the corner to use on the coldest nights. Violet would come out and bank it before bedtime. She bragged that she never lost a plant to the weather."

Faith felt another surge of family pride. "She was so imaginative."

"She used every asset she had available. I patterned myself after her."

Faith was afraid to follow that particular train of thought. "We've found three signatures now. Millicent, Violet and Candace. That's it."

"Why is Millicent's name in the attic?" Alex asked.

Dottie Lee patted his shoulder. "Millicent was quite the thespian. She wanted to be an actress. She spent huge stretches of her childhood in that attic putting on plays with the other children in the neighborhood. It was her creative home."

"You, too?"

"No, dear. I was a charming little girl, and they recognized my real talent. They sent me door-to-door to sell tickets. I sold a great many."

Faith couldn't help but smile. "Pavel, Dottie Lee's going to help me reconstruct Violet's garden."

Pavel was examining the stones. "I could rebuild the greenhouse on this spot. Maybe there's a photograph somewhere of the old one."

"Thanks, but I don't want to raise plants for a living."

"Then a summer house. An open air gazebo, where we could sit in the evenings and look out over the lights."

She wondered if the others noticed how he had incorporated himself into her future. "I couldn't ask you to do that."

"You didn't."

"Violet would approve. She spent so much time out here." Dottie Lee turned and swept the air with her hand, to encompass the yard. "Are you ready to sketch, Faith?"

Faith held up the tablet.

"Then let's get to it, before I expire. At the back of the house were camellias. Three, I believe. No sign of them now. A lovely carmine pink. A white. A lighter, shell-pink."

Dottie Lee closed her eyes as if envisioning the past. As she spoke, trees emerged, a blue spruce, dogwoods and redbuds. Azalea and wisteria followed on their heels, along with a list of perennials that changed with the seasons. Trillium bloomed in the shade of a long-dead sweetbay magnolia, and white clematis the size of saucers climbed a trellis that had decayed to dust decades before. Old-fashioned hollyhocks and sunflowers shaded the greenhouse windows in the hottest days of summer.

Dottie Lee faced Faith. "But the most remarkable thing she

grew, of course, were the poppies. Surely Lydia told you about the summer of the poppies?"

"Poppies are those red flowers, right?" Alex asked.

"They can be any color, but these were indeed red," Dottie Lee said. "Bright red. In the summer of 1941 half of Washington came to see them."

"The garden tour." Faith hadn't thought to ask Dottie Lee about the tour. Lydia had been too young to remember details, but Dottie Lee was older.

"Violet's garden had Georgetown talking. That's why she won a spot, because everybody wanted to see it."

"What was so special about poppies?" Alex asked.

"That summer, 1941, a great deal of the world was already fighting World War II, but the United States hadn't gotten involved. Violet planted red poppies to remind her neighbors that war is very serious. Hundreds of them in every available inch of garden soil. You have never seen such a sight. It was breathtaking, like bright red smoke covering the ground. The flowers even grew between the paving stones on the walk leading down to the greenhouse."

Alex had been listening closely. "Pearl Harbor was in December of '41, right? We studied it last year. But what do poppies have to do with anything?"

It was the second time that the right poem had occurred to Faith. "There's a famous poem about World War I. It starts off 'In Flanders fields the poppies blow, between the crosses, row on row.' Now red poppies are a reminder of the men who died fighting."

Dottie Lee finished the explanation. "Because of James, Violet knew that war is always sad for someone. When the U.S. finally joined the fighting, she was every bit as patriotic as anyone else on the street. But she had no illusions that what was happening was glamorous. She knew better."

Since moving into the house on Prospect, Faith had given up one life, but almost without her permission, she was being woven into another. Her ancestors were supporting her in her time of crisis. Even their decision to hold on to this house had changed her life, for without it she wouldn't have grown and changed herself. The women who had lived and loved here had made everything possible for her.

She felt Pavel's hands on her shoulders, and she leaned against him. Her gaze flicked to Dottie Lee's face. Dottie Lee was looking at her; and at Pavel's proprietary grasp.

"I know more about this house and the things that happened here than anyone in the world," Dottie Lee said. "Don't forget that, Faith. When you need answers, I have them." Her aged eyes lifted to Pavel's. "But only when you're ready to hear them."

 23

Faith half expected Remy to disappear after school the next afternoon, but she was waiting at the appointed spot when Faith
came to pick her up. For the most part Remy was silent, spitting
out monosyllables in answer to Faith's questions about her day, but
Faith simply counted her blessings.

Alex had gone home with a friend and wouldn't be back until
nearly dinnertime, so without other obligations, Faith began stripping the wallpaper in her bedroom. An hour later she was surprised
to find Remy standing in her doorway, watching her.

"That stuff is sick. Who would want to look at it?"

Faith, up high on her stepladder, was down to wide strips in the
center of the wall, but above it, in the area she'd learned to call a
"frieze," she had discovered a stylized landscape of a cypress
swamp at sunset.

"Sick? I love it. I wish I could salvage the whole scene. I've been
trying to find a way, but there were so many layers on top of it, it's
taken a beating."

"Who wants a mural at the top of a wall?"

"It must have been stylish at the turn of the last century. I've been
thinking about dark green in the middle, with a landscape up here
and a simple border along the edge of the ceiling. I've found a
source online for reproductions."

Remy was silent for so long that Faith thought she'd gone back to her room, but a glance proved otherwise.

"You really like the history here, don't you?" Remy said.

"When I was a little girl I fixed up my closet like a time machine. I'd crawl inside and imagine I was in Queen Elizabeth's court or battling Attila the Hun."

"You? A soldier?"

"It's easy to pretend you're anything."

"I pretend I'm old enough to leave home for good."

"I'll bet you do." Faith began to scrape carefully under the paper and was rewarded when several inches peeled away.

"The wallpaper in my room is awful."

"I know." Faith continued to lift and peel. It was a job for someone with infinite patience and time, both of which were in short supply these days.

"The room's not too bad, though. The lights are pretty at night."

Faith was amazed she didn't fall off the ladder. She kept her voice neutral. "They are. You have the best view."

"The kittens are almost old enough to give away now."

"I've been wanting to talk to you about that." Faith had finally managed to get Guest and her babies to the vet. They were in good health, and the requisite vaccinations had begun. Guest was still aloof, but the kittens, thanks to Alex and Remy, were well socialized.

"Guest is used to this house. I know how she feels, you know? It's a strange situation, us being here, but she's adjusted. If we try to give her away, it'll just be too much for her."

"Do you think she'll ever be a good pet?"

"She's kind of used to me. She jumped up on my lap yesterday."

Faith wanted to abandon the ladder, find the cat and give her a big smooch. "If you want to keep Guest, we will. But she has to be spayed. No more kittens."

"I'd like to keep Pinto Bean, too."

Pinto Bean was the tortoiseshell. Not surprisingly, all the kittens had names now. "Two cats?"

"I'll take care of them." Remy didn't say please, but her tone implied it.

Faith knew her daughter had only summoned up good manners

so she could plead the kitten's fate, but it was a revelation that Remy could still be polite, so Faith was willing to make allowances.

"Okay?" Remy said.

"I'll tell you what. I'll bribe you. You let me help you fix up your room, and I'll let you keep Pinto Bean."

"What are you going to do?"

Faith backed down the ladder. "For starters, we could see how many layers of wallpaper we have to remove. Once it's gone, you can paint, or find some pretty paper and put it up."

"You think I'd do a good job?" Remy sounded uncertain.

"Remy, I have complete faith in you. I think you can do anything if you try hard enough. That's why this school problem has me so worried."

"I don't want to talk about that."

"Let's talk about wallpaper."

Ten minutes later they were sitting side by side on Remy's floor, putty knives and sponges in hand, lifting strips of wallpaper from one corner.

"This room wasn't used as frequently before your grandmother rented out the house, so I'll bet there are fewer layers here than in my room," Faith said.

"Who picked out this stuff?" Remy was scraping away the top layer. This room was gratifyingly easy. Faith suspected her mother had found the cheapest paper hanger in D.C.

"Someone who was trying to save money. Your grandmother."

"You know what I think? I think she was trying to cover up Hope's wallpaper. So she wouldn't have to look at it and remember. You know?"

Obviously Remy was thinking more about family dynamics than she let on. "I bet you're right, but not this layer. I bet there'll be a couple of layers before we get down to Hope's nursery. That was so long ago."

"The way everybody talks around it, it seems like it wasn't that long ago."

"What do you mean?"

"Well, usually people avoid fresh things, you know, things that hurt them recently. But nobody in our family talks about the kidnapping, even now."

"The moment a baby's born, she feels like a person you've known and loved all your life. So even if my mother just had Hope for a few days, it was like having an arm or a leg ripped away."

"Is that how you'd feel?"

"I don't know if I could have lived through it." Faith weighed her next sentence, but decided to go ahead. "Mother lost a piece of her heart, and she's guarded the rest of it ever since."

"You mean that's why she's so...I don't know..."

"Distant?"

"Mean."

Faith had to smile. "Well, of course I didn't know her before."

Remy giggled. "Maybe she was always mean."

"She just pushes people away. And not so much since we've moved here. Have you noticed?"

"Maybe you think so because you don't have anyone else to talk to now that Daddy's gone."

Faith took heart that Remy had mentioned David. The whole conversation seemed charged with miracles. "Maybe I'm just more approachable."

"You're mad at *me* all the time."

"With no reason?"

Remy didn't answer.

They scraped in silence, getting enough of the top layer off to start in on the next. That one was ugly, too. A Peter Max wanna-be had designed it. At least the pop art hearts and flowers made a stab at whimsy.

"This looks like late sixties, maybe early seventies. Something straight off a Beatles album."

"Hope was born when?"

"1962. So if I'm right, we'll find at most one more under it before we get to her nursery paper."

"What did Grandmother put in *your* nursery?"

"Armed guards." Faith took another stab at the paper. "Actually, I have seen pictures. It was teddy bears of all shapes and sizes. And after I was born, people all over Virginia sent teddy bears, too. Dolls and teddy bears."

"Because of Hope?"

"Your grandparents packed them all off to children's hospitals, but I saw a newspaper article about it recently. I never knew."

"I guess all those people were glad you were okay."

"People need happy endings."

"I used to think that was the only kind there was."

Faith was touched. "You need to stay around for the next installment of this story. Sometimes the bumpiest roads save the best scenery for the end."

"That's really dumb, even for you."

Faith burst into laughter. "You keep me honest. I'll give you that, kiddo."

They scraped and lifted, nudging each other as they changed position, at one point leaning back-to-back companionably. The third layer was navy-blue with tiny white fleur-de-lis in symmetrical rows. Plain and serviceable, it was more fitting for a study than a bedroom.

"I bet this is the last layer before we find Hope's wallpaper," Faith said. "It's dark enough that it would easily cover any trace."

"It's so dark, this room must have felt like a morgue."

Faith thought it must have felt like a morgue anyway to the two people who'd had their child stolen from inside these walls.

They kept scraping and lifting, sponging with the big sponge and solution Faith had brought from the other room. The next layer wasn't what they'd expected. It was an elegant emerald and gold stripe, formal for a bedroom, but in keeping with the traditional lines of the house.

"Where are the ducks and clowns?" Remy set down her putty knife.

"This *is* very odd." Faith rested, too. The hearts and flowers had obviously been from the late sixties or early seventies. Since that point, she and Remy had gone down two more layers. That seemed like a lot of wallpaper for a ten-year span. "My best guess is that someone moved in, hated the paper and put up more."

"College students?"

Silently Faith conceded the point. "One more layer, then we'll quit. My curiosity's stirring."

Two layers later, they admitted the obvious. Quite clearly Hope Huston's loving parents had brought their daughter home to a room of formal emerald-green or studious midnight-blue. No ducks. No clowns. No grinning teddy bears.

"Did you decorate my nursery?" Remy asked.

"Fairies and butterflies. I spent weeks picking out the paper."

"I had baby wallpaper. You had baby wallpaper. Why didn't Hope?"

It was a mystery. Faith was left to wonder if her mother had experienced so little maternal feeling Lydia hadn't cared enough to fix up the room.

"What would you say if I painted this room black?"

"I would say no."

"It's my room, isn't it?"

"A room, not a cave."

"What if I find wallpaper I like? Dark wallpaper. You're doing dark green."

"That would be fine. But I get to see it first, just in case."

"What do you think I'm going to do? Buy something with gang graffiti scrawled all over it?"

"Is there such a thing?"

Remy giggled. Faith put her arm around her daughter's shoulders for a quick hug.

Remy picked at the wallpaper after her mother went downstairs to make dinner. Now that they had a kitchen, Faith was trying to pretend things were just the same as they'd been in McLean. As if Remy couldn't see straight through all her efforts. Cinnamon rolls and chicken and dumplings didn't make a family. Neither did new kitchen counters or fresh wallpaper. Faith was just playing house, the way Remy had as a little girl.

The telephone rang, but she didn't bother to answer it. It was never for her anymore. Megan had stopped calling because Remy had nothing to talk about. She didn't want to tell Megan anything about the guys down the street. If she did, Megan might tell her mother, and her mother might feel she needed to tell Faith. If that happened, Remy figured she would never be allowed to leave the house again.

She didn't know why she'd agreed to strip her wallpaper or why, for a little while at least, she had believed her mother was anything more than a warden. She didn't really live here and never would. She didn't know why she'd said that stupid thing about the lights being pretty. They only reminded her that there was another world outside this house, a world she would join just as soon as she was old enough.

In the meantime, she had lived for the few hours each week when she could escape this Georgetown jailhouse and see Enzio. Now that she was in solitary confinement, even that diversion was going to be denied her.

Faith knocked on her door again, and Remy called a lethargic "Come in."

"That was Alex. He and Sammy wrote a play, and they're putting it on for Sammy's mother and me before he comes home. Do you want to come and see it?"

That was too dumb for an answer. Remy rolled her eyes.

"Can I trust you here by yourself, then?" Faith asked. "I'll probably be gone for a while."

"Like what am I going to do? Play with matches? Drink drain cleaner?"

"Don't go anywhere. I'm not sure when I'll be back," Faith said at last. "But I'll expect to find you right here."

"Seig heil!" Remy gave a mock salute.

Faith shook her head and closed the door behind her.

Remy waited until she heard the front door close. Then she ran to Faith's bedroom window and watched her mother disappear down the street. Back in her own room, Remy slipped on her shoes and combed her hair. Not that there was much of it left to comb. The new cut made her feel older and more sophisticated, like a different person. One fully capable of doing whatever she wanted.

Outside, she locked the front door and started toward Enzio's house. She knew this was his afternoon off.

Enzio still didn't know how old she was, but she'd told him and the other guys at the house that her mother was psycho and didn't want Remy to do anything except work and study. She'd had to tell them something just to make sure they didn't stop by the house and ask for her.

And wouldn't Faith love that? She'd already noticed Enzio the day of their shopping trip. What would she think if she knew how much time Remy spent with him? Faith would lock her in the attic until she was a withered old lady. Remy would be reduced to carving her name on rafters, too.

The door was ajar when she arrived. She nudged it open and called inside before she walked in. Selim was in the living room, fastening Bear's leash to a studded collar. He got to his feet and started in her direction.

"Going for a walk?" Remy stooped to ruffle the fur around Bear's oversized neck.

"Down to the canal to meet some people."

"Colin home?" She didn't want to sound like she was only there to see Enzio.

"Somewhere."

"Enzio?"

"Yeah." Selim nodded goodbye as Bear yanked him toward freedom.

"Remy!" Colin wandered in from the kitchen and flashed a huge grin. He was the warmest of the roommates, a big-brotherly guy who liked everyone and managed to make everyone like him, too. "What'd you do to your hair?"

"Chopped it all off. Do you like it?"

He came over and placed a palm against each of her cheeks, squinting studiously. "Cute," he pronounced.

"I don't want to be cute. Short people are automatically cute to start with."

"What do you want to be?"

"Gorgeous."

He stepped back. "That, too. Are you just stopping by?"

"I can't stay long. I just wanted to say hello."

"Your mother keeps you on a tight leash, huh?"

"She wants me to get into a good school next year."

"Where have you applied?"

"University of Virginia. William and Mary." Remy shrugged, as if college was no big deal.

"Not Georgetown?"

"Who wants to live at home?" Remy wondered what she would do next year when she started high school and the guys in this house thought she was supposed to be in college. It was probably too early to worry about it.

"I'm off to the library," Colin said. "I think Enzio's around someplace."

"I'll find him and say hi."

Colin grabbed a pile of books off the water-stained coffee table, pushing aside a pizza carton and two half-finished glasses of milk to search for a notebook. He found it and added it to his pile. Then, with another dazzling grin, he sprinted for the front door and slammed it behind him.

Remy wondered if Paul, the fourth roommate, who practically lived at his girlfriend's house, was home, too, or if she and Enzio were alone.

"What's all the noise?" Enzio, bare-chested, stretching as if he'd just woken up, came halfway down the stairs.

"Colin doesn't know how to close a door quietly."

"Where're Selim and the mutt?"

"They left before Colin."

Enzio sank to the landing, as if he was too tired to make it all the way downstairs. "So what are you doing?"

"I just stopped by. I can't stay long. My mother would have a cow if she knew I was here."

"Why do you let her push you around?"

"She feeds me. Besides, next year I'll be out of there."

"I got you something."

Remy had moved to the bottom of the stairs. She leaned against the newel post, looking up at him. "Yeah?"

"I'll get it." He stretched again, the muscles in his chest flexing. "Be right back."

Her curiosity built as she waited. If Enzio really had gotten her something, that meant he thought about her when she wasn't with him. That felt big. That felt huge, like her life had suddenly made a sharp turn for the better.

"Here." He took the steps two at a time and thrust a shocking-pink Lawford's shopping bag into her arms. Remy caught it and peeked inside. The lime-green skirt and jacket with the rhinestone zipper tab were stuffed under a wad of tissue paper.

"Enzio!" She pulled out the jacket, a little wrinkled now, but still an awesome piece of clothing. She held it to her chest. "This cost a lot, didn't it?"

He shrugged. "No big deal."

"But it is a big deal. I remember what this cost."

"Some chick bought it and decided she didn't want it. When she returned it, I just forgot to put it on the rack. Okay?"

"You mean you didn't pay for it?"

"Looked to me like maybe she wore it before she brought it back."

She didn't know how these things worked, but she guessed Enzio knew what he was talking about. "Well, thanks a lot."

"Put it on."

She looked up at him. "Now?"

"Yeah. I want to see you in it again."

Remy looked down at her jeans and T-shirt. "I don't know."

"Go in the bathroom and change. It will only take a minute."

"Yeah, sure." She took off for the bathroom beside the kitchen. "I'll be right back."

A few minutes later she stood in the tiny room tugging on the skirt—which barely covered her rump. She felt strange in the outfit, like somebody she didn't know very well.

When she came out, Enzio was in the kitchen making coffee. He lived on coffee and always smelled like it. She thought of him whenever her mother brewed a pot for herself. She thought of him a lot.

"What do you think?" She struck a pose, one hand on her hip, one behind her ear.

"Sweet baby." He cocked a brow. "Pull that zipper down a little and let me see some skin."

Her hand flew to the rhinestones. "It's fine just like it is."

He laughed and started toward her. "We're shy today, huh? Here I bought you a big present, and you won't even show me your collarbone?"

She laughed nervously, feeling like an infant. "Stay there and I will."

"Sure. I can see just fine."

She inched the zipper down until it nestled between her small breasts. She had shirts that exposed more skin, but she felt funny unzipping the jacket with Enzio's gaze on her.

"What are you so afraid of? Nobody ever seen you naked before?"

"Nobody's about to, either."

He smiled without showing any teeth. "You made it through high school a virgin? Isn't that some kind of world record?"

"Well, I'm not through yet."

"That's right." The smile broadened. "C'mere, little girl. Show Enzio how grateful you are."

Remy knew that the moment had come to put a stop to this. A stop to something that was whirling out of control. A stop to the most exciting thing that had ever happened to her.

Instead she took one step, then another. He slipped his arms around her waist and pulled her the rest of the way, leaning down to nibble at the top of her ear. "Why'd you cut your hair?"

"I don't know." Her knees felt like rubber.

"So I could do this?" He grazed her ear with his lips and tongue, tracing the curve, nipping at the lobe. "And this?"

"May...be..."

He kissed her throat, lingering at the hollow. One hand slid under the jacket and inched up as he continued to kiss her. At first he simply stroked her back; then two fingers slipped under her bra, and before she knew what he'd done, the clasp was free and as fast as lightning he was pressing his palm against one breast.

"Mmmm... Nice."

Remy was so shocked she didn't know what to do. It had all happened so fast. She had been thinking about what his lips were doing, and now his fingers were plucking and pinching her nipple.

"I don't think—"

"Don't think, baby." Enzio turned her head with his free hand and covered her lips with his, pushing her against the refrigerator. His hand was still between them, inching the zipper down from inside the jacket. In a moment the jacket hung open and both hands were kneading her breasts.

She was dizzy with sensation, pinned lightly against the cold metal by the warmest hands imaginable. His tongue thrust between her lips, and his hips began to dance against hers. She wanted to squirm away; she wanted to push her body harder against his.

She didn't know which to do, and suddenly she knew she couldn't do either. Because the front door slammed.

"Fuck!" Enzio stepped back.

Remy grabbed the zipper with both hands, trying to fasten it. She barely had it zipped before Colin sprinted into the kitchen. "I forgot a book. Enz, have you seen that book on the Korean War I've been reading?" He stopped and looked at Remy. "Is that what you were wearing before? How'd I miss it?"

Remy was sure her cheeks were bright red and that the trail Enzio's lips and hands had made was blinking neon.

"I gave it to her," Enzio said. "What do you think?"

Colin looked surprised. He frowned at Remy, then at Enzio. "You gave it to her?"

"No big deal. Just something we were getting rid of at the store. I thought Remy would look good in it."

Colin still looked a little worried. "Sure. You look good, Remy. Great."

"I've got to get home." She had never felt so flustered. "I'd better change. My mother has a thing about short skirts."

"Maybe your mother knows what she's talking about," Colin said.

Enzio reached in his pocket for a cigarette. "Butt out."

Colin shrugged.

Remy made her escape. In the bathroom, she tugged on her jeans before she removed the skirt. Her fingers were trembling so hard she had to remove her bra and turn it in front of her to fasten it again. By the time she emerged, Colin was gone and Enzio was standing at the sink, smoking.

"Wish I didn't have to run." She wasn't sure that was true, but it sounded like the right thing to say.

"Next time we'll make sure he's really gone for good."

Next time. That possibility warmed all the places he had touched and simultaneously sent a chill through her heart.

"Thanks for the outfit," she said.

"Save it and wear it for me next time we're alone."

She smiled, or hoped she did.

She let herself out. For one brief moment on the sidewalk she found herself hoping that her mother had already gotten home so she would have to tell Faith where she'd been and what had happened there. But the house was empty.

She sat down at her great-great grandmother's spinet and began to play a song she'd memorized when she was still a little girl.

 24

"I believe I liked it better when it was covered with weeds. At least it was green."

Faith and Lydia had just walked down to see Violet's name chiseled in the mill stone. True to his word, the Can Man had finished the ivy removal the day before. The yard looked like a desert.

"I know it looks horrible. But on Monday an arborist is coming to take out all the dead trees. It's expensive, but I figure with all that firewood I won't need to turn on the heat for years."

"And then?"

"Then Alex and I are going to put in the new trees and shrubs I'm getting from a wholesale nursery. Little ones, but they'll be similar to what Violet had here. I'll refurbish the beds with perennials in the spring, when I can wheedle divisions from you and my friends in McLean, and there's still time to put in discount store bulbs this fall."

"You'll be busy. Are you sure you want to tackle such a big project?"

"I'm excited about it, and we need a place to retreat. The biggest news is that Pavel swears he's going to build a gazebo where the greenhouse used to sit. If he does, I thought I'd plant wisteria as an overhead canopy."

"Mr. Quinn is spending a lot of time here and making rather large commitments for the future."

"He's not the kind of man who expects anything in return." Faith wasn't sure who she was defending, Pavel or herself.

"I've never met a man without some sort of expectations." Lydia took a break from her survey to look at her daughter. "You like him, don't you?"

"What's not to like? He's funny, intelligent, charming. I don't have to be anyone but myself with him."

"I've heard border collies described the same way."

Faith's defenses crumbled, and she laughed. "I think if I'd met Pavel when I was married to David, I would have felt guilty. Because the attraction would have been there, wedding ring and all."

"Then maybe you understand David a little better now. And the entire range of human beings who've slipped away from their wedding vows, even momentarily."

Faith couldn't believe what she was hearing. "When did you become such a liberal, Mother?"

"You mean when did I begin to have thoughts and opinions of my own? Or when did I realize the world was filled with moral ambiguity?"

"Both."

Lydia had obviously reached her saturation point. She turned back to the yard and swept her hand to encompass it. "I think my grandmother would be pleased with you and terribly displeased with me. I'm so glad you're making things right."

"No one would ever blame you for not wanting any part of this house."

"It's a home again."

Faith backed into the question that had been nagging at her. "And speaking of home, Remy and I began to strip the wallpaper in her room. I was surprised at the designs we found."

"There's no accounting for taste."

"Did you choose any of the wallpaper?"

"I put the house in the hands of rental agents. They made all the decisions."

Faith tried a different tack. "We found a dark blue paper and a formal green stripe under the surface papers."

"I'm sure Remy doesn't care for either."

Faith was stumped. Without asking her mother directly about the absence of baby wallpaper, she wasn't going to get the answers she sought.

Lydia glanced at her watch. "I need to go home. We're having company tonight. A slew of wealthy constituents your father's trying to impress. An intimate little gathering of between sixty and eighty."

Faith was surprised Lydia wasn't already at home fussing over the preparations. She remembered her mother suffering migraines after smaller parties because she had worked too hard and worried too much.

"You're invited, of course," Lydia said. "I forgot to tell you."

"You know I'm not. The senator hasn't spoken to me since the night the lights went out in Georgetown."

Lydia didn't deny it. "He doesn't like to be reprimanded. He broods."

"He behaved badly that night." Faith paused. "But I'll make peace with him. For your sake. And the children's."

"Are Alex and Remy concerned?"

Faith doubted her kids had noticed. Joe was so remote that he figured only superficially in their lives.

"*I'm* concerned," Faith said. "Families are supposed to stick together."

"A platitude that might need to be reexamined, like all the other platitudes we've lived with."

"Mother?"

"I need to go home and put my seal of approval on the preparations." Lydia's gaze lifted to the hedge that separated a portion of Dottie Lee's garden from Faith's. Dottie Lee was just emerging from her house. "There's that woman. Now I really do need to leave."

"You were friends once upon a time."

"Stay and talk to her if you like." Lydia leaned over to kiss Faith's cheek. "I'll look forward to seeing this yard in bloom again." She started toward the basement stairs.

Faith strolled to the hedge when Dottie Lee beckoned and stepped through into the other woman's garden. The landscaping here was beautifully manicured and spare, with carefully tended evergreens, artistically placed gravel paths, and a narrow, raised rectangular pool adorned by lily pads and a carved stone statue of a little girl squatting to see her reflection in the water.

"That's me, you know," Dottie Lee said, pointing at the little girl. "My father commissioned it when I was three."

"I didn't know." Faith had been in Dottie Lee's garden before, but they had talked of other things.

"What an anachronism I am, living in one house all my life. Letting the world come to me." Dottie Lee sounded quite pleased with herself.

"Did you ever want to live anywhere else?"

"Oh, once, perhaps. I fancied myself in love, and I thought I might follow him wherever his career took him."

"But you didn't?"

"There was the small matter of a wife."

"I never know when you're teasing."

"I never tease." Dottie Lee lowered herself to a bench with a view of towering rhododendrons. She motioned Faith to join her. "I saw your mother."

"She had to leave. I'm sorry."

"Dear, your mother hasn't spoken to me for years. She's afraid of what I know."

Faith felt her heart accelerate. "What you know?"

"I've told you this before."

"Not exactly. What you said was that you knew things that could hurt my father's career, or rather, you implied it."

"I've lived on Prospect Street all my life. I lived on Prospect before your mother and father moved in. I've heard things and seen things, and, worse, I remember them all. The curse of an active mind."

Faith felt as if she was being asked to put a puzzle together. Dottie Lee didn't volunteer information. Faith always had to ask, and she had to ask the right questions. She knew from experience that the more general she was, the more general Dottie Lee would be.

She wondered if she could learn from Dottie Lee what she hadn't been able to learn during her brief conversation with Lydia. "I came across something the other day that interested me. Would you like to hear about it?"

"I have nowhere else to go."

"Remy and I were stripping the wallpaper in her room. It's the one that was Hope's nursery."

"Go on."

Faith wondered if she was just making too much out of this. "There were layers of paper. Just as you'd expect with a house as old as mine."

"And?"

"And there was no wallpaper fit for a little girl's nursery. It was all very dark and formal, as if no one had prepared for a baby. Does that make any sense to you?"

"Sense? As in what would I have done if I were preparing for a new arrival?"

"No. Sense, as in knowing my mother, doesn't it seem out of character that she didn't prepare? She does her Christmas shopping in July. The gifts are wrapped in August. By September she's made diagrams of what decorations she'll use that year, where they'll go and when each segment will be put up."

"The woman you know and the one I knew are not the same."

"You mean she wasn't always compulsive? I can understand that Hope's kidnapping changed her, but I can't believe she wasn't organized enough to fix a nursery. Was she ill?" Faith hesitated. "Depressed? Did she hate the house even before Hope was taken?"

"Let's take the questions one at a time."

"All right. Was she ill? Is that why she didn't fix up the nursery?"

"I don't believe it was a difficult pregnancy. Not physically."

That last part had been added almost as an afterthought. Faith built on it. "Then was she depressed? Was the pregnancy difficult because she was unhappy?"

"Sometimes the truth is best learned from the people most affected by it."

"Dottie Lee, my sister's kidnapping is an open wound."

Dottie Lee was silent for a moment. "She wasn't happy, Faith dear. I don't believe the pregnancy was a good time in your mother's life."

Faith knew if she asked why, Dottie Lee would evade answering. She struggled for something more specific. "Was she unhappy with my father? With all the responsibilities of his office?"

"Why do you suppose his job was the problem?"

Faith thought back to something she'd read in the library scrapbook. In one of the many heavily manufactured stories she'd scanned, a reporter had interviewed family friends, looking for some whiff of scandal. The resulting profile of her parents had seemed odd to Faith. They kept to themselves. Lydia seemed to dislike Washington's social whirl and only participated when required. Joe, who had proudly showed off Lydia at first, had encouraged her to retreat during the pregnancy. At the time, Faith had assumed it was only one reporter's solution for filling a front page column. Now she wondered.

"I know she wasn't very active during the pregnancy. If she wasn't ill, maybe it was simply the nesting instinct. But she doesn't seem to have done the usual nesting."

"No, she didn't. Before she and Joe brought Hope home, the back room was your father's study. I don't believe they did anything more than move in a crib and a bassinet."

"Didn't she want the baby? Is that it? Was Hope an accident?"

"I wasn't living in their house. I certainly wasn't sleeping in their bed."

Faith tried to piece together what she knew for sure and what she could build on. "My father's difficult to live with. I'm sure adjusting to him was hard. And a baby on top of that... But I can't believe Mother didn't care enough to make a nursery." She looked up, inspired. "Unless my mother and father were having such serious problems that Hope was an unwanted link. Maybe Mother saw Hope as a barrier to divorce."

"Lydia never mentioned divorce to me."

"Was she unhappy enough to want one?"

"Your mother liked being the wife of a congressman. She grew up in a political family. She wanted to relive the happy years when her childhood home was filled with interesting and influential people. No, there are other ways to leave a marriage."

Faith didn't know what to say to that.

Dottie Lee got to her feet. "Have you seen photographs of your mother, dear? When she was newly married?"

Oddly, Faith could remember only a few. The kidnapping photographs, of course. Photographs of her father with important political figures. One with President Kennedy several years before he was assassinated. Another with a youthful Nixon during his unsuccessful campaign for governor of California. Lydia had been in the photographs, too, but very much a bit player.

Dottie Lee didn't wait for an answer. "Lydia was a lovely young woman. I was never quite sure why she chose Joe Huston. She had the looks, the education, the background and contacts to make a better match. I'm sorry for saying so, but it's true. I believe she saw something in your father that wasn't necessarily there. But there were other men who had her in their sights. Some more prominent and more deserving."

Faith rose from the bench, too. "Are you saying she had an affair? Or wanted to have one? With a colleague of my father's?"

"I'm merely saying she was an attractive young woman trapped in a marriage that wasn't made in heaven. Certainly a pregnancy could have made that marriage seem even less of a bargain."

Faith tried to imagine her mother at that age. Lydia seemed almost sexless to her, a woman who didn't like physical affection, a woman who shook hands with her grandson and stood stiffly when she was hugged. Had Lydia looked at her marriage and wished for more? Had she hoped for more in the arms of another man, a hope that was cut short by an unwanted pregnancy?

And what did any of it have to do with Hope's kidnapping?

Dottie Lee picked a dried leaf off a spray of perfectly disciplined holly. "The authorities tried and failed to find your sister's kidnapper. What makes you think you'll uncover the truth?"

Faith wondered if she really wanted to.

Dottie Lee dusted her hands. "You won't like what you find. Secrets are never kept because they're too delicious to share. Secrets are hideous, squirmy little creatures, and once they've been set free, they'll follow you forever."

"I'm afraid they follow you anyway."

"You're becoming wiser, Faith. Just watching that makes living in this old body worth the trouble."

* * *

The party was a success, but that didn't surprise Lydia. Over the years she had put together a list of professionals who knew what she liked and how to provide it. Caterers, florists and window washers went the extra mile in exchange for generous tips. Marley supervised the cleaning and final preparations, and Lydia waltzed in at the last moment to nod her approval. She no longer rearranged the flowers or agonized over whether to use champagne saucers or flutes. Over the years she had learned the hard way what was important—and how it felt to live without it.

"Well done as always, Lydia. I think everyone enjoyed themselves." Joe had changed out of his suit into pajamas that were nearly as formal. The leather of his slippers was good enough to see duty on the Senate floor, but he was on his way to his study, where he would stay up half the night perusing impending legislation and making phone calls to various members of his staff.

"I'm glad you're happy." Lydia flicked off the light in the dining room, now completely emptied of silver trays and canapes.

"Are you going to bed now?" When she nodded, he didn't offer to change her mind, merely gave a brief nod himself and left, his thoughts on the work awaiting him.

She flipped off the lights, checked the security alarm and the outdoor floodlights, and called down to the guest house to assure Samuel that all was well and they were turning in for the night.

In her bedroom, Lydia closed the door and stood with her back to it, as if to bar anyone from following her. No one would, of course. She couldn't remember the last time Joe had joined her here. Not since his heart attack. Not since well before it. As a young man, sex had been high on his agenda, but as his career blossomed, his sex drive had waned. Sublimation of some sort, she thought, and lucky for her.

She went through the familiar bedtime rituals. In her nightgown at last, she stood by the window, looking over the woods that protected their house from even the hint of neighbors. Somewhere a dog barked, then was silenced. She thought she heard a plane overhead, and as she concentrated, she heard the whisper of CNN coming from the television in Joe's study. He never worked without the news at full volume, as if listening as he dictated memos on obscure political technicalities would put him squarely in the middle of world events.

Her love affair with Joe Huston had ended almost before it began. A brief honeymoon, mere weeks in their own home together, and she had realized what a terrible error she'd made. She had mistaken rigidity for strength, craftiness for intelligence, obsession for idealism. She'd had no one to intercede for her, and no one to offer counsel. Too young to know better, she had tried to weather the storms of her marriage, but she had been adrift in gale force winds.

And then Dominik Dubrov had appeared at her front door.

Arms folded over her chest, she watched moonlight gild white pines at the forests' edge. Somewhere beyond their lacy branches lay the life she should have led, the one filled with tenderness and intimacy and shared values. That life was always out of reach, just beyond the trees or clouds or sweep of her fingertips.

But the little piece of it that she'd known was never far from her thoughts.

"Dominik, I, well, I'm surprised." Lydia pushed a silver-blond strand behind the velvet headband that kept her hair out of her eyes when she was working. She hadn't expected to see Dominik today. "Did you tell me you were coming? I thought Sandor was going to work on the wallpaper."

Dominik Dubrov shifted from one foot to the other, but not uneasily. He was a confident man, properly deferential, yes, but never unsure of himself. He was a poor man, a crudely educated man, but still one who was supremely sure that the homeowners who hired him were getting the best. Dottie Lee Fairbanks had assured her that Dominik was the only man to do the renovation of the Hustons' row house, and Lydia had come to agree.

Today Dominik was holding a wool knit cap at his waist, as if he had removed it just before knocking. Her gaze flicked to it, watching in fascination as his broad hands stretched and kneaded the cream-colored yarn. Gently, as if he were plucking the strings of a lute.

"Sandor had another job, and I finished at Miss Fairbanks' house early." The words were accented and faintly guttural. His command of English was excellent, but Lydia suspected his thoughts spun out in some Slavic dialect. At their first meeting she had tried out her college Russian on him, and he'd only smiled.

Dominik's smile was memorable. A little gap-toothed, a little lopsided, and impossible not to respond to.

"You want I should start on the wallpaper in the back today? I can measure and prepare."

Joe hated the wallpaper in the room he'd chosen as his study. He despised green and insisted that gazing up at the wide stripes made him seasick. She had lugged home book after book of samples, and he had finally, grudgingly, chosen a navy blue with tiny fleur-de-lis marching in symmetrical rows.

Three months into their marriage, and she was already fed up with Joe's insistence on controlling every detail of their lives.

Lydia stepped aside to let Dominik in. "Whatever you can do would be appreciated. I've been painting the trim."

"This is something you like to do?"

"I like to do it all. I've always wanted to make a home. We moved so much when I was growing up...." She realized she was telling the handyman the story of her life.

"I also moved as a child. I understand."

He stepped past her, careful not to brush her skirt as he passed, although he was a large man, and that wasn't easy. The dress was an old one. She could have told him as much, but she appreciated his consideration. The first few weeks that Dominik had worked for her, she had found his presence hard to get used to. He was a man and a stranger, and being alone with him in the row house begat an intimacy she found disturbing.

Lydia started toward the kitchen. "I was about to get myself a glass of water. Would you like something?"

Dominik followed her. He had stripped the wallpaper there and prepared the surface. She had painted the walls a sunny-yellow and set three hand-thrown Italian plates on an iron display rack in the corner. A majolica rooster perched on the counter beside cobalt-blue canisters. Joe had objected strenuously to the rooster, but so far Lydia had withstood that particular barrage.

"Cock a doodle doo?" Dominik fingered the rooster's wattle as Lydia retrieved ice from the freezer and ran it under the faucet to separate it from the metal tray.

"Do you like him?" Lydia snapped the ice onto a fresh dish towel beside the sink.

"Very much. He's for smiling, yes?"

"I wish you'd tell my husband."

"A serious man?"

"To a fault."

Dominik leaned against the counter and watched her fill two glasses with ice, then with tap water. He took up much of the kitchen. He had wide shoulders and long muscular legs. His hair and eyes were black, both a little wild, as if the good manners he displayed in the workplace were the flip side of something darker. He had a ruddy complexion, prominent bones and strong features, particularly his nose, which was curved and beaklike and utterly barbaric.

She could see Dominik Dubrov in a Cossack's saddle, saber at his side, fur hat on his head, sweeping across the frontiers of Mother Russia.

"If a man cannot smile, a man cannot love," he said.

"An old Soviet proverb?"

"Just another reason to be happy."

Lydia handed him a glass and a napkin to put under it when he set it down. "As if we should need reasons."

"Some people, they seem to."

She thought Joe might be one of those.

"Are you happy?" She wasn't sure where the question had come from. It wasn't a question a woman asked her handyman. But during the weeks Dominik had been coming to work on the house, she'd stopped thinking of him that way. He had a quiet wisdom that was a foil to something else, something she could only term animal magnetism. It was a phrase *Photoplay* or *Silver Screen* might choose for Marlon Brando or the late James Dean, but it fit Dominik, too.

"I have a son. My Pasha makes me happy."

"A little boy?" She made a cooing noise. "How old is he?"

"Two. A hell raiser? This is how you say it?"

"That's how we say it." She hadn't known Dominik was married. He wore no ring, but that wasn't uncommon for a man. Joe had chosen to wear one, but only, she suspected, because it made him seem more settled, dependable and worthy of votes.

"He began to talk very much at only one year."

Lydia's knowledge of children was fuzzy, but since Dominik was proud, she suspected this must be early. "And I bet he chatters all the time now."

"And I am chattering too much. There is no one in the bedroom?"

"No, you can go up."

He held up his glass. "Thank you."

"Dominik, does having a child make a marriage stronger, do you think?"

He didn't seem surprised by the question. "This is what they say."

"What do *you* say?"

His face sobered. "I say that some marriages, they cannot be made stronger, not by anything."

She knew he was talking about his own, and, strangely, she was glad. She wasn't one to revel in other people's misfortune, but just knowing that Dominik faced the same problems she did made her feel even closer to him.

"I guess that means having a baby with Joe won't make our marriage better."

He was silent, as if he was fighting with himself. She wasn't sure whether he had won or lost the battle when he spoke. "You aren't happy, Mrs. Huston?"

"Lydia. We've grown beyond Mrs., don't you think?"

He shrugged, a marvelous shifting of his broad shoulders that spoke volumes.

"I'm not happy." She wondered what else she would tell him today. First the story of her life. Now this.

"You are young. This is new."

She shook her head. "I made a mistake. I don't know how to fix it. I don't want a divorce, and I don't want to stay married." Tears sprang to her eyes. Perhaps it was easier to say these things to a virtual stranger. Perhaps it was simply that Dominik was there when she needed to talk.

Perhaps it was simply that Dominik was Dominik.

"Divorce is not possible?" he asked.

"I don't believe in divorce. I think one makes choices and one sticks by them."

"I think the same. And my wife is Catholic and would not consider such a thing."

"What a pair we are."

"I did not mean to pry."

"I didn't mean to bend your ear." When he looked perplexed at her slang, she managed a teary smile. "I talked too long about myself."

One tear refused to be tamed and slid to her cheek. Dominik set down his glass; then he reached out and caught the tear on his fingertip. She closed her eyes as he drew his finger tenderly across her cheekbone, trying to erase her sorrow.

"I'm sorry." She swallowed hard. "I don't know what's wrong with me this afternoon."

She felt his arms around her, strong, soothing arms. He pulled her to his chest to comfort her. She slipped her arms around his waist as naturally as if she was married to him and not to a man who would have pushed her away after one impatient pat.

She laid her head against his shoulder, expecting sobs to pour forth. But the tears had dried up now, and what was left was very different.

She felt a shudder run through Dominik's body. It was answered by a wave of excitement in her own. He felt so good against her, and comfort was now only a small portion of that.

She told herself she should move away before she no longer could. She wasn't afraid of Dominik. As strong as he was, she knew he wouldn't force himself on her.

She was more afraid of herself.

Neither of them moved. At last she looked up. He was gazing down at her, his expression hooded. He didn't move away; he didn't move forward. He stood still and waited for her to tell him what to do.

The whole world seemed poised for discovery.

* * *

Now, as a woman who hadn't been held with that terrible, ferocious longing for thirty-nine years, Lydia held herself instead. She wrapped her arms over her breasts and leaned her forehead against the window.

 25

"Casual, then, and warm," Pavel told Faith when they made arrangements for their Saturday date. The children were invited to her mother's for the night, and Faith had no curfew.

She pried a little harder and learned that he didn't mean casual like going for pizza on M Street. That was formal. Faith wasn't able to get anything more out of him, since he insisted that wherever they were going was a secret. But at least as she got ready on Saturday afternoon she wasn't obsessing about what to wear again. She chose jeans that still buttoned comfortably and her favorite kelly-green turtleneck.

She was brushing her hair when Alex came into her bedroom to say goodbye. She gave him a bear hug. "You've got everything you need?"

"Mo-om...." Disgust made it a two syllable word. "I'll bring my Legos, and Remy can bring her Barbie dolls."

"Funny guy. I just don't want you to get bored."

"We're going to the movies tonight, and tomorrow we're going to a horse show in Maryland."

She wasn't sure why she was fussing. Joe was in Richmond for the weekend, and Alex and Remy would be fine with her mother. Even Remy seemed resigned to the visit. Of course, in Great Falls she was no longer grounded.

Faith went through a mental checklist. "You closed your bedroom door so Guest won't eat Lefty?"

Alex rolled his eyes in a very good imitation of his sister. Faith bit back a suggestion that he pack his toothbrush and clean underwear. "Don't forget I'll have my cell phone if you need me."

"I'm going to wait on the steps."

"Is Remy already out there?"

"I don't know."

Lately Faith had noticed that Alex became evasive whenever Remy's name was mentioned. Alex, usually incapable of repressing a thought, seemed to be repressing a great many. But now was not the time to probe.

"Have fun, and I'll see you tomorrow." She gave him another hug, and this time he hugged her back before he disappeared into the hallway and down the steps.

She was fastening gold studs in her earlobes when she realized Remy was standing in the doorway, watching her.

"Need anything before you go?" Faith asked.

"Like what? Clean diapers and a new teddy bear?"

"I'm not sure what time I'm coming home tonight, so this will be easier."

"Like that had anything to do with me staying alone tonight while you're on your date." The word "date" was uttered like a particularly offensive profanity.

Faith fastened the second stud. "I want to be able to trust you again."

Remy turned away. "Have a great time. Don't think about *us*."

Faith marveled that somehow, without help from the people who loved her most, Remy had become the grandmaster of sarcasm.

In a moment the front door slammed. Faith hoped her mother arrived before her children had a fistfight on the stoop. Her wish was granted when a car stopped out front. Lydia's greeting drifted upstairs, along with the conversation of Georgetown students biking past. By the time Faith opened the front window to call her last goodbye they were gone, all three of them.

She closed it, turned and leaned against it. She was free. No one expected anything of her tonight. Pavel was taking care of all the arrangements, and she only had to show up. Not even that, since he was coming to pick her up.

She only had to let him in.

Faith realized she was smiling. Not the obedient smile she'd learned as a child, or the untouchable good girl smile of her adolescence. Not even the perfect wife and role model smile she'd mastered during her years with David. Something brighter and more connected to her real hopes and fears. Something so brilliantly genuine it realigned the muscles in her face.

She was ready when Pavel arrived. She opened the door and admired the way a snug pair of jeans outlined his hips and thighs. He wore a red Scavenger sweatshirt with a navy-blue collar and logo. A brand-new one, she guessed, by the absence of spots or wrinkles. He probably owned a hundred.

"New line." Self-consciously, he pulled the sweatshirt away from his chest with one hand and held up a shopping bag with the other. "More, for you and the kids."

Faith was touched. Even if Remy used her shirt to mop up spills or polish her shoes, Alex would be in seventh heaven. "That was so thoughtful. I'd wear mine now, but it would look like we're going steady." She realized she was standing in the doorway. She took the bag from his hand and ushered him inside. "The kids are already gone."

"Any chance your mother might decide to keep Remy?"

She grinned. "Mother's a lot of things, but never a masochist."

"Are you close to her?"

"Mother? As close as I'm allowed."

"I've only met her in passing, but she's nothing like you, is she? You're warm and giving and easy to be with. I'm not sure she's any of those things."

Faith savored the way he had characterized her. "She's getting more like that. It's funny, but she's opened up so much since we moved here. And you'd think the opposite would apply."

"Maybe everything that happened in this house wasn't bad. This was her first real home with your father, wasn't it?" He seemed to read her thoughts. "Not necessarily a good thing?"

"Maybe not." She changed the subject. "Anyway, where are we going? What's the surprise?"

"Gotta know what's under the wrapping paper, huh?"

"I've been patient most of my life. I feel that phase coming to an end."

"Grab a coat, then, and let's see what happens."

"It's not that cold outside, is it?"

"You never know."

She snatched a wool jacket on the way out. When she locked the door behind her, she felt the weight of daily life lifting from her shoulders. "I'm ready for anything."

"I'll hold you to that." He smiled as he said it, but his eyes flashed something different. She wasn't sure which message to believe, but she suspected she was going to find out.

She wasn't ready for West Virginia. Not for Interstate 80, leading to the cottage David had bought for her. Not for the turnoff to Granger's Food and Gas, and particularly not for the stop Pavel made there.

She had fallen asleep somewhere along the way. After they drifted into a comfortable silence, Pavel turned the radio to soft jazz. She closed her eyes, and when she opened them again she was horrified to find she had been sleeping and now they weren't far from the place where she'd found her husband in the arms of another man.

As she fumbled for a way to tell Pavel, he pulled off the road and into Granger's parking lot. He glanced at her and saw she was awake. "Hey, sleeping beauty. Stay here and sleep some more."

She snuggled down in the seat and prayed no one would come out to see if they needed gas. "What are we doing here?"

"Just forgot something." He opened his door and stepped out, closing it behind him.

Faith wished she could disappear.

He took forever. She sat in the car and wondered if she should tell him the truth, that being here, simply breathing the West Virginia air and gazing at the familiar blue haze of the mountains, made her heart ache. She scooted farther down in her seat and turned her head as a car pulled beside Pavel's. The door slammed, and she heard footsteps. When she risked a glance in that direction, she found Tubby staring at her through the window.

She sat frozen until she realized he was waiting for her to roll it down. She pressed the button, but nothing happened, because the engine was off. Silently cursing the twenty-first century, she opened the door and got out.

"Tubby." She managed a smile and leaned stiffly against the car.

"Miz Bronson." Tubby's grin could ignite a bonfire. "You're a sight for sore eyes."

"You, too." Silently she asked forgiveness for the lie.

"Those folks that bought your cottage come by here every week or two, but it ain't the same, you know? He won't talk to me like your David did. Don't care what I think about nuthin'." Tubby hiked one strap of the ubiquitous overalls to punctuate that sentiment.

She didn't know what to say. She fell back on good manners. "We always enjoyed talking to you."

"You doin' okay?"

"I am, thanks. I'm living in the city now."

"And the mister?"

"David's okay." She didn't know how much to say. She was in the heart of conservative America. Certainly he'd heard about their divorce and the story behind it. As much as she liked Tubby, she was fairly sure of his views on homosexuality.

"He got a job yet?"

Her spine was rigid. She was still waiting for Tubby to turn on her. "He's having trouble finding the right job."

"Now that's a shame. He's a good man and a smart one." He waved away unspoken protests, as if they were zinging around his head like a flock of bees. "Oh, I know what people say, and I know it was a terrible shock for you and all. I was angry at first, you know? Why'd he keep that kind of thing a secret and pretend he was different than he was? But then I got to thinkin'. We don't live in a world where a man can just come out and say what he is, do we? What choice did we give him?"

Faith was surprised. "You've really been doing some thinking, I guess."

"Had to."

She looked up and saw Pavel coming toward them. She was

afraid Tubby was about to get another shock from the Bronson family. "Tubby, this is a friend of mine, Pavel Quinn."

Tubby turned. "Hey, Pavel. Good to see you again. Just passin' the time with Miz Bronson here. We're old pals."

Pavel looked genuinely amazed. "You are?"

"She seen that place of yours yet?"

"We're on our way up there now."

"Well, don't let me keep you." Tubby turned back to her and winked. "You just keep your eye on him, you hear? He like to have burned down that house of his one night when the wind turned."

"I was burning trash," Pavel explained. "Just a little too close to the house."

"Good thing you didn't set fire to it," Tubby said. "Prettiest place in these parts." He stepped away. "You stop by anytime, Miz Bronson. I'll make sure we keep some of those green apples you like, just in case."

Faith waved as they drove off. She hadn't even turned in her seat before Pavel spoke.

"How do you know Tubby?"

"*Your* house, Pavel? You have a house *here?*"

"That's where we're going." He put his hand on her knee. Just a quick squeeze, but the message of support was clear. "Okay. Your turn."

"David and I had a cottage just down the road. This is where I found him in the arms of Abraham Stein."

"Jeez." He looked as if he was going to pull over.

She put her hand on his wrist. "Don't you dare turn around."

"The scenery's pretty familiar, huh?"

"I think that's okay." She hesitated. "Maybe not okay, but getting there."

"You don't feel like you're back in a nightmare?"

She didn't. Her first reaction was gone, and in its place she felt relief. "Tubby greeted me like an old friend. He didn't blame me for anything. For that matter, he doesn't even seem to blame David. The mighty fell, but Tubby saw us for what we were. Just human beings with flaws. We weren't nearly as important as I thought. I can't tell you how much I like that."

"We can still head home."

"Let's. To *your* home in the mountains." She paused. "It wouldn't happen to be on Seward Road, would it?"

"I'm two mountaintops away."

"Good. That would have been more than I could handle." She laughed. The feel of it was cleansing.

Just as he'd predicted, Faith loved the house. Pavel was hopelessly in love with it himself. Technically the land and everything on it belonged to Scavenger, and sometimes the board or employees used it for corporate retreats. But Pavel had first claim on scheduling.

The house itself was gray cedar and glass, with windows looking over the mountains and, at closer hand, a huge pond. A cottage sat five acres away out of sight, a cozier version of this one, housing their jack-of-all-trades caretaker and his wife, who was a gourmet cook. Lolly had plotted with him to have dinner ready when he and Faith arrived, and the smell had greeted them the moment they opened the door.

They ate in front of a massive stone fireplace, sitting cross-legged with their plates on their laps, despite a dining room with a view of forever. Lolly served platters of roast pork, penne pasta with vegetables and a lemon butter sauce, and for dessert a curried fruit compote so mouthwatering that Faith threatened to chain herself to the front porch unless she got the recipe.

Pavel selected a Hungarian red wine to go with the pork, and after the meal he was pleased to see Faith was on her second glass.

"What did you say this was?" she asked, holding the wine to the firelight.

"Bikavér. Bull's blood."

"I could get used to this. I'd better remind myself to sip, so it lasts longer."

"There's more where that came from."

"Judging by this pleasant buzz in my head, I won't be having another glass."

"That's a particularly good vintage. Wine making in Hungary suffered during Communism. It's taken some time to get back on track."

"You know your wines. I'm a babe in the woods."

He settled more firmly against an ottoman, stretching his legs toward the fire. "I know wines, but only a little about Hungary."

"You haven't been there?"

"I've made a few hit-and-run business trips to Europe, but none that far east. I'd like to go someday. I've had plans to travel for years, but Scavenger sucked all the life out of that."

"Sucked enough that you're really serious about going on to other things? Like traveling?"

"That surprises you?"

"In the world I come from, people don't leave important jobs. They continually negotiate for bigger ones, unless scandal brings them down."

"Did your father want to be president?"

She swirled what was left of her wine. "When he was younger. Before his heart attack. But he made one serious career mistake a long time ago. He remained a Democrat when most conservatives fled the party, and he lost his chance to move up and on. I've never been quite sure why. A rusty sort of idealism, I guess. If Joe Huston had been fighting for the Confederacy, he never would have surrendered."

"Maybe he's not as political as you think."

She looked up at him. "Oh, don't make that mistake. He's terrifyingly political, but he's stubborn, too. He's at war with himself, and I'm glad. For the sake of our country. Joe Huston should never be in charge."

He wondered if that was the wine talking. "You don't like him very well, do you?"

"This isn't personal. I just think his brand of politics isn't what we need in the Oval Office. He's a Democrat, but he doesn't really believe in democracy. He's an unrepentant backroom pit bull. He may sound like a populist, but he really doesn't like the common man. He just likes to think he knows what's best for him."

"That's quite an indictment."

"That's quite a bottle of bull's blood."

"I'm trying to understand here. You say this, but you were married to a man who's even more conservative than your father."

She inclined her head. "David's conservatism is both honestly compassionate and intellectual. He truly likes people and believes the best about them. He just doesn't believe the government should run their lives."

"What about you?"

"I'm so confused I'm not even sure who to vote for next month. I'm spending this year trying to forget everything I thought I believed. Then I'm going to think for myself." She smiled, although that admission was more poignant than humorous. "And you?"

"I know who to vote for. I'm so liberal Joe McCarthy would have had me at the top of his hit list."

"My father thinks it's an honor to be named Joe." She raised the glass in toast. "Three cheers to you, Pavel. We neatly got off the subject of your life and on to the subject of mine. Are you just a great listener, or do you really hate to talk about yourself? I know so little."

"What do you know?"

She cocked her head. "A test, huh? You were born in the area, but you grew up in California. And you were educated somewhere in the Midwest?"

"Chicago."

"You came to visit and stayed to found Scavenger. You've never been married, because you don't like long-term relationships."

"Wait a minute. You're hypothesizing there."

"Am I wrong?"

He couldn't deny it.

"Then there's that house," she went on. "A long-term project if ever there was one."

"I'm easily bored. I need a house that has endless potential to keep me busy."

"But not a woman?"

"Do you know any women like that?"

The moment he said it, he was sorry, but Faith only laughed. "Do you need a woman who keeps you on your toes? Somebody who indulges in temper tantrums and sweeping flights of fancy?"

"I grew up with a woman like that. Even though she kept me on my toes, the view from that position was decidedly bleak."

"I'm sorry. That doesn't sound good."

She *was* sorry. Empathy sang in her voice and softened her gaze. Exactly the kind of woman Pavel had always tried to avoid.

"My parents separated when I was little, and I never saw my father again. My mother drank her way in and out of depression more times than I could possibly count."

"You said she died before you left California?"

"Her life was wasted on regret."

"Not wasted. She had a son."

"And occasionally she remembered, and then life was sweet for a while. Until she started drinking again."

"That's a hard way to grow up."

He supposed it was, although years ago he had learned not to feel much about it. "Good things came out of those years. I spent every hour I could at school so I wouldn't have to go home. I learned to make friends easily for the same reason. Both of those things helped make a success of Scavenger."

"I bet." She finished her wine and set down the glass before she spoke again. "Do you remember anything about your father?"

"That he didn't stay around to see me grow up."

"Sometimes life seems like one big club for people with unhappy childhoods."

She looked so solemn, he had to laugh. "Faith, it's all right. I'm not unhappy now."

"I just wonder how I'll hurt my own children. Maybe I have already. Or maybe knowing their father is gay will be an insurmountable hurdle for them."

"No, because you're involved in their lives in a way that makes the difference, and from what little you've said, so is he."

"You would have been a good father."

"Do you think so?" That surprised him. What surprised him more was how little thought he'd ever given to it. With no good role models of his own, he hadn't been eager to chance it.

"You're terrific with Alex," she said. "You're even good with Remy, and that's the litmus test."

"You liked the part where I told her I wanted to turn her over my knee?"

That sexy Dietrich laugh rumbled in her chest. "I liked the part where you didn't do it."

Pavel set down his glass and told himself not to pour another.

Because with one more glass of wine warming his libido and cooling his inhibitions, he was fairly sure what he would do next.

He got to his feet and stretched; then he held out a hand. "Let's walk off that food."

"The sun's going down, isn't it?"

"Not fast enough to catch us."

"I was just hoping the sunset would be spectacular and the stars would come out on the walk back."

"We might see a few. You'll need your coat."

She let him take her hand to pull her up, stumbling a little as she got to her feet. He put an arm around her to steady her. "Whoa there."

"Don't worry. It's not the wine. My leg was asleep." She looked up at him, pale eyelashes framing the summer sky-blue of her eyes. "That was a lovely dinner, Pavel. Thank you."

He considered forgetting the walk. Faith had been a married woman for years. He suspected she had yet to redevelop the defense strategies single women used routinely. He doubted she understood what she was doing to him with that unfettered gaze and the weight of her body in his arms.

On the other hand, he wondered if she understood completely.

"I'm glad you enjoyed it." He released her, waiting a moment to be sure she was steady on her feet. "You'll enjoy the fresh air, too."

"I'm looking forward to it."

His eyes flicked to the huge, soft pillows they had dragged to the Persian rug in front of the fire and the still flickering flames. From the stereo system a Liszt symphonic poem breathed sensuality into every corner of the room.

He forced himself toward the hallway coat closet. "Let me get my coat."

"Mine's by the front door. I'll meet you outside."

He spent a full minute digging through the closet and wishing that this woman, like every other woman in his life, meant nothing important to him.

Faith was feeling particularly exhilarated. She wasn't sure whether to blame the wine, the food, the clear mountain air or simply Pavel's company. The question seemed important. The fact that she wasn't sure seemed important, too. On some nearly subliminal level she understood that the answer, whatever it was, was the key to some part of her future.

"It's as beautiful as I thought it would be," she said, breaking a long silence.

They had strolled around the pond to a crude gazebo that looked out on the valley below. She wasn't sure how long they had been sitting side by side on an old wooden glider with a carpet of evergreen needles at their feet. Long enough to watch a crimson sunset fade to twilight. Long enough to watch a harvest moon begin its ascent and stars punctuate the sky.

Pavel had put on a heavy wool sweater, and now he pulled the collar up to shelter his neck. "I try to spend weekends out here when the leaves are turning and the air's crisp."

"I wouldn't have pegged you for a country boy. This place alone would be an incentive to stay with Scavenger."

"I can buy the whole thing outright if I leave. It's in my contract."

She imagined that if he ever left Scavenger, he would have enough surplus cash to buy all of West Virginia. "You don't act like a wealthy man, Pavel. I never would have guessed."

"You *didn't* guess, as a matter of fact."

"The paint-spattered Rolex should have been a clue, huh? Not that it matters one way or the other. Except that sometimes wealthy people retreat into their own private worlds, and you're a regular guy."

"Because I drive a beat-up Subaru and do my own renovations?"

"Because you come visiting with chicken curry and pad Thai in brown paper bags, and crawl under my sink to check for leaks."

"Do you know how many dot coms fail every year? Scavenger was a good idea, but so were a thousand others. I was lucky. I don't see why that should turn me into a different person."

She poked him in the arm. "Humble, to boot."

"Hey, I had humble beginnings. I was born at D.C. General, to parents who couldn't pay the hospital bill. I was raised on potatoes and cabbage, Mom's Irish roots. That's one way I've changed. I don't eat cabbage. I don't even want to smell it cooking." He turned to smile. "Just in case you're really planning to have me over to dinner sometime."

"The cook here is an act I can't live up to."

"I like your company better."

They hadn't touched since leaving the house. She was grateful to Pavel for not pushing intimacy, for seeming to understand her conflicts—or possibly his own. At the same time, she missed the feel of his skin against hers.

She placed her hand on his in one more of a short list of daring gestures. "I like your company, too. And I promise you dinner soon. I'll even scratch my favorite cabbage soup off the menu."

"I would be more than grateful." He turned his hand and captured hers. "Shall we start back? We've still got a long drive home."

She knew the evening had to end. Yet her sadness that it was about to was familiar. She recognized it, of course. She had been haunted by this so many times in her marriage, times when she wanted to deepen the intimacy with David and was lovingly rebuffed. These circumstances were different, of course. Pavel was not her husband, and they had never been lovers. Their relationship was new and uncharted, and might be nothing more than a close friendship.

She was still sorry the evening was ending.

"You're right." She got to her feet, holding his hand. "Do we walk back the same way?"

"It's shorter in the other direction."

She supposed shorter was better. "You're going to have to come quietly, mister. I can't pull you up."

Their eyes met and held; then he pulled her down instead, with one fluid twist of his wrist and a groan. She was on his lap before she could take a breath, and he was kissing her before she could take another.

He cradled her face in his hands, his lips simultaneously soft and insistent. She drew a startled breath; then the desire that had been simmering all evening boiled over in sensation so intense it had no precedent.

"Faith..."

She was kissing him back. Thought fled immediately. A starving woman would have torn into bread the same way. No manners, no plan to nourish anyone else, no worries about what might follow. She kissed him as if he might disappear the moment she stopped. She inhaled the masculine scent of him, absorbed his warmth through layers of clothing, listened avidly to the moaning murmur deep in his throat.

He pushed her away. "This is not the place."

She gauged the distance back to the house and measured it in regrets and fears. "Your fault." She kissed him again, and he tugged her against him hard, wrapping his arms around her to hold her there.

Even if she had wanted to make the trip to the house, it was impossible now. Along with thought, her ability to maneuver fled. At the moment she couldn't have found her way out of a phone booth. And Pavel was no guide. He, too, seemed incapable of more than exploring her mouth with his tongue, her back with his hands. He unhooked her bra, and the feel of his palm against her breasts severed the final link to sanity.

The air was cold where her skin was bare, and with the rising of the moon had come a heavy blanket of mist that rose heavenward like steam. She didn't care. The carpet of evergreen needles was soft and dry as they tumbled to it together. They worked at each other's clothing, pawing, pushing, tugging.

A man stripping away her clothes like so much annoying wrapping paper was new to her. Pavel had large, sturdy hands, but they were surprisingly skillful at small details. Her jeans were unbuttoned; her leather sneakers went flying. She felt the rough denim scraping her skin as her legs were bared. The green sweater found a new home under a towering spruce.

She could smell resin and woodsmoke and the unique, earthy fragrance of Pavel's skin. Between them they made short work of the sweater and Scavenger sweatshirt. In the faint moonlight she saw that his chest was wide and hard, not sprinkled lightly with hair but defined by it. The muscles rippled against her palms, and his skin was as hot to the touch as if they were in front of the fireplace after all.

She had a moment of sanity when he was naked above her. One moment when she wondered what she was doing and how she had come so quickly and effortlessly to this place. They hadn't spoken.

There hadn't been any words of love or even affection. She didn't think love had much part in it yet. She wanted him. She wanted to feel like a woman who wanted a man.

She needed him to make her feel like a woman.

He rummaged in a pocket of his jeans, graceful, capable hands seemingly incapable now. He muttered something, and she heard frustration, not words. Then, still cursing, he finally pulled out a small, familiar-looking plastic bag and from it a foil wrapped package.

She knew why he'd stopped by Granger's Store.

Even with the first blaze of desire melting all her inhibitions and stealing her sanity, she heard herself laughing. "Oh, Pavel, you got that at Granger's, didn't you?"

"Busted." Poised above her, he hesitated. "You're ready for this? You're sure, Faith?"

"Being sure has nothing to do with it."

He smoothed on the condom, taking precious seconds away from her; then he covered her with his body and drew her underneath him.

"I'm absolutely sure I want you," he said.

She stretched out her arms, welcoming his weight and the hard thrust of his hips against hers. She gave herself up to the fierce pleasure and the quick release that came immediately after.

 26

She wasn't sorry, although every instinct she possessed told her she ought to be. Not because legally she was still a married woman. Not because she had always followed the rules others laid down for her. Not even because now she would have to cope with the fall-out and renegotiate her relationship with Pavel.

She wasn't sorry because she was so very happy. And despite a lifetime of questioning her right to feel this satisfied and secure in her sexuality and feminine powers, now she believed she deserved it.

She had awakened this morning on the farthest edge of Pavel's bed, his hairy arm thrown over her naked breasts and his knee prodding the small of her back, unsurprised to discover that he sprawled outrageously. After the first shock, she knew she would never be sorry for the night they had spent together or for Pavel's foresight in buying an entire package of condoms, and particularly not for the restoration of her confidence.

Because what woman could doubt her own attractions when a man like this one couldn't seem to get enough of her? And when the opposite was every bit as true? She had thought she was attracted to David. She had not understood.

"Faith?"

Faith looked up and realized that Lydia had asked her a question. This afternoon Faith had beaten her mother and the children home from their horse show by a scant half hour, just in time to change her clothes and delete the messages on the answering machine—in case someone noticed she hadn't been home all morning to receive them.

"I'm sorry. I didn't sleep well last night. I guess I'm tired." She managed not to smile.

"I asked if you had fun last night."

"Uh-huh. I did."

"Did you eat somewhere nice?"

"Out in the country. Very casual, but the food was great." Faith realized she had begun making coffee for her mother but hadn't moved beyond filling the pot with water. Now she rummaged for a filter.

"Well, the children seemed to have fun this morning. Remy especially liked the horse show. She saw some girls from your old neighborhood and went off with them. I didn't see much of her again until it was over."

Faith was glad her daughter had reconnected with old friends. Right now she and Alex were upstairs getting ready for a shopping trip, but Faith hoped she would hear more about the horse show then.

"Faith, are you ever going to put the coffee in that filter?"

Faith looked down. "Yes, but slowly. Very slowly."

"You really didn't sleep well, did you? You have circles under your eyes."

"There's a lot to think about these days." Faith forced herself to finish the preparations and turn on the coffeemaker.

"Like what?"

Faith scrambled for something to say. "Well, I've got to finish fixing up the house and the garden, and I want to do it right."

"Right?"

"I have a lot of painting left. I'm trying to pay attention to both history and comfort. I should probably just go next door and ask Dottie Lee what she remembers about the interior colors so I can stop obsessing. She remembered everything about the garden."

Faith looked up. "She as much as told me there was nothing about this house that she didn't know. But she's doling the facts out one at a time. She waits for just the right questions. I think she wants insurance I'll keep visiting her."

"What did she mean, she knows everything?"

"She said she remembers more about this house than anyone else in the world." Faith searched her memory, then shrugged. "She's older than you are, so she remembers further back. And she lived right next door from the day she was born. Makes sense to me."

Lydia fell silent. Despite her own preoccupation with the events of last night, Faith noticed her mother was brooding.

"She told me the other day just how beautiful you were." Faith watched her mother's head snap up. "And I told her how few photographs I've seen of you as a new bride. Wedding photos, yes, but nothing much after that." She hesitated and decided not to pussyfoot around. "Except newspaper photos after Hope was kidnapped."

"How did that come up?"

"I was asking her about those early years. Hope's a strong presence in this house. Not a ghost," she hurried to add. "It's just that there's a strong sense of something not finished."

"That was almost the worst part of it, you know, waiting for answers that never came. Next to knowing that she might be dead or in pain or crying for me..."

"Oh, Mother." Faith put her hand on Lydia's. "I'm sorry."

Lydia shook her off. "You're the one who brought up the past. With that woman."

"I live here now."

"There's nothing to be gained from dredging up the kidnapping. Do you think you can have a couple of conversations with Dottie Lee and solve a crime the FBI couldn't?"

"I just wanted to understand a little more. That's all. It's the great blank in my past, the elephant in the middle of the room. She was my sister. I was affected, too."

"After it happened, the only way I could survive was to put the kidnapping out of my mind. At first just for minutes, then for hours, and later, much later, for whole days at a time. I couldn't have borne it otherwise."

"I know how hard it is, even now."

But Lydia wasn't finished. "I thought having another child would help heal the wound. Then I had you, and every time I looked at you I wondered what Hope would have looked like at your age; or if she would have walked earlier or later or liked the same kind of toys you did. She was dark-haired, like your father. Sometimes when you were little I'd be shopping, and I'd see something that would suit a dark-haired child, and I'd have to fight myself not to buy it for Hope. When you walked down the aisle to marry David, I wondered how she would have looked in her wedding dress."

Lydia had been staring at the kitchen table. Now she looked up. "I loved you, Faith. Don't make the mistake of thinking I didn't. But so many times I looked at you and thought of your sister. And that was another reason I tried to put the whole thing behind me. Because it wasn't fair."

"And I'm dredging it up again."

"Don't. Just don't. For everyone's sake."

Faith remembered the things Dottie Lee had said and, more importantly, the things she hadn't. The hints. The silences that had led Faith in new directions. She couldn't let it go. "Was Hope the beginning of all the sadness in your life?"

"I don't know what you mean."

"I mean I grew up in a house with two unhappy parents. Would things have been different if Hope hadn't been taken?"

"How can I answer that?" Lydia's tone had changed considerably, a cold front moving in after a warm spell.

"Losing a child is the hardest thing parents ever have to deal with. Even in a perfect marriage."

"There's nothing to be gained from this, Faith. The past is exactly that."

Faith knew there was nothing to be gained right now by continuing. Her mother had opened up as much as she was going to. "I'm sorry. I'm not trying to pry. Just trying to understand."

"Why? So you'll understand yourself a little better? Or maybe you're suddenly interested in relationships because you just spent the night with a man and your own life's topsy-turvy?"

Faith realized she wasn't as blase about what had happened with Pavel as she'd thought. Her cheeks were warming like a high school sophomore's. "How did you know?"

"I may be growing old, but I recognize the glow of a satisfied woman."

Lydia hadn't knocked on Dottie Lee's front door in almost forty years. As she made the journey, she noted that the house was less than half a dozen steps away. There were no stairs to climb, since Dottie Lee's entry was at street level, no landscaping to skirt. Twenty seconds from their door—or Faith's, as she needed to think of the row house now—and suddenly she was staring at the deep magenta trim and gray brick that belonged to Dottie Lee.

The doorknocker was a brass dragon's head, a fanciful—and, to Lydia's mind, outrageous—touch.

Dottie Lee herself answered the door dressed in a royal-blue sari and copious gold bangles. She didn't look at all surprised.

"I've been expecting you," she said.

Lydia glanced down at the yapping, snapping Chihuahua at Dottie Lee's feet, a breed that was nothing more than a neurosis with a tail. "You'll still be expecting me unless you quiet that dog."

"Titi!"

The dog fell silent.

"Alex adores her," Dottie Lee said.

"Alex is far too easy to please."

"Does Faith know you're here?"

"Are you going to invite me inside?"

Dottie Lee stooped—slowly, Lydia saw with a pang—and gathered the tiny dog against her chest. Then she straightened and stepped aside.

Faith *didn't* know that Lydia had come. She and the children were shopping, and Lydia had promised she would lock up after she finished another cup of coffee.

"It's changed since you were here last," Dottie Lee said. "Have a look around."

"As I recall the interior changed with every new lover. How many were there? Two senators and at least one congressman that I'm aware of." She paused. "An ambassador."

"No dear. Two ambassadors. Lovely men, both of them. One from India." Dottie Lee gathered the sari in one hand as if making a point. "But you've underestimated badly, and I'm quite wounded, because most people give me credit for at least one president. Of course, I never actually counted, although I still could, I suppose. The men went away, but the memories didn't. I remember them all so fondly."

Lydia stepped farther into the room, examining the exotic rosewood and mahogany antiques. "The last one must have spent a great deal of time in the Orient."

"He was *from* the Orient. A charming, tawny-skinned Chinaman. Oh, it's probably not politically correct to say it quite that way, but we've never stood on ceremony, you and I."

"And you never married a one of them. Did they ever ask?"

Dottie Lee laughed, and although the woman was so much older, the laugh was not. "Frequently."

"But you couldn't leave this house, could you?"

"You know me so well. Even after all these years."

"Does Faith know you're terrified to go outside?"

"Does she know I try never to venture past my own garden? I doubt it. I've been to your house since she moved in. She hasn't noticed that I don't go farther, or she believes it's simply my preference."

"You never tried to get help?"

"I never needed it. Yes, it was inconvenient at times, and yes, before you ask, there was a man or two who might have intrigued me enough to make the effort had I given him the encouragement. But I learned so much from living inside these walls." Dottie Lee gestured to the room. "They came to me, you know. The diplomats and the statesmen. I entertained them in ways that made them come back until I tired of them."

Lydia wanted to fault her childhood baby-sitter and friend, as she had for so long. Yet hadn't they both made concessions to their fears? Hadn't they negotiated the hands that had been dealt them to their best advantage? She had continued her marriage to Joe and borne another child. Dottie Lee had found ways to make a prison into a palace.

"This is not a social call," Lydia said.

"I suspected as much. You haven't wanted to be caught with me since marrying Joe Huston."

"You have an unsavory reputation."

"And I am so very proud of it." Dottie Lee led her toward the sofa. "Shall I ask Mariana to fix tea? Or something stronger?"

"Nothing. I'm not going to stay long."

"Then sit and have at it, Lyddy. Do you remember visiting here as a child? You were a rascal. Your grandmother paid me to play with you so she could get some rest, and you wore me to a frazzle, too." She smiled fondly. "Much like your grandson. Full of questions and ideas and vigor."

Lydia was tired simply thinking about it. She remembered those long-ago days, when her parents had traveled to faraway places and she had stayed with her grandparents until her mother could make a home to receive her. She remembered coming here as she waited, to this very house, and to Dottie Lee's humor and patience.

"I'll get right to the point," Lydia said.

"I'm sorry to hear that."

"You're filling Faith's head with facts she doesn't need to know."

"She told you this?"

"She told me that you claim to know everything about our house, and I am certain, knowing you as I do, that you're taking advantage of that to ignite her interest in the past."

"Not *the* past, dear. *Your* past. Don't generalize."

"Nothing good can come from this. I want to know what you've told her. And what you're planning."

"Planning?"

"Faith says you only drop tidbits of information, that you seem to be waiting for her to ask the right questions."

"Is that what she said?" Dottie Lee smiled. "She's a clever girl. Have I mentioned how much I like her? She reminds me of your mother. She would have made a wonderful ambassador's wife, just like Millicent. So accommodating. So aware of how to make others comfortable. But with enough backbone to survive the petty politics of the State Department." Dottie Lee paused. "I must be getting old. Faith would make a wonderful ambassador herself. Times have changed, haven't they?"

"Not enough has changed for you to be telling her things best left secret!" Lydia leaned forward. "What have you said?"

"As I told you, she's a clever girl. She figured out that you and Joe weren't happy, not even before the kidnapping."

Lydia's breath caught, although she wasn't really surprised. She had known from the direction of Faith's questioning that her daughter was moving in that direction. "What did you say to that?"

"Lyddy, let's not dance around it. We won't resurrect the dead by uttering a name. I did not tell her that you had an affair with Dominik Dubrov. I believe that's for you to tell her. But your daughter suspects there may have been another man in your life."

"How dare you!"

"No, how dare *you?* You have shared nothing with her. You are a stranger to your own child."

Lydia sat back. "You know nothing."

"I know Dominik was more than a handyman. You had an affair. Yet you never came forward with that information, not even when the poor man was suspected of stealing your baby."

"You are delusional."

"I know the facts, Lyddy."

"You're testing a pet theory."

"I'm repeating the truth. And you are trying to lie your way out of it, just the way you did when you were a winsome child of four."

Dottie Lee set the Chihuahua on the sofa beside her, and the dog snuggled into a pillow and fell asleep before Lydia spoke again.

"I was unhappy. The affair was brief and doomed. I'm the one who ended it. It was impossible."

Dottie Lee nodded, waiting.

"I always wondered if you knew," Lydia said at last.

"I always wondered why you didn't come forward when Dominik was under suspicion. Would you have, if they had accused him and taken him off to jail?"

"What good would the truth have done? Never mind what harm."

"He spent untold hours at your house, more than seemed necessary. A personal relationship would have explained some of them. He seemed particularly emotional after Hope's disappearance, more so than a stranger should have. That concerned the authorities."

"You know why I didn't tell. I would have been tying the noose around his neck. He was the strongest suspect they had. He had access to the house. He had opportunity. He was familiar with the layout. He had a key!"

"But he didn't have a motive," Dottie Lee said.

"A jealous lover is a motive for any crime. I knew what the police would say. Dominik was angry that I had broken off our affair, so he kidnapped Hope in retaliation. Or he took her because he was a crazy Slavic immigrant who felt entitled to some of my happiness, or because he wanted ransom money to ease his personal suffering."

"There was no ransom note."

"Because she died, or because he got frightened. Don't you see? I knew the way the authorities would view this. My announcement would have provided them with the one thing they lacked. And for what? To explain his presence in my house? His work explained it well enough. The rest was simply speculation."

"So once I made up an alibi for Dominik, you felt free to remain silent?"

"*Made up* an alibi?"

"All these years, Lyddy, have you believed that nonsense?"

Lydia couldn't look away from Dottie Lee's face. "You lied? He wasn't here with you that afternoon?"

"I knew the FBI and that monster in charge of it. Hoover was willing to do nearly anything to close the case quickly. An hour after Hope was reported missing, I suddenly realized poor Dominik was in danger of being railroaded. It was only a matter of time, and I saw no reason to allow that."

"If you were going to lie, why not go all the way? Why did you make up that part about the hardware store? Because of that, he was still under suspicion until the day he died. Afterward, too."

"I couldn't say he was here the entire afternoon because a friend stopped by to see me, and of course he didn't see Dominik in the house. So I made up the story about the hardware store because Dominik had gone there earlier that day on an errand for me. I told him to use the story if he was questioned. Dominik, bless him, had trouble understanding why we should lie. But he'd spent enough years under Communism to be persuaded that innocent men are easily convicted. Even in America."

"Then where was he, if he wasn't with you?"

Dottie Lee sat back. "Do you suspect him even now, Lyddy?"

"Where was he!"

"Walking. Trying to make sense of his life. Trying to decide what to do with the rest of it. No witnesses, of course. Only his word."

Lydia couldn't think about Dominik now, not about his whereabouts on the day her child was stolen or the feelings she'd had for him. "How many more people would have been destroyed if I had admitted to the affair?"

"In retrospect?"

"Joe's career would have suffered. I would never have been able to hold up my head in Washington again. Dominik had a wife and child who needed him. I would have destroyed everything. And for what end? Honesty?" Lydia gave a bitter laugh.

"And yet you must have wondered if, by keeping even this one detail a secret, you hindered the search for your daughter."

"Just as you wondered if a false alibi for the strongest suspect might have hindered the search, too?"

"And now your daughter's digging away at the truth, one speck at a time."

"I want you to stay away from Faith."

"She'll discover what she needs to know without me. I'm merely a conduit. *You* would be a better one."

"Me? Do you really think I'm going to sit her down and tell her I was an unhappy bride who had an affair with my handyman? That somehow that will set things right between us?"

"I've always believed I would still be alive when the truth about all of this finally came out. I've depended on it."

Lydia got to her feet. "Or have you believed that someday you would force your version of the truth into the open? Is that it, Dottie Lee? You sit in this house day after day, looking for ways to enrich your life because you have nothing else. And now that Faith's fallen into your path, you're using her to enliven your miserable isolation."

Dottie Lee rose. Slowly, Lydia noted, as if she were suddenly weary to the bone. "I can stay away from Faith, of course. But it won't do any good. There are forces at work here that are beyond our control."

"What do you mean?"

"I mean that sometimes, dear, there's very little we can do except watch. And tell the truth as we know it."

Lydia started toward the door. Clearly there was nothing else to be said. Too much had been revealed already.

"Lyddy?"

She turned in the doorway and found Dottie Lee just behind her.

"We're family here on Prospect Street," Dottie Lee said. "Oh, there aren't so many of us left now. There are strangers in too many of our houses. They move in and out, and leave nothing of themselves behind. But you and I...the ties that bind us are strong. I won't be the one to sever them. But I can't stop outside forces from ripping them to shreds."

"You're an old woman, Dottie Lee. And old women imagine things."

"Come and visit again. We can be old women together, old women talking of old times."

Lydia reached for the doorknob to let herself out. Dottie Lee stood tall, her white hair twisted back from her face with mother-of-pearl combs. For a moment Lydia saw the young Dottie Lee, a black-haired vixen with enough allure to fascinate the high and mighty.

Lydia could not come this close to her past again. She shook her head. "I'll come to your wake."

Lydia didn't go home. She went back to Faith's, because she wasn't sure if she had turned off the coffeemaker. She was increasingly absentminded these days, although she knew it was preoccupation and not the onset of dementia. Heaven help her if she ever did lapse into Alzheimers. Joe would sweep her under the carpet like an afternoon's worth of dust. Then, once she was safely out of the way, he would wax eloquent on the need for better health care for seniors—while he voted down every attempt his own party made to institute it.

Joe Huston, the worst mistake of the many she had made.

In the kitchen she saw that the coffeemaker was indeed on, and she poured one last cup before she switched it off. She wasn't sure why she didn't just leave, or rather, she *was* sure and hated to admit it. She was here because this house still echoed with the voice of Dominik Dubrov. And even though Dottie Lee had insisted that talking about him wouldn't resurrect the dead, of course it had.

Thirty-nine years later his face was as clear to her as if she were staring at him.

They had been standing in this kitchen the first time he kissed her. They hadn't planned it, of course. She had been so far above him in status, a fact that had mattered more to her than to Dominik, who believed himself any man's equal. They had been married, and both of them had taken their marriages seriously, although for different reasons. He from a deep sense of responsibility to his wife and child, she because...

Lydia set down her cup and put her head in her hands. She because her father was a powerful man, and power was everything to her. She had grown up with privilege and a sense of entitlement. She *deserved* marriage to a man who could ensure both. So she married Joe, but she fell in love with Dominik.

She had never grown tired of him, never dreaded his appearance at her door or the feel of his body in her bed. He asked for nothing except those all-too-brief hours together. If she had fantasies of asking for more, she eradicated them before the words were formed. It was enough just to share their forbidden, ecstatic pleasure. She hadn't envisioned the future, because she had known what she would see.

She just hadn't known exactly *how* it would end.

Dominik was a passionate man, at home in his body—and in hers. There were no neutrals in Dominik's world. Wild, glorious color splashed everything he saw and saturated each moment. For a man with little education, he knew something about everything. He understood the real heart of politics, the flickers of idealism, the compromises that often extinguished them. He could sing entire arias in credible Italian, and once he bought her a cheap print of Botticelli's *Birth of Venus* just to show her the shade of green he envisioned for her living room.

He wept over dew on a rose petal, raged over a candy wrapper in the street. Each time he invited her into his heart, she fell in love more deeply. She lived for the moments they shared and refused to think of the day when they would cease.

Until the day they did.

Dominik was late that afternoon. She knew his son was often ill and required medical intervention. Dominik's wife was angry at fate. She was a good mother, he claimed, but since fate was unavailable, she blamed Dominik for the boy's asthma. He didn't work hard enough, fast enough, long enough, and their relative poverty meant hours in clinic waiting rooms. She couldn't work, because the wheezing Pasha couldn't be left with a baby-sitter. Her only recourse was to rail at her husband.

Lydia didn't want to hear about Dominik's marriage, although she understood his need to talk. When they were together, she tried not to mention Joe. She wanted their time to be private, without the shadows of their marriages intruding. Joe traveled so frequently and invited her to join him so infrequently that she had days, sometimes weeks, when she could pretend she wasn't married at all.

Now the fantasy was over.

Dominik arrived nearly an hour after she had expected him. His dark hair was ruffled, as if he had been digging his fingers through it all morning. His face was drawn.

"I'm sorry, this could not be helped."

She nodded and held the door wide, although he had a key and could let himself in. He entered, removed knit gloves and stuffed them in the pocket of his threadbare overcoat before he removed that, too, and slung it over his arm.

"You are alone?" he asked.

"Joe's out of town again."

He didn't move to embrace her. He was always hesitant, as if he needed confirmation that she really wanted him.

Today she couldn't give it to him. She crossed her arms over her breasts, a posture she had taken up since her marriage. The young woman who had been alive and open to anything was learning to close herself away.

"Your son is ill again?" she asked.

"The doctor, he says perhaps the Christmas tree makes him sick. We had to take it to the side of the road for the garbage men. He cried so hard." Dominik looked as if he had destroyed his son's childhood. "Sandor, he promised Pasha a new tree, a little one all shiny and gold. But this is not a Christmas tree."

Lydia understood why Dominik was unhappy, but nothing about

the situation moved her today. She had too much to think about, and too much to tell him.

And no words.

She fell back on training. "I'm sorry. I hope he'll grow out of this."

"Time is our best hope." He reached out tentatively and traced a fingertip along Lydia's cheekbone. "You are all right?"

"No, I'm not, Dominik." She stood very still, afraid that if she moved, she might launch herself into his arms.

"You are ill?"

"I am pregnant."

He dropped his hand.

She could see the thoughts running through his head. He had been wise to leave the Soviet Union, for if Dominik had been compelled to hide secrets from the Communist authorities, he would have failed.

"It's Joe's baby," she said. "You and I have been careful." They had, in fact, used Joe's own condoms, kept beside their bed but never used by him. Several months ago Joe had decided it was time to have a child. Lydia, far less sure, had secretly been fitted for a diaphragm, which she used whenever she had adequate notice to prepare.

But there had been times when there was no notice, times when Joe mounted her and found his release without so much as a loving word of warning. He found this sexy, she thought, controlling their lovemaking as he controlled the rest of their lives, making sure she understood who made the decisions.

"*We* have been careful, yes," Dominik said, "but *he* has been gone. How is it that he could get you with child?"

"It only takes once, and he does come home now and then." She felt her bottom lip begin to tremble. She bit it. Hard. "He wants a baby, Dominik. He's been trying, and I've been, well, lying to him. I've been using birth control. But not always. I don't always have the chance."

"And the timing is correct?"

She didn't know, because she wasn't sure exactly how far along she was. Unless she was in Dominik's arms, she'd felt tired and discouraged for the past several months. Joe's job made demands on her time and energy. The house made demands, as well. She had refused to hire a maid, so the housework had fallen to her, too.

Her period had been late, then scanty, then nonexistent. She had attributed each change to exhaustion and depression. She had wanted so badly not to have Joe's child that she hadn't acknowledged the possibility.

"It's Joe's baby," she said. "He never comes home without demanding sex. Even when he's only home long enough to change clothes between trips."

Dominik's posture was rigid, a rarity, since he was so at ease with his body. He fingered the overcoat, rubbing his fingertips over the wool, back and forth, like a toddler with his blanket. "This changes everything."

Her lip trembled again, and she couldn't control it. "Yes." Her voice trembled, too.

"How will you go on?"

How would she go on without him? That was the question he was asking, not from conceit but from compassion. He knew how much their time together meant to her. When she was with Dominik, she was the woman she'd been born to be. When she was with Joe, she was an appendage.

"How will *you?*" she asked.

He shrugged. When he'd appeared on her doorstep, he'd looked tired. Now he looked stricken, his ruddy complexion pale, his eyes lifeless. "I have Pasha. Without him?" He shrugged again.

They had never talked about their differences, as if doing so would widen the chasm that separated them. Now there was no point in skirting the truth.

"I wish I were strong enough to leave Joe," she said. "If I were stronger, I would. I would find a job and raise my child without him. I would wait for you in a tiny apartment in the city, live for the nights when you could slip away from your family and come to me. But I'm not that strong, Dominik. I need the other things Joe can give me. And he wouldn't let me go, not without a fight. Not without trying to prove I'm unfit to raise our child."

"I also have wishes that will never be."

"We have to say goodbye today."

"There is still work to do on the house."

"I can take care of the little that's left. I'll hire someone else if I need to."

"No, I will send Sandor."

She wanted to say no, that this tie to him would be too painful, but she understood that sending Sandor was the only way Dominik could still give her something of himself. She lowered her head, one brief nod, but she couldn't raise it to look at him again.

"I've learned there is little happiness in the world. What I've found, I found with you," he said.

Tears spilled from her eyes, but she didn't look at him. "I think you'd better go."

"I wish you a healthy baby. A girl? Would that please you?"

She didn't care. The reality of motherhood seemed very far away. "That would be...nice."

"Then that's what I'll wish for."

She felt his fingers under her chin. She let him lift her head so their eyes met.

"Something to take into the years," he said.

"Please go."

He dropped his hand and sighed. Then he turned. He didn't put on his coat, although a light snow was falling. He went to the door and let himself out. Quietly, and without passion.

In the silent house, Lydia wept.

Thirty-nine years later, Lydia wept again.

 27

Early most mornings, Pavel came to see Faith on his way to work. She had coffee waiting, and before he left for Scavenger's headquarters in northern Virginia they shared their plans for the day or their amazement at the twists and turns in the presidential election.

And sometimes, like this morning, he wasn't in a hurry to leave.

"I can't get over the fear that one of my children will walk in on us." Faith lay in her own bed, her head pillowed on Pavel's shoulder. He was an athletic lover, capable of great tenderness and even more enthusiasm. She was always wrung out after their lovemaking, as if he had squeezed every drop of response out of her.

"They're in school." He stroked her hair, seemingly in no hurry to be gone, despite a board meeting that afternoon.

"I know they are. Rationally. But I think it's a leftover inhibition. Maybe I'm afraid someone will finally figure out I'm a sexual being. Who worse than my children?"

"You? A sexual being?" Laughter rumbled through his chest.

"You know, if you had been my first lover..."

"What?"

"Well, I would have realized that what David and I had together was..."

"You're having trouble talking. Did we permanently alter your brain today?"

"This is embarrassing."

"You can be embarrassed? After what we did just now?"

Now it was her turn to laugh. She was sure what they'd done was an entire chapter in the Kama Sutra. "At first David and I made love often enough that I believed all was well. But even then, we just didn't find this kind of joy. We shared, but we didn't take. Does that make sense?"

"Perfectly."

"The warning signs were there. I just didn't know enough to heed them."

"And now that you've had me, you won't make the same mistake twice?"

She tugged a tuft of his chest hair in retribution, and he yelped. "You think you're funny, but now that I know what's been missing, maybe I'll pattern the rest of my life after Dottie Lee's. I'll take lovers. Dozens of them. I'll be known all over town as 'that woman'!"

"On one level, I'd like to see that. The spectacle of you as a fallen woman would be highly entertaining."

"And on another level?"

"I'd miss knowing I'm the only man you're waiting for in the mornings."

"Well, maybe I won't start on the high life right away."

She and Pavel had never discussed their feelings for each other. Perhaps that wasn't odd for Pavel, but it was certainly odd for her. She had always believed sex, love and marriage were three lobes of the same leaf.

She wasn't ready for a discussion of that kind. Their relationship was centered in the moment. She was evolving as a person and as a woman, and right now, at least, she didn't want to make commitments or even begin that long, helpless, terrifying spiral into permanency. And Pavel had clearly never wanted to begin it with any woman.

"Do you understand your husband a little better now?" Pavel said.

"Do I understand David's desire for Abraham Stein because I understand passion a little better?"

"A *little* better?" He pretended to be offended.

"The word smidgen comes to mind."

He rolled her on top of him and stared into her eyes. "Do you want to see a smidgen more, then?"

"You're kidding. That would be a record. Even for you."

"If I can set records in the business world, I can certainly set them here."

"I feel a challenge coming on."

"Is that all you feel?"

Pavel was gone by the time she got out of the shower. They had made a date for dinner. She was going to take the giant step of leaving Alex and Remy alone while she was gone. A conference with Remy's teachers on Monday morning had gone well. All of them reported a slight improvement in cooperation and test scores. Remy's choral teacher had lingered afterward to emphasize how talented Remy was.

Since things at school appeared to be better, Faith was going to reward Remy with a little responsibility and leave her alone for the evening. If that went successfully, she would lift the restrictions one at a time.

Once she dressed she started laundry and stacked the dishwasher before she got her coat for the trip to the library. She was putting the finishing touches on the history of the row house to give to Lydia, and before long she would begin work on one for Joan and Carter Melvin, Pavel's friends. She suspected Pavel had spurred Joan to call and ask her formally, but she didn't care how the Melvins' business had come her way.

She had her first commission. She was thrilled.

In the Peabody Room she settled at her favorite table. Dorothy was behind the desk today, and she greeted Faith by her first name when she asked for an out-of-print textbook that detailed the history of Georgetown's west end.

"I'm glad you're here. I have something else for you." Dorothy left and returned with a volume of what looked like tabloid newspapers. "This just came back from the bindery. Inside are copies of a local weekly that only stayed in business for a little while in the early sixties. We haven't even catalogued them yet. Someone found them in an attic and thought to bring them to us. The circulation was so low the paper wasn't even on our radar screen."

Faith took the book from Dorothy's hands. "Why did you think of me?"

"Somebody on their staff was bucking for the Pulitzer. It's not your usual weekly. There are in-depth articles about the kidnapping in nearly every issue. I thought you ought to have a look. I haven't had time to read all the way through, but it looks like interesting stuff."

"Thanks. I'll check it out and tell you what I find."

But Faith didn't tell her, because an hour later she set the volume back on the absent Dorothy's desk and left the library.

The Scavenger board meeting absorbed all Pavel's attention until nearly six o'clock. What had started as an eccentric group of computer geeks with creative ideas and limited business skills had been transformed, through the years of their success, into a well-oiled international business machine.

For the past two years he had been delegating more and more authority, and now Pavel knew the "Pascal" was on the wall. The moment he began to let control of Scavenger slip through his fingers, he had as much as announced his resignation. He'd sat through today's meeting as the titular head, but everyone knew that these days he had as much to do with leading the company as Queen Elizabeth had with governing England. Either he had to take back his power, and soon, or he had to resign. Scavenger wasn't languishing terribly, even in a difficult economy, but rifts were opening, tiny cracks in both confidence and mission. Stronger leadership was required, and soon the stockholders would begin to sense it.

He drove straight home, refusing to join his cohorts for their usual play-by-play over drinks at McCormick & Schmidts. That was yet another sign he was losing interest in his job. There had been a time when he would have drunk every one of them under the table and still argued coherently and at length. He would have relished every minute of it, too, and if there had been a woman waiting for him, he wouldn't have remembered until he was on his way back to Georgetown.

But he remembered Faith.

He showered and didn't wonder until the water was beating against him what he was trying to wash away. Not stale cigarette smoke, because no one was allowed to smoke inside the Scavenger building. Not sweat, because since showering at Faith's, he hadn't lifted more than a ballpoint pen all day.

He supposed he was trying to wash away the decision that faced him. That was his habit, after all. Wash away anything unpleasant. Store it, beat it into submission, bury it. Get rid of it at all costs. Better yet, don't get near anything messy or unpleasant in the first place. Not life-altering changes, not the sorrows of the world.

Not relationships.

He dried and dressed and even considered shaving, but that seemed too extreme. They were only having dinner at nearby Filomena, with its apple-cheeked mamas preparing pasta from scratch in the front window. Faith had never eaten there, and he was looking forward to introducing her to this particular pleasure.

He remembered what she had said this morning, about the other "pleasures" he had introduced her to. She had no idea how ingenuous she was, how she wore too much emotion where others could see and destroy it. She was a strong woman with a soft heart. Although he had met other women who possessed that combination, he had never met anyone who was so unguarded. She had been hurt, and badly, less than a year ago. But she hadn't closed herself off.

She didn't take after her mother—or his.

He was slipping back into his favorite loafers when his doorbell rang. Since he had arranged to meet Faith at her house, he wasn't expecting anyone, but he threw open the door without checking and found her standing on his front porch.

"Well, hey!" He felt a rush of pleasure, as if he'd just been given a surprise party. He was aware, on some subliminal level, that the pleasure was far too close to joy and far away from his normal reaction, fear. Usually when a woman began dropping by his house unannounced, he knew it was a sign he had to oust her from his life.

"Hello, Pavel. May I come in?"

He sobered immediately. She hadn't smiled. She hadn't leaned forward for a kiss. She looked composed, but he knew her well enough to realize it was an act.

"Of course you can come in." He stepped aside. "I was just on my way to your house."

"I timed it that way."

"Faith, are you all right?"

"No, I'm probably not."

"Has something happened to one of the children?"

"They're at home doing schoolwork. They're fine."

He was relieved. "Are you ill? Because we don't have to go to Filomena. We can wait until you're feeling better."

She didn't answer. She walked into his parlor and stood stiffly beside the fireplace.

He was anxious to make her comfortable. "Have a seat. I'll get us something to drink, unless you'd rather just go home and forget tonight."

"There's a lot I'd like to forget, Pavel."

He paused in the act of heading for the kitchen. "Do you want—"

"I don't want anything from you. Not a drink. Not dinner." She hesitated. "Well, I guess that's a lie. I do want one thing."

"What's that?"

"An explanation."

He understood then, both what she meant and what he had tried to rid himself of in the shower. "I guess you think it's about time, huh?"

"I guess I do."

"At least have a seat."

"I doubt this will take long enough to need one. I'll shorten your part. Here's what I know. You weren't born Pavel Quinn. You were born Pavel Quinn Dubrov, to a man named Dominik Dubrov and his wife Maureen Quinn Dubrov. Your father did repairs on our house on Prospect, and he was a suspect in the kidnapping of my sister."

Pavel took the seat he had offered her, sitting forward with his forearms on his knees. "How did you find out?"

"An old newspaper article. Someone with too much time on his hands did an in-depth biography of your father. He mentioned the name of Dominik's son and the maiden name of his wife. You said your mother was Irish, but your *last* name is Irish, which doesn't fit, does it? The facts were staring me in the face."

Pavel wished it had never come to this, but how could it not? He had waited too long. He simply hadn't known how to make this right.

"He called me Pasha. In Russia that's a nickname for Pavel. My mother told me when she was on a memorable weekend drinking binge. I don't remember, of course. I have no memories of him. He was dead before I was three. We were living in California by that time, without him. My mother thought the climate would be better for my asthma. We settled in a small community near Palm Springs, and she cleaned houses to support me, nearly until the day she died."

"I'm touched."

She wasn't. Even that dash of sarcasm was so unlike her that it trumpeted her anger.

"What else do you want to know?" he asked.

"For starters, why you didn't tell me."

"What could I say, Faith? That I came back here when I graduated from college to see what I could find out about my father and his part in the kidnapping? He's the perennial suspect, you know, always mentioned in discussions of the case. That's why my mother left him and changed my last name. She couldn't live with the shame."

"She left him because he might have done something? Or because she knew he *had?*"

"I've never found any evidence that my father kidnapped your sister. Not in all the reading I've done. Not even the cops who were involved really believed my father did it. Two of them told me so."

"What cops? I tried to find somebody who worked on the case and was told they had all retired."

"They have. Now. But when I started looking I found one who was still on the job and another who had moved to a town near Myrtle Beach. It made a nice weekend trip."

"I'd like their names."

"I'll be sure you get them, but they said nothing of interest. Just that my father's alibi couldn't be shaken, and no one could come up with a motive for the crime. They searched our apartment, my father's pickup, even the house where his assistant lived. They didn't turn up any evidence, not so much as a grain of baby powder."

She slid one finger along his mantel, as if measuring it along with his story. "This is why you insinuated yourself into my life, isn't it? You want answers. You want to prove, once and for all, that your father didn't steal my baby sister."

"I owe him that."

"What did you owe me? I'll answer that. The truth, right from the beginning!"

She had finally raised her voice. He could see now how furious she really was. He felt ashamed, but he still wanted her to understand.

"What would you have said if I'd told you at that first introduction? I can see it now. Hi, I'm Pavel Quinn, only that's not my real name. It's Dubrov, and I'm the son of the man who the world believes kidnapped your sister."

"I would have said it's a small world, but of course, it isn't. You were standing in front of my house not because watching two men move a piano is interesting, but because the *house* was interesting to you. Interesting enough that you've explored every inch of it under the guise of helping me decide what renovations to do."

"Faith, I came to Washington to see what I could find out about my father. I discovered very little. In the meantime, I fell in love with the city, got involved with Scavenger." He turned up his palms in supplication. "I stayed. When the time came to buy a place, I bought one in Georgetown. Not because my father worked here— at least, I don't think so. Because I fell in love with Georgetown, too. And sometimes I would walk along Prospect Street, yes. Did I think I'd see my father's ghost? Did I think someone would stop me and say, 'Oh, by the way, you look a lot like a man I used to know named Dominik Dubrov. He was accused of kidnapping a congressman's baby, but I know differently. Would you like to hear the story?' "

"*Did* you think that?"

"I'm not that obsessed. After my investigation turned up nothing I reconciled myself to not discovering the truth. Then one day I saw a moving truck in front of your house."

"And the rest is history."

"Not quite." He rose and joined her beside the fireplace. The room seemed cold, and he wished he had built a fire on the grate. "I never planned to have a relationship with you, Faith. At first I was intrigued you were moving into the house. It was a twist of fate, and I appreciated it. I thought I might find out something about our mutual past, but almost immediately I discovered you knew even less than I did."

"So why didn't you tell me then?"

"Because I was afraid if I did I would never be welcome in your house again. And I didn't want you to shut me out. I decided to wait and see. I thought the right time would present itself."

"You mean after you had a chance to snoop some more? Maybe after an introduction to my parents? Was meeting my mother exciting for you, Pavel? Seeing the flesh-and-blood mother of the kidnapped baby?"

"That's beneath you."

"But lying about your identity wasn't beneath you? Getting close to me for reasons you didn't reveal wasn't beneath you?"

"I've been Pavel Quinn since I was three years old. That's who I am. I didn't lie about that."

"You're splitting hairs, and I'm going to leave now." She hiked her purse over her shoulder. "Please don't come around anymore, Pavel."

He knew he owed her more than rhetoric. "Faith, I was afraid to tell you. The deeper we went together, the more afraid I was." He put his hand on her arm. He could feel her tense. "I didn't care about meeting your parents, and I knew there was nothing to learn from you. I could have told you then, gotten it out in the open and gone on about my business."

"But?"

He was repeating himself, and he knew it, but he didn't know how to fix this. "I liked you. I cared about the kids, and I didn't want you to think things were all about the past. I felt..." He ran out of words. The ones that came to mind were unfamiliar, and now they would be unwelcome to her.

"Pavel or Pasha or whatever your name is, here's God's simple truth. I just left a man who lied to me about who he really was. And now I've gone to bed with another. I must be the world's worst judge of men, don't you think?"

"David lied because he couldn't face the truth about himself. I lied because I didn't want *you* to face it. Not yet, anyway."

"On moving day you had a five-minute window of opportunity to tell me who you were. It closed, and it's been boarded up ever since. I learn slowly. I may be reality impaired, but I do learn."

He knew she was going to leave, and he knew he couldn't stop her. Now the only thing he could affect were the words she heard in her head on the walk home.

"You're important to me, and you were growing more important every day. I didn't tell you who my father was because I didn't want to lose you. It's that simple. I was looking for a way to tell you the truth."

She started toward the doorway, her head high, her back still rigid. In the hallway, she turned for a parting shot. "You did lose me, Pavel. But consider yourself lucky. A woman who's such a rotten judge of character is a bad bargain. Go to Filomena by yourself tonight and celebrate your good fortune."

 28

By the following week, Faith could tell herself she was lucky. One miserable week during which she questioned every part of herself. By week's end she had managed to substitute philosophy for shame. Considering how long it had taken her to discover the truth about David, she had discovered the truth about Pavel in record time. No serious damage had been done. Her heart was still intact, if a little worse for wear. She had not compromised any state secrets.

She had only lost a friend and lover. Again.

Welcome to the sisterhood.

"I don't see why I have to go."

What was left of the Bronson family was getting ready for a trip to Great Falls for Joe's birthday celebration—or supposed to be getting ready. In her bedroom, Faith looked up from choosing shoes to gaze at her pouting daughter. "You have to go because he's your grandfather."

"But I have a test tomorrow, and I have to study or you'll ground me again. I want to be free over Thanksgiving."

"You studied this afternoon, didn't you?"

"Not enough."

"You knew we were going to your grandparents' for this birthday party. If you didn't study enough, that was bad planning, wasn't it?"

"I thought you'd be reasonable!"

Faith didn't feel reasonable. She felt discouraged and lonely. She felt like something was missing in her life. "Go change, Remy. We're leaving in fifteen minutes, and you're not wearing that to Great Falls."

"Why not?" Remy's black T-shirt ended two inches above her navel; her capri pants started two inches below. All she needed was a ring dangling from her belly button, an adornment that so far they had avoided.

"Because it's November," Faith said. "Because the temperature dropped below fifty this afternoon and it's cold outside. Because your grandparents don't want to see as much of you as you want to show them. And neither do I."

"You're hopeless."

Faith slipped on one shoe, then the other. "So very true. But not helpless. You aren't going to Great Falls looking like that, and if you don't get ready in a heartbeat, you aren't going anywhere for the next millennium. Get my drift?"

Remy stared at her. The threat was so unlike Faith that for a moment Faith, too, wondered if she had been momentarily possessed.

"You're nothing but talk." Remy got her bearings again and started down the hallway. "Talk, talk, talk." Her door slammed.

Faith sat down again and rested her head in her hands. She was edgy and easily annoyed, and her children deserved better. But darned if she would apologize.

In half an hour they were on their way to Virginia. Remy had changed into an acceptable skirt and sweater, and Alex was wearing a pale blue sports shirt and the only pants he owned that weren't made of denim. Faith's parents would approve of the clothing, if not of any of the things that made them children. For Alex and Remy's sake, Faith hoped the birthday celebration would be mercifully quick.

"We're the only ones who are going to be there?" Alex asked as they neared the turnoff to Great Falls.

"As far as I know. We'll eat dinner, have cake and ice cream, give your grandfather his birthday briefcase and leave. You've got school tomorrow."

"Thank God!" Remy said.

"My science teacher liked my proposal for the science fair."

Faith almost missed Alex's remark, but the last few words snagged her attention. "Science fair?"

"Uh-huh. You know, I told you all about it last week."

She didn't remember. Not one word, but then, she had spent the past week trying to block out the world. "Refresh my memory."

"I'm going to write a computer program that predicts animal behavior, using Lefty as my subject. See, I watch him for fifteen minutes every day for a week. Different times each day. I count stuff like how many times he gets on his exercise wheel, how many times he drinks water—"

"How many times he craps," Remy said.

Alex ignored her. "Then I enter the data in the program I'm writing. When I run it, the program will predict how many times he does those things in a day, broken up into time periods."

"That's just adding and averaging," Remy said. "Anybody can do that in their heads."

"No, it's not. Because the answer is going to be broken down and dependent on certain variables. I want to be able to predict as accurately as possible, to see if rats really behave the same way over time. See, I'm going to try some different stimuli. Do one chart for his behavior when there's a light on, one for when it's dark—"

"That's stupid. If it's dark, you won't be able to count."

"Remy!" Faith turned back to Alex. "This sounds ambitious. Do you know enough about programming to be able to figure out all the computer stuff?"

"Pavel can help if I don't."

She hadn't told her children about Pavel, and the time had come. "I don't think he's going to be coming around," she said, trying to keep her voice light. "We've decided not to see each other anymore."

"How come?" Alex said. It was an indictment, not a question. "That's not fair. He's my friend, too."

"He likes you a lot, and this has nothing to do with you or anything you've done. It's a grown-up thing."

"Wow, a real live lovers' quarrel." Remy's tone was scorching.

"The day you start really getting your kicks from other people's suffering, Remy, will be a black day in your life. Don't let it happen." Faith nearly missed the turnoff, but she saw it at the last minute. She took it too fast, skidding until she had slowed enough to regain control.

Remy squealed. "Great, Mom, get us killed over this, why don't you?"

Faith waited until she was steady again. She lowered her voice. "Alex, your dad can help you with the programming part. He's not as knowledgeable as Pavel, but he knows enough for this, I'm sure."

"Yeah." Alex sounded disgruntled. He wasn't unhappy because he had to ask David for help. He would just miss Pavel. The two were soul mates.

"It sounds like a wonderful project," she said.

"Yeah. I'm going to use graphics and everything." He sounded discouraged.

She wished the evening were over.

The previous week, Faith had stopped by the Senate office building to make a vague apology to her father. His expression hadn't changed. He'd nodded, and that was that. He asked about the children's health, and she answered politely. The rip in the fabric of their family was mended.

Since then, as a sign of renewed favor, Joe's secretary had called her twice. Once to see if she wanted a ticket to a Kennedy Center gala, and once to see if she would help hostess a Christmas party for children from Richmond's inner city. She had turned down the ticket but agreed to play hostess, since the planning was nearly finished.

By the time she parked, gathered up Joe's gift and followed the children down the sidewalk, she was steeling herself to endure this party, too. Holiday celebrations in the Huston family were notable affairs. The food was delicious; the house was always beautifully decorated. If a cake was called for, it always came from the area's finest bakery.

But an underlying current of disenchantment spoiled all the picture-perfect trimmings. Faith hadn't known how much fun birthdays could be until the girls in her freshman college dorm threw her an impromptu surprise party and she discovered that laughter and gluttony and irreverence were the stuff birthdays were really made of.

"This is where you always tell me to chew with my mouth closed." Alex pointed to the bottom step. He pointed to the next one. "And this is where you tell me not to pick up cake with my fingers."

"You'll thank me one day when you're president and the king of England comes to dine."

Marley opened the door, and as Faith ushered the children ahead of her, Marley gave them each a rough-and-tumble hug.

"What's the temperature reading?" Faith asked when it was her turn.

"The senator's chilly as a mountain stream. Storm coming."

Faith thought that sounded about normal for a holiday. "What's for dinner? Your wonderful jerk chicken?"

Marley started toward the back of the house. "Country ham, black-eyed peas, corn bread, turnip greens, sweet potatoes."

"Shades of his heart attack. Is that what he asked for this year?" Faith came to a halt in the hallway, an idea dawning. "Marley, is a reporter coming?"

"Photographer. Coming up from the south to take happy family photos and find out what your daddy thinks about the sorry state of this country."

"When did this happen?"

"While ago, seems, but no one told your mama."

Faith was sure of that, because if Lydia had known, she would have called Faith to warn her and make sure the children were "presentable."

"Where's my mother?"

"In her room, changing clothes."

She didn't ask where her father was. From long experience she knew he was locked away in his home office and couldn't be disturbed until the food was on the table. "That's where I'll be if you need me."

In Lydia's wing she rapped softly. Something crashed behind the door, and her mother muttered incoherently before she shouted, "Come in."

Faith poked her head in first, scanning to be sure she was safe. "What did you drop?"

"A lamp. A stupid, stupid lamp. I brushed it with my arm."

"Break it?"

"I don't think so." Lydia motioned her inside. "Did you just get here?"

"Just in time to hear we're having a photographer immortalize our little celebration."

"You know your father. He never lets a little thing like family togetherness get in the way of ambition."

Faith was surprised. The unhappiness in her childhood home had never been vocalized. She hadn't witnessed fights. Arguments had been dispensed of in a few well-chosen sentences, and neither of her parents had criticized the other out loud.

"It's a good thing I made sure the children were nicely dressed," Faith said.

"You were well taught." Lydia fastened an earring. "The photographer is coming from Lynchburg, so he'll be a while. I'm sorry to put you through this. I suspect you have better things to do and better people to do them with."

Her mother meant Pavel. Faith lowered herself to the bed. "As a matter of fact, I don't."

"Mr. Quinn's out of town?"

"Mother, I found out something about Pavel that makes a relationship with him impossible."

In the act of fastening the second earring, Lydia swiveled. "Faith, if you tell me *that* man is gay, I'm not going to believe you."

Faith had weighed this conversation carefully. She had no real reason to tell Lydia who Pavel was, but she wanted to see her mother's reaction. Maybe she was poking and prodding needlessly, or, worse, sadistically, she wasn't sure. But she wanted answers.

"Pavel Quinn isn't really Pavel Quinn," she said carefully. "Quinn was his mother's maiden name."

"You're saying the man's illegitimate?" Lydia frowned. "Does that matter to you? You surprise me."

"I'm not saying that. His parents were married, Mother. His father's name was Dominik Dubrov."

Lydia paled. She lowered her hands, the earring forgotten. "Dominik's son?"

"Did you know he had a son?"

"A little boy. Pasha."

Faith was surprised, both that Lydia knew this and had remembered it so well. She supposed the circumstances surrounding Hope's kidnapping had been burned into her mother's brain, but it still seemed odd.

"Pasha was just a nickname. His mother changed his last name so no one would know who he was."

"It worked." Lydia sank into the chair at her dressing table. "This must have been a shock."

"*You* seem shocked."

"It's just—" Lydia looked up. "I...It was all so long ago, but it continues to rise up and slap me in the face."

"I know Dominik Dubrov did quite a bit of work for you, Mother. But you must have been friends or you wouldn't have known his son's name."

"It's a row house, Faith, a narrow, cramped row house. We ran into each other in every room and hallway. And we consulted constantly about the renovations."

Lydia began to work on the earring again, but she couldn't get it in place. "Dominik seemed like a nice enough man. I asked about his wife and son, like any polite employer. The boy was sick so much." She paused. "You wouldn't know it, looking at the man."

"Dominik was in and out of the house a lot, wasn't he? The article claimed he had a key."

"Of course he had a key. He worked when I wasn't there more often than when I was. What did Pavel say when you confronted him?"

"He said he was looking for the right time to tell me. He was afraid I'd suspect he ingratiated himself to get more information about the kidnapping."

"What does he want to know, for heaven's sake? His father was never charged."

"Maybe he wants to know why his father hung himself."

Lydia was silent for so long that Faith got to her feet and started for the door. "I'll go see what Remy and Alex are doing. With luck I can keep them quiet until the party begins."

"Faith?"

Faith turned. "Yes?"

"After Hope was taken, I suspected everybody. I lay awake at night and made up scenarios. This one had taken her to get even with Joe for some slight. That one had taken her because she was infertile and couldn't have children of her own. I nearly drove myself crazy with my imaginings. But I was never able to imagine Dominik doing it. He was a gentle man, honorable to the bone. His son should know that."

"His son will have to find that out from someone else."

The next morning, Joe was already at work when Lydia finished putting away her good china. The party had gone as well as could be expected. Her grandchildren had acquitted themselves nicely, posing for the photographer the way they had for campaign literature during the past election. Joe liked to project an image as a family man. Lydia had never objected, since whenever the media was present, he was kinder and less officious.

Faith and the children had made an early exit, and the photographer had departed at ten. She had been left to think about Dominik's son.

She had always known Pasha was out there somewhere, although she'd never considered looking for him. What would she say? I was your father's lover? I loved him more than anyone else ever did, most especially your mother? I want to remember him when I look at you? She had hoped the best for the little boy, hoped he had grown out of his asthma, hoped he had enough food to eat and the education his father had yearned for. Hoped he grew up to be half the man his father was.

What would Dominik think of his son? Pavel Quinn, a dot-com success story. Son of an immigrant suspected of a infamous kidnapping.

Only in America.

Now she knew what Dottie Lee had meant when she said there were forces at work that were beyond their control. Somehow that woman had known Pavel's real identity. Perhaps Lydia herself had even sensed it, because at that first meeting he had seemed familiar to her; she had been startled but unable to place him. Now she knew why. Pavel didn't look like Dominik, not really. But there was something of his father about him, something about the way he carried himself, his build, the expression in his eyes.

"You done with that china yet?" Marley bustled into the dining room. "I don't know why you won't let me put it away. I ever break anything in this house?"

"This was our wedding china. The vegetable dish came from Mike Mansfield. The tureen came from the White House, compliments of the Kennedys. Joe wanted to send it right back, but of course he couldn't. He hated Jack Kennedy like a junkyard dog hates the night watchman. They had to work together. He had to take orders. But he would have bitten him in the leg, gnawed it right down to the bone, if he could have gotten away with it."

Lydia looked up and saw Marley staring at her, eyes wide. "Yes, occasionally even I talk too much," Lydia said.

"Not all that occasionally. Maybe that's the first time."

"Maybe it won't be the last. Pay no attention." Lydia stepped back from the cabinet, admiring the perfect placement of every piece. "I'm going out for a little while. Do we need anything? I'm just going into town."

"Why don't you stop somewhere, have a cup of coffee? Just sit and relax a little. You looking tired."

"I might."

"Or call that massage woman."

Lydia wondered how many knots she was tied in. "You have a nice morning."

In the car, despite what she'd said, Lydia turned away from Great Falls. In Reston, twenty minutes later, she parked and entered a small bank. Inside, she looked for the manager and told him what she wanted. In a few moments he was escorting her to the safety deposit boxes, where he left her alone to open hers.

Joe didn't know about this box, although he probably suspected she had one somewhere. This one was registered in her maiden name, and in case of death, her personal attorney had instructions on how to deal with the contents.

She wasn't sure why she was here today. She felt reasonably secure that Joe, despite his exalted position, could not secure a key, even if he traced the box's location. She kept original documents here, but there were copies hidden in other places. Joe knew she was no fool. The only way he could be sure of her silence was by honoring the deal they had made long ago.

But sometimes, like this morning, she just had to make sure the papers were still here.

Lydia opened the box and stared inside at the small stack, just a few pages, really. A few pages that had changed her life forever and could change Joe's in the blink of an eye.

She fingered them, lifting the top sheet to be sure the ones beneath were all there. Then, satisfied, she locked the box again. She clasped her hands on top of it and closed her eyes, almost as if she was in prayer.

But Lydia felt no peace.

 29

In the middle of December, Faith, bundled against the cold weather, trudged to the middle school for the preliminary round of the science fair. Earlier that morning she had helped Alex pack up Lefty, David's portable computer—which he had loaned Alex for the fair—and his presentation board covered with charts and photos. Alex had barely contained his excitement. The science fair had brought David and his son closer, and the project reigned as Alex's most positive learning experience.

She and David had planned to attend later that afternoon—their first appearance together since their separation—but plans had changed. An emergency meeting with Remy's teachers had been called for two o'clock, and Faith, who was tired of bearing the parenting burden alone, had asked David to attend that, too. In their brief phone call, he had sounded pleased.

At R Street, from habit, Faith nearly turned toward the library. Over the past weeks she had thrown herself into all her projects with a vengeance. Although Lydia hadn't yet seen it, the history of the house on Prospect was complete, and the Melvins' was finished, as well. Faith's discovery that the ordinary little bungalow in Glover Park had once been the residence of a notorious bootlegger had so delighted Joan that she carried the history everywhere. Last week Faith had received three phone calls from people

Joan had bragged to. One homeowner had already sent a retainer, and no one had blinked at the cost. It seemed Faith might be in business.

The row house was comfortable and homey now. She had finally settled on colors, a deep sage-green for the living and dining rooms, ivory for the kitchen. Her own room was newly wallpapered, and, in a surprise move, Remy had chosen a soft violet paper reminiscent of the turn of the century for hers. Between observations of Lefty and hours at the computer, Alex had helped remove the wallpaper from his room, and together they had painted his walls a soft brick-red. Pictures were hung; boxes were unpacked; new pillows graced the sofa.

Christmas was coming, and the divorce would be final soon. Faith had jump-started her new life. The problem was that she wasn't looking forward to the rest of it. Now that she had stopped madly whirling from project to project, what would she find in the quiet spaces?

The school came into sight, and David was waiting beside the front entrance. He looked better than he had the last time she'd seen him. Not as gaunt, not as haunted. He smiled as she approached, but they had been married too many years for her to be easily fooled. David wasn't sure how he would be greeted.

She stopped just in front of him, pleased that she could see him these days without feeling as if the oxygen in her body had dispersed.

"You look good," she said. "A little more relaxed."

"Things are going well." He didn't elaborate.

In their perfunctory conversations he never mentioned Ham, and Faith never asked. Now she took that step. "You're still living with Ham?"

"Yes."

"He's been a rock through all this."

He clearly wasn't sure what to say about that. "You look good, too, Faith."

"I look tired. There's been so much to do."

"Alex keeps me up to date. The house is nearly finished?"

"Until I hit the lottery and call an architect to redo the third floor. That's phase two."

They started through the halls. Faith had been to enough meetings here to know her way around, but it was David's first trip.

"It's not the academy," he said, when they were halfway down the hall.

She struggled not to react. "It's not the same world anymore."

"The change has been good for Alex. We should have considered who he was when we chose his school. I was only looking at who I wanted him to be."

Faith was surprised to hear him say so. "Who did you want him to be?"

"Me." He grinned, almost the old David. "Except straight."

"I don't know why I let you influence me so strongly on that and everything else. If things hadn't changed between us, I would have gone to my grave thinking my own opinions weren't worth the gray matter they were imprinted on."

"I never bullied you. I respected your opinion."

"As long as it fell in line with yours." She tried to soften her words. "But why should you have been any different? I was an adult. I could have objected. Somebody turned on my 'yes, ma'am, no, ma'am' switch when I was born, and it froze in place. But nobody's ever going to make me doubt myself again."

"Good for you." He sounded like he meant it, and that surprised her.

They arrived at the gym where the science fair was being held. Kids streamed in and out, and parents slipped in between groups of Alex's cohorts. David and Faith waited their turn.

Inside, the walls were rimmed with tables, and more tables stood end to end throughout the center of the room. Somebody was making announcements over a microphone, but the system was so bad and the room so noisy that only the occasional word was audible.

"Do you know where he set up?"

"We took the stuff to his classroom. I guess we'll just have to wander around."

They passed exhibits measuring the insulating properties of air, the conductivity of various liquids, the whitening power of various toothpastes. One enterprising young man had found a way to gauge the absorbency of half a dozen name-brand paper towels. Faith made a mental note to buy the winner.

Halfway through the life science row—it was not a happy day for earthworms—they found Alex, surrounded by an admiring audience.

Faith saw why immediately. She knew her son's project was clever, and he had gone into astonishing detail. But even though she had helped him put together the presentation board with all its charts, she had never seen the *piece de resistance.*

"Look at him go! Wow! Dance, you old rat!" A boy who looked to be closer to Remy's age than Alex's was standing just in front of the table. When he moved and Faith got a clearer view of the object of his attention, she was astounded.

Lefty—or a clever cartoon version—boogied across a kitchen complete with window curtains and appliances to a refrigerator, which opened to reveal a water bottle. He removed it and drank. Four times in a row. He flipped his little tail and his beady eyes glistened mischievously.

"See, according to my study," Alex was explaining, "midday, if the room is quiet and the light is low, he'll go to his water bottle four times. Now if we program in a different time and different conditions," he made the adjustments on the computer, "the number of times will change."

This time the cartoon Lefty made the trip and drank three times.

"Mrs. Bronson?"

Faith looked up to see the man who taught Alex's science class. Mr. Salter was young and athletic looking, more physically suited to being a coach than a science nerd. Alex reported that all the kids thought he was cool, because he had once played professional hockey. She introduced David; then she gushed. "I'm overwhelmed. He never showed me the graphics."

"He says he spent hours on them." Mr. Salter looked at David suspiciously. "How much help did he have?"

"Very little. He got stuck once or twice, and I helped him figure out the problem."

"I didn't help at all." Faith held up her hands. "Alex helps *me* with the computer."

"This project is so good it deserves a ribbon. It's not the most advanced science I've ever seen, but it's creative and clever. This son of yours has a wonderful mind."

Faith was warmed by the praise. "He's a wonderful kid."

The crowd—and Mr. Salter—moved on, and Faith moved in on her son. "Hey, kiddo, can you make the rat dance for me?"

"Mom! I thought you were coming later." Alex looked up to see both his parents watching him. His eyes widened when he saw them together.

Faith could almost read the thoughts going through his mind. This was the first time in a year that the three of them had been "family." She and David and their son. Not in crisis. Just together, enjoying Alex's achievement.

"We're so proud of you," she said, stressing the "we." "What a great project."

"Are you surprised?"

"Am I! I had no idea it was this complex." She thought—as she too often did—of Pavel and how much he would enjoy seeing what Alex had accomplished. And almost as if she had conjured him, Pavel strode toward the table.

She understood Alex's reaction now. She had told her son she was coming that afternoon, just before school let out. At the time she hadn't known she and David would be meeting with Remy's teachers.

Alex had invited Pavel to come to the fair in the morning, because his mother wasn't expected. He had invited the president of a major Internet search engine to come to a middle school science fair and see a cartoon rat cavort across a computer screen. And Pavel had come.

Pavel saw her at the last moment and stopped just before the table. "Hello, Faith."

She felt David watching her. She felt Alex watching her. She struggled to be gracious. "Scouting for new talent?"

"The first place I always look." Pavel turned his attention to Alex. "Let me see what you've got here."

Alex mumbled an explanation, then typed in the information Pavel gave him—evening, low light—and Lefty did his dance.

"Hey, I'm impressed. That's great." The two launched into a discussion of graphics that Faith couldn't follow.

"Who is this guy?" David asked quietly.

Faith grasped for an answer. "A friend from Georgetown," she said, after a pause.

Pavel was edged aside by a mob of students, directly toward Faith and David. She introduced him, and the two men shook hands. "Alex has mentioned you," David said.

"That son of yours is a creative thinker. He has every right to be proud of this project." Pavel glanced at Faith. "How are you?"

She heard a million questions in the three words, although his expression gave none of them away.

"Busy," she said. "How's the house?"

"Coming along." They stared at each other, surrounded by pushing middle schoolers and flanked by a soon-to-be ex-husband. She didn't know what to say. She had worked for a month to put Pavel Quinn out of her mind. Now here he was, and immediately she was back to square one. She hadn't succeeded; she had sublimated. The difference was huge.

She fumbled for something, anything. David wasn't helping. He seemed intrigued. "It was nice of you to come all this way to see Alex," she said after an awkward pause. "Did he call you?"

"I'll take the Fifth."

"He misses you." She wasn't sure where that had come from. From a tongue that wasn't working properly, a heart that wasn't nearly as cold as she'd hoped, a buzzing in her ears when she looked at this man and remembered the feel of his hands and lips on the most intimate places of her body.

"I miss *him.*" His eyes flicked to David, then back to her. "Not just him."

She steeled herself. "Well, I'm glad we got to see you." It sounded like a lie, even though she tried to sugarcoat it with sincerity. "I think we'd better finish looking at the other exhibits. There'll be a test when Alex gets home tonight."

Pavel nodded at David. "It was good to meet you. You have a terrific son."

"Thanks. I know."

"Faith..." Pavel nodded goodbye.

She told Alex they were leaving and started down the row. In the middle of the next row she realized she hadn't seen a single thing. She wouldn't be able to comment on the other exhibits after all.

"Have you had lunch?"

She realized David was still beside her. "I didn't have time."

"We have an hour before we see Remy's teachers. I saw a place just a couple of blocks away where we could sit and talk."

She didn't know what they had to talk about. Cozy conversation belonged to the happily-married couple who'd had the world at their fingertips, Mr. and Mrs. Moral Majority. Now they were dropouts, aliens.

"We've made a start toward building a working alliance," David said. "Let's see if we can broaden it. Okay?"

Oddly, the thought of being with David was almost appealing. Once upon a time she had been able to relax with him. He understood her. She nodded.

"Say the names of every exhibit. You'll remember at least one by the time you get home."

She took his advice.

The restaurant was nothing more than a deli, with molded benches and Formica-topped tables set behind display shelves of imported pasta and porcini mushrooms. They ordered at the counter, then took their sandwiches and bottled tea to a sunlit corner, where they could have privacy.

"Since when did you become a vegetarian?" she asked. At the counter David had carefully stayed away from everything except cheese and fresh vegetables.

"Ham doesn't eat meat. I've just gotten in the habit."

"This man has a powerful effect on you." The words were said with no venom. Today she was more curious than hurt.

"There are some things we probably shouldn't talk about."

"David, if we made a list it would stretch to Nepal. Let's face it, we're going to be thrown together for the rest of our lives. We can tiptoe around reality and make our children uncomfortable, or we can talk like two people who used to be friends."

"I don't want to hurt you any more than I already did."

She considered that. "I think you've lost the ability."

He bit into his sandwich, and she opened her chips.

"Does Mr. Quinn have something to do with that?" he said after he'd chewed awhile.

Now it was her turn to be uncomfortable and silent.

"Yes, Ham's had an effect on me," David said at last. "He's completely comfortable with himself in a way I'll never be."

"You mean he's comfortable being gay?"

"Mostly that, yes. But he's comfortable with his flaws, too. Not that he doesn't try to change them, but he accepts himself while he works away."

In all her ruminations on the subject of David, she had never really considered what it must be like to have some part of you that could never really be reconciled, to believe that some basic, intrinsic part of you was unholy. Even if David adjusted his thinking, all the years of believing homosexuality was a sin would stay with him.

She opened her tea and poured it over ice. "You always tried too hard to be perfect."

He smiled a little. "Look where it got me. Pride goeth before a fall."

"I don't think you were proud. Just serious about doing what you thought was right."

"I had some rethinking to do, didn't I?"

"And Ham's helped you do it." She felt a pang, just a twinge, but noticeable. *She* hadn't been able to help David rethink his life. He had needed someone else for that.

"Ham; and admitting who I am," he said.

"How's the job front?"

"No, it's your turn now. Who is Pavel Quinn?"

She was surprised he was interested enough to repeat the question. "He's the president of Scavenger. He helped me plan some of the renovations."

"Alex mentioned him but never said what he did. I bet he didn't want me to feel inferior about my computer skills."

"Alex is surprisingly sensitive these days."

"I picked up vibrations between you and Mr. Quinn. What gives?"

She considered both the question and him. "Why do you want to know? You don't want to date him, do you?"

When he saw laughter in her eyes, he smiled a little. "I'm monogamous."

"Unless you're in the middle of a lifestyle change."

"Touché."

"I slept with Pavel." She watched his gaze shoot to hers. "You wanted to know."

"Maybe not that much."

"It gives me a certain amount of pleasure to tell you that even if you didn't want me, another man did, David."

"The claws have been unsheathed, huh?"

"And sharpened."

"Well?" he asked.

"Well, what? Was it good? Because that's a place we won't go."

"Try well, are you glad? Are you happy? Are you fulfilled?"

"It's complicated."

"You're monogamous, too."

She bristled. "You don't know what I am anymore."

"I think I do."

She couldn't believe it had come to this. Discussing her love life with the man who was still officially her husband. A year ago, if an angel had descended to show her the future, Faith would have recommended a heavenly psychiatrist or a career writing divine soap operas.

"Back to the job front," David said. "That's part of what I want to talk to you about."

"Talk away. Have you had any luck?"

"I want to go into the ministry, Faith."

For a moment she thought she hadn't heard him correctly. After Arnold Bronson's death, David had received routine inquiries every year about taking over his father's pulpit. "You're thinking about taking over your father's church? The door is still open?"

He grimaced. "That door is locked so tight my shadow couldn't get through. They're praying for my soul every Sunday. No, have you ever heard of the Metropolitan Community Church?"

She hadn't, and he explained. The church was a traditional Christian community that was radically different in only one way. Congregations consisted mostly of gay, lesbian, bisexual and transgendered Christians.

Faith realized there was an entire vocabulary she had to brush up on.

"I've been led to this," David said. "I know it's a shock, but I've always wanted to be a pastor. I just knew, deep in my heart, that I couldn't stand up and condemn others. Now I know why I've gone through this experience, why I've had to struggle to reconcile my faith and my sexuality."

They had been married fifteen years, and he had never told her he wanted to be a minister. Of course, if he had, there would have been so many other things to explain. "You're ready now?" she asked.

"Not quite."

"What's stopping you?"

"You are, Faith."

She frowned, not even sure which question to ask. But it didn't matter, because he continued, although not before he had balled his napkin in his fist.

"I need to ask your forgiveness."

"Why? Is that on the application somewhere?" She was sorry she'd been flip the moment the words emerged, but David only shook his head.

He was staring at the table now, as if answers might be ingrained in the Formica. "No, I need forgiveness because I've lied to you. And how can I help other people achieve peace if I can't find it myself?"

She spoke carefully. "I'm coming to turns with how hard this was for you to admit to yourself. Both of us have to move on, and I know that now." It wasn't forgiveness, but it was close.

He looked up. "I knew I was gay when I was thirteen, Faith."

She stared speechlessly at him.

He looked away. "That's the thing I haven't been honest about, the thing I'm asking you to forgive. I've told you, I've told everyone, that this was buried so deep I just didn't see it. But, Faith, I knew. Of course I knew. Before I married you, I knew I had to tell you the truth, but I just couldn't. I knew I would lose you, and I believed you were my only chance to be straight. So I told myself it was okay, that I wasn't a homosexual if I didn't act on my fantasies. I loved you. I really did. And I thought the love and the desire to make a home with you would carry me past the rest of it, that once I was safely married, the other part of me would die away."

"You had that debate with yourself? Fifteen years ago?"

"It's my final and worst confession."

She should have been furious. Some part of her knew that. She should have condemned him for his lies and the wreckage they had left behind. But the compassion she felt left no room for fury.

David had used her. Yes. He had kept the truth from her when it could have saved them both, but never out of disdain or disregard. Out of shame and out of love. He had hoped she could save him from himself. In his own way, David *had* loved her.

She reached across the table and rested her hand on his. "What happens if I can't forgive you?"

"I have to ask. You only have to do what feels right, but there can't be any more lies in my life." His eyes filled with tears. David, who never cried. "I am so sorry. I hope you know that. Not for who I am, but for keeping it from you."

She didn't know what to say. She tried to imagine what life would have been like if she had never married him. She wouldn't have enjoyed fifteen years of David's companionship. She wouldn't have Remy or Alex. Yes, there had been lies, but there had also been laughter and warmth and moments when they had shared their hearts.

David had lied, but did that lie cancel out the rest? Or now, with the truth in front of her and his deep sorrow about it so apparent, could she simply, finally, lay this burden to rest and make room again for the good things? Since the divorce, she had been notably absent from church, but she still believed all the tenets of her faith, forgiveness being foremost among them.

"I'll try," she said at last. Despite this most damning revelation, her heart already felt lighter. Some of the love she'd once felt was surfacing, and she realized that maybe, finally, she could face that, as well.

He cupped her hand and squeezed.

"Can you forgive yourself?" she asked.

He cleared his throat. "I'm easier on myself now, more willing to accept God's grace and love. And I think I have something to offer. I understand intimately what it's like to be gay and struggle to be a Christian, too."

"They'll accept you into the ministry?"

"I've made inquiries. I already have the degree. I'll need to do some things before I'm accepted to pastor a church, some additional education, probably an internship and a hospital chaplaincy program. But there's another hurdle."

He leaned forward, the open, emotional David she hadn't seen since their separation. "I'll never be rich if I do this, Faith. I'll be able to pay child support, but my income will be a fraction of what it was. And to make things more complicated, I've been offered a position as a lobbyist for a biotech firm, where I would make considerably more money."

"You would hate that."

"I can survive it."

"So this is my decision?"

"I want your input before I make it."

It was time to tell him about the architectural history business. He listened intently, nodding his approval.

"Perfect. Your eyes light up when you talk about it."

"But *I'll* never get rich."

"What's better for Remy and Alex? Rich parents? Or parents who are enriched by what they do every day? Parents who are giving something back?"

"You're already a preacher, David. I can't believe I didn't question you harder about your real calling when we were married. Let me think a little, okay?"

He sat back. Neither of them smiled, but neither of them averted their gaze. She thought that, for the first time in a year, they were finally really looking at each other.

He spoke at last. "We have a few minutes before we have to go back to school. What are we going to hear about Remy today?"

She heard the way his voice tightened when he said his daughter's name.

"I had her on a tight leash for a while, and it seemed to help. She made marginal improvements in her schoolwork. Then I loosened the restrictions, and she's back to failing every subject except music."

"Faith, I know you don't want to hear this, but I still think she needs counseling."

Faith waited to feel annoyed or even angry that David was asserting himself. But she didn't. Gratitude stole over her and crept inside the hollow places that had stayed empty since David moved out of the house. She might not have a husband, but her children had a father who loved them and wanted to share the burden of raising them. A good father. A good man.

She only had to open the door.

"Will you find someone for us?" she asked.

"Us?"

"All of us. Remy's not the problem. We need to see someone together. We should have done it right away. We all have issues we need to talk about if we're going to be a family again."

"Remy won't go if I'm there."

"We won't give her a choice. She needs you, and letting her decide when to reconcile isn't working."

"You weren't there the day she attacked me."

"No, but I will be if she tries it again." She put her hand over his once more. Briefly. The hand of a friend. "The only way through this is together. The four of us."

He covered her hand with his. For the first time in a year they really smiled at each other.

The conference with Remy's teachers went as expected, although having David along made it more bearable. Together they came up with strategies to deal with the problems of homework and studying for tests. They left with the names of several agencies that specialized in family therapy and troubled teens.

Remy spent the afternoon and evening in her room, furious that once again her free time was going to be restricted. She reminded Faith at the top of her lungs that Christmas vacation was coming and now she would have to sit home the entire time. Faith heard the corollary, that her daughter would be making everyone else's holiday miserable, as well.

Remy refused to come down for dinner, but that didn't subdue the ebullient Alex. He was riding high on his science fair success.

His teacher had hinted he might get a ribbon. Alex, who until now had only won ribbons for showing up on time.

"Next year I'm going to invent something," he said with his mouth full. "A new computer chip, or a time machine."

"You'll probably need a new computer chip if you're going to invent a time machine."

Absorbed in his fantasies, he finished the meal in silence. He might come in just a little short of a time machine next year, but whatever project her son hatched was going to be spectacular.

In a vain attempt to lure Remy from her room, Faith had made a complicated spaghetti sauce recipe, and the kitchen had suffered accordingly. She cleaned while Alex worked on his homework at the table. Now that problem solving was a larger part of it he had a new, budding appreciation for math. In an unguarded moment he'd admitted that Pavel was the reason. Pavel had said if Alex wanted to be an inventor, or a computer whiz, or even just a garden variety genius, he would need math skills.

By the time she finished cleaning, he was staring into space.

"All done?" she asked.

"Are you mad I asked Pavel to come to the fair?"

"Just surprised. You didn't exactly warn me."

"I miss him. He knows how I think." Alex stood. "I'm going to take my shower and go to bed."

"Call when you're ready. I'll come up and say good-night."

"You can say it now."

She felt a pang. She had stopped tucking Alex in years ago, but they had continued the nightly ritual of a final "sleep tight" and hug in his bedroom. She had a feeling that now her young scientist might have grown beyond that part, too.

"Sleep tight, then." She kissed his cheek.

"Thanks for, you know, coming with Dad today."

Both restless and wrung out, she made a pot of tea after he left, just for something to do. She had planned to work on an ad for the *Georgetowner,* a local bimonthly with a healthy circulation. Unfortunately, she didn't feel like working tonight. Even reading her newest how-to volume for small businesses lacked appeal. Her conversation with David played and replayed in her mind.

And her reaction to seeing Pavel still unsettled her.

She was on her second cup of Earl Grey, staring at the same scratch on the oak table, when the lights went off in the upstairs hallway. The music pouring from Remy's room—that had been yet another fight—stopped midphrase and the house fell silent.

She was about to give up and go to bed herself when she heard a car door slam in front of her house. She wandered into the living room and realized Pavel was standing on her stoop. She let him in, closing and latching the door behind him.

"If you want me to go, I will. No struggle." He didn't smile.

She had told him not to come around anymore, yet here he was, and she didn't want him to leave. She started back toward the kitchen. "I was just having tea. Would you like something?"

He followed. "Just a chance to talk."

Tea she could have handled, but conversation was a step toward intimacy. When she didn't respond, he went on. "I have something to offer you. If you send me away, you'll never know what it is."

"You're appealing to my curiosity?"

"*I* wouldn't be able to resist."

She was reminded of what Alex had said tonight. *Pavel knows the way I think.* For the past month Pavel had probably twisted and pulled apart every detail of their last meeting to see what he could mine from it, just the way Alex would have.

"Are you curious about the kidnapping?" he said.

She motioned him to a chair. Once he was seated at the kitchen table, she pulled the pocket doors shut for privacy. She stood with her back to the old wooden panels. "Why? Do you know something I don't?"

"That's why I came. We both want to know what happened the day your sister disappeared. We can work on it separately, or we can work together. Personally, I think we'll move faster and further together."

She wasn't sure she wanted to work on it at all. What had she learned so far? That almost from the start her parents weren't happy together? That her mother, her prim, proper mother, might possibly have had an affair? She had no idea how or even *if* any of this related to her sister, and she was afraid that the more she probed, the more the gap between her parents would widen.

"Let me make you an offer," Pavel said, when she didn't answer.

"I didn't tell you everything I know. The last time we spoke, you were too angry."

"Betrayed."

"I didn't betray you. I just didn't know how to tell you about my father. You had become too important to me."

It sounded too much like what David had said earlier that day. But these circumstances were vastly different. How would it feel to believe Pavel? Would she feel like a fool or a saint? Or just a woman giving a man she cared about the benefit of the doubt?

She went to the stove again, got the teakettle and filled it, then set it back on the burner to boil, although she had no plans to drink more tea. Finally she faced him. "How can we work on the kidnapping? It happened so many years ago. There are no clues, no witnesses."

"By comparing what we know. By taking it one step at a time from there. By asking the right questions of the right people."

"Dottie Lee?"

"For one, yes."

"My mother?"

"That's up to you. I didn't come here tonight to pressure you."

She could see the future clearly. If she chose to go along with him, they would be thrown together frequently. If she chose not to, some part of who she was would remain a mystery. No, two parts. The part that needed to find out the truth about her sister's kidnapping, and the part that needed to find out the truth about Pavel.

"Tell me what you know," she said.

"I will, whatever you say next. But will you work with me afterward? Will you help me piece together what we can?"

"I reserve the right to step back or out if someone else is about to be hurt."

The kettle whistled. She turned off the burner. "Last chance for tea."

"Come sit with me."

Warily she joined him, sitting stiffly across the table, hands folded. "What didn't you tell me?"

"Do you remember how I said I didn't know anything about my father until the weekend my mother went on a drinking binge?"

She did remember, because, despite everything else, that gloomy glimpse into Pavel's childhood had tugged at her. "Did she tell you something else?"

"She poured out her heart. I don't know why. She'd kept so many secrets. I grew up believing my father had deserted us. Suddenly I discovered he had hung himself from a rafter."

"Why did he kill himself? Did she say?"

"Because he lost the two people he loved."

"Your mother and you?"

"No. *Your* mother. And me."

She didn't know what to say. He nodded to confirm it. "Faith, your mother had an affair with my father. That's a large part of what drove my mother to California. Not just the kidnapping, but the fact that he was unfaithful."

"And you believe this?"

"She wouldn't have left him otherwise."

"Maybe she left because he really *did* kidnap Hope."

"She swore on her deathbed he didn't. She had nothing good to say about him, but she insisted that much was true. She passed out of this world claiming he was innocent of that crime and guilty only of adultery."

"With my mother."

"Right after the kidnapping my mother found out about the affair—she didn't say how—but she confronted my father, and he admitted the truth. He said the relationship with Lydia had been over with since the day she learned she was pregnant. With a baby on the way, Lydia was determined to make her marriage work, and my father recommitted himself to his own. He asked my mother to stay with him for my sake, but she was too disillusioned. She was a strict Catholic, so divorce was out of the question. Instead, she hocked her wedding ring and bought bus tickets to California. Neither of us ever saw him again."

Faith could imagine how Pavel's mother had felt, and how she must have felt later when she learned her husband had killed himself.

Pavel locked his fingers behind his head and leaned back in his chair. Faith thought the casual posture was a defense, the antithesis of what he really felt.

"You're surprisingly calm," he said. "I expected an angry denial.

At the least, reminders of the differences in their status and the fact that your mother would never have dallied with the handyman."

"You can be wrong."

"And have been."

She shrugged.

He dropped his hands and sat forward. "Your mother stared at me when we were introduced. I only have a few pictures of my father. I don't think I resemble him, but maybe there was something about me that was familiar."

"When I told her who you were, she seemed stunned." She owed him the remainder of what Lydia had said. "Mother said she was never able to imagine your father as the kidnapper. He was a gentle man. Honorable. She wanted you to know that."

"And you didn't tell me?"

"It was an opinion, not proof."

"It would have meant something to me, coming from Hope's own mother."

"I didn't expect to see you again."

"Did you really think I would let this drop?"

She was growing angry again. "I should have known better, right? I saw firsthand what you do to get answers."

"I'm not talking about the kidnapping. I'm talking about *us*. Faith, I made one mistake, and yes, it was no small thing. But I never set out to hurt you. And nothing else that happened between us was part of a conspiracy to get information. Right from the beginning, it was clear you were more in the dark than I was. So why did I keep hanging around?"

"I don't know, Pavel. You tell me."

"Because this was where I wanted to be."

She was a woman who accepted responsibility for every mistake, even if she wasn't in the room when it happened. But she had learned a lot in a year, and she was wary now of being hurt again. "I'm not ready to pick up where we left off." That much she was sure of.

"I understand."

"Let me think about this. All of it."

"What are you going to do with what I've told you?"

She refused to be pushed. "I just need to think."

He got to his feet. For that moment he towered over her. "Well, thanks for listening." Clearly he had hoped for more, perhaps even a return to their easy give-and-take.

Maybe she missed him just as much, the anticipation of hours in bed together, the knowledge that there was one person in her life who saw her as something more than a problem solver and caregiver, a man who saw her as a woman. But for too long she had trusted her heart. Nowadays she only trusted it to keep beating.

She got to her feet, slid open the door and stood back to let him pass. "You can count on one thing. I'll let you know if I learn anything else."

"I appreciate it."

Outside, he hesitated on the stoop, examining the pine wreath wrapped with plaid taffeta ribbon she had hung to celebrate the holiday. "Good night."

"Good night, Pavel." She softened a little. "Pasha. It suits you, you know. Your father must have loved you very much."

"He died at Christmas. It's not a holiday with much meaning for me."

It was the most personal thing he had ever said to her. His father's suicide must have haunted him for years.

"He must have felt a lot of pain," she said.

"I visit his grave, and I tell him I understand, but I don't know if I really do." He straightened his shoulders a fraction of an inch. "Tell Alex I'll be in touch."

 30

For Lydia, Christmas was a series of tasks to check off until the holiday season was blessedly over. A week before the big day, the worst was finally behind her. Her personal gifts were chosen and wrapped. The house was resplendent with traditional arrangements of evergreens, citrus fruits and magnolia leaves. White candles glowed in every window, and cinnamon and pine boughs scented the air.

Last night she and Joe had given their traditional party for his D.C. staff and their families, an elaborate buffet that culminated in the singing of Christmas carols and a visit from Santa Claus, who gave a different keepsake ornament each year. This year Santa presented silver-plated cutouts of the White House, as close to laying claim to that particular residence as Joe was likely to get. Through it all, she hadn't squeezed out a drop of Christmas spirit.

Today she was feeling marginally merrier as she parked her car outside the row house. She had presents to put under Faith's tree. In the past months she had spent so much time with her daughter and grandchildren that she'd had no trouble knowing exactly what they wanted. Alex talked of nothing except upgrading his computer, so she'd bought him a gift certificate to a computer store. She'd bought his ridiculous rat a gift, as well, a cage with mazes and tunnels and platforms that was as much like the Hilton as a rat could expect. An impulse buy, but she was looking forward to seeing Alex's face.

Remy hadn't been hard, either. At the horse show she had expressed an interest in learning to ride, so Lydia was giving her granddaughter ten lessons at a Great Falls riding stable. In the spring Lydia would pick Remy up after school and take her there every Wednesday afternoon. It would give them a chance to get to know each other better.

And since she was at the pet store anyway, she had bought those attic strays a padded scratching post.

Faith had been harder. Her life was in flux and her future uncertain. She had no time for hobbies, and soon enough she would be looking for a job. A business suit seemed a practical solution, but a cold-blooded one. Instead, Lydia had sorted through boxes and memories and chosen photographs of her family, the women who had lived and loved on Prospect Street. She'd had them restored and beautifully framed. They would look lovely in the stairwell.

Perhaps she felt a drop of Christmas spirit after all.

She made two trips to the car before she rang the doorbell. Faith answered, and her eyes widened. "I didn't know Santa was on the way. The kids are at rehearsals. Christmas program coming up."

"I have to put in an appearance at the farewell party at the vice president's residence. I thought I'd drop by on my way."

Faith took an armload of packages, and Lydia stooped to retrieve the others. "You look lovely," Faith said. "Is that a new dress?"

Lydia's personal shopper had picked out the dark red sheath. "Just for the occasion."

They deposited the gifts under the Christmas tree, a Scotch pine festooned with ornaments the children had collected each year since they were old enough to point. *Southern Living* would never feature Faith's Christmas decorations as they had Lydia's, but the house fairly reeked of Christmas spirit.

"Do you have time for some wassail?" Faith asked.

"Real wassail? Or a teetotaler David Bronson variation?"

"I can spike it with Dottie Lee's Scotch. It's not authentic, but that's all I have."

"I could use it."

"Seasonal Christmas blues?"

"Am I that obvious?"

In the kitchen, Faith removed a pitcher from the refrigerator and poured some of the contents into a saucepan, while Lydia settled at the table.

Faith faced her mother. "You know what? I'm going to give you a Christmas present now."

"There's still a week to go."

"It's just us, and I want you to have time to savor this one. I'll get it."

Faith had always loved surprises. As a child, she had worked for hours in her room on homemade cards or scarfs woven on a childish loom. Her daughter's enthusiasm was the bright spot in a grim holiday, and Lydia had tried not to quench it.

Faith returned with a box and presented it to her mother. "Here you go."

"Is this something you made?"

"Have I taken up quilting or knitting? No."

"I still have the scarf you made me when you were seven."

"Now that surprises me."

Lydia looked up. "Why?"

"Well, it's very sentimental, that's all. It wasn't much of a fashion statement."

"You mean purple and orange weren't featured in Milan that year? Of course I kept it. Some year I might go to Mardi Gras. Practical, not sentimental."

"You'll like this better."

Lydia untied the ribbon and slipped the paper off carefully. Then she lifted the top off the box. Inside, a slim leather-bound volume nestled on sheets of tissue paper. On the front was a watercolor of the row house, with the address printed in gold below.

"Faith, what on earth?" Lydia flipped the cover and began to read. "What have you done?"

"It's a history of the house, Mother. I've been working on it for months. It's my thank-you for letting us live here, for handing the house over to me when I needed it most."

"You did this?" Lydia was amazed. She turned page after page, admiring the beautifully printed text, the photographs, the maps and copies of deeds and documents. A chapter was devoted to each of the women who had owned the house, anecdotes from their personal histories, even copies of newspaper articles that related to them or to the area at the time.

When she looked up at last, she saw that Faith was watching her. "It's wonderful." Lydia clasped it to her chest. "I had no idea. How on earth did you find all this?"

"I've become quite the expert on researching architecture. In fact, I'm starting my own business. I've already done another history, and after the holidays I'll start on a third. All that and I haven't even advertised. It's just word of mouth so far."

"You won't need another job, too?"

"The more historics I do, the less time I'll have to spend figuring out logistics. I'll have a backlog of information, more contacts, better skills. Who knows, eventually I may have to hire an assistant."

"You amaze me. This is the best gift I've ever been given."

"I didn't want you to associate it with Christmas. But this seemed like the right moment."

Lydia put down the history to savor at length when she was alone. "Am I that obvious?"

"You mean have I always known how much you hate the holiday?"

Lydia started to protest, but Faith lifted a hand to stop her. "I know why Christmas has always been a bad time for you."

Lydia was surprised this particular conversational thread hadn't already unraveled. "It's a lot of work, that's all. More appearances to keep up than usual."

"Then it doesn't have anything to do with the fact that Dominik Dubrov killed himself over the Christmas holidays?"

Lydia was caught off guard. For a moment she forgot to breathe. Then anger ballooned inside her. "Faith, this isn't a subject I want to discuss."

"Mother, I know Dominik was your lover. You don't have to hide it from me anymore. You've been hiding it for years, and you've never had anyone you could talk to about it. Maybe I'm not the best person, but I'm the one who knows."

"I think you've spent too much time looking into the past. Now you're seeing things that aren't there."

"It's the truth."

"That woman made this up, didn't she? She's lying."

"Dottie Lee prepared me, but Pavel told me. His mother left his father because of your affair. She refused to stay with him, even when he told her the affair had ended months before."

"Why are you doing this?"

"I'm tired of secrets. Don't you think I wondered why Christmas at our house was so cold and gloomy? Why you had to bite your lip to get through it? I always thought it was *my* fault, that I wasn't lovable enough or good enough to make it worth the effort. Even after Pavel told me about the affair, it took me a while to work that part out."

"Dominik's been dead longer than you've been alive. Leave him to rest. Leave *me* to rest!"

"I don't think so." Faith's voice remained calm. "I considered that. But nobody knows about secrets and the harm they can do better than me. I will not let my life be defined by them any longer. I won't let *your* life be defined that way, either."

"You have no idea what you're saying."

"Why? Do you think I'll hold this against you? I've watched you and Dad all these years, and I know what it's like to live with him. You were young. You probably felt lonely and confused. Dominik walked into your life, and the rest is history. When you found out you were pregnant with Hope, you told Dominik goodbye and recommitted yourself to my father. What else could you have done?"

For once Lydia's anger eclipsed caution. "You think you know so much? Well, here's a little more, Faith. I wasn't committing myself to the baby's father. Hope wasn't your father's child!"

On the stove, the wassail began to scent the room.

"I'm leaving," Lydia said. She got up and started around the table.

"Oh no, you're not." Faith blocked the doorway. "Let's finish what we started."

"What *you* started."

"Hope was Dominik's baby?"

"Do you feel cleansed?" Lydia grabbed the history from the table and shoved it into Faith's hands. "Why don't you put the truth in here somewhere, so everyone will know?"

Faith set the volume on the counter, took her mother's hands and clasped them between her own. "How do *you* feel?"

Lydia didn't know. She was trembling. She was ashamed. She was furious it had come to this.

She was frightened that now, Faith would never really love her.

"Sit down," Faith ordered. "I don't want you fainting in my kitchen."

Lydia didn't move. Faith poured the wassail into a mug and added Scotch. Then she set it on the table. "Drink."

Lydia was too upset to do anything else. She sat, cupped the mug in her hands and sipped.

"Pavel doesn't know Hope was his father's child," Faith said, "or he would have told me. I guess his mother didn't know, either. Who *did* know, Mother?"

Lydia began to speak. Slowly at first, then faster as the words tumbled out. She had never planned to share this story with anyone, most particularly not her daughter. But now that she had begun, she couldn't seem to stop or censor herself. The truth was like a prisoner burrowing to freedom.

At first Lydia was convinced her obstetrician was wrong. She couldn't be as far along in the pregnancy as he thought. Joe had been away for almost three weeks during the time the doctor swore she had conceived. Dominik had been her only lover.

The facts were so clear. Dominik had religiously used condoms. Joe had not. Joe had wanted her to become pregnant. Dominik had been afraid she might. The baby had to be Joe's.

But when the pregnancy developed according to her doctor's timetable, she faced the awful truth. The child inside her belonged to an immigrant handyman, and her congressman husband was too intelligent to be fooled. Joe wouldn't know *whose* baby this was, but the moment he did the math he would know it wasn't his. Unless a miracle occurred and she carried the baby several extra weeks, Joe Huston would know his wife had been having an affair.

When the worst of the shock was over, Lydia began to consider alternatives. She could have an abortion, go away and find a back-alley practitioner to perform one and tell Joe she had miscarried. She had the means, but she also knew the risk of complications. Abortion was an illegal procedure. Even women who could afford a real doctor were at risk. Women with pregnancies as advanced as hers were playing with fire.

Beyond that, despite her panic, the thought of an abortion upset her. This was Dominik's baby fluttering happily inside her. Hormones surged through her system, put there by Mother Nature to preserve the human species. Perhaps she was the victim of her own biology, but she couldn't bring herself to explore that possibility further.

She was left with three choices. She could hope for the best and pray that the baby came late or that Joe knew too little about timing to be suspicious.

She could tell her husband the truth and hope that Joe, fearing for his career, would pretend the child was his own.

Or she could cash in a little "insurance" she had set aside.

At the beginning of her sixth month the choice was taken from her. Joe, pleased at her announcement and solicitous of her health, had eased his demands and encouraged her to rest. He stopped complaining about the row house, the traffic on Prospect Street, the Jesuit university hovering at the horizon. He voluntarily moved his home office into the windowless middle bedroom so the baby could have cool summer breezes from the river.

Then, on an unusually warm spring evening, a different Joe confronted her. That morning he had awakened to the butterfly movement of the baby under his palm, and he had been as proud as a sultan at this proof of life. She didn't admit she had been feeling movement for weeks, afraid that might alert him to the truth. Instead she celebrated with him, pasting a happy smile on her face, but the tears in her eyes weren't from joy.

He was pale when he walked through the door that evening, and he waved away the iced tea she had made for him. "Is that what you did today, Lydia? Made tea and prettied up for me?"

The evening might be warm, but the temperature in the room had cooled dangerously. She counseled herself to be calm. Joe was prone to tantrums if things didn't go his way, and as a junior member of Congress, they seldom did.

She set the glass on the edge of her grandmother's mahogany table. "I cleaned the house and did some gardening. Read a little. And I made a casserole for dinner because I wasn't sure what time you would be home."

"I lost my appetite about four o'clock. Do you want to know why? I got this reminder from my secretary." Joe thrust out a slip of paper.

Frowning, Lydia took it. The paper had been crumpled, then smoothed. The words were in pencil, and the light was dim. She couldn't make them out. "I can't read it."

"It's from your obstetrician's office. You have an appointment tomorrow?"

"Yes, but—"

"They couldn't reach you at home, so they left the reminder with my secretary. Apparently they had my office number in case of emergency."

"I was home all day, Joe. But I was outside for part of it, pulling weeds in the garden. It was such a beautiful day I—"

"Let me tell you the best part. You don't know the best part, Lydia. She wasn't just reminding *you;* she was reminding *me.* Because your doctor likes to have the fathers come at the end of the second trimester, and I'm expected at this appointment."

She pretended she didn't understand, desperately trying to buy time. "I didn't ask you because you're so busy. I figured I could tell you everything you needed to know afterward, I—"

"Needed to know, Lydia? Like the fact that you're a full month further along than you told me? Like that? Like the fact that you got pregnant when I was away from home? Like that?"

He was shouting now, and moving toward her. She backed away, but the table was behind her, and she was trapped. He slapped her hard across the cheek. Then he clasped his hands around her throat and began to choke her.

She grabbed his hands and tugged at them. "Joe!" She couldn't breathe. The plea was expelled on her last breath. Frantically, she tugged harder.

Something crossed his face, some semblance of reason, perhaps only the realization that if he continued, his life would change forever. He dropped his hands, but he didn't move away. He trapped her there, the bulk of his body a barrier to escape.

"I called your doctor and told him I was confused about dates. He went over them with me, Lydia, including conception times. This isn't my baby, is it? Say it!"

She knew better than to lie. She shook her head. He closed his for eyes a moment, as if to gather the strength not to finish what he'd started. Then he stepped away.

"You whore."

She put her hands to her throat. Moments went by before air was passing normally through her lungs again. Despite the attack, she wasn't frightened of another. Joe was not a physical man, and until now he had never lifted a hand against her. He controlled with words. The attack had been one moment of pure unadulterated rage, completely out of character.

"I didn't know," she said. "Not at first. When I told you I was pregnant, I thought the baby was yours."

"Even though you'd had an affair?"

"We—I was careful. I thought pregnancy was impossible."

"You need a few lessons in biology, don't you?" His expression was menacing, but his hands were locked behind his back. "Who's the father?"

She shook her head.

"I'll find out."

"It doesn't matter. I haven't seen him since the day I found out I was pregnant."

"What? He didn't want a pregnant mistress?"

"I told him goodbye, Joe. I thought I was having your baby."

"And when you determined differently?"

"He still doesn't know."

"So you were going to pass it off as mine? That was your answer?"

"I didn't know what to do. And for a long time I thought the baby might be yours, after all. I hoped..."

"If wishes were horses, huh?"

"I know how you must feel."

"I doubt that, Lydia. But since you think you can read minds, what am I planning next? What does the future hold?"

"If you divorce me, the truth will come out. And everyone will know that Joe Huston was cuckolded by his own wife."

"Yes, but there's always the sympathy factor."

"You don't want sympathy. You want power."

"If divorce makes *me* look weak, it will make *you* look like a fallen woman."

"With time my letter *A* will fade until nobody remembers."

"In the capital, everyone remembers everything."

She tried to appeal to his better side. "I don't want a divorce. Do you?"

"No, but I don't want this baby even more. So here's what we're going to do. I've had the afternoon to give this some thought. You're going away, somewhere nice and quiet, because you're having problems with the pregnancy. You'll deliver out of town, and the baby will unfortunately be stillborn—or that's what we'll tell people. You can do whatever you want with it at that point. Leave it on someone's doorstep, give it to some childless woman, I don't care. Just be sure no one ever discovers the truth. Then you'll come back here, we'll stay together for a year, after which we'll file quietly for a divorce. Nobody will connect the two events."

"I'm not giving away my baby like a CARE package. And there's no such thing as a quiet divorce for a politician. Someone will snoop. Someone will discover the truth."

"If our despicable president can cover up *his* shenanigans, we can keep this a secret!"

"I'll tell the whole world the truth before I'll give this baby away."

His eyes were blazing, but his hands were still locked behind his back. "Then what's your plan, Lydia?"

"I married you in good faith. I thought we could make a wonderful life together, but you drove me to this affair with your demands and your criticism and your lack of affection. You have some responsibility. So here's what *we're* going to do. We're going to stay together, and you're going to claim this baby as your own. You're going to help me raise it, and as much as you're capable, you're going to love it. In return I'll be the perfect political wife. I'll do everything in my power to help you. On the surface we'll be the ideal American family."

"You're crazy."

"Do you think so?" She was trembling now, about to play her final card.

"Why would I stay with you? Why would I accept a child who isn't mine?"

So she told him. She watched his eyes widen and watched, for the first time in their marriage, fear steal over his features and over-shadow conceit.

"And that's why," she finished at last. "Because in the end, you have no choice."

He stared at her for a long moment. As she watched him, she wondered if he would explode again, perhaps kill her. But he was too much of a political animal for that, because by now he probably realized that if she died under any circumstances except the most natural, he would be an immediate suspect.

Her attorney would see to it.

"So Dad realized the baby wasn't his flesh and blood," Faith said. "And for some reason he was willing to accept it and move on? I can't buy that, Mother. Joe Huston doesn't have a forgiving bone in his body. And what about Dominik? Did he find out Hope was his? Is that why he killed himself? Because *his* daughter had been kidnapped? Or did he take Hope after all, because he thought she belonged to him and something terrible went wrong along the way?"

"Dominik figured out the truth," Lydia said. "After Hope was born, Dottie Lee told him that the baby had come a little earlier than expected but we were both doing fine. Dominik worried all along that he might be the father, even after all my assurances. When he counted backward from July, he knew he'd been right. The three weeks your father was away were the three that we were together the most."

"Surely he came to see you when he discovered whose child it was. What did he say?"

Lydia could talk for hours and not tell it all, not the terrible emotions that had filled her, not the despair that she and Dominik could never escape together with their child and start a new life.

The last time she saw him was as clear to her as the past few minutes. The man himself was dead. The child had only been hers for a week. But the tragedy would be engraved on her heart forever.

The birth wasn't easy. 1962 was the year of the Thalidomide tragedy. Lydia finished the pregnancy convinced that her sins would mark her child, that somehow the things she had done with Dominik would imprint themselves on her son or daughter for the world to see.

When labor began, Joe took her to the hospital and dropped her off, giving instructions to the nursing staff to call his secretary when the baby arrived. She was left to labor alone while she fought every contraction, hoping the labor would stop and she could go back home, her sins yet undiscovered.

The hospital was advanced, and hygiene was considered more important than comfort. The nurses only visited to chart her contractions. When the time came to deliver, she was so heavily sedated that the doctor had to use forceps to usher Hope into the world. Hours passed before Lydia learned she had a healthy daughter.

The first sight of Hope allayed months of fears. She was a beautiful baby, with masses of dark hair and chubby cheeks. The nurses bragged she was the prettiest child in the nursery and couldn't understand when Lydia clasped her baby daughter to her chest and wept.

Unfortunately, the nurses owned her child. They brought Hope to be fed every four hours and whisked her away when twenty minutes were up. Breast-feeding was out of the question, not the style and not considered the scientific alternative. Lydia longed to try anyway, but she knew Joe would be furious. The sight of someone else's baby at his wife's breasts might be the final straw, so she let the nurses bind them and took the drugs they prescribed. And she dutifully placed the rubber nipple between Hope's lips, whether the baby wanted it or not.

The nurses told her Joe had come to see her while she was still sleeping, and that he had made a fuss over Hope. Lydia didn't see him until the day after the birth, when he arrived with a photographer to record the happy event. She smiled dutifully and let him hold the baby for the photos.

Late that evening she lay awake, staring at the ceiling and praying she had made the right decisions. At Hope's final feeding that night, she had been fussy and unpleasant, as if she sensed her mother's tension. In front of the photographer and nurses Joe had kissed her and promised to visit again tomorrow, but Lydia doubted he would be back. She was alone in an antiseptic hospital where visitors were discouraged and her baby was sequestered.

The night nurse came with a routine sleeping pill, but when the woman turned to pour ice water, Lydia slipped it under the covers. The nurse left and turned off the light, and, wide-awake, Lydia stared at the shadows creeping across the ceiling.

Sometime later the door squeaked, and she shifted to see what the nurse had forgotten. Dominik moved silently across the room to stand beside her bed.

She sat upright, pulling the sheet to her breasts. She was wearing a hospital gown, and she felt exposed and ugly.

He held a finger to his lips. "I have been waiting for her to leave this wing. She won't be back again, will she?"

"Not for hours, but—"

"Good, then." He rested his hands on the metal railing that enclosed her bed. She had asked the nurse not to raise it, but it was hospital policy, even for healthy new mothers. Now she felt as if Dominik were a visitor at the zoo.

"What are you doing here?" she demanded.

"I came to see my daughter."

Something rose in her throat. A denial, perhaps. Or simply bile, but in the end she swallowed both. "I didn't know," she said. "Not for a long time. When I told you she was Joe's, that's what I believed."

"And you didn't think to tell me differently? This was something you didn't consider?"

"What good would it do? She's Joe's daughter now. The birth certificate has his name on it."

"And he knows she is not his?"

"Yes, he knows."

"What kind of man accepts this?"

"One who has no choice." There was only dim light from the street lamps outside her window, but she saw that he didn't believe her.

From the beginning she had considered whether to tell Dominik the whole story. Someday Joe might discover Dominik was Hope's father, and she didn't want him to punish her lover or harm his family. She was only too aware that a man like Joe could pull any number of strings. If Dominik knew the truth, he might be able to protect himself. Now that was all she could give him.

She spoke quietly, but she leaned forward, still holding the sheet against her chest. "Last year, after the Bay of Pigs, Joe and several other political leaders discussed assassinating President Kennedy."

She lowered her voice even more. "Joe hates the president. He thinks he's a traitor, and so do the others. So they came up with a plan. They were going to use Cuban nationals to kill him. Then, if any of the men were caught, they could claim they were under orders from Castro."

"He hates the president this much? He would order a man killed in cold blood because he hates his politics?"

"He hates everything about him, Dominik. He thinks Kennedy is leading us to hell. He's sure he's going to push civil rights legislation and integration, and if Johnson becomes president, *he* won't dare. Johnson's a Southerner, too, don't you see? They feel safer with him. And they think Kennedy is soft on Communism and too liberal to do what he needs to in Cuba. Joe was in Cuba; he's rabid on the subject. He and the others think Kennedy's a poisonous moral influence."

"They think the president is a poison, but they don't think killing him is bad?"

"Assassination's the ultimate solution in American politics. Our government killed leaders in Guatemala, the Dominican Republic, the Congo. In the secret corridors of Washington, there are plenty of men who believe the end justifies the means. It's not just the Soviet Union where people die without a trial."

"They tried this?"

"No, no! I'm not sure the plan was anything more than talk all along, a chance to feel they were taking control, even if it was only in a back room somewhere. And too many things went wrong right from the beginning. The Cubans demanded exorbitant sums of money. One of Joe's colleagues changed his mind and threatened to expose them if they went forward. Kennedy's schedule changed."

"How do you know this?"

"My husband was careless. There are notes in his handwriting, logs of meetings and telephone calls. I found them when I was preparing to move his desk into the middle bedroom. I thought I would remove the drawers to make it lighter. When I took out the first one, I found the file wedged in a crack above the runners, where Joe probably thought no one would ever see it. I'm not sure why he kept the papers after they changed their minds. Maybe he wanted a weapon to use against the others, if any of them ever turned on him. The notes explained who said what and when. They were convincing. And there was a letter from one of the others that he'd kept as evidence, and the draft of a letter to one of the Cubans."

"You have these papers?"

"Until I told him, he didn't even know they were gone. I forged lookalikes and put those back in the file. I put the originals in a safe deposit box. I'll move them every couple of years, for safekeeping."

"Why have you told me this?"

"Someday you may have to protect yourself. Someday Joe may come after you. If you have to, you can come to me, and I'll make sure you're safe."

"And what about *her?* Who will protect our daughter from this man?"

"Joe won't hurt Hope. That's the one thing we can be sure of. He's not a man who would harm a child. Do you think I could stay with him if I thought so? Perhaps he won't love her. Perhaps he'll be cold toward her. But I'm as sure of her safety as of anything in the world."

"You can't live like this. Come with me. Bring our daughter. Hope. You named her Hope. Do you have hope for us?"

Her heart was breaking. "There's no hope for us. You don't want to leave your wife and son, and I don't want to live in sin with you.

We have no future together. The best we can do is pick up our lives and move forward."

"I saw her. I came to the nursery today during visiting hours and saw her through the window. She looks like my Pasha."

"Joe's hair is dark. No one will suspect she's not his. In time, maybe he'll think of her that way."

"You don't believe this."

She didn't. She knew the most she could hope for from Joe was an absence of overt cruelty, but that would have to be enough.

"I believe I'm doing the best I can," she said. "If things get too bad, I'll leave Joe and start over. But I'm going to try. I'm going to see if we can make the marriage work."

He reached through the rail for her hand, clasping it. "Then you want me to go? For good?"

"You have to. Right now Joe doesn't know who Hope's father is. We can't ever give him reason to suspect you. You shouldn't have come here."

"You will tell her about me?"

Lydia tried to imagine that conversation. She couldn't, in good faith, promise it would ever take place.

When she remained silent, his expression darkened. "She is my daughter, Lydia. I cannot willingly give her up so easily."

"I'll do what's best for her. I can promise that. She's the one we have to consider now."

"You must protect her. I don't know how, but I'll be watching. From a distance, I will be making sure."

"She'll be safe, Dominik." She lifted his hand to her lips, kissed his palm and folded his fingers over it. "I'll do everything to protect our daughter."

He looked as if he wanted to say more, but he didn't. He withdrew his hand, resting it on the railing for a moment, drinking in this last sight of her. Then he turned and left as quietly as he had come. In a moment the room was empty.

"I will protect her, my love," Lydia said into the darkness.

But, of course, she hadn't.

"And with all this, with two men who were torn to pieces by my sister's birth, you actually believed that someone *else* might have kidnapped Hope?" Faith sounded incredulous. "There were two strong suspects, my father and Dominik, but you never told the FBI the real story? They investigated the kidnapping without knowing any of this?"

Lydia wanted her daughter to understand. She had been trying to protect both men, denying the possibility that either could have kidnapped her baby. Joe's future was at stake, because he knew that if Lydia suspected him, she would come forward with the papers in her possession. And Dominik? What reason did he have? He had a wife and son to consider, and nothing material to offer Hope. Besides, at the time, Lydia had been convinced Dominik would never hurt her.

"How could I tell the FBI?" she said. "I didn't believe either man had done it. Both of them had too much to lose."

"You can say that, knowing the bad judgment my father showed when he went along with this Kennedy plot?"

"But he *didn't* go along with it. In the end he spoke against it and severed his ties with the others. When Kennedy was assassinated the following year, I was absolutely sure your father had nothing to do with it. He was a hothead, yes, but a politician first and foremost. The whole thing scared him so badly he learned his lesson. "

"You believed or you hoped?"

"Faith, try to understand. I didn't know what to do. For a long time I believed the FBI would find Hope and return her. And what if they had, but by then the whole world knew she wasn't really Joe's daughter? Can you imagine how that scandal would have followed her for the rest of her life? I was trying to protect her. I was trying to protect Joe. I was trying to protect Dominik."

"You were trying to protect yourself."

"I don't deny it."

Faith was at the stove now, pouring herself a cup of wassail. She added Scotch, but she stood with her back against the counter to drink it. She looked shaken. "When did you begin to realize you'd never see her again?"

"Months." Lydia set her mug on the table. "I didn't give up for a long, long time."

"And afterward, Mother? Why did you stay married to Dad? Why did you have another child?"

Lydia fumbled for words. "When Hope was taken...your father seemed genuinely sorry. I was so in need of comfort, I believed what the public saw. I...I believed that he had forgiven me."

Faith shook her head in disbelief.

"You weren't there," Lydia said. "The newscasts, the pleas for her to be returned. He put on a tragic face. Even at home, where there were no reporters...he was solicitous and kind. I was in no condition to think rationally about what was happening. Then, in December, Dominik killed himself."

She cleared her throat. "What was left of my world fell apart, but your father was the Rock of Gibraltar. I...I clung to him, and as the months went by we drifted back into a real marriage. I set out to help him, the way he had helped me through the worst. I forced myself to rejoin the world at his side."

"And you had me."

"I owed Joe a child of his own."

"He told you that?"

"Faith, I was a hollow shell. For a long time I simply gave up. I let your father tell me what to do, and I was grateful when he did. Besides, I desperately wanted another baby. Hope was only one week old when she was stolen from me."

"So you got pregnant. With me."

Lydia had no desire to continue. "That's everything. You know it all now."

"I don't think so."

Lydia didn't look at her. "I don't have anything else to add."

"Just one more question, Mother. I grew up in that house, re-member? You say you wanted me. You say you wanted to give my father a gift for all his support. But I was *there*. There was no warmth or gratitude in that house. What happened? You say you were making a new start? When did it end?"

"I've told you too much already."

"What happened? You owe me the rest of it. This was my life."

Lydia considered the table in front of her. The faint ring where a child had set a wet glass and forgotten it, the crack in the finish at the edge of one panel.

She traced a finger along the crack. "When I was eight months pregnant, your father asked me why I'd had the courage to have another baby. We'd had a fight about something, just a silly spat. The pregnancy was difficult so soon after the last one, and I was tired. I challenged him, stood up to him again, the way I had before Hope disappeared. I told him I was having this baby for him, because I wanted to start a new life together and create a family."

She paused, remembering. "He was smiling a little. I'll never forget that. And he said he was glad that this baby didn't belong to the handyman, too."

"Then he knew all along who Hope's real father was?"

"I don't know how or when he figured it out. Maybe it was only a guess. But when I didn't deny it, he said that of course a baby's parentage doesn't have any effect on fate. Lightning isn't supposed to strike in the same place twice, but I should never let folk wisdom guide me. Wouldn't it be a tragedy if I lost his baby, too?"

She looked up. "I asked him what he meant, and he said that obviously it hadn't been a difficult matter to make Hope disappear. Someone had taken her, somebody with everything to gain, and I should be careful."

Faith was pale now. "He as much as said he kidnapped Hope?"

"No, that was the beauty of it, of course. He didn't say it. He just hinted at the possibility, and, worse, that you wouldn't be safe, either, unless I did what I was told."

"But you had evidence against him. You had the Kennedy evidence. My God, the Warren Commission would have been all over it!"

"It was a standoff, Faith. I had the papers, but could I really tell the world the father of my new baby had once plotted to kill Kennedy? And Joe had you. He never *said* he would harm you or make you disappear, but the threat was there. Dominik was right to worry about Hope's safety. With one twist your father let me know I'd been a fool, that I'd never had any reason to trust him or depend on him. I'd been weak, and because of it, I had lost my chance to be free. If I left him, you would be in danger forever. Perhaps only in a custody battle, but the threat was imminent."

"So you stayed with him?"

"He never threatened me again, but of course he never had to, did he?"

Faith's eyes glistened with tears. "Maybe I'll be able to understand this someday, I don't know, but, Mother, I've been an adult for twenty years. I've been safe for decades. And you're *still* with him. You can't blame me for that."

Perhaps this was the hardest part to admit, the part where Lydia had no good excuses. Not passion, not a desperate need to protect a child. Simply, ultimately, cowardice. She looked away from her daughter.

"I've considered leaving him a hundred times or more. But I'm old. All I have left is the life Joe and I made together. As much as I despise him for what he did and said that day, my roots in that life are too deep to untangle. And it was all such a long time ago."

"Please tell me that if you'd *really* believed he'd kidnapped Hope, you wouldn't have stayed with him for any reason. Tell me that much."

Lydia didn't know anymore. "Joe had reasons to kidnap Hope but more reasons not to. He tortured me with the possibility by not denying it, but it was one conversation in the heat of anger. There's never been one bit of evidence he was involved."

Faith's tone softened. "Then you don't think he did it?"

Tears filled Lydia's eyes now, tears that had never really disappeared. "Once upon a time there were *two* men who were unhappy my beautiful baby daughter came into this world. So many years later, and still, that's all I can be sure of."

 31

Ham had never had a Christmas tree. He was Jewish by birth and a humanist by conviction, two strikes against celebrating the holiday. But when David arrived home from an interview with the dean of admissions at Wesley Theological Seminary, he found a tree—a living tree, of course, since that was more environmentally acceptable—sitting in a galvanized pail in the corner of the apartment.

"You needed something familiar," Ham said. "But I draw the line at decorating it. I borrowed some ornaments from a friend who isn't putting his up this year. They're under the table."

David stared at the little Norfolk pine. Burlap peeked from the top of the pail. Clearly Ham had been to a nursery, not a Christmas tree lot. "What's next? Speaking in tongues? Baptism?"

"Sure, and I'm the new Messiah. Dream on."

David embraced him. "You didn't have to do this."

"It's a pagan ritual. I'll pretend I'm a Druid if you will."

"I'll let Alex decorate it this afternoon."

Ham stepped back to get a better look at David's expression. "You're bringing him here?"

Alex would be spending Christmas day with his mother and grandparents, but David had booked a cabin in western Maryland for the weekend so he and Alex could have their private celebration in the country. They were going to hike, cross-country ski if the weather cooperated, and play chess in front of a roaring fire. He hadn't told Ham the rest of it.

"I spoke to Faith last night and told her I wanted to bring him here before we head out of town. I want him to see where I'm living."

"And she said yes?"

"Without a struggle." David had considered that his first gift of the season.

"I'll make sure I'm gone."

"No, I told her you'd be here. She said that was fine."

"She didn't warn you not to have sex in front of the kid?"

"I think she's giving me some credit for good sense. Maybe she's even giving you some, too."

"You'd better be careful. Someday I might learn to like that woman."

"You *would* like her, if you had the chance to know her. Maybe you will yet."

"Miracles of the holiday?"

"She's had a hard time."

"And you still care about her." It wasn't a question.

"Would you want me to say no?" David asked.

"No, that's who you are."

Faith was trying to help Alex pack for his weekend with David, but her mind wasn't on it. Last night, as she'd tossed and turned, she'd thought of nothing except Lydia's visit. This morning, just after dawn, she had come to a decision. She had to tell Pavel what she'd learned. She had promised she would tell him if she discovered anything new about the kidnapping, but even if she hadn't promised, Hope was Pavel's sister, too. Faith and Pavel shared a half sister they had never known.

"Mom, I don't need six pairs of underwear. Let me pack my own stuff." Alex grabbed the briefs and socks out of her hands, embarrassed.

She didn't point out that she still did her son's laundry, that she had washed, dried and folded these particular items approximately one million times in his young life. She just nodded, as if his was the most sensible protest in the world.

"Go ahead. You know what you'll need better than I do."

"Dad's not coming till three. I don't have to be packed till then."

"Why put it off until the last minute?"

"Because that's the way I want to do it."

She wondered what life was going to be like with two teenagers in the house. Alex had just turned twelve. She was on the brink of discovery. "Fine, you take care of it. Just don't forget Dad's Christmas present, all right?"

Alex had made a screen saver for David's computer from a lifetime of school photographs of himself and Remy. Faith suspected she might have a copy under the tree, too.

"You think he'll like it?" Alex asked. "You don't think having Remy's pictures in it will make him sad?"

"Of course he's going to want her pictures, too."

"I asked her to go with us to Maryland."

Faith was certain of the outcome. "That was nice."

"You're going to let her go to Megan's?"

Alex wasn't given to policing family rules or wanting to exact just punishment for his sister. But now he sounded unhappy that Remy, too, was going away for the weekend.

"She needs to get away, just like you do. And school's out, so she won't be missing any schoolwork."

"You'll be here all alone."

"I'll be fine. Remy hasn't seen Megan in ages, so they'll have lots to catch up on. I'm going to finish my Christmas shopping and clean the house. Hey, I might even bake those peppermint swirl cookies you like so much."

"I've already got a whole tin of cookies to take this weekend."

"I need to bake more so I can take them to all the neighbors."

"Maybe Remy ought to stay home and help."

"Are you afraid I'll be lonely?"

He shrugged.

"Sometimes at my age a quiet house is nice." She left him to pack and worry alone. She was sure once he left with David, his mind would be on other things.

Next she stopped by Remy's room to see if she needed help.

From the doorway it appeared Remy was no further along than her brother. "Got everything you need? I have a tin of cookies for Megan's mom."

"Megan's mom makes a million Christmas cookies every year. She doesn't need yours."

Faith heard more than rejection. "It's a hostess gift. Aren't you glad to be getting together with Megan and your other friends, sweetheart? You said you wanted to go."

"I don't care."

Faith hoped Remy would go back to McLean, renew old friendships and turn back into the happy young teen she had been. Of course Faith also believed in a virgin birth, wise men bearing gifts and angels appearing to lowly shepherds.

"You can stay home," she offered, knowing she would be turned down. "There's still a lot to do around the house. I could use the help."

"You're so obvious. I'm trying to get ready, okay?"

Faith went downstairs. Off duty for a few minutes, she called the Scavenger office and asked for Pavel. His secretary agreed to take a message but warned her that he probably wouldn't be in for the rest of the day.

She tried him at home and left a message on his voice mail. She was staring at the narrow wall beside the telephone, adorned only by a calendar, when the day's date suddenly clicked. Back upstairs in her room she shuffled through her copies of the newspaper articles from the library scrapbook until she found the one she was looking for.

Thirty-eight years ago on this date, Dominik Dubrov had hung himself from a Georgetown rafter.

She dropped to the edge of her bed and wondered if Pavel knew. Did he ignore the date of his father's suicide, or did he commemorate it in some way? She wondered what she would do under the circumstances.

A few minutes later she was dressed in her warmest coat, although she was only going next door. "I'll be back in a few minutes," she called upstairs. "I'm taking Dottie Lee some cookies."

Although she had salted them twice that morning, the steps were icy. She took a moment to scrape off an accumulation of snow before she gingerly descended. Next door, Mariana welcomed her and took her coat.

Dottie Lee's holiday decorations were unorthodox but festive. Multicolored origami animals were strung in doorways. Pysanky eggs from Eastern Europe adorned a tabletop Christmas tree. A papier-mâché witch rode a broomstick across the opening of the fireplace.

"La Befana," Dottie Lee said from the stairs. "On twelfth night she brings candy to good Italian children and coal to bad ones."

"I'm not sure my children could wait that long to see which they were getting." Faith held out a colorful tin when Dottie Lee joined her. "For you and Mariana. And an invitation. We'd like you to come for Christmas supper. We'll be going to my parents' house early in the day, but we'll be home in time for a celebration of our own."

Dottie Lee considered. "Why don't you come here instead?"

"I don't want you doing the work. I want you to be our guest for a change."

"I don't often go out, you know."

Faith assumed she was talking about the winter weather. "If it snows, Alex and I will come and get you. I don't want you slipping on the ice."

"Faith, dear, the only times I've been out of my house and yard in years and years were the brief times I've been in yours."

"Oh..." Faith was chagrined that she hadn't understood. She had missed all the signs that Dottie Lee was housebound. "I'm so sorry. Are you afraid to leave?"

"I suppose I am."

"But you did come that once. And you've been to my front door."

"Both visits seemed imperative."

"Do you want to try again?" Faith asked gently.

Dottie Lee chewed her lip.

"The houses are connected," Faith pointed out. "If there was a doorway right here—" she tapped the wall that separated them "—then my house would be your house, too."

"There is no doorway."

"I don't want to make you uncomfortable. It's just that you feel like part of our family now."

Dottie Lee thought about it, then nodded. "No, we'll come. I might leave a bit early. Would that be all right?"

"We can make it a progressive dinner. If you get tired of being at our house, we'll follow you over here."

"Does your mother know what a blessing you are?"

Before Dottie Lee sidetracked her with flattery, Faith shifted to the most immediate reason she had come. "Dottie Lee, I've got something else to discuss."

"I'm delighted to leave my neuroses for the moment." She gestured to the sofa, but Faith shook her head.

"I'll launch right in. I know my mother had an affair with Dominik Dubrov. And I know Dominik is Pavel's father. I'll bet you've known that for a while, haven't you?"

Dottie Lee didn't seem surprised by either fact. "Does your mother realize you know?" When Faith nodded, Dottie Lee sighed. "Good."

"I also know Dominik Dubrov killed himself thirty-eight years ago today."

"Yes. A tragedy."

"I'm trying to find Pavel. And I wondered, well, if you happen to know where his father is buried?"

"You think Pavel might be there?"

Faith knew it was a long shot, an impossibly long shot. But Pavel himself had said he visited his father's grave. What better day for it?

"I think it's a possibility," Faith said. "And even if he isn't..." She had no reason to visit the grave. Her mother's affair with Dominik Dubrov had set the stage for her own unhappy childhood. At the same time, she was drawn to his story. He had become a tragic figure in her mind, a man left with nothing, who, in the end, had taken his own life to escape the pain.

Dottie Lee interrupted her thoughts. "Do you have something you need to say to him? To Dominik, that is?"

Faith supposed she did, although she didn't know what. "I know what you told the police, but are you sure he didn't kidnap Hope?" She didn't add that Hope had been Dominik's daughter. For all she knew, Dottie Lee had figured it out already, but that was Lydia's secret to share.

"I believe in the end you'll find everything is tied together, dear. I never thought a stranger wandered in and took the baby."

"But you were Dominik's alibi," Faith probed.

Dottie Lee didn't confirm that the alibi had been genuine, a fact Faith made note of. "If I hadn't told the police what I did, perhaps Dominik would still be alive. They might have arrested him, and he would have found it harder to kill himself in jail. So when no one claimed his body, I did. I buried him in my family's plot at Oak Hill, with senators and statesmen. He deserved better than a pauper's grave. No matter what you think of him now, Dominik was a good man. Tell him I still believe it, will you, when you visit today?"

Remy didn't want to go to Megan's house. All her old friends were coming for a sleepover, and they would be talking about things Remy had no part in anymore. She had seen some of them at the horse show, and although they were friendly, she just knew what kinds of things they'd said about her after she left.

Besides, they seemed so young now. Some of the guys they talked about weren't even in high school yet. She hadn't told Megan much about Enzio, afraid Megan would tell her mother and she would call Faith. So far Remy had been able to keep that particular secret.

For weeks now her mother had made it nearly impossible for her to see Enzio, but Remy had found ways. The easiest was to sneak away when her mother went out and left her at home with Alex.

Alex knew Remy was sneaking out and around, of course. He also knew that if he ever told Faith, Remy would hate him for the rest of his life. Alex wanted to be cool and grown-up. He liked to think he was both, which was pathetic, of course, but something she used in her favor. So far he had kept his mouth shut.

She'd gone to see Enzio directly from school, too. Once she left early and went to Enzio's house while the other eighth graders spent the afternoon at an assembly. She'd returned to school, exhausted from jogging most of the way, just in time for Faith to pick her up.

She even skipped classes to go to Lawford's. The first time she was nearly caught, but she lied and said she was in the library doing research. Luckily, before her teacher could check, he was distracted by a fight in the hall.

The second time, when she found out Enzio wasn't working that day, she went down the street to visit Ralph, because there wasn't time to go to Enzio's house. Ralph remembered her from the shopping trip with her mother and asked why she wasn't in school. When she told him, he'd been really cool about it, listening and nodding his head as if he actually understood. He'd said that he had hated school, too, because he was different, but now he was going to college part-time, and that she ought to stick it out. He said that finding new friends could be hard, but if she looked she would find people who liked her the way she was, that *he* had.

Ralph wasn't like anybody she'd ever known before, but she guessed, despite his stupid advice, that *she* liked him the way he was, too.

She was staring at the ceiling, wondering what she would say to anybody at Megan's party, when Alex came into her room. Her mother was next door at the old lady's house, and Alex lounged in her doorway like they were friends or something. Lounging or not, he still looked uncomfortable.

"You're going to Megan's?" he asked.

"So?"

"You're not going somewhere else?"

"Megan's having a sleepover."

"You could still go to Maryland with Daddy and me."

"Like I'd want to be in the same place, any place, with him."

"He misses you, Remy."

For a moment she didn't know what to say. She didn't really care if David missed her, but for just a moment her throat felt thick. "I'm not going."

"Jesus said we should forgive each other."

"Let Jesus forgive him, then. When did you turn into a creepy little evangelist?"

"He's our dad. He's the same dad he always was."

"Not the same. He's a flamer, or did you forget?"

The front door creaked, then closed. Faith called upstairs, "You two all right?"

"What does she think?" Remy made a face and reached for Guest, who was strolling across the bed as if she owned it. Guest and Pinto Bean still hung out in Remy's room most of the time. They were the only reasons Remy ever wanted to come home.

"We're okay," Alex shouted into the hallway.

"You know, one of these days you're going to figure out Mom just asks those dumb questions because she's nosy. She doesn't really care if we're all right. It's just something she has to ask." Remy hugged Guest to her chest. After a wiggle, the cat settled in, resigned to her fate.

"That's stupid." Alex sounded disgusted. "You hate everybody."

"Yeah, mostly you."

"You know, I used to wish I was you, but now I'd hate to be like you." Alex left.

Despite herself, she was hurt. She didn't want to be Alex's friend. What would be the point of that? But she'd always liked knowing that he looked up to her. She was the smart one, the popular one, the good one. He'd always been jealous, and that hadn't been so bad.

She tried to forget him by throwing a few things in her backpack to take to Megan's. By the time Faith came up to check on her again—like a prison guard doing a head count—she was nearly ready.

"Sally's going to be here in a little while," Faith said.

"You don't have to keep reminding me."

"Alex is ready, too, and I've got an errand to run. Do you mind if I leave now? Alex says he doesn't mind staying alone if you leave before he does."

Remy put her fist to her chest in a feigned heart attack. "You mean I'm allowed to stay in this house without you for more than fifteen minutes?"

Faith's eyes narrowed. "Maybe not."

Remy knew she had overplayed her hand. "Of course you can go, Mom. We'll be fine. I'll make sure the door's locked when I leave, and I'll remind Alex."

Faith studied her. "I don't want to feel like a jailer."

"You're way too serious."

"This feels serious to me. It doesn't to you?"

"I just want to be left alone. I don't want people hanging over me, deciding everything about my life."

"You want to be an adult, and you're not."

"Let's pretend for a while, okay? Just for, say, half an hour? I'll stay here, and you can leave. And I won't burn down the house or snort cocaine while you're gone."

"Remy, do you ever listen to yourself anymore? Do you want everybody who loves you to wish they didn't?"

That sounded too much like what Alex had said. "Just leave me alone!" She grabbed her pillow and wrapped her arms around it because Guest was out of reach.

"We'll talk when you get back from Megan's."

"I don't want to talk."

Faith looked as if she wanted to say more, but something persuaded her not to. "Forget about it for now and have fun."

In a few minutes the front door closed. From Faith's bedroom window, Remy saw her mother cross the street and start down the brick sidewalk to the spot where their car was parked today. She waited until she was sure Faith had driven away. Then she closed her mother's door and reached for her telephone.

She prayed while the telephone rang. On the fourth ring Megan picked up. "Hey, Meg," Remy said. "I was afraid I wouldn't catch you."

She listened to her friend recite where she'd been and why she hadn't answered quicker. Sometimes Megan could be so lame. "I'm not coming," Remy said when Megan took a breath. "I'm...sick. I'm going to wait awhile and see if I feel better. If I do I'll come later." She figured she had enough money saved to take a taxi to McLean. It meant she wouldn't be able to buy a Christmas present for Alex, but she was too angry to buy one anyway.

She listened to Megan jabber on. "Look, I've got to go," Remy said. "I'll call you in a while. Just tell your mom not to come and get me, okay? And don't call here, because I might be sleeping." She hung up before Megan could start a new topic.

She had the rest of the afternoon. She couldn't believe her luck.

She could spend what was left of the day with Enzio, then take a taxi over to Megan's late in the evening. Faith would never know.

She wished it weren't winter, that she could wear something sexy and fun—not that her mother let her have anything revealing. But she put on a black top and a bright yellow shirt over it, tying it above her waist. She slid into red capris so her midriff was bare and finished with her clunkiest platform shoes. She hated to spoil the effect with a coat, but she knew if she showed up at Megan's without one, Megan's mother would say something. She could take it off just before she got to Enzio's.

She hoped, she double hoped, he was there. All the other roommates had gone home for Christmas, except Colin, who had stayed behind to finish up a research project. He spent all his time in the library, though. Remy thought there was a good chance that if Enzio was there, she would find him alone.

Alex was already downstairs, picking out a one-fingered melody on the piano. "What's that supposed to be?" she said.

"'Say My Name.' You know, Destiny's Child?"

She pushed him to one side and played it the first time perfectly. Then she added some chords.

"Hey, that's good."

She closed the piano, embarrassed. "I'm going. Megan's mom's going to pick me up on the corner. I told her I'd wait so she doesn't have to park."

"You're lying. I heard what you said on the phone. You told her you were sick and decided not to go."

"You heard wrong."

"I'm not deaf. My room's right beside Mom's."

"I'm going now. I'm not going to be here when your father gets here. I'm going to wait for Megan's mom."

He ignored the part about David being "his" father. "Where are you really going?"

"I told you." Remy got to the door and turned. "It would be a real shame if you told somebody what you think you know. Because I could lie about you, too. I could think of a million lies, and you'd have soooo much trouble proving I was wrong." She shut the door behind her before he could respond.

Outside, she started down the street, but even though she should have felt excitement at the unexpected freedom, she didn't. Alex had spoiled that for her. Alex, with his stupid worried eyes. Alex, her dumb baby brother, who was trying to tell her what she should feel about everybody and everything.

She was older than he was and knew a lot more. She was old enough to attract a college guy like Enzio, and she was old enough to make her own decisions. It was too bad everyone was treating her like a baby, but she was willing to take that matter into her own hands. Maybe Enzio was a little old for her, but she could handle him. She could handle her life. She could prove to everyone she was old enough to be left alone.

 32

In the mid-nineteenth century, Georgetown's Oak Hill Cemetery
had been part of a new revolution in the design of burial grounds.
Instead of overcrowded churchyards, rural "landscape" cemeter-
ies like Oak Hill featured winding lanes and spacious terraces with
sweeping views, the precursors to modern public parks.

Oak Hill, with its Primrose and Violet Lanes, English Gothic
chapel and sculptured marble monuments, was a protected Georgetown oasis that was nearly as difficult to get into alive as dead. But
Faith had attended funerals here for her father's colleagues, and she
felt at home exploring the fifteen-acre expanse.

Dottie Lee had given her the family plot number, and with the
help of a caretaker—who was impressed enough by her family
name to allow access—she pinpointed the right path. She made
slow progress, taking care where she stepped, since a thin layer of
snow covered the ground and in places had turned to ice. She
passed only a few stalwart visitors. One woman swathed in a calf-
length mink wept silently beside a trio of stone cherubs marking
a gravesite. Christmas wasn't always a time of good memories.

Faith didn't really expect to find Pavel. He could be anywhere,
perhaps even blissfully happy in the arms of another woman. The
impulse to visit the cemetery had overtaken her good sense, but she

didn't care. Walking toward Dominik's grave, she felt one step closer to solving the riddle of Hope's kidnapping.

As she picked her way along the path, she tried to imagine the black depression that had driven Dominik to suicide. His wife and son had moved to the opposite coast, but certainly he could have joined them to attempt a reconciliation. His baby daughter had been taken from her mother's home, but only five months had passed since the kidnapping. Had suspicion that his daughter had met some terrible fate spurred him on?

Or had he known her fate for a certainty?

She turned and started downhill past three towering hardwoods. She could begin to read tombstones and markers once she reached the area below, but as it turned out, reading wasn't required. Once she passed the trees, Pavel stood fifty yards away, looking down at what had to be his father's grave.

She came to an abrupt halt, feeling like a trespasser. What was simply a question mark in her life was an exclamation point in his. His father's death had, as much as anything else, made him the man he was. He had no memories of Dominik Dubrov; he didn't even carry his father's name. But the man who would rest in a pauper's grave except for the kindness of one eccentric woman was the central figure in Pavel's history.

As she watched, he rocked back on his heels. He held a wool cap in his hands, and when he turned and began to pull it back over his head, Faith moved forward to meet him.

She knew the exact moment when he recognized her. He didn't look either pleased or surprised, merely wary. She wished it had never come to that.

"Faith?" Pavel pulled his hat over his ears with gloved fingers. "What are you doing here?"

"Dottie Lee told me where your father was buried. I wanted to see the grave."

"There's not much to see. A simple marker."

"How long have you known where he was buried?"

"After I got here, I did a little research and turned up a death notice on microfilm. I could have put up a more elaborate marker, but I would have needed Dottie Lee's permission."

"You didn't want her to know Dominik was your father, did you? But she wasn't surprised when I told her today."

"She's had it figured out for a while. She made it clear when I first started seeing you, although she never said it in so many words."

"Why didn't you just tell her? You were curious about your father, and she was his friend."

"I thought I might do better just watching and waiting."

Faith had an urge to zip his dark leather jacket. Pavel looked as if he needed a good night's sleep and a hot meal. His father had succumbed to depression. She hoped the son had better resources.

"I guess I'm here to reward your patience," she said.

"What does that mean?"

"My mother told me something you need to know. That's the real reason I came looking for you."

"Not to console me, huh?"

She realized consolation had been part of it, something she hadn't admitted to herself. She was still linked to this man, and not only by the circumstances of their childhoods.

"Hope was only my half sister." She crossed her arms over her chest, as much for protection as warmth. "And your half sister, too."

For a moment he looked weary enough to have problems putting that together. Then it clicked. "My father's child?"

Faith told him the story.

"Then my father knew? And your father?"

She hadn't told him about Lydia blackmailing Joe. Even the word seemed overwrought, a cop-show motive for murder. She danced around it. "My father had his own secrets. Nothing to do with the kidnapping, but something my mother could use against him. So under pressure he agreed to raise Hope as his child."

"It's a toss-up, isn't it, whose family was crazier?"

"This puts a whole new spin on everything that happened," Faith said. "There's no possibility now that your father kidnapped Hope out of revenge. But maybe he took her for other reasons. Today Dottie Lee as much as told me that she made up his alibi. I don't think he was working for her that afternoon."

He didn't seem surprised. "You're saying he might have wanted to raise Hope on his own?"

"Or protect her."

Pavel frowned. "From your father?"

"My mother forced my father to accept Hope as his child. The senator's not a man who gives in without using every weapon at his disposal. Your father may have realized that."

"So my father took Hope to protect her from yours?"

"It's one scenario. Maybe he took her and something happened in the process. Or maybe he didn't take her, and afterward he realized my father arranged to have her kidnapped. Maybe your father felt guilty he didn't do more to stop him."

Pavel looked increasingly weary. "We can't ask my father. He took his secrets with him when he threw that rope over the rafter."

Faith knew Pavel would never erase that particular image from his mind. "The suicide bothers me, Pavel, not only because a man killed himself, but because the solution was so extreme and I can't believe the situation called for it."

"Knowing everything you do, you can't understand why he was depressed?"

"The dark, brooding Russian personality's a stereotype, isn't it? Did your father really suffer from depression? Or did he learn something so terrible he didn't want to live anymore? Was he placed in a situation so desperate that he saw no other way out?"

"There's one person who might know the answer. Unfortunately, he dropped off the face of the earth."

Faith must have looked puzzled, because he explained. "Sandor. My father's assistant. He was a distant cousin of my father's, remember? From the Hungarian side of his family."

"I just know Sandor did some of the work on our house." Faith was trying to put pieces together now. The kidnapping had happened so long ago, and Sandor, like so many others, had been a bit player.

"Apparently my father was training him. Sandor did the scut work, and my father did anything complicated."

"But surely the authorities interviewed him," Faith said. "From what I've learned, they talked to everyone who had the slightest ties to our family. They asked for the list of guests at my parents' wedding, acquaintances who attended any party they had been to, anyone who'd contributed to Dad's campaign."

"They interviewed Sandor," Pavel said. "He swore my father wouldn't have done such a thing, that he had never even hinted at that possibility."

"Sandor and your father were cousins. He might have lied to protect family." She considered her own words. "You say he dropped off the face of the earth?"

"The men in my family don't seem to have much staying power. Sandor married a few years after my father's death and had two children of his own. Before they even started school, he left without a word to anybody. Eventually his wife remarried and his children grew up, but to this day they have no idea where he went. They're the ones who told me he had been interviewed by the FBI."

"You checked into this." She was stating the obvious.

"Sandor was my cousin, too. I had some vague notion of reestablishing family ties. Unfortunately, his children want nothing to do with their father or anyone who reminds them of him."

"Pavel, the last time we talked, you said you'd told me everything."

He tugged at his cap. "I didn't think about this. I was more hopeful about finding a cousin than a kidnapper. Nothing I learned about Sandor seemed important to the case."

"Everything's important."

"This has begun to possess us. We have lives. I have a job in turmoil, and you have children who need you. But we're standing in the cold, in the shadow of a stranger's grave, talking about something that happened decades ago as if it could change our lives."

"It already has. Not just because of the way we were raised, but because we've been thrown back into it."

"And at each other."

"Was there more to us than that?" She'd hoped to sound detached. She didn't.

"There was. There is."

She wanted to deny it, but whatever had passed between them still simmered under the surface. She was here not simply because she wanted answers to the past, but because she needed answers to take her into the future.

"If anybody knows where Sandor went, it's Dottie Lee," she said.

"She's the one who recommended Dominik to my mother. He worked for her first. Sandor probably did, as well."

"Will she tell us what she knows?"

Dottie Lee doled out information when she thought the time was right, but now Faith wondered if there was more to the old woman's reluctance than a need for attention, a need to be the center of things.

Dottie Lee might have a more important reason.

Faith raised her eyes to his. "Pavel, she's protecting somebody. I should have realized it before."

"She's been protecting my father. She buried him in her family plot."

"Your father's dead. Dottie Lee's old, but she doesn't live in the past. She's protecting somebody who's still alive."

"Your mother?"

Faith wondered if she could be wrong. "Have coffee with me. I'm freezing. Let's talk this over and come up with a strategy. We have to find a way to encourage Dottie Lee to tell us everything."

"It's been a while since we sat down at a table together."

She heard the corollary. He had missed that intimacy. He had missed her.

And she had missed him.

"It's a cup of coffee," she warned.

"I'll take it."

No wreath hung from Enzio's door; no lights adorned the scraggly bushes in the narrow strip along the house. Somebody had taped construction paper snowflakes to the front window, but Remy guessed that was Colin's doing. He tutored first graders in an inner city Catholic school, and she would just bet the snowflakes were some little kid's art project. Colin was always talking about eye-hand coordination.

The house seemed unwelcoming today, as dark inside as the slate-colored sky. For a moment she reconsidered her plan. There was still time to go home, admit she had changed her mind and call Megan. If Megan's mother couldn't come to pick her up, then Remy could call a taxi, the way she had planned.

She didn't have to do this.

Remy wasn't sure exactly what was bothering her. Alex had something to do with it. So did lying. At first, lying had been an adventure. By not getting caught, she proved she was smarter than her parents. They weren't the people she'd always thought them to be; now she'd proved they were stupid, to boot.

Lately, though, lying wasn't its own reward. She was still angry, still determined to twist the knife whenever she could. But there was little pleasure in it now that the initial thrill was over.

Enzio had something to do with it, too. They hadn't been alone for more than a few minutes since the day he nearly undressed her in his kitchen. She'd thought about that day ever since. The feel of his hands at her breasts, the grinding of his hips. Maybe she was only fourteen, but a lot of girls her age did the nasty, and with more than one guy. Billie was proud of her own personal scorecard.

Remy had been careful until today to make sure Enzio didn't get her alone for long. She was nervous just thinking about it, but excited at the same time. He was a man who knew his way around, and she was just a kid. Of course, he didn't know how young she was, but that hardly mattered. She had to start sometime. Her parents had taught her the importance of virtue, but look at the way they lived their own lives.

What would they think if they knew a college guy wanted to have sex with their little girl?

She let the brass knocker fall against the door and waited for someone to answer. Enzio came to the door at last. His eyes lit up when he saw her, and he pulled her inside.

"Your timing's good," he said. The words came out slowly, spaced like the dripping of a leaky faucet.

"Why?" She was puzzled by the size of his pupils and the grin that seemed to have no origin.

"I just got some verrry good bud. I'm checking it out."

"Marijuana?" She tried to sound matter-of-fact.

"You're from another planet, aren't you?" His laugh was a little off the mark. "Ever smoke weed on your planet, little Martian?"

She hadn't even smoked a cigarette, although she'd inhaled enough secondhand smoke from Enzio's to count for something.

He laughed. "Come try this with me. I'm soaring over rooftops."

She wondered what that would be like. If she soared over

rooftops, she could leave Georgetown and everything that had happened in the past year behind her. No more father. No more mother. No more little brother who disapproved of every breath she took.

She told herself not to be a baby. "Where is it?"

"Up in my room." He must have accurately read the look on her face, because he laughed again. "We'll leave the door open. Jesus, you're such a kid."

She didn't want to be a kid. She wanted to be ten years older and living a different life. Right now this was as close to the fantasy as she was liable to come.

"Lead the way." She linked her arm through his.

David listened for the chime of Faith's doorbell, but the house was silent. Despite what she'd said, the row house still needed work, including a new bell. He knocked, listened, then knocked again, but no one came to the door.

He was certain he had told Alex when to expect him, and Faith knew his plans, of course. For a moment he wondered if she had done this on purpose. Was she making a point about the holidays? He didn't deserve consideration because it was his fault their family wouldn't be together the way they had been every Christmas of the children's lives—until last year?

No, that particular surge of guilt wasn't coming from Faith.

The steps were too icy to sit on, so he settled for leaning against the newly painted iron rail. He would wait a few minutes, then head back to the car to find a telephone. He could try Faith on her cell phone, although that was a long shot.

He passed the time and ignored the cold by remembering other Christmases. Seven years ago Alex had gotten his first new bike. He had refused training wheels, although he had taken more than a few spills while he learned to balance.

Nine years ago David had built a dollhouse for Remy, and Faith had painted the tiny rooms and furnished them. He wondered where the house was now. He hoped that, in her quest to rid herself of everything that reminded her of him, Remy hadn't destroyed it. He had hoped she would pass it on to her own children.

A blast of wind rattled the shutters on the row house. Snow was expected again tonight, and if he and Alex didn't leave for Maryland soon, they might be driving in it. David checked his watch and saw it was even later than he'd thought. He started back toward Ham's car, which he had borrowed for the trip.

Halfway to the car, he saw Alex walking toward him. His son had his head down, but the coppery curls were a giveaway. Alex was scuffing his boots as he trudged along the brick sidewalk. Years of parenting told David that something was bothering him.

"Hey, Alex."

Alex looked surprised at the summons, as if he had forgotten that David was expected. "Dad?"

"Where have you been?"

Alex didn't answer. David read indecision on his son's features. "Alex? I've been waiting at the house for you."

"I...I heard something at the end of the street. Like a crash or something. I just went down to see, you know, what it was."

David had very little practice uncovering lies. Alex was a straightforward kid who was more likely to tell the truth in excruciatingly accurate detail than to misrepresent it, but even he could tell that something was wrong now.

"Did you find out anything?" David said.

"No. Everything looked okay."

"Where's your mom?"

"She had an errand. She left us—me. She knew you were coming."

"Then Remy's at home?"

"No."

"Did she go somewhere?"

"She's supposed to go to Megan's house for the weekend."

David knew he was getting to the truth, but it was taking too long. He was chilled to the bone. He stamped his feet as he walked to warm them. "Alex, where's Remy?"

Alex shrugged. "Maybe she heard the noise, too."

"Then she would have told you, right?"

"I don't know."

He did know. David was sure of it. Alex was keeping something from him and not enjoying it one bit.

They were at Faith's house now, and Alex opened the door. David followed him inside and continued his interrogation. "One of the problems with having a sister is that you feel loyalty to her and loyalty to your parents. Sometimes it's hard to figure out which is more important."

Alex didn't say anything.

"But sometimes it's pretty easy," David said. "Like when you're afraid your sister might do something to get herself in trouble."

"She doesn't tell me anything. She thinks I'm a geek." Alex got as far as the stairs up to his room before he turned. "She already hates me."

"She doesn't. Not really. Someday the two of you will be great friends."

"Not if I tell you."

"Tell me what?"

Alex was clearly torn. David made it easier for him. "You have to tell me the truth, Alex. I'm your father. You don't really have a choice."

"I'm going to get in trouble."

David considered that. "Because you didn't tell sooner?" He watched his son nod. "You haven't been sure what to do. But now you know."

"Remy's been lying a lot."

David needed to hear this, but he didn't want to. "About what?"

"About where she goes when she's not home. There are some guys down the street—college students, I think—and Remy goes over to their house whenever she can. She hasn't been going to Billie's after school. She's been going over there. One of the guys works at a clothing store, and she goes to his store, too."

"She's over at the house now?" David couldn't imagine what Faith had been thinking to leave Remy and Alex alone.

"She was supposed to go to Megan's house. It was all planned, but she called Megan as soon as Mom left and told her she was sick. Then she took her stuff and went down the street. I waited a long time, hoping she would come out again, but she didn't."

"Is that where you were coming from?"

"I followed her, just to see if she was lying. She said I'd heard her wrong, that she was meeting Megan's mom at the corner, but she wasn't telling the truth."

David was rapidly growing more concerned. "You didn't tell your mother any of this?"

Alex looked down at the floor. "Mom doesn't know. She watches Remy real close, but Remy lies, and Mom wants to trust her. I wanted to tell her, but I knew Remy would be really mad at me if I did."

"Don't worry. You've done the right thing now. Let's go get her."

"You're going down there?"

"Does your mom have her cell phone? Call her right now. She needs to come home."

Alex took off for the kitchen phone. When he returned, he was shaking his head. "It just rings and rings. Then I get her voice mail."

"Did you leave a message?"

"Yeah, but it doesn't work. It never works."

David put his arm around Alex's shoulder to propel him toward the door. "Let's go."

Outside, Alex turned in the direction of Ham's car. David wondered by how many minutes he had missed his daughter. If he had arrived a few minutes earlier, would he have seen her?

They crossed one street, then another. At the beginning of the next block, Alex slowed his pace. "It's that gray house."

The house was a little run-down, much as Faith's had been. Otherwise it was a typical Georgetown row house. "You're sure that's the one?" David said.

"I've seen her go in there before. And I stood here and waited almost forever."

"Okay. Go home now. And try your mom again. Stay by the phone in case she calls back."

"You don't want me to come?"

"No, I'll get your sister and bring her home."

Alex looked relieved. He turned around and started back.

David steeled himself for the coming confrontation. At the door, he knocked and waited, but there was no answer. Frustrated, he knocked louder, then tried the knob. But the door was locked.

He stepped back on to the sidewalk and shouted up at the front window. "Remy!"

"May I help you?"

David turned to see a young man coming down the block toward him. In the seconds before the young man stopped in front of him, David noted blond hair and clean-cut features, a harmless enough Georgetown student.

"Are you looking for somebody?" The young man's smile was polite but wary.

"My daughter's in there."

"Daughter?"

David held out his hand, although he wanted to shake the kid by the scruff of his neck. "David Bronson. Remy Bronson's father."

"Colin Fitzpatrick." Colin dropped his hand. "You're Remy's dad? I thought her dad was dead."

"She'd like everyone to believe that. Is she here?"

"I don't know. I've been at the library most of the day. She might be with Enzio. They hang out together."

"Unless Enzio is fourteen, too, we have a problem."

"Fourteen?"

David knew Colin wasn't faking surprise. Colin was genuinely taken back—and alarmed. "That's right. Fourteen. She's been lying to you if she said differently."

"She said she was a senior in high school."

"And you didn't question it?"

"She's short, but she looks old enough. Why'd she lie?"

"Because she knew you'd send her back home if she told you she was in the eighth grade."

"Eighth grade!" Now Colin looked truly alarmed.

"I want her out of there, and I want her out of there now."

Colin fished in his pocket, pulling out a key. Without another word, he stuck it in the lock. "How come you didn't put a stop to this earlier?"

"I didn't know. She's been lying to everybody."

"She's a good kid." Colin looked worried.

The door seemed to take forever to open. Despite the cold, David's hands were sweating. If Enzio was anything like Colin, they probably didn't have too much of a problem. But not every college age male was honorable.

"Look, Remy and I have our problems," David said. "She's going to resist coming with me. But she has to, so please don't interfere."

"She sure can't stay here." Colin finally jiggled the lock until it clicked and pushed the door open. In the foyer, he shouted her name. "Remy!"

Silence was the only reply.

"I'm going up to Enzio's room and check," Colin said.

"I'm coming with you."

Colin looked alarmed. "I don't know what's been going on with them. I came home once and, well..."

"Well what?" David demanded.

"I just thought maybe things had gotten a little hot and heavy, and I was glad I walked in. I asked Enzio later, but he said that was stupid, she was like the house mascot or something."

"Let's go."

Colin took the steps two at a time. "Hey, Remy, there's somebody here to see you." He stopped in front of a closed door. "Enzio, you in there?"

David wasn't as polite. He turned the knob, but the door was locked. "Remy! It's Daddy. Are you there?"

He heard something like a cry of distress, a muffled cry. That was all he needed. He pushed Colin to one side and rammed the sole of his shoe against the door. Once, twice, then a third powerful blow that jolted up and down his spine but did the job.

The door flew open. The room was dark, but he saw Remy on a mattress on the floor and the lithe figure of a young man pulling up his pants in the corner.

He wasn't sure how he crossed the room. One moment he was in the doorway, the next he had Enzio by the shoulders and he was slamming him against the wall.

"Hey!" Enzio tried to shake loose, but David had a death grip on him. "Hey, we didn't do anything, man."

David shoved him so hard that Enzio's head snapped back and he slid to the floor, dazed. David dropped him and knelt beside the mattress. Remy was pulling her shirt down and sobbing.

"Are you okay?"

"Daddy..." She launched herself into his arms. David held her against his chest and stroked her hair.

"It's okay, sweetheart. You're okay, now." He wasn't sure it was true, though he had never wanted so badly for anything to be true.

"She's fourteen!" Colin was on the floor beside Enzio, shaking him.

"Remy, tell me what happened here," David said. "I have to know whether to call the police."

She was sobbing so hard he wasn't sure if she could talk. But she stammered out the words. "We—came up to—get high. I—I— we smoked a couple of joints. I—maybe I—I fell asleep. And when I woke up—he was taking off—my clothes."

David's heart was breaking. "Did he rape you, Remy?"

"No. He was trying to take—off my—" She began to sob harder. "He had his hands all—over me, then you shouted—and he told me—to be quiet—and I called you, but you didn't hear—"

Enzio tried to push Colin away. "The little bitch! She told me she was eighteen."

David closed his eyes. "Get him out of here, Colin. Before I kill him."

"It's my fault. It's my fault!" Remy clung to David even harder.

He stroked her hair and whispered reassurances as Colin hustled Enzio out of the room, but he couldn't dispute that she'd had some fault in this. She had lied to everyone, and the lies had caught up with her.

When she was calmer, he helped her straighten her clothes and put on her shoes. Then he got her to her feet, his arm around her shoulders. He grabbed her coat, recognized her backpack on the floor beside the door and scooped that up, too. "Can you make it downstairs?"

She nodded. "I'm sorry, Daddy. I'm sorry...."

"I know. Let's just get out of here."

Colin was the only one downstairs. He looked upset, as if he felt responsible for everything that had happened.

"Where's your roommate?" David asked, as Remy sobbed softly beside him.

"He left."

"I'm going to press charges unless he moves out of here and away from Prospect Street."

"I'll make sure. Nobody likes him anyway."

"You can tell him I'll come by on Monday to check. If his stuff isn't gone, I'll report this as attempted rape of a juvenile."

"He'll be gone." Colin stole a glance at Remy. "Hey, Remy, are you okay?"

She just cried harder.

"She's a good kid," Colin told David. "She was just playing at being older. I don't think she knew what could happen."

"She found out." David tightened his arm around his daughter. "Let's go, sweetheart."

"Are you going…to tell Mom?"

"You know I have to."

"She'll hate me! She'll never trust me again."

"She won't hate you." Trust was a separate issue. He pulled Remy's coat closed and buttoned it, as he had buttoned it hundreds of times when she was little. Then he helped her toward the door.

Outside, the cold air seemed to revive her. She gasped when it hit her, but it seemed to clear her head. By the time they reached the row house, her sobs had diminished.

The door was unlocked. David pushed it open and ushered Remy inside. Faith stood in the foyer with Pavel Quinn beside her. "Remy?" she asked.

Remy began to cry again. Faith grabbed Remy's hands and held them to her cheeks.

"Remy, are you okay? David, is she okay?"

She wasn't okay; and wouldn't be for a long time. But for the first time, David was absolutely sure she was going to be.

"She had a close call," he said. "She's been lying and hanging out with some college guys up the street. She was lying to them, too, about her age. One of them nearly raped her."

Faith let out a cry and pulled Remy to her chest. Remy went without resistance. David glanced at Pavel. The man's eyes were blazing, and David realized he had an ally. In a different time and place, Pavel would have been strapping on his six-shooter to avenge Remy's honor.

"I took care of it," David told him. "He'll be moving out."

Pavel nodded. "He'd damned well better."

"How did this happen?" Faith said. She was trying to get answers from Remy, but David put his hand on her shoulder.

"I'll tell you the whole story. I promise. She's too upset to go into it again."

"She was supposed to go to Megan's house. I thought that's where she was. Then I came home, and Alex told me—"

David cut her off. "Remy and Alex are coming with me to the cabin for the weekend."

Faith looked up. "No, she's upset, David. She can't go—"

Remy pulled away from her mother. "I'm going with Daddy." She crossed her arms, as if to comfort herself. "That's...where I want to go."

David watched Faith and the parade of expressions that crossed her face. He was relieved to see acceptance bringing up the rear.

"Okay. I can see you do." Faith smoothed Remy's hair back from her forehead. "That's the best place for you right now. Shall I throw a few extra things in your backpack so you can stay warm?"

"Thank you." Remy sniffed.

David rested his hand on his daughter's shoulder. "Why don't you go wash your face while your mom packs?"

"You'll wait?"

"I'm pretty good at waiting for you," David said.

Her eyes met his. A smile trembled on her lips, then died. It was a start.

 33

By the time David and the children drove off together, Faith knew the whole story. David had conveyed the rest of it while she packed warmer clothes for Remy's trip to Maryland. Now, as she stood at the window and his car passed the house, heading out of town, she felt her shoulders sag and the muscles of her throat tighten in protest.

"You must be feeling a million different things."

She hadn't forgotten Pavel's presence, but his words startled her, as if he'd seen directly inside her heart. "I'm worried about Remy. She's been through so much, now this."

"What a great mother you are. Anybody else would be furious."

"Of course I'm angry, too. What were those young men thinking? How could they believe Remy was a senior in high school? And the one who almost—" The word lodged in her throat. She couldn't say it. "He's lucky he's getting off so easily."

"Not as easily as he thinks. I have friends on the police force. They'll be interested in his extracurricular activities."

"No, David's right. We can't drag Remy through anything else. And the fact that she's been lying about her age would make it harder to prosecute him."

"I'm talking about drugs. He'll be out of business shortly, and he'll be out of Georgetown shortly, too, if he knows what's good for him."

Faith hugged herself. Remy was lucky. She had two men who cared about her and wanted to protect her. She had a mother and a brother who would do anything they could. She had behaved badly and taken foolish risks, but she was going to be all right. She had all the help she needed.

That realization didn't calm her as much as it should have. Faith was still angry, and not only at Enzio Castellano. "*I* should have realized. I knew how hostile she was, but I thought if I was just patient, if I left the door open, she'd come back to me. I know her better than anybody does. But I never guessed my own daughter was capable of that kind of deceit."

"She's a teenager, and like you said, she's been through a lot. Rebellion comes with the territory, doesn't it?"

"She lied to *me*. Over and over, and I couldn't see it. My God, I must be the stupidest woman in the world."

He came up behind her and put his hands on her arms, rubbing them slowly back and forth. "But it's okay now. She's safe, and judging from what I saw, she learned a huge lesson."

"And when am *I* going to learn?" She faced him, her anger growing. "When am I going to figure out that nobody's the person I think they are? Not even a child I raised. I hovered over her. I taught her my values, and I thought that was all I needed to do. I never thought she would turn everything I believed about her inside out."

He didn't say anything. He seemed to know she wasn't finished.

Her next words were more emphatic. "Nobody's told me the truth since the day I was born. Not my parents, not my husband, not even my beloved daughter!"

"Not me."

"Right. Not you." Anger was slowly turning to fury. She had been terrified to discover how close Remy had come to disaster. Terrified of all the things that might have happened but hadn't. Terrified that she herself had made such a huge mistake in judgment, that she hadn't looked closely enough or intervened. Fury felt better than terror.

Pavel cocked his head, as if he were a spectator watching a

storm spin out of control. "What is it, Faith, that makes people lie to you? Maybe you were just born gullible. Do you think that's it? Or maybe it's a plot. All of us who've ever cared about you get together on a regular basis and decide how best to deceive you. A secret society of liars, devoted just to Faith Bronson, and our only purpose is to shatter your belief in yourself."

There was no sarcasm in his voice. He asked the questions as if she might really know the answers.

"How dare you!" Her eyes narrowed, and her fists balled. "You think this is funny? Do you think what you did to me was funny, Pavel? Passing yourself off as somebody you're not?"

"I'm not a master of psychology, but here's something I learned in the business world. The things we hate most in other people are the things we don't like about ourselves."

Her hands were trembling. "I—am—honest. I don't lie about who I am. I don't pretend to be somebody I'm not."

"Then let's hear a little of that famous honesty. You're angry at your daughter for lying to you, even though you know she's just a kid like a million others. You're angry, even though you know deep inside that this isn't about you."

"It feels like it's about me. It keeps happening. Over and over again!"

"No, I think it reminds you of something important about yourself."

"You think you know what I'm feeling? Right now I'm feeling like I never want to see you again." She stepped closer. "You of all people have no right to lecture me. Look at your track record in the honesty department."

"How many times in the last months have you used that line in your head? If you focus on the lies everyone else has told you, then you don't have to focus on the lies you tell yourself, do you?"

"What lies?" She shouted the words.

"Come on, what are you feeling, Faith? Besides anger? Besides hurt that somebody lied to you again?" He put his hands on her shoulders and pulled her one step closer. "What in the hell are you feeling?"

"They left without me!" She shoved his chest with her palms, but he didn't move. She didn't know she'd said the words out loud until Pavel tightened his grip.

"They abandoned you?"

Her stomach churned, and her palms began to sweat. For the first time she realized how David must have felt all these months. His life had been severed from theirs. What had been four was suddenly one. Alone. Yes, he had Ham, but all the people he'd loved before were gone. His beloved children were gone. Life as he'd known it was over.

And she had *wanted* it that way. She had lied to herself since that day at the cottage. She had wanted to hurt David the way he'd hurt her. Deeply. Permanently. All year long she had tried to stop being the good girl, but she had never been a good girl to begin with. She was just like everyone else. Flawed, dishonest, unforgiving.

She choked out the next words. "I didn't realize how much I liked having him on the outside looking in. It seemed like just punishment. Maybe he left me for a man, but I had the children and he didn't. Three of us against the world. And him. And now that's over."

He rubbed her shoulders with his palms. "You know how natural that is, don't you?"

"But it's not me! That's not who I thought I was. I thought I was above that. When I recovered from the shock, I told myself I was going to do the divorce perfectly. Make a home for the children, be calm and sensible, restart my life, be an anchor for everybody else."

She was crying now, and she didn't care. "And what I really wanted...deep inside, was to hurt David...and keep him out of the family. I wanted to prove...I was the one who could be counted on."

"Okay, but I've been watching, remember? Maybe that's what you were feeling, but that's not the way you acted. You rose above it, Faith. Maybe you wanted to punish David, but you didn't. Okay, you didn't extend a hand to help him back into the family, but you allowed him back in as fast as he could find his way."

But this wasn't about what she had *done.* Faith knew it was all about who she *was.* Never the good girl. Never the paragon. A human being with a dark side. Like the other human beings in her life. Like the other human beings she loved.

Pavel shook his head, then pulled her to his chest. "Faith, Faith..." He wrapped his arms around her. "Didn't you know you were just a nicer version of everybody else?"

She was crying too hard to answer. He held her close, stroking her back while she sobbed. The tears went on and on, a well of tears she had never cried. Finally, when she could, she choked out the most damning statement of all.

"What I knew...what I *know*...is that nobody will ever really love me unless I'm perfect."

"So you convinced yourself you were both. Lovable and perfect, the magic combination."

She shook her head, wiping her wet cheeks on his shirt. "Not lovable. Not deep down...not where it counts."

"And when the rest of us lied to you, it made you doubt yourself more, huh? Because if you'd just been a little more perfect, we wouldn't have lied in the first place."

"There were things I could have done to help Remy find her way back to David. I...could have gotten us into therapy. We're going to do it after the holidays, but...I could have agreed to it sooner. Maybe...maybe I was afraid it would work?"

He stepped back and held her away. "Look at me."

She wiped her nose with the back of her hand. "I'm a mess."

"I like you this way. Look at me."

She did. Eyes and nose red, cheeks flushed and damp. Imperfect.

"You were angry at David," he said. "Of course you didn't want him back in the family. But you're a good mother, and you did what you thought was right."

"I've been lying to myself. I've been fooling myself."

"Welcome to the club."

She took a deep, shaky breath, then another. Finally she tried to smile. She failed, but it was a start. "How do the rest of you stand it?"

He smiled for her. "We've had years of practice. Most of us figured out a long time ago how imperfect we are. We forgive ourselves."

And that made it easier for them to forgive each other. That was the unspoken message, the one he didn't want to hammer home. But she heard it anyway, and she was ashamed.

The conversation wasn't about Remy anymore. It wasn't about David, or the lies her own parents had told her. The conversation was about them. She knew it, and she knew that this conversation was as important as the others. Because this one was about her future.

Pavel Quinn was a good man. Flawed, yes. Just as she was. Shaped by the traumas of his childhood. Just as she was. Wary of emotion. Capable of deceit. Just as she was.

But still, beneath it all, a good man.

"I wish you had told me right away who you were," she said.

"I know. So do I."

They couldn't change the past, but she could change the future. She saw that now. She could change it for everyone she loved, beginning with herself.

"I'm not perfect," she said. "Can you forgive me for that?"

"Faith, I've known all along. I revel in it. Perfection doesn't appeal to me."

"I understand why you didn't tell me about your father. I've understood ever since the night I confronted you. I just couldn't..."

He sighed. "You couldn't forgive yourself for being duped again. I know."

She felt hollow until he smiled. He had a wonderful smile, filled with warmth and promise. The smile was honest, because Pavel himself was filled with warmth and promises, too.

He tilted her chin so they were eye to eye. "It's okay. I knew that you'd figure this out. I've just been waiting."

She sniffed. She remembered what he had said about himself the night the stove caught on fire. "For somebody who's just an inch deep, there's an awful lot you understand."

"I guess I've been lying about that, too."

She tried another smile and this time nearly succeeded. "Two inches deep?"

"At least."

She didn't know where to go now. She felt cleansed and empty at the same time. She didn't know what she had to offer anymore.

She didn't know who she was. She didn't know what she had a right to ask for.

He understood. She could see it in his eyes right before he kissed her. He pulled her close, and his lips were warm against hers. She pressed her body closer to his, lifted her arms to encircle his neck, gratefully let the kiss go on and on.

When it ended, he stepped away reluctantly. "We started in the wrong place, Faith, and we've still got too many unanswered questions fogging our lives. I want to start over with you, but not now. Not until there's nothing in the way. Not secrets. Not lies. Not a past we don't understand."

Not until she understood herself a little better. He didn't say it, but she knew that was the biggest part of it. He didn't want to take advantage of her now and risk losing the trust they were rebuilding.

"You realize we may never get answers?" she said.

"We'll need to let go of our parents' lives at some point, but that time's not here yet. And you're still too raw for another complication in yours."

"You're a complication? You can admit it?"

"Find your feet. I'll be here."

She knew he was right. As much as she wanted him—and she hadn't stopped, not during all the weeks of anger—he was right, and she was grateful for his insight. Because she knew, from the kiss, that it wasn't easy for him to wait.

"And now I think I'll get out of here while I still remember how," he said. "You need some time alone, and you're not ready for another confrontation today. We can question Dottie Lee another day."

She didn't want Pavel to go. What would she do for the rest of the weekend? Wonder how she had fooled herself for so long? Question why she hadn't tried harder to get Remy into counseling months ago? Ask what might have happened if David hadn't taken it on himself to find Remy today?

Ask herself who she wanted to be when she finally and completely confronted who she was? And whether she wanted Pavel to be there to witness it.

She rested her hands on his. "No, please. I don't want you to go."

"You're sure?" He waited until she nodded. "Then I won't."

"Let me wash my face and recover a little, then let's go next door and talk to Dottie Lee. The sooner we do, the sooner we can move on."

"It could lead to more bad news. We may not want to hear what she has to say."

"I want to get this over with. I can handle whatever we hear."

"All right. I hope she's home."

She squeezed his hands. "That's one thing we can be sure of, Pavel. Let me tell you why."

 34

Pavel had been strong for Faith, but he was quietly grappling with his own reality. Remy's close call, a shootout with the woman he was coming to love. And the new and painful knowledge that Hope Huston, the little girl who had made headlines around the world, was as much his sister as Faith's. Not only had he lost a father, but he had lost a sister before ever glimpsing her face.

He only rarely admitted to himself how much Dominik's loss had affected him. He concentrated on the few positives of his childhood and the things he had gained from the negatives. Now, as he and Faith stood on Dottie Lee's stoop and waited for Mariana to come to the door, he realized how much he needed answers. Years ago he had come to Washington for them, and he had never really let the matter rest. He had always watched and listened and hoped that someday he would discover the truth.

"She might not cooperate," Faith warned. "We can't depend on this conversation."

"It's the next step."

Mariana opened the door and invited them inside. She motioned them to the sofa and went to get Dottie Lee.

Pavel didn't want to sit. He paced, while Faith tried to settle herself against the cushions. "I wonder what work my father did here."

"He remodeled the entire back of the house," Dottie Lee said from the kitchen doorway. "Come and I'll show you."

Pavel followed her into the dining room, and Dottie Lee swept her hand toward the windows facing her small garden. "He did this. The house was closed off from the world, but Dominik opened it up for me. He said if I was going to live every day here, I must bring the world to me. So that's what he did. The upstairs is the same. All glass and river and city lights at nighttime. I can see the Kennedy Center and pretend I'm listening to the world's finest orchestras. In the seventies, I could stare at the Watergate and imagine its secrets."

Pavel tried to imagine his father here, exposing the world for Dottie Lee to enjoy from a distance. "It's wonderful."

She faced him, and her eyes were misty. "Your father was a wonderful man. I knew who you were almost immediately. The very first time I saw your photograph in the *Post* business section. He called you Pasha, but once, when he brought you here to meet me, he told me your real name was Pavel. And you look like him, of course, just enough to convince me."

"Then I was here as a child?"

"Oh yes, he liked to show you off. But, of course, you wouldn't remember that. I can tell you he was so very proud of you. He was sure you were remarkable, and as it turned out, he was correct."

Faith joined them. "Dottie Lee, we've reached the end of the road. We don't know where else to look for the truth about the kidnapping."

"You know your mother and Dominik had an affair, Faith. Do you know anything else?"

Faith looked at Pavel, and he shrugged, as if to say that the choice of what to tell Dottie Lee was hers.

"We know Dominik was Hope's father," Faith said, and prayed her mother would forgive her.

Dottie Lee didn't look surprised. "Your mother told you?"

"Yes, and she told me my father knew Hope wasn't his. We think you lied to the police about where Dominik was that afternoon. We know he committed suicide months later, but the reason for that is still a mystery. Unless he was involved in the kidnapping, what made him take his life? He never even tried to reconcile with Pavel's mother."

When it seemed Dottie Lee wasn't going to answer, Pavel continued for Faith. "I think there's someone who might be able to help. My father had a cousin who worked with him—"

"Sandor," Dottie Lee said.

"Do you know what happened to him? Would you have any idea how we might find him?"

"Do I know what happened to him? Yes, of course I do. And so do you, Faith. Where to find him is a more difficult question."

Faith's eyes met Pavel's. He read concern that perhaps Dottie Lee wasn't as alert as they'd thought.

"I know him?" Faith said.

"Sandor is Hungarian for Alexander, dear. He goes by Alec now. Alec Babin. You know him as Alec the Can Man." Dottie Lee turned to Pavel. "You met him the day you came to Faith's house. He was pulling ivy in her garden."

Faith could hardly believe it. "And my mother doesn't know?"

"She wouldn't, not unless she spent a great deal of time around him now. He's changed dramatically. He came to my house one day some years ago, looking for work. I gave him odd jobs. A week passed before I realized who he was. He's hardly the same man."

"But why would he come back here?"

"That he's never told me. We can be certain, though, that it's not a coincidence. I, for one, don't believe in them."

"What else do you know?" Pavel had tired of tact. Dottie Lee had known so much, and they had known so little.

"You believe I know it all, don't you? Don't you think, if I did, I would have gone to the authorities? I may be old, and I may pride myself on my peculiarities, but please give me credit for also being law-abiding and concerned for Faith's mother."

"But you've been protecting Sandor," Faith said.

"Protecting him from whom? He was never wanted by the police. Who should I have told? He was questioned after the kidnapping but never detained. Perhaps I should have found his family and told them he was here. I've debated that. But I knew if I did, he would disappear and never be seen by these old eyes again. So I've kept silent, and I've given him work whenever I can."

Faith remembered their first conversation about the Can Man. "He slept in your basement."

"For a while he did, yes, almost every winter. This year it's been ready for him just in case, but he hasn't been here. I haven't seen him in weeks."

Pavel hoped Sandor hadn't left town again, not now, when they were so close. "Did he tell you anything at all? Anything we should know?"

"Everything I know about Dominik and the affair with Lydia came from Sandor. I had my suspicions. He confirmed them with a word or two. Since then, he's refused to discuss the past. I believe Sandor knows more than he's ever told anyone. He and Dominik were close. If Dominik talked of this to anyone, he would have talked to Sandor."

"We have to find him." Faith addressed that to Pavel, as if to convince him. Her next words were addressed to Dottie Lee. "Do you have any idea where he might be?"

"He's an alcoholic, but he still exercises moderately good judgment. I think that if he hasn't been here, he's found a better, warmer place."

"A shelter?" Faith said.

Dottie Lee gave one brisk shake of her head. "He likes to be alone. But there are several programs in the city that offer vouchers for hotel rooms. He mentioned something like that once. The hotels are what we once called flophouses, but they have beds and bathrooms. That might be a place to look. Of course, he may simply have found a basement he likes better."

Pavel read Faith's expression. They were gaining ground, but unless they could locate the Can Man, they had little hope of gaining more.

Faith repeated her earlier question "Why did he come back? You agree it's not a coincidence he ended up on your doorstep. There were a million places he could have gone. Places with more favorable weather and better resources."

Dottie Lee led them to the door. "He ended up here because he has something to say. But I don't think he's ever found the courage to say it. I've no idea how many bottles of alcohol that man has drunk, but he's never found courage at the bottom of any of them."

* * *

The Can Man wasn't a resident at any of the hotels they tried. Even if he had been, Faith wasn't sure they would have gotten a positive answer at the reception desks. Men came and went, but most of them had no faces to the clerks who took whatever form of payment was offered and handed out keys.

They stopped for dinner at a run-down Italian restaurant on a block near two of the hotels and sat silently by the flyspecked window, watching residents stream in and out. They dragged out their meal with coffee and surprisingly good cannoli, but they knew they were no closer to finding Sandor.

"We ought to call it a night," Pavel said. "You look whipped."

She was. She was also too keyed up to sleep. "There are two places we didn't try."

"They're not exactly in safe neighborhoods."

"Neither is this restaurant. Be glad you drive an old car."

"I've never done a thing to improve the world." Pavel was staring out the window.

She was surprised. "You created a search engine used by millions of people every day."

"And made a fortune off of it. Scavenger gives to charity, and so do I, but I haven't actually *done* anything."

"Pavel, are you listening to yourself?"

He switched his gaze to her. "There's a difference between throwing money at a problem and trying to solve it."

"What else can you do?"

"I could create jobs. Computer training and job placement. A place to start over."

"At Scavenger?"

"No, I'm resigning, effective this summer."

Faith was surprised, then hurt. "That's a big decision. And you didn't even tell me."

"We weren't exactly at that level anymore, were we?"

She picked at a loose strip of the red-checked vinyl covering their table. "I missed not knowing what was going on with you."

"You missed *me?*"

She looked up at him. "You're pushing."

"I'm feeling bad about my life. I just want you to feed my ego a little."

"Of course I missed you."

"What did you miss exactly?"

"Your ego doesn't need that much fodder." She looked out the window again. Two men were walking slowly together, one with a pronounced limp. Their clothing was shabby and thin, and the man whose gait was unimpaired was carrying a backpack over his shoulders. Both looked as if they belonged to the streets, as if they had been honed into the men they were by hopelessness and despair.

"This is no life for anyone," Faith said. "And Sandor chose it over his wife and children. Why?"

"People make terrible decisions. Sometimes it's impossible to go back."

"Particularly if you have something in your past you can't surmount."

"What couldn't he get beyond?"

Faith rose. "Let's see if we can find out."

"You're sure you're up for more bored clerks?"

"I don't think I'm going to be sleeping very well tonight anyway."

"I could help with that."

Despite herself, she smiled. "Weren't we going to back up a little?"

"I know the moment I'd like to back up to."

She was sure it was the same moment she would choose if she could. One of many at his West Virginia hideaway.

The clerk at the next hotel was surprisingly attentive and completely useless. Unfortunately, Alec's description matched a thousand other men who had walked through his door. They talked to several residents who passed in the postage-stamp lobby, but no one had any help to offer.

"One more," Pavel said. "Then we're out of leads. Tomorrow we can make the rounds of the parks and talk to people to see if anyone knows Alec."

"I wouldn't be surprised if he went south for the winter. That's what I would do if I didn't have a roof over my head."

"He had the offer of one, remember? Dottie Lee's basement. And I suspect it's more like an apartment than a dirt cellar."

"Maybe he doesn't want to be that close to the scene of the crime."

"We're trying to second-guess a man we hardly know. It's impossible." Pavel put his hand on her back, a protective gesture that staked a claim of sorts.

"Let's try the last hotel, then call it a night."

The last hotel was the nicest of the lot. There were few vacant storefronts on the block, and an apartment building on the corner appeared to be undergoing renovation. The brick hotel was old, but inside it smelled of pine cleaner. The reception desk sported an artificial tree decorated with twinkling lights, but there was no clerk on duty.

The reason became apparent immediately. In a small room to the right, a Christmas party was taking place. Men huddled around a table overflowing with food, and carols vibrated from a tinny portable stereo. Several helpers in coats and ties or party dresses were chatting with the men and dishing up plates.

Faith spotted Alec immediately. He was waiting his turn in line, but when he got to the front he took a glass of punch and a cookie. Nothing more. When he turned away, he saw her. For a moment he didn't move. Then, with something like resignation, he started toward them.

"Alec." She managed a smile. "Merry Christmas."

"What are you doing here, Mrs. Bronson?" If he remembered Pavel, or even noticed that he was with Faith, he gave no sign.

"Alec, is there some place we can talk? I don't want to take you away from your party, but—"

"I'm done here. Got my cookie."

"Would you like to go somewhere and eat?"

"Had my dinner already."

"Where might we talk?"

"You can come up to my room, I guess. Can't have guests after ten, but that's not for a while."

"You're sure you don't mind?"

He started up the stairs, and Faith followed him, while Pavel brought up the rear.

Alec's room was only slightly larger than a jail cell. A radiator hissed under the lone window overlooking the street. A small dresser, a plastic chair, a narrow single bed with a wool blanket, and a shelf for any extra belongings were the only furniture. Still, the paint was fresh, and the carpet wasn't more than a few years old. The effect was spartan, but clean and comfortable enough.

Alec gestured Faith toward the chair and Pavel toward the bed. He leaned against the wall. "The old lady told you, didn't she?"

She didn't play games. "Dottie Lee told me you're Sandor Babin, Dominik Dubrov's cousin."

He shrugged. Not with hostility but resignation.

"Alec, this is Pavel Quinn, Dominik's son. You probably knew him as Pasha."

For the first time Alec looked at Pavel. "I know who you are."

"Since we met in Faith's yard?"

"Yeah. Your mother changed your name to hers, huh?"

"She was ashamed."

"Wasn't any reason to be. Your father was a better man than most."

"I'm glad to hear that."

"Weak, though. Maybe it runs in the family."

"How so?" Faith asked.

"My family left Hungary. His left Russia. Maybe we learned to turn tail when things get tough, I don't know."

"My father didn't run, he killed himself," Pavel said.

"There's a difference? A man takes whatever avenue is open to him. And that was the only one your father could see."

"Why?" Pavel demanded. "What boxed him in until the only solution was to take his own life?"

"Why do you need to know?" He turned to Faith. "Why do *you?*"

"Pavel and I share a sister," Faith said. "We know Dominik was Hope's father, and that he knew it. We also know that somewhere along the way my father discovered the baby was Dominik's. Can't you see why we need to know what happened? I suspect my father of the kidnapping, and Pavel suspects his. That's no way to go through the rest of our lives."

"What do you want from me?"

"Whatever you know. Anything that might help."

"Maybe it won't help. Maybe it will make things worse."

"Alec," Faith said gently, "that's not up to you. Not anymore. I think you've been protecting somebody, but it's time now to tell the truth. Let it go. Let us decide what happens next."

He closed his eyes, fighting some interior battle. "I need a drink."

"Please, not now," Faith said.

Alec's face was taut with tension. "What you know, that's old news to me. I know a whole lot more than that."

When he didn't say anything more, she prompted him. "Will you tell us? Please?"

He was silent for so long Faith was afraid he wasn't going to answer. Then he began. "Your father found Dominik, and they had a fight while your mother was still in the hospital."

Pavel encouraged him. "Tell us what happened."

"Dominik went to see the baby in the nursery, sneaked in and peeked at her, and somebody told the senator, only he wasn't a senator in those days, just a congressman. Dominik said the bastard had been paying people to watch and see who showed up at the nursery."

"What happened when my father confronted Dominik?" Faith said.

"He threatened to deport him. And Dominik believed he could do it. In Russia, in Hungary, things were simpler. The people in charge could do what they liked. Members of our family died just because somebody in authority wanted them dead. The rules changed every day, depending on who was making them."

"That's why he killed himself? Because he was afraid of deportation?" Pavel didn't sound convinced. "I can't believe it. Maybe if a hearing was imminent and he was sure he was about to lose—"

"My mother had promised to protect him if it ever came to that," Faith said.

"That wasn't the only thing the senator said." Alec opened his eyes and looked at Faith, as if he was weighing the rest.

"Alec, I want the whole truth," she said. "I already know my father is capable of many things, not all of them good."

When he spoke again, his voice was low. "He threatened the baby."

She knew if she protested, that would be the end of his secrets. She forced herself to nod. "Go on."

"He told Dominik that he'd only agreed to raise Hope because he had no choice, but he also said that things happened to babies, bad things. Sometimes they just died and nobody knew why. Sometimes it looked like they'd just stopped breathing, like someone put a pillow over their faces and pushed and pushed...."

He sank to the floor with his knees up to his chin and his arms wrapped around them. He began to rock back and forth.

Faith didn't realize she was crying until tears were rolling down her cheeks. The threat was too much like the one her father had used against her mother to deny it. "Alec, did my father kill Hope?"

He continued to rock, eyes closed. "Dominik, he couldn't go to your mother and tell her. She'd warned him that the senator might threaten him if he ever found out Dominik was Hope's father, but she was convinced the baby would be safe. There was no proof Senator Huston had talked to Dominik, and Dominik was afraid your mother would think he was making up the story to force her to leave him."

"So he kidnapped Hope," Pavel said. "Because he felt he had no choice?"

Alec opened his eyes. "What do you know about your father? You think he loved the baby more than the mother? You think he could have done such a thing to Mrs. Huston?"

"Then what happened?" Faith demanded.

"I watched him suffer. He couldn't decide what to do." Alec's gaze locked with Faith's. "And so I made the decision for him. I took her."

Faith stared at him. The answer to everything had been right in front of her. Sitting right in front of her, and she hadn't guessed it. She had been sure that either she or Pavel would leave Alec's room as the child of a kidnapper.

She felt Pavel's hand on her shoulder. "You?" he asked.

"It wasn't as hard as the papers made it sound, though I had to make all the preparations fast. I cut through backyards to get to the house. I took Dominik's key and let myself in through the basement. The baby was asleep and stayed that way when I lifted her from the crib. Your mother was playing the piano. There was no pause, not even after I closed the door behind me. I knew a young mother who agreed to help me get the baby away once she heard the story. I knew I could trust her, and I had a place for the baby to go."

"Where?" Pavel said.

"My family came into this country through Canada. A Hungarian family we knew in Ontario wanted a child and couldn't have one of their own. They had been trying for years and years. By then they were almost old enough to be grandparents. The papers were easy to forge. They knew who to ask for a new birth certificate, and how much to pay and how to have it done quickly. We, all of us, had practice with false papers. My family couldn't have come to America without them."

He was speaking faster now, as if he had waited a long time to tell someone and was afraid he might not have time to finish. "My friend took Hope across the border using her own baby's birth certificate for identification and gave her to the Canadian family to raise. She told them the baby was illegitimate, a teenager's baby, and the girl's family would disown her if they ever found out. She said the girl had gone away to have it out in the country by herself, and nobody could ever know the circumstances of the baby's birth. They wanted a baby so badly that they didn't ask any questions."

"Canada?" Pavel's hand was a heavy weight on Faith's shoulder.

"I knew if I tried to keep Hope in the United States, she would be found. I did it for Dominik. He was my best friend, more like a brother. I did it to protect his daughter and because he wouldn't do it himself."

"And you never told anyone? Not all these years?"

Alec stopped rocking. "Tell? No, but Dominik knew. He figured it out."

"And nobody else knew except the woman who helped you? Not even the people who raised her?"

"Why should I tell anyone? I knew I was right. I was sure I had prevented a murder. She was a baby, just a little baby. Dominik's baby. She deserved a life, didn't she?"

"But it ate at you, didn't it?" Pavel said. "Just the way it ate at my father until he killed himself."

"Once he knew, Dominik figured out there were no good choices. Hope was safe, but Mrs. Huston was nearly crazy from grief. In the end your father died from grief, too. He couldn't turn me in to the police. I was his cousin. He couldn't tell Mrs. Huston. He couldn't rescue Hope and give her back, because he was afraid for her life, too."

"And so he killed himself," Pavel said.

Faith couldn't let that go. "And after all that, you still thought you'd done something good? Something right?"

For a moment he looked defensive. "I was sure I'd done something good." His face crumpled a little. "Then I had kids of my own. One day I looked at them and I knew what I'd done after all. And that's when I started to drink."

There were unanswered questions, but one loomed above the others. Faith couldn't make herself ask it. Not yet.

"At that point, why didn't you tell somebody?" Pavel asked. "Why didn't you turn yourself in when you realized how serious this was and how many lives you'd destroyed?"

"You think it would have been that easy?"

"I just want answers," Pavel said.

"Because I still believed the senator would harm the little girl! And she was a little girl by then. A pretty little thing, and happy. So happy with her new parents. They weren't rich, but they thought she was a miracle, and they gave her everything they could. So if I told the police where she was and what I'd done, I would have destroyed one happy family to fix an unhappy one. How could I do that? In the end there was nothing I could do. Just like Dominik."

Faith knew she would be sorting this out for months. Years. But one question still hadn't been answered. The most important one. She asked it at last. "Alec, where is Hope now? Please tell us. It's time to set the record straight. Nobody can harm her. She's thirty-eight years old."

"She's alive. She's happy." Alec fell silent.

"Please, I have a sister," Faith said. "You don't know what that means to me. Hope has a sister—" she glanced at Pavel "—and a brother, and it's not your duty to protect her. She's old enough to know the truth and figure out what to do about it."

He sat very still, considering. Faith was almost afraid to breathe. At last he got to his feet and went to the dresser. He opened the top drawer and lifted out a neatly folded pile of clothing, reaching under it for something. Then he replaced the clothing and turned.

"I have a picture." He held it out to Faith.

She took it, her hands trembling. She expected to see a baby, the baby she had only glimpsed on the pages of newspapers. Instead an adult stared back at her from a torn sheet of heavy tan paper. A pretty woman with dark curly hair. She had the body of someone who preferred eating to dieting, a warm smile and laughing dark eyes. In the crook of each arm was a small child, a boy and a girl.

"This is Hope?" She couldn't take her eyes off the photograph, which seemed oddly familiar. She felt Pavel move closer to gaze at it, too. "This is my sister? But I've seen this photograph somewhere."

"She writes books for children. I go to the bookstore and look at them sometimes. I tore that from the jacket of one."

Faith looked up at last. "Not Karina Gililand?"

"That's her name."

"Faith?" Pavel took the picture from her hands. "You know something about her?"

"I read her books to my children when they were little. She was their favorite author, one of the only things they ever agreed on. We have them all. I even kept them after we moved so I could give them to my grandchildren someday. They're packed away in the attic."

She put her hands to her cheeks. "In *my* attic. In a corner, right under the rafter where my grandmother carved her name."

She began to cry again. She felt Pavel's arms come around her, but she wasn't sure which of them needed the comfort more.

 35

This year the Christmas tree at the Hustons house was adorned with icicles of hand-blown glass and delicate antique ornaments from Germany. The ten-foot blue spruce sported bundles of cinnamon sticks tied with plaid taffeta ribbon, and dried slices of oranges and lemons. Lydia was sitting beside it, waiting for Faith to arrive.

The clock had already ushered in midnight, and even though Faith was aware her mother never fell asleep until the early hours of the morning, this late-night visit was uncharacteristic. Lydia knew her grandchildren were gone for the weekend, but that didn't explain Faith's phone call an hour ago. She hadn't asked if she could come to Great Falls; she had announced an impending visit.

"You're still up?"

Lydia turned to see Joe in his flannel robe, standing in the doorway. He seemed annoyed that he didn't have privacy for his nocturnal wanderings.

"Faith's stopping by."

"At this hour?" He sounded even more annoyed. "You should have taught her better manners."

"Her manners are perfect, but yours are beginning to upset me."

"I'm not in the mood for company. Tell her I went to bed. And don't let her stay long. We have a prayer breakfast tomorrow morning at the Mayflower."

"I'm going to insist she spend the night."

He snorted, but he left without another thrust and parry. She was grateful.

The house was silent by the time she heard Faith's car in the driveway. Thanks to Samuel, no one else would have made it that far. She met Faith and ushered her inside, taking her coat and hat with a minimum of discussion to hang them in the hall closet.

Faith followed Lydia back to the living room, where tiny white lights twinkled on the tree. "Have a seat," Lydia said. "Would you like something to drink?"

Faith declined. She'd said little since entering the house. She shivered now, and Lydia crossed the room to light the gas fireplace. The room was already warm, but the temperature outside was below freezing. Snow had fallen, and more was expected.

"You'll have to stay," Lydia said. "I won't let you drive home this late. What were you thinking, to come all the way out here in this weather?"

"I was thinking I couldn't wait."

Lydia wasn't sure what to say. "Did the children get off all right? Alex is with his father?"

"They're both with David."

Lydia, on her way back to the sofa where Faith had perched, slowed in surprise. "You're joking."

"No, Remy asked to go with him. There was a nasty incident, Mother. She's been hanging out with some college boys—men— down the street. I'm not going to go into it all right now, but she's okay. David got her out of a bad situation, and they've reconciled."

Lydia joined her, lifting a Christmas afghan crocheted from filmy white mohair off the back of the sofa to tuck around Faith's legs. "So that's why you're here. No wonder you're upset."

"Mother, you don't know the half of it."

"Remy's all right? Really?"

"I think so. And David will take care of her. That's not why I'm here."

"There's more?"

"I don't know how to tell you this."

Lydia's heart began to speed. "That's the worst possible way to begin a conversation. Just tell me."

Faith leaned forward and took Lydia's hands. "Mother, we've found Hope."

Pavel Quinn, Dominik's son, was flying to Canada later that day to search for his half sister. He knew executives at several publishing houses in New York, and he was sure he could learn Hope's address. No longer Hope, of course. Karina now.

Karina Gililand, a woman with a house and a family and a career.

Despite Lydia's protests, Faith had gone home after telling the whole story, convinced Lydia and Joe needed to be alone to resolve this. Somehow Lydia had walked her to the door, even kissed her daughter's cheek and watched her drive away. But hours passed before a sense of reality returned. She stared at the ceiling and trembled for most of the night. When she finally fell asleep just before dawn, the familiar nightmare began, but this time the music was gentle and sunlight sparkled through the rooms. This time she found her way to Hope's nursery, where the dark-haired infant slept peacefully in her crib.

When Lydia awoke, she didn't know what to say to her husband, but she did know Faith was right. She had to say it in private.

By seven she couldn't stay in bed another minute. She covered her nightgown with a robe and went to make coffee. Marley had the day off, but for once Lydia was grateful to be alone with her husband.

At seven-thirty Joe came into the kitchen, fully dressed for the day. They weren't scheduled to leave until nine-thirty, but true to form, he would spend the next two hours working in his study.

"Sit," she said. "We have to talk."

"I have phone calls. Can't it wait?"

"No, it can't." She took a tray with the coffee service and a platter of toast into the breakfast room, and reluctantly he followed her.

"Is this about Faith?"

"No." Lydia set the tray on the buffet and poured coffee for herself before she turned. "No, Joe, it's about Hope."

Joe was fiddling with the Roman shades at the window closest to his chair. He turned, frowning. "What hasn't been said already?"

"That she's been found."

His expression didn't change. She knew he didn't believe her.

Lydia's knees threatened to buckle. She crossed to the table, coffee cup in hand, and sank into her chair. "Her name isn't Hope Huston anymore, of course. It's Karina Gililand. I have a photograph. Would you like to see it?"

"This is preposterous!"

"Sit down, Joe."

The shade thudded against the window; then his chair scraped the hickory floor. "What are you trying to feed me?"

"The truth." Lydia couldn't hold the cup any longer. She set it on the table. "Hope lives in Canada, most likely in a suburb of Toronto. She's lived in Canada all these years. The family who took her in named her Karina, but they were much older than we are, and they're dead now. Pavel Quinn found some facts about her on the Internet. Karina married a man named Bob Gililand and had two children by him, but they're divorced. She writes children's books. Faith has them all. I even read them to our grandchildren."

"You're not making any sense." Joe got up and crossed to the buffet to pour coffee for himself. "What makes you think this stranger is Hope?"

"Because the man who kidnapped her told Faith the whole story. She and Pavel are checking, of course. But there's no reason to believe it's not true. Everything fits."

"You would believe that baby was carried off on a spaceship if an idiot in a Star Trek uniform told you he'd seen blinking lights in the sky that night."

"No, Joe, I wouldn't. But I believe this."

He flung himself into the chair across from her and slammed his cup on the table. "Who took her?"

"Sandor Babin, Dominik's cousin and helper. Dominik had nothing to do with it. He didn't know until later."

"Why? There wasn't a ransom demand."

"Because you threatened her, or that's what Dominik believed. You went to him and threatened him with deportation, then you talked about how easily a baby could be smothered—"

"I—did—no—such—thing!" Joe sounded furious, but there was something that didn't quite ring true about his performance.

Lydia examined him. She wanted to believe him. She didn't love Joe Huston. She didn't even like him. But she wanted to believe, more than anything, that Joe had never planned to murder her daughter, and that Dominik really had misunderstood.

Otherwise, how could she live with herself?

She finished the story, still searching his face. "Sandor knew what you told Dominik, so he took matters into his own hands. He claims he was afraid for Hope's life."

"Where is this man now?"

"Homeless. Broken. The kidnapping caught up with him. All of us..." She swallowed tears. "All of us were so damaged. Even you, Joe."

"What does that mean?"

"I've believed for years you might have been responsible. You know I have. You said things that made me suspicious. You know what that's done to our marriage. This house has been an armed camp. We never had a chance."

"We've done the things we had to."

"There's one more thing we have to do. If Karina Gililand really is Hope, we have to tell the world. This secret's going to get out, the way secrets always do. Once we make contact with her, someone will sniff this out. We need to be sure the story is told with sensitivity and discretion."

Joe was on his feet before she finished. "We damn well won't make contact, and we won't tell anybody! Do you want to parade your affair in front of the world? Admit your connection to Dubrov? Tell everyone your baby girl was illegitimate? Leave well enough alone, Lydia. Leave this woman alone!"

"I won't be cheated out of knowing her. She's my baby, my little girl! I don't care if some of this will be hard to explain. If she wants to know me, I want to be her mother. I won't be kept from her any longer."

"You? *You!* This is all about you. What about my career?"

"We have to consider how best to tell the story and to whom. We—"

Joe was too enraged to listen. "If I'd wanted the whole world to know about Hope, I'd have told the truth years ago!"

"Years ago there was no point. You didn't want to tell the world I was an adulteress—" Lydia stopped, watching the expression on her husband's face. The rage was tempered now by something else. Caution? For a moment she was at sea, adrift in the nuances of what he'd said and his own reaction to it.

Then she understood.

She rose on trembling legs. "You're not talking about my affair, are you? You *knew* who took her. All this time you knew where she was and what happened to her. Joe, you knew!"

"Of course I didn't know. I was talking about you and Dubrov and—"

"You liar!" His rage was nothing compared to hers. "You knew my baby was alive. You knew where she was! And you kept it from me! You watched me suffer. You watched me bleed one drop at a time for decades, watched my heart ice over. You bastard!"

This time he didn't deny it. His expression changed to something close to satisfaction. "You deserved it. After what you did to me? Yes, I knew, because that man Babin was an idiot. He dropped a religious medal in Hope's crib that day when he bent over to take her. The Hungarian St. Elizabeth, the patron saint of poor people. Isn't that perfect? I found it between the mattress and the slats while you were downstairs calling the police. I'd met Sandor Babin when he was painting the row house. I knew his family emigrated from Hungary and he was Dominik's cousin. He might as well have left his calling card."

Lydia sank to her seat. She stared at the man she had been married to for almost forty years. She had remained married to Joe even when he plotted against a president, and afterward, when she worried about his involvement in the kidnapping. She had stayed with him, borne him a child, stood by his side on the campaign trail. And all the while he had been silently torturing her. He had never forgiven her for her sin, never assumed any blame for it. He had simply gotten even.

"You can't stay in the Senate," she said at last.

"Have you lost your mind? Do you want to destroy everything we've both worked for?"

"Yes, I do. You're evil, and I won't let you spread your poison any further. Your heart attack was convenient, Joe. Now you can use it as an excuse when you resign. By then the public will know some of Hope's story. How much they know will depend on how quietly you go. If you fight me, if you try to stay on, I'll tell the world that you knew all along where Hope was, even when you were pleading with her kidnappers on camera."

"No one will believe you."

"Quite possibly. But then I'll tell them about your plans for President Kennedy, and no one will dispute that, because I have the documents. You know I do."

He tried one more threat. "You've kept those documents hidden all these years. Any consequences to me will be yours by proxy. You'll be tarred by the same brush."

Her smile felt precious and new, the first of a long line of smiles in the years she had left. The bleak years were over. The rest of her life was ahead of her.

"I have my daughters, Joe, and four grandchildren who need me. They don't have to elect me. I don't have to campaign. I just have to show up. I have everything I need and more than I ever knew I wanted, and I will *not* have *you* in my life. Because the day you resign from the Senate is the day I'll file for divorce."

Pavel thought Washington was cold in December. He'd also known—on a theoretical level—that Toronto would be colder. He piled on layers, topping them with a jacket bought for the West Virginia ski slopes. But there weren't enough clothes in the world to make up for the biting Canadian wind. On the airplane a proud Torontonian had mentioned—gleefully—that Toronto was the battle zone for frigid Arctic air from the north and warm, moist air from the Gulf of Mexico.

Mother Nature had declared war, and Pavel was a pacifist.

The skies were dark by the time he made his way to the Park Hyatt in historic Yorkville, which was dressed in full regalia for the holiday. He was used to the hotel, since he always stayed there on business trips, and Karina lived near the university, which wasn't far away. He had gotten her address through a ruse, and he planned to use the same ruse when he called her.

He checked into his room and took a long, hot shower in the elaborate marble bathroom. Ten minutes into it he had thawed sufficiently to speak without stuttering. He dried and slipped on a robe, but he still didn't lift the receiver. Faith's final words before he left for the airport played and replayed in his mind.

"Don't scare her, whatever you do, Pavel. Get to know her a little first. Make her comfortable. Then you can tell her that her entire past is a sham."

He had added his own twist. "And that as soon as the story gets out, she's going to be hounded unmercifully by the press."

"And that my mother needs her desperately and her heart will break if Hope—Karina rejects her."

"If she lets me take her out to dinner, that should get us through the appetizers."

Faith's expression had been the midpoint between a frown and a grimace. "I'd come with you. I really would. But I don't want to frighten her too much."

"You're the one who's frightened."

She had admitted it with a nod.

Pavel was frightened, too. He had been alone in the world, and for the most part that had seemed fine. His experiences with family were less than stellar. A father who killed himself, a mother who drank herself to death, distant cousins who turned him away, and now their homeless father, who would probably disappear for good.

Sandor—Alec the Can Man—had too much sense to stay in Washington. After their conversation, Pavel and Faith had wished him well, and Pavel had slipped the old man every cent in his wallet and his spattered Rolex to pawn. On the way home he and Faith had agreed not to tell the authorities about Karina until they had to. Alec would have a running head start until the news was made public. Pavel was certain no one would ever see him again.

Pavel wondered if Karina was going to be the next in his string of failed relationships. He hadn't made it as a son or a cousin. He had no record to speak of as a significant other. What kind of brother would he be? And the biggest question of all: Would she give him a chance to find out?

Eventually he had to pick up the telephone. He dialed the number he had wheedled from Karina's literary agent and waited for her to answer.

A child answered instead. His niece, he suspected. Her voice was high and sweet, and after she dropped the receiver, she came back on and apologized. Then she went to get her mother.

As he waited, he cleared his throat twice, observing his own nervousness with something close to horror. When she answered, he cleared it again.

Karina didn't sound like Faith, for which he was grateful. He wasn't sure he could have gotten past that; he might have been in danger of blurting out the truth in his first sentence. Instead he introduced himself as the president of Scavenger, who was in town for a business meeting. Then he launched into his chosen lie.

"We're looking into developing a Web site for young children. A safe place where they can play games, read books online, learn some computer basics." He filed the idea away, since it wasn't a bad one. Alex would probably have some ideas on the subject.

He finished. "Your name came up as a potential consultant, and your agent thought you might be interested."

She spoke softly, as if she had no need to project or assert herself. Not like a woman with no confidence, but one for whom confidence had never been a problem. "Mary Ann called to say you might be contacting me."

Pavel was thankful the stranger had paved his way. "I'm sorry this is so last-minute and so close to Christmas, but this trip was just arranged. And now I find myself here with a free evening. Is there any chance you could meet me at my hotel for dinner?"

She couldn't, which didn't surprise him, since she had young children to consider, but she agreed to come later for a drink at the hotel's Roof Lounge if a neighbor would baby-sit. He promised a roaring fire and a view of the skyline. By the time he hung up, he was already planning what he would say to her. He had hours to perfect it.

Four hours later he was waiting on a sofa near the enormous fireplace when she came through the door. He had positioned himself to watch for her. She was shorter than he'd expected, although still taller than her sister. Her hair was longer than it had been in the photo, a dark curly mass that nearly touched her shoulders. She wore a navy-blue sweater dress that extended to the tops of dark boots, and she carried a simple cloth coat over her arm. When he stood, she came toward him and extended her hand.

"Mr. Quinn?"

"Pavel." Her hand felt warm in his and gave him courage. She seated herself beside him. "The Roof Lounge has a reputation as a watering hole for well-to-do writers. Suffice it to say I don't come here often."

"Children's books aren't a gold mine?"

"Only if I had thought of Harry Potter first." She looked absolutely at home and expectant.

His well-planned segue into the story evaporated. "Karina, I haven't told you the whole truth about why I invited you here."

She raised one sculpted eyebrow. "No? Have you told me the truth about who you are?"

"I really am the president of Scavenger, not some maniac stalker. But my business with you isn't professional. It's personal."

She regarded him for a moment; then she smiled tentatively. "Are we family, Pavel?"

He couldn't remember the last time he'd cried. Perhaps at his mother's funeral, perhaps not. But now his eyes filled with tears. For a moment he couldn't speak. Instead he nodded.

She put her hand on his, a sister's warm, soft hand. "I've been waiting for you to find me. What took you so long?"

36

The reunion had to take place on Prospect Street. Lydia thought of it as a circle coming together, a circle that would surround and enclose them all, together at last. Faith liked the idea.

It was ten days after Christmas, and Alex and Remy dug through the attic all morning to find toys to entertain Jody and Jeremy when they arrived with their mother. There were packages for Karina and the new cousins under the tree, which still resided in Faith's living room, but no matter how tirelessly Faith argued, the Bronson children weren't convinced the handheld computer games and fancy Lincoln Logs would hold the younger children's interest.

To keep Lydia busy, Faith had invited her to help with the hunt, but Lydia had elected to stay downstairs on the sofa, afraid the trip to the attic where her mother's name sentimentally graced the rafter would finish her off. She was already hanging by a thread.

Lydia had spoken to Karina twice. Once on the day after Pavel told his half sister the story of her kidnapping. Once more as they made plans for this reunion. Both times she had been so nervous, so overwhelmed, that Karina's words bounded through her mind. She still wasn't sure exactly what had been said.

Not enough. Surely not enough.

"Lydia, here's something for you."

Lydia looked up, and a cup of tea appeared magically in front of her. Pavel waited for her to take it. "I thought you could use this."

"That was very thoughtful." She took the cup, feeling stiff, foolish and old.

He flopped down beside her. "You don't have anything to worry about, you know. Karina's taken this entire situation in stride, even the fact she is *the* Hope Huston. She's just happy we found her. She always hoped someone in her biological family would show up on her doorstep. I think she was expecting me."

"She had a good life, didn't she?" Lydia couldn't seem to stop asking that question.

Pavel had reassured her before, but he seemed happy to do it again. "She did. Her adopted parents adored her. She showed me the house where she grew up. Nothing fancy, but a big yard in a neighborhood with lots of children. She had cousins to play with, good schools. She's still close to her extended family."

Lydia was glad, so glad, but a part of her still mourned. "It was a better life than she would have had with Joe and me."

"You don't know that," Pavel said. "You don't even know you would have stayed with him if she hadn't been abducted."

"But I did. I stayed with him and raised another daughter in an angry house. I made so many bad decisions."

If he was surprised she was talking this frankly, he didn't let on. "You had Faith. I'm the last guy in the world to believe that was a bad decision."

Lydia couldn't lift the cup to her lips, no matter how badly she needed it. She set it down. "I want to thank you."

He looked surprised again. "You don't need to. Let's face it, I did this for myself. I needed answers."

"Do you always do that?"

"What?"

"Attribute the good things you do to selfishness?"

"I'm no saint, Lydia."

"Are you a good man?"

He seemed to consider. In the end he shrugged. "Not such a bad one."

"I loved your father. I want you to know that. And he loved me. It was never simply a...a physical thing."

"I'm glad you loved him."

"He would be so proud of you. Of course, he always was, but now he'd be proud you found Hope and brought her home."

"And cleared his name."

She wanted him to understand. "No, Dominik had pride, but that's not the reason he killed himself. He was an impulsive man, and a passionate one. When we lose everything and see no choices ahead, life becomes unbearable. He came to this country to be free, and instead he found the worst kind of prison. It was just too much for him."

"Maybe. I wish he'd stuck around anyway."

Lydia rested her hand on his. "I'm sorry for my part in this. I hope—" She cleared her throat. "I hope that having Karina in your life will make up a little for Dominik's loss."

If there had been any lingering question that Pavel *was* a good man, he satisfied it now. He covered her hand. "You've suffered enough, haven't you? Let's both enjoy this gift without any more regrets."

Faith was glad Karina was due to arrive early. Thus far Alex and Remy had managed a truce, so enchanted by the thought of cousins that they had forgotten their long-standing war. But she wasn't sure how much longer that would last without reinforcements. She left them to finish their search and took the stairs to the living room, where she found her mother and Pavel in quiet conversation.

Even Lydia was falling under Pavel's spell. Faith couldn't imagine why she'd ever thought she had a prayer of not falling under it herself.

"They've found Remy's dollhouse but not the furniture," she announced. "She's pretending she only wants it in her room so Jody can play with it, but I'll bet it never sees the attic again."

Her gaze flicked to Pavel's, and she smiled. She realized she was smiling a lot these days. She was free in ways she'd never thought possible, and every moment seemed precious.

Lydia looked away, perhaps because the smile seemed too private. When she stopped fiddling with her cup of tea, Faith addressed her. "It's time for Pavel to pick up Karina and the kids at the airport."

Lydia looked at her watch, the watch she had shaken half the morning, apparently convinced it had stopped ticking. "Already?"

Pavel got to his feet, and Faith strolled over to kiss his cheek. "We'll be waiting," she told him.

He went to the front closet for his coat, and she helped him into it. "Don't do any sightseeing on the way home, okay?"

"You're sure? I was sure they'd want to see all the monuments first." He smiled to let her know he was joking.

She lowered her voice. "This day probably ranks with the day Hope was taken for sheer emotion. I don't know how long Mother can hold out."

"She's strong." He brushed an errant strand of hair off Faith's cheek. "Like her daughters."

"I'm glad you'll be here."

"Wouldn't miss it for the world. I'm part of the family now. Almost like your brother."

"Don't even go there."

"You don't think of me that way, huh?"

She thought of him a hundred different ways, none of them vaguely fraternal. "One thing at a time, remember?"

"My idea, unfortunately, and a bad one." This time, when he touched her cheek it was simply a caress. Then he disappeared out the door.

Faith rejoined her mother. Lydia was pale, and she was twisting her hands in her lap, such a departure from her usual poise that Faith's heart went out to her. No matter how profoundly Lydia had changed, this kind of display would probably be rare in the future.

"Are you positive you want Alex and Remy here?" Faith said. "I can call David..."

"No, they'll make Karina's children feel at home."

She was frightened of meeting Karina's children. Lydia had two grandchildren, eight and nine, that she didn't know. The photos Karina had sent showed Jeremy with red hair like Alex's, only straight as a board. Jody's hair was dark and curly, like Karina's, Pavel's— and Dominik's. But they were still strangers, absolute strangers, and Faith knew how worried her mother was.

"I haven't been an exemplary grandmother to your children," Lydia said. "What if I can't learn to do better?"

"You'll love them, and they'll love you."

"Remy and Alex aren't sure what to make of me."

"Well, you've changed so much in the last few months, they're a little confused. But they're delighted with the grandmother who's emerging."

"I don't know what to say to anybody."

Lydia had a lot she was going to have to say eventually, but so far nobody outside the family knew that Hope had been found. They wanted their reunion first, before either law enforcement or the media made a three-ring circus of it.

Faith thought this was a good subject to distract her mother. "I have an idea for someone you can talk to when you're ready. I know the right person to tell this story."

Lydia sounded cautious. "You and Pavel have worked a miracle, and I couldn't trust either of you more. But I don't want someone in the conservative media—"

"You're assuming because I was married to David all those years those are the only people I know?"

Her mother's silence was answer enough.

"Those are also the people who would bend over backward to dig up Dad's side of the story," Faith said. "Not something he would appreciate, either."

"Who then?" Lydia asked at last.

"Ham."

"David's lover?"

"Boy, do I hate the sound of that. Yes, that would be the one. Abraham Stein. He already knows the story. Alex and Remy spent a couple of afternoons last week with Ham and David at their apartment. Alex loves to talk about Karina with his dad, since we've made him keep silent everywhere else. And—"

"You let them go there? To the apartment?"

"Their dad's gay, and his lover's a nice guy. More or less a step-dad."

"Faith!"

Faith laughed. "You know, you're going to have to get used to this. I doubt I'll ever be truly objective about the guy, but I can see clearly enough to appreciate his moral compass."

"You're certainly not the woman you used to be."

"Look, he's the one to tell the story. He'll be fair and accurate, and he'll use discretion. He has too much to lose if he doesn't, because David won't stand for anything that might hurt the kids." Faith could see she had succeeded in diverting her mother. Lydia was examining her as if she needed to unravel all Faith's secrets.

"You're over David, aren't you? You'd have to be, to be so nonchalant."

"I'm really hoping we can be good friends again someday. He gave me two wonderful kids. I'll always be grateful for that."

"If you're counseling me to reveal our family scandal to your ex-husband's lover, then you're already friends." Lydia patted the sofa, and Faith joined her.

"I have decided one thing," Lydia said. "I'm putting the house on the market. I'm going to leave Great Falls."

Faith wasn't surprised. The move was inevitable. Her father was already living in a downtown hotel. "You can live with us. It's still your house. We can make an apartment upstairs, or the kids and I can find another place to go."

"I want to be closer to my family, but please, not *that* close. And this house is yours now. That's the way I think of it." Lydia paused for effect. "Besides, I'll need to be closer to my new job in Alexandria."

"Job?"

"I'm going to be looking for a house in Old Town, Faith. I hope you'll go house-hunting with me."

"Job?" Faith repeated.

The words rushed out, with just a tinge of embarrassment. "Starting next month I'll be working for the National Center for Missing and Exploited Children, in their Office of Public Affairs. Just a volunteer, but full-time. They've been asking me to help them publicize the plight of missing children for years, but I was too close to the issue. Now I can do something to help. I take good care of myself. I still have time left to do some good."

"That's so perfect." Faith squeezed Lydia's hand. "I'm proud of you."

"Are you?"

"Are you kidding?" Faith paused. "Does Dad know?"

"We communicate through lawyers now, and of course I don't

need his permission. But he agreed to sell the house and divide all our property, so we won't have any financial problems, either of us. I can do anything I want."

"He's still not returning my calls." At the moment Faith was just as glad. She wasn't sure what she would say to her father when the time came.

"You found Karina, and that will cost him his seat in the senate. Keep trying. Someday maybe he'll come to terms with it." Lydia moved on. "What about the other man in your life?"

The questions and revelations were coming faster than Faith could cope with them. "This year I lost a husband, found a sister, lost a father, rediscovered my mother, nearly lost my daughter. What makes you think I've had time to think about Pavel?"

"How could you not?"

Faith was surprised Lydia understood so well. All the years she had yearned for this intimacy, and now she hardly knew what to make of it.

"Do you love him?" Lydia asked.

"Mother, these days I'm not even sure of my own name."

Lydia leaned closer. "This is going to take some getting used to, I know. Talking about things that really matter. I'll have one reunion today, but I'm selfish. I want two." Lydia chewed her bottom lip, another uncharacteristic sign of lack of poise. "I loved Hope, and I lost her," Lydia said. "And somewhere along the way I lost you, too. You said you rediscovered a mother. Have we really started to find one another?"

Faith cupped her mother's hand. Lydia's insecurity touched her more than anything else could have. "Just in time. Because once we opened that door, there was room for Hope, too."

Remy wandered downstairs and perched on the sofa's edge. Still holding Lydia's hand, Faith put her free arm around her daughter's waist, and Remy didn't move away. There had been a reunion of sorts there, too. Since her reconciliation with David, Remy had been more affectionate with Faith. At least temporarily, their good times outweighed their bad.

"What do you think, kiddo? Ready to meet your new family?" Faith asked.

"I think this whole thing is really weird."

Faith glanced at Lydia. "I hope you won't put it quite that way when you meet Aunt Karina."

"Give me credit for a little sense." Remy still didn't pull away. "Alex found the furniture. I dusted the dollhouse and got it ready."

"Jody will love it."

"She'll probably make me play with her."

"And you'll hate every minute, right?"

"I'm not a little kid anymore."

"Not a kid and not quite a grown-up," Lydia said. "But a pretty decent in-between—if you ask an old grandmother."

Remy shot her a grateful smile. "I'm going to call Megan."

"You can't tell her about Karina," Faith said.

"That's so lame. Finally something interesting happens to me that doesn't involve getting grounded, and I can't tell anybody!" Remy punched her mother lightly in the side before she broke away. She glanced at her grandmother; then she grinned and punched her, too.

Faith thought it was definitely a love punch. From her mother's expression, she was pretty sure Lydia agreed.

The final leg of the flight was held up by an hour. Bad weather, holiday air traffic, a stopover for the President's plane in New York that stranded passengers in cities all over the continent. Pavel claimed the delay was a combination of all those things and simple bad luck. He was still at the airport, but in their last phone call he had assured Faith that Karina and the children were in the air now and expected momentarily.

Lydia wasn't certain she would survive the wait, even though Faith had made a point of keeping her informed at every turn. Now, thirty-five minutes after Pavel's call, Faith settled herself on the sofa again, where Lydia herself had been rooted since his departure.

"Are you going to make it?" Faith asked.

Lydia tried to sound strong. "I've had practice. I used to imagine a reunion with Hope, but I always thought the fantasy was as close as I'd come."

"At least you had a chance to prepare."

"Thirty-eight years."

A car door slammed in front of the house. The fact that some-one had found a parking spot on Prospect was something of a mir-acle. Lydia thought if that someone was Pavel Quinn, the miracle would be complete.

Faith left her to go to the front window and peek outside. She turned, her eyes shining. "Lord, she looks like Pavel, Mother. More than in her photographs. He didn't tell me."

Lydia's bones seemed to dissolve. What had been a skeleton was now elastic.

"Maybe you should sit," Faith said. But it was too late, because Lydia was already struggling to her feet. A perfunctory knock was their only preparation. Pavel pushed the door open before Faith could reach it. He stood back.

Karina, followed by two wide-eyed children, walked through the doorway.

Karina's eyes went immediately to Lydia. There was something of a pause, although for Lydia time meant nothing. Then Karina smiled; her father's crooked smile.

"Hey, Mom," she said softly. "I'm home."

 Epilogue

The house on Prospect Street rested on a foundation of stone, laid there by an expert mason more than a hundred years before. Faith discovered that in February while she was shoveling snow away from the basement door. She hadn't given much thought to the foundation until that moment, but immediately the symbolism appealed to her. As she cleared away drifts that had hidden the transition between sandstone and cherry-red brick, an idea formed.

This morning Faith had awakened to a spectacular sunrise, but she wasn't alarmed, because she understood this particular announcement. Something momentous *was* going to occur, and she could hardly wait. Now, with springtime sun warming the newly landscaped garden where she and her family stood, Faith handed a slender chisel and wooden mallet to her mother.

"Really, Faith, you're sure this will do the job?" Lydia had already printed her first name in chalk in the area they'd decided on together. It was six feet from the door, and someday it would be framed by the new camellias that were waiting in five-gallon pots for Faith to plant.

Faith had already given verbal instructions and a short demo. "I experimented. The stone's soft enough to work with. Give it a try. You don't have to be Michelangelo."

Lydia, still wearing the raspberry-colored suit she'd put on that morning to hear David preach his first sermon, stooped and began to tap the chisel with the mallet Faith had provided.

"Do you have a camera?" Karina asked her sister.

"Oh, I'm glad you remembered." Faith motioned for Alex, who was chasing Jeremy around the yard. "You two, don't step on the daffodils."

The two boys joined them, and Faith asked Alex to retrieve the camera. "How come Remy can't do it?" he complained.

"She's gone to get Dottie Lee." Faith looked toward her neighbor's house and saw the old woman coming through the hedge, Titi tucked under one arm. Remy held the branches back so that Dottie Lee could step through. Jody was helping.

Alex muttered something about slave labor and started for the basement door.

Faith felt Pavel's arms circle her waist, and she leaned back against him. "Maybe we should have set up a tent," he whispered in her ear. "Had the event catered."

"It won't take that long. We're only doing first names. Except Karina. She gets two."

"Karina Hope," Karina said. "Not all that catchy, but it does the trick."

Pavel pulled her in for a hug, too, one woman in each arm, and the sisters watched as their mother struggled with the chisel. Alex arrived and shot a photograph.

"Violet did it," Faith said, when, like her grandson, Lydia muttered something unflattering under her breath. "And the millstone is granite."

"I don't see why we couldn't just sign a bedroom wall in Magic Marker."

"Yes, you do."

Lydia grumbled, but she went back to chiseling. When Jeremy volunteered to help, she embraced him and helped him hold the mallet.

"This is a pretty nice moment," Pavel said.

Faith agreed. It was that and more.

They were a different family than the one they had been last year at this time. Faith and David's divorce was final, and Joe and Lydia's was underway. Last week Lydia had closed on a house in

Alexandria, and now she was in the process of moving in and unpacking. Karina and her children, who were out of school for spring break, had driven down from Canada to help.

The happy conclusion of Hope Huston's story had, as expected, been a major news item. Ham broke it with an exclusive, although the public would never know the entire truth. There were no revelations about Hope's true parentage, and Joe and Lydia's separation was explained as a mutually agreeable, though painful, solution to a marriage that had suffered too much emotional trauma. If anyone wondered why Joe was never photographed with his long-lost daughter, they would wonder eternally.

Joe had announced his plans to retire from the senate at the end of his current term. Although he still refused to see Faith, he had told her during a brief phone call that he intended to make a permanent home in southern Virginia, where he had roots and supporters. She knew from Lydia that he was already negotiating for a consulting position.

The police and the FBI had questioned the family extensively, but so far the scanty details Faith and Pavel had revealed about Sandor Babin had borne no fruit. Alec the Can Man hadn't yet been found. Faith and Pavel hoped he would live out his final years in peace.

"I see you started without me," Dottie Lee said.

"Listen, you can do the work yourself if it makes you happy." Lydia got to her feet. "All right, I've made a start."

Faith squinted at the foundation stone. "Mother, you've barely scratched it."

"My name's clear enough. There'll be plenty of time for me to gouge it deeper for all posterity to see. Let Karina take her turn now." Lydia handed her oldest daughter the chisel.

Karina laughed. Faith loved the sound. This sister of hers, this phantom who had haunted her life, was warm, funny, intelligent and as well-grounded as any human being Faith had ever met. Faith was looking forward to a life of getting to know her better. They had already booked a cruise for later in the spring. Just the two sisters and Lydia.

"I'll take my turn," Karina said, "but I've got more to chisel than anybody else."

"Don't forget the line between your name and Mother's." The three women had decided to connect their names. They had been separated long enough.

"I was absolutely certain I would live to see this day," Dottie Lee said.

Lydia walked over to stand beside her. "You did your share to make it happen," she said grudgingly.

"Why, Lyddy, that almost sounds like praise."

"Mark this day. How often have *you* heard praise from a woman?" The two old friends looked at each other and smiled.

There was noise from the basement stairwell, and David and Ham emerged from the house, David still in his suit, Ham in a sportscoat and jeans. "Did we miss the big event?" David asked.

"If you come back in ten years you won't miss it," Faith said. "It's going to take some time to do it right. But we're making a start."

Remy and Alex flanked their father, and he put an arm around each of their shoulders. The four Bronsons had been in counseling together for three months, and as painful as the experience had been, it had made important changes in all of them. Remy's behavior wasn't perfect, but when Faith had problems with her daughter, she and David worked on solutions together. Reports from the middle school were encouraging, and Remy was seriously studying piano now and loving it.

"Thank you all for coming this morning," David said. "It meant a lot."

Faith was proud of David. He was interning at a church downtown, and today had been his debut in the pulpit. He had chosen forgiveness as his topic, and he had been both inspired and inspirational. David had found his calling.

She caught his eye and smiled. "You were great." She smiled at Ham, too. "Didn't you think so?"

Ham grinned. "Good enough that I might go back in twenty years to see if he gets any better."

"We came to steal the kids," David said. "But we can wait."

Karina, who had been chiseling steadily, got to her feet. "Okay, okay. It's harder than it looks. But if you squint, you'll see the start of something good here. Faith, take your turn and let these kids get out of here."

Faith took the chisel. Like Lydia, Karina had done little more than scratch the surface, but there was plenty of time for all of them to perfect their efforts. Faith hadn't chosen stone to be contrary. It seemed the perfect medium. Their names would be hard-won, but they would be right here, together, forever.

Faith knelt and began to add her own, connecting it to Karina's. Like the others, it needed hard work and time, but she wasn't going anywhere.

When she finally stood, everybody clapped. Then, one by one, they left. David and Ham with Remy and Alex. Lydia with Karina and her children. Dottie Lee back through the hedge.

Faith was alone, at last, with Pavel.

"Wasn't that something?" she asked him, her eyes shining. "I never imagined we'd have a day like this one."

"A new beginning."

In the months since they found Karina, Pavel had bided his time, helping everyone make the transition into new relationships, using his contacts to be sure the family got fair coverage in the media. He had spent long hours at Scavenger, wrapping up his tenure there and figuring out how and if he wanted to fit into the company in the future. Like the rest of them, Pavel had quietly transformed his life.

Faith waited, but he didn't say more. Pavel had supported her every step of the way, but although he was always affectionate, they had rarely been alone, and they had never become lovers again. She had been waiting for him to say "more" for months now. But he was obviously waiting for her.

"Well?" she said at last. "Elaborate a little. What kind of new beginning?"

"I guess that's up to you." He rocked back on his heels.

Faith had spent more than a year taking control of her life. She was proud of everything she had accomplished, as well as all the things she had given up. There were a lot of things in her former life that she could do without.

The man in front of her was not one of them.

She held out her hand and he took it. "Have you just been trying to prove how patient you are?" she said. "Because sometimes you've been so patient I've wondered if maybe you'd just gotten tired of having so many people in your life. Too much of a good thing."

"Patient? Yes, I have been patient, haven't I? I ought to get a commendation. And let's not forget trustworthy."

"You know I'd trust you with my life, Pavel."

"Funny you should put it that way. Someday I might ask you to do exactly that."

She smiled up at him. Today her heart had been filled to overflowing, or so she had thought. But Pavel's love was the hidden spring, the source of joy now and for the future. Pavel, and all they could share, was the final measure.

She was certain of that now.

"You'll take me, warts and all?" she said.

"Right now I'll just settle for taking you to my house until your kids come home. Will you come with me?"

She squeezed his hand, or rather, she gripped tightly. "I was going to offer you dinner, a real home-cooked meal. Just the two of us. You never got the one I promised the day you saved my piano."

"You can cook at my house."

"We'll be eating late?"

He drew her against him for a kiss. It was all the answer she needed.